# Fascists in Christian Clothing

# FASCISTS IN CHRISTIAN CLOTHING

## The Vast Right Wing Conspiracy

*Is America Nuts? A Trilogy—Part II—The Strange Marriage of Evangelical Christianity, Conservatives and the Moonies*

Richard J. Weisman

iUniverse, Inc.
New York Lincoln Shanghai

**Fascists in Christian Clothing**
The Vast Right Wing Conspiracy

Copyright © 2005 by Richard J. Weisman

All rights reserved. No part of this book may be used or reproduced by any means, graphic, electronic, or mechanical, including photocopying, recording, taping or by any information storage retrieval system without the written permission of the publisher except in the case of brief quotations embodied in critical articles and reviews.

iUniverse books may be ordered through booksellers or by contacting:

iUniverse
2021 Pine Lake Road, Suite 100
Lincoln, NE 68512
www.iuniverse.com
1-800-Authors (1-800-288-4677)

ISBN-13: 978-0-595-35737-6 (pbk)
ISBN-13: 978-0-595-80215-9 (ebk)
ISBN-10: 0-595-35737-7 (pbk)
ISBN-10: 0-595-80215-X (ebk)

Printed in the United States of America

# Part II
# The Vast Right Wing Conspiracy

## Chapter One

Whenever I get a hankering for Mousaka, I head over to Mykonos, a Greek restaurant on Madison Avenue. Today I had a hankering. I took my favorite seat by the window so that I could check out the pedestrian traffic as I completed reading The New York Times.

"Hello, Angelina," I said as I glanced down at the floor.

"Doc, how did you know it's me?" she asked.

"Cause, you got a great pair of sticks," I answered.

"Doc, you have a beautiful fiancée, why do you always flirt with me?" she asked. Men, all men have a thing for waitresses and I'm no exception.

After 9-11, Spiro and Olympia Papanicholas, the owners, had cable television installed. CNN became institutionalized background noise to every conversation and meal. I asked Spiro to turn it off whenever I visited but he insisted that it was necessary for his survival. He needed to watch the news just in case there was another terrorist attack.

I could hear Wolf Blitzer during his "Late Edition" program talk about Sam's opponent's claim that he would conduct a sensitive war on terrorism. The word "sensitive" gave rise to an all out attack by Sam's supporters. Getting the killers of 3,000 innocent World Trade Center victims would require resolve not sensitivity. Sensitive was a poor choice of word and the candidate should have known better. It didn't make a difference that I knew what he meant; Sam's supporters would spin the word into some Northern liberal elitist pabulum that would clearly define Sam's opponent as soft on the international war on terrorism.

Angelina came back with lunch and lingered at my table.

"Not sitting with your back to the wall, facing the kitchen?" she asked.

"No, not today," I replied.

Angie was referring to our favorite game that we played for years. I would sit with my back against the faded mural of the Acropolis and Parthenon and watch Angie walk back to the kitchen. Angelina would oblige my stare with an exaggerated butt swagger. The mural had recently been restored in honor of the Greek Olympics. The moment was perfect: Angelina, The New York Times, Mousaka, the beautiful Madison Avenue women in their latest designer fashions and an unusual balmy dry August afternoon.

Angelina gripped my shoulder and motioned to stop talking. The ubiquitous "BREAKING NEWS" flashed across the screen, except that the word "MAJOR" preceded the phrase. One third of the patrons watched the television and stopped talking. The noise level fell accordingly. Within seconds, one by one, each patron ceased talking and stared at the television. Wolf Blitzer had a silent, unknown, captive audience at the Mykonos diner on a beautiful day.

"Fifteen minutes ago, CNN received an e-mail in Arabic which we have translated into English. Prior to this announcement, CNN contacted the Office of Homeland Security and the Center for Disease Control. We have been working for the last fifteen minutes to gather our experts to bring you insight into the events as they occur. Based upon our loose translation, the e-mail reads as follows:

'For the past three years, the African Missionary Movement has been in contact with various Christian missionary groups in the United States. After developing a working relationship, several American groups invited the AMM to visit America as their guests. Accordingly, we dispatched a group of 200 martyrs. In medieval times, an invading army, to aid their conquest would hoist over a walled city, soldiers infected with the plague. We have done the same. May Allah grant martyrdom to our infected missionaries. Fourteen days ago, fifty of our missionaries, left for the United States infected with a particular virus bound for the

West Coast from Seattle to San Diego. Fifty missionaries were dispatched to the East Coast ranging from Albany to Miami and an additional fifty missionaries, broken into two groups of twenty-five each were sent to Chicago and New Orleans. These two groups were infected with two different viruses than the first group. The one hundred fifty missionaries have been in the United States for a sufficient period of time that symptoms of the injected diseases have developed or will develop shortly. We will e-mail you another letter in twenty minutes. Signed Dr. Junin Lassa Marburg.'"

The diner was stunned into silence. The cooks in their dirty aprons left the kitchen and stood by a counter watching the broadcast. Angelina glanced down at me looking for comforting words but I had none to offer. The announcement created the silent shocked disbelief that occurred three years ago as everyone watched the planes crash into the Twin Towers. No one could believe what Wolf Blitzer just read. Conversation resumed during a break. There were three different camps: (1) the report must be true as CNN would never air it if it wasn't (2) CNN was irresponsible for airing the report and (3) the report wasn't true. Angelina left my side. I glanced out the window and watched as an increasing number of people stopped to answer their cell phones and then either ran down the block or increased the speed of their gait. Some people cried openly as they listened to what they were told by a loved one or friend on their phone. Several people rushed into the diner to watch the report. Fights broke out over cabs. No one in the diner moved.

Wolf reappeared and the trailer under the banner MAJOR BREAKING NEWS stated that America might have suffered a major biological attack. Wolf held his finger to his head set and listened carefully.
"We have just been informed by the CDC that there is no Dr. Junin Lassa Marburg. The name is actually the name of three viruses; the Junin virus, the Lassa virus and the Marburg virus."
He stopped listening to his director in his earphone. He continued.
"Our staff in Atlanta, CNN headquarters, is calling every major hospital in the United States. We have contacted the White House. Our own team of medical and biological experts will be with us shortly to assist us in this major breaking story."

At this point, an arm reached across Blitzer's desk and handed him a piece of paper.
"I have just received the second e-mail and it reads, loosely translated, as follows: 'we are sure you are wondering what happened to the other fifty martyrs of the group of two hundred. Those fifty Muhajadeen, our most dedicated warriors

were sent to the Plaza Hotel in New York City. Four of them were infected with bubonic plague. The remaining forty-six stayed with the four infected martyrs until they developed symptoms and secondary pneumonic plague. The forty-six became infected with the bacterium by respiratory droplet. Upon inhalation of these droplets, many of the forty-six will develop primary pneumonic plague. Upon infection, the forty-six missionaries were then dispatched to small town America. The fatality rate for pneumonic plague is fifty-seven percent. May Allah crush the infidels and protect the innocent. Signed Muhajadeen Bio-Terror Brigade.'"

CNN arranged a conference call with the Director of the CDC. She explained the families of the different viruses, filoviruses and arenaviruses. The arenaviruses contained the Lassa and Junin strain each causing Lassa fever and Argentine hemorrhagic fever, respectively. The Filoviruses caused Marburg and Ebola hemorrhagic fever. I envisioned bleeding from all orifices of the human body. The Director of the CDC was most concerned with primary pneumonic plague. Junin, Lassa and Marburg viruses needed contact to spread. Pneumonic plague spread by air. The news streamer under Wolf indicated that the market plunged 476 points since the airing of the report. Trading was suspended and the stock market closed for the day. Angie came over to my table and said "what's gonna be, Doc?" "I don't know Angie, I just don't know," I replied. An elderly woman seated two tables from mine sneezed and everyone turned around to look. A simple sneeze turned itself into an act of suspicion. I knew panic was going to set in. Blitzer stated that initial reports from the CNN staff indicated that approximately 57,000 people at the country's major hospitals were admitted with unknown illnesses. Everyone's wish that what we were witnessing on television might be false was destroyed. The bleeding from the eyes, ears and nose had not started. Wolf pressed the Director for an answer to the number of people that could become infected and the anticipated number of deaths. She resisted. The scene outside the window became more chaotic. People were now running. Madison Avenue was choked with traffic. Cars had their trunks and back seats stuffed with personal belongings in a desperate attempt to escape the city. I stared at the Mousaka in front of me. I could not hold on to one thought, as thousands raced through my mind. The market would collapse and be closed indefinitely. The malls would be empty as well as the supermarkets after the initial burst of panic buying. The streets, subways and office buildings would be deserted. A nationwide quarantine would be self-imposed. Fatal viruses were descending on America. The Director of the CDC collapsed under the constant pressure of Blitzer's pressing for an answer for a forecast and stated that "with the limited information available at the present time, an estimated eight million people would become infected and that three million would die." CNN provided coverage of two of 300 hundred patients that had been admitted to a major hospital in Chicago. They were bleeding from the eyes and ears. A spokesman for the hospital stated that he thought it might be the Marburg virus, however, confirmation would come in several days after an Antigen-capture enzyme-linked immunosorbent assay (ELISA) test was conducted. Bits and pieces started to flow in from various sources. Fifty robes had been discovered in the Plaza Hotel. The Bio-Terror Brigade missionaries were presumed to be in ordinary clothes. The address that the American Christian evangelical missionaries were corresponding with was a mailbox in the capitol of Gabon. I looked out the window into the chaos that had descended upon Madison Avenue. Upon seeing the footage of the bleeding eyes, eight patrons bolted from the diner and immediately disappeared into the madness that now engulfed the street. Everyone glanced at each other in an effort to determine whether they too should exit. For the moment, no one budged. Video footage from San Francisco showed one patient being carried in on a stretcher. The spokeswoman stated that the patient had symptoms of high fever, pain behind the chest wall, sore throat, back pain and facial swelling. Her initial diagnosis indicated Lassa fever. Again, an ELISA test was being conducted. I suspected that the Marburg virus was in Chicago and the Lassa virus was in San Francisco. I assumed that the Junin virus was on the East coast. The Junin virus was a member of the Arenaviruses and airborne transmission had been reported in some cases. I realized that all airline traffic from the United States would be banned internationally and that jets in flight from foreign countries would be turned around if the planes had enough fuel to return to their home base. The Canadian and Mexican authorities would post soldiers on their borders preventing all Americans from escaping the states. The terrorists must have planned their attack carefully in order to insure maximum exposure. The infected missionaries must have visited high traffic areas, the malls, airline terminals and subway stations. Blitzer reported that a large number of patients had been admitted to an Akron, Ohio hospital with high fever, cough, shortness of breath, chest pain and bloody sputum. Pneumonic plague arrived in the heartland of America. The CDC Director stated, in medical terms, most of which were incomprehensible, that the bacteria migrate through cutaneous lymphatics to regional lymph nodes where they are phagocytosed and resist destruction. They rapidly multiply, causing destruction and necrosis of lymph node architecture with subsequent bacteremia, septicemia and endotoxemia that can lead quickly to shock, disseminated intravascular coagulation and coma. In short, you're a dead man in forty-eight hours. After hearing this last explanation, the balance of the patrons bolted for the door and they too disappeared into the madness of the twilight. I sat alone with Angelina standing next to me. Spiro was in the kitchen and Olympia was next to the cash register. I was reminded of Edward Hoppers painting of two people alone in a corner diner.

Spiro came out of the kitchen and locked the door to the diner. Madison Avenue was deserted. Olympia turned off the television and I knew intuitively that Spiro was going to have his version of the last supper. Spiro placed two small tables together and Olympia set the table. Angelina grabbed my hand and stood next to me while we silently watched. Spiro invited everyone into the kitchen and advised us that "tonight, we are going to cook the most wonderful Greek dinner together." He reached for a hidden bottle of Ouzo, took out four small glasses, poured and handed each of us a glass. "To life, salute," he said and all of us raised our glasses and said, "to life." Our small, as of yet uninfected group was going to cook, eat and dance together and hopefully, smash glass against the wall at the conclusion of our evening. Ouzo was freely poured and all of us were buzzed halfway through preparing the meal. We made a Greek feta cheese salad and a lamb main dish. Dessert was Baklava. Seated at the table, Spiro raised another glass of Ouzo and said, "May God be with us." "Amen," all of us replied. The day's events were never mentioned. We had reached that point in time when there's nothing left to do except celebrate. We did. Half way through the meal, Spiro put on Greek music and we all danced around the table. More Ouzo blurred the line between the tragedy that was unfolding across America and the drunk stupor of carefree merriment that we created. Spiro picked up a glass and flung it against the wall. Within seconds, all of us were throwing whatever breakable dinnerware we could find. With each glass that Spiro broke, he yelled "to life." After three hours, all of us were exhausted and gathered around the table for espresso.
"Angie, you're coming home with me. I'm not letting you go out alone," I told her.
"O.K., Stan, no problem."
Angelina knew exactly what I meant. If we participated in the last supper then Angelina was going to be my last screw. I was going to wrap my legs around her and never let go. Angie and I kissed Spiro and Olympia good-bye, possibly our last good-bye and headed around the corner to my apartment. Before we left, Spiro handed me another bottle of Ouzo.

Entering my apartment, I decided that Angelina and I would sit on the back deck overlooking the garden. Angelina peeked into my office and said nothing. I turned on the light above the oven that cast a low glow through the kitchen win-

dow, intentionally setting the mood. I put on the soft sounds of John Klemmer's sax and brought out two glasses with the bottle of Ouzo. Both Angie and I were highlighted with a soft golden glow. I was sure we looked appealing to each other. As I raised my glass for a toast, Angie moved her head in a pointing manner, indicating that I should look behind her. Half hidden behind Angie was Sam. "Well, Well, Well. It's my best friend Sam," I told Angie sarcastically.
"I know who it is," she said.
"Sam, this is not the best time," I told him.
Angie was finger tapping on the table and quietly singing, "it's the end of the world as we know it," over and over. I looked at Angie. She stopped singing.
"Don't worry Warlib," she said. "We'll take care of business and then we'll take care of business. You know what I mean." I nodded with approval and had a slight smile on my face.
"So, Sam, what brings you here? Have an Ouzo," I asked Sam. He didn't answer. Sam, Angelina and I continued for thirty minutes having a lighthearted conversation. It seemed nobody wanted to bring up the scourge that the terrorists had inflicted on America. All of us temporarily suspended reality. The mood was relaxed and easy.
"So, Sam, what *really* brings you here?" I asked.
"Just wanted to know if you still don't believe in terrorists?" he asked.
"Domestic or foreign?" Angie asked. Angelina no longer appeared as much as a waitress as she had before. She exhibited varying degrees of attributes that I never noticed. "Angie, how many degrees do you have?" I asked. I expected high school would be her answer. She answered, "almost three," emphasizing that the last degree would be a doctorate in sociology. She was presenting a thesis about the role of female waitresses in American society. She looked at me and shrugged her shoulders. "Oops," I blurted out.
"Waitresses as surrogate mothers, I suppose," I said.
"Something like that, Stan," she answered.
"O.K., let's answer Sam's question. Does Dr. Stanley Warlib believe in terrorists? Sounds like a foolish question as 200 human bio-bombs are running around loose throughout the United States," said Angie.
"Why is Sam asking you if you believe in terrorists?" Angelina asked.
"Long story, Angie. Let's just say a long time ago, I told Sam that I didn't believe in terrorism to the extent that he likes to portray to his family. In my opinion, Sam was gas lighting his family and trying to make them more nuts than they already are."
"Like the Ingrid Bergman movie," Angie said.

"Yeah, like the movie," I answered. I poured Angie and I another Ouzo.

"Want a drink Sam?" I asked.

"Sure, why not. I don't think God will punish me," he answered. Angie excused herself and looked for a glass in the kitchen. "In the upper left hand cabinet, above the sink and bring back some ice, please," I yelled out. I told everyone to watch what happened to the Ouzo when I put ice into the drinks. The Ouzo turned milky white. No one was impressed. I felt like a little kid. We continued drinking. Eventually, Sam got high.

"It's the 800 pound gorilla sitting in the middle of the living room that no one wants to talk about," I said.

"What gorilla?" Angelina asked.

"God in American politics," I answered. "It's the third political rail that you can't touch and everyone is embracing God. It's what scared people do. Take, for example, Lt. Gen. William Boykin in full military regalia preaching in Christian pulpits that Osama bin Laden and his terrorists would be defeated if we came at him in the name of Jesus. I mean he's the damn Deputy Secretary of Defense for Intelligence. At twenty-three churches, Boykin went on to say that Satan was the mastermind of the terrorists and that he wanted to destroy Sam and his Christian army. His boss Rummy didn't even get upset. He praised the general for his outstanding record."

After I finished, everyone sat there unimpressed. My complaint was small in comparison to the plague outside.

"And another thing," I continued. "In Horry County, North Carolina, local officials opened their council meeting with a prayer to Jesus, despite the fact that our Supreme Court declared it unconstitutional. During a recent confirmation hearing of J. Leon Holmes for a seat on the federal bench, his supporters stated that the Senate is anti-Christian because they questioned Holmes religious writings." Sam interrupted.

"I once told you Stanley, that political correctness is now on the right. It's Christian political correctness. Let it go."

"You guys are going to spend what might be, perhaps, our last few healthy hours on earth talking about politics. I had something else in mind, Stan," Angie declared.

"Your boyfriend Stan is a little anal. Once he gets on to something he doesn't let it go. Obsessive-Compulsive, you know," Sam said.

Angelina was right.

"Angie, you're right, but just let Sam and I finish. I want to answer his question whether I believe in terrorists. You know, unlike you conservative ideologues, us liberals can change our minds. I think the terrorism threat was a lot of hype until a few months ago. I changed my mind. Ever have a moment, Sam, like a moment of truth, a moment of enlightenment or a moment of awareness where everything becomes crystal clear. There are also fighting moments. I mean, like real fights. In all the fights I had, I knew that I would win 49% and lose 49% of the fights. If there were a hundred fights, there were two fights that I didn't know what was going to happen and when I locked with my opponent there was this moment when I realized that I could take this guy. I had a chance. Remember the first Rocky movie, where the music dramatically changes in the fourth round. That's the fighting moment. Rocky realizes he could take this guy. He wasn't going down and the real fight began. Well, I think that's where we're at right now. The terrorists are having a fighting moment where they realize they can take on big, bad Sam and you state, in your infinite wisdom, 'bring em' on.' Well, they did and it's right outside my freaking door. You know, you and bin Ladin are having a moment in history. Both you guys are joined at the hip and can't exist without each other. He's your best campaign manager. You've replaced the Statute of Liberty as the single most important American symbol and Osama is the biggest symbol for your war. You don't want him captured, dead or alive and he doesn't want you to lose your position as head of the family. Your locked together destined to write bad history."

"O.K., fight fans, this party is over," Angelina said.

Sam took his leave and Angie led me by the hand to the bedroom.

"This could possibly be our last night on this planet and you want to talk politics. Geez, Stan," Angie exclaimed.

I knew Angelina was worried that I wouldn't be in the mood and so instead of telling her that I was still in the mood, I showed her. I lit a joint. Angie and I smoked as we sat on the bed. I let a sufficient period of time pass until I slowly removed her clothes in synch with the music. All memories of politics, viruses and bleeding from the eyes had vanished. It was just Angie and I and this was our moment. Angelina pushed my hip with her hand and slowly slid on top. I paused and let her gain her rhythm and cadence. I wanted to see what she was going to do. I adjusted to her movements and we got lost in each other. Angelina liked making love at a medium speed with a lot of pressure pressed against my bone. She was massaging her clitoris. We worked up a sweat in a short period of time and she placed her hands on both my shoulders and leaned into her movements. Her hands kept on slipping off my shoulders and stopped at the base of my neck. I opened my eyes and checked Angie out. Her eyes were closed. I closed mine and we both let our respective genitalia speak to each other. The Ouzo and John

Klemmer were a powerful partnership as were Angie and I. I didn't realize exactly what was happening but I started to gasp for air and when none was available I opened my eyes. Angelina had her hands around my throat and was choking the life out of me and it wasn't Angie but the fucking bitch bastard Elicia who had shot me three weeks ago.
"You're a sick fuck. Trying to kill me and come at the same time. Fuck you," I screamed. My hands shot straight up to her throat and in one movement I pinned her to the wall. Her feet were dangling two feet off the ground.
"You're dead. You're fucking dead," I screamed.
"Stan, Stan, Stan, wake up," Gabby screamed.
I sat up straight and the sweat ran out of my pours. The sheet was soaked.
"Stan, you had a nightmare. I'm Gabby. It's Gabby. This is Southhampton."
My heavy breathing subsided but the sweating continued. I looked at Gabby and slowly realized what was going on.
"What a fucking nightmare that was," I told her. "What a fucking nightmare," I repeated. "Was it the usual horror show?" she asked.
"No, this was different than my usual nightmare and totally off the fucking wall," I said. Gabby placed her arm around me and stroked my head with her hand. "Look," she said, as she pointed to TazTwo, my Labrador Retriever, who sat at the side of the bed with his head half-cocked staring at me with a puzzled look. "You scared your buddy and you scared me," she said. "I'll meet you downstairs."

I took a shower in an effort to calm down. In the kitchen I fixed myself a cup of coffee and headed out to the dunes and stared at the ocean.
"Must have been quite a nightmare," Mr. Westerfield said. Charles was ten feet behind me sitting in his Adirondack chair with a cup of coffee in one hand and The New York Times in the other.
"Yes, quite a nightmare. Different than the usual one," I told Charles "and a lot more frightening," I added. "It seems Sam and Elicia invade every part of my life," I told Charles.
"Look, Stan, about three weeks ago, Elicia shot you under the rotunda of the courthouse. You suffered a tremendous traumatic experience. You can't expect to forget it in three weeks. That's why I wanted you to recuperate in Southampton. I thought it might be less taxing. It wasn't the usual nightmare?" Charles asked.
"Same cast of characters but a different plot," I answered.

I continued staring at the ocean. Without provocation, I uttered under my breath, "you shall not lie with a male as with a woman; it is an abomination. If a man lies with a male as with a woman, both of them have committed an abomination; they shall be put to death, their blood is upon them."

"Sorry Stan, I couldn't hear you. What did you say?" Charles asked.
"Leviticus 18:22 and Leviticus 20:13," I answered.
"Quoting scripture. Stan, you really need a rest," said Charles.
I walked back from the top of the dune and sat down next to Charles.
"You know what Charles?" Before he could answer, I continued. "I think all of us should stop fooling around and let the red states and the blue states go at it. Good versus evil. Armed rebellion. Sam has commenced a new civil war for this new millennium. I hate them and they hate me," I said.
"Where is all this coming from?" Charles asked.
"I don't know, I guess I woke up on the wrong side of the bed," I answered.
"You must be getting stronger. I haven't seen you this upset in a long time. It seems resting at the estate and Gabby's care is doing you a world of good," he said.
"Gabby is terrific," I declared.
"You know where all this crap is coming from? When I came downstairs I realized that under no circumstances would Sam be defeated in November. If Sam's religious and financial buddies used to be in the sub basement of a ten-story building they're now on the third floor and they will let nothing stand in their way. Nothing, absolutely nothing. Oh, I remember. What set me off was a little clip that I saw on PBS showing Nancy Pelosi trying to hide behind some guy at a multi million-dollar bash given by AOL-Time Warner. I was witnessing a total convergence of money and politics by both parties. Money is king. I know this is baby stuff but I always hold out hope that maybe things might change. They won't and when I realize they won't, I get upset. Don't tell me, I'm naïve," I concluded.
"Stan, I'm taking you out tonight for a little fun," said Charles.
"I mean if the boys think the election is too close they'll drag out the bones of a dead Osama! Or start the trial of Saddam Hussein! Or get some good old White Supremacist and blow up some buildings prior to the election just in case Sam's family forgot they're in a war. After all, what's a couple of hundred dead people when the boys are advancing their cause and going to save one million six hundred thousand aborted fetuses next year. From a professional standpoint, I learned that between a histrionic and paranoid personality disorder, paranoid is going to trump histrionic, all the time. You can't be you if you're dead. Sam's opponent is trying to outdo Sam on Sam's turf. Sam is the Commander in Chief," I said. Charles interrupted me.
"Stan, calm down. Take a deep breath and just calm down. I didn't realize you were such a political junkie," Charles said.

"I'm not, but I'm witnessing an incredible transformation before my eyes and I can't do anything about it. I'm helpless and I hate feeling helpless. Can you imagine a march of 400,000 people in New York City and it's 'proudly peaceful.' What bullshit! We need more black shirts out there," I said referring to anarchists. "And another thing that's pissing me off is that Sam's religious buddies are putting a face on their war. It used to be the war on terrorism, but now, a face is appearing. A memo must have gone out advising everyone to start using the word Islam. Terror is a method used by someone and that someone is an Islamic Muslim. In the second and third tier media outlets, I have been hearing the 'the war on Islamic terrorists,' or the 'war on radical Islam,' or the 'war on extreme Islam.' Now I read in the venerable New York Times, David Brooks in an op-ed piece writing that Sam is fighting the war on radical Islam with tenacity and constancy. Hollywood is coming out with a movie on the crusades. Charles, I feel a set-up and it's happening right before my eyes and I am powerless to stop it," I said. Charles looked at me with a stern face and said "enough."

"One last thing and I'll stop. Last month I heard Sam's Attorney General give a speech at a Take back America for Christ convention and I know Ralph Reed wrote a book in the 90's about how to make America a Christian nation and that's exactly what they're going to do," I said.

Charles got up from the chair and said, "let's take a walk. If you didn't have enough on your mind, I'm going to give you more."

We both walked down a path to the open beach with Taz in tow. I turned around and saw Gabby wave. I picked up a stick and threw it ahead of me. Taz fetched it. Even though Charles was attempting to clear my head, the walk wasn't doing any good. Sam was slowly getting his family comfortable with the fact that him and his religious buddies were going to declare war on one billion Muslims. Islam was evil.

"Stan, this might not be the best time to bring this up, however, now is as good a time as any. First, I'm sure you are aware that a pre-nuptial agreement with Gabby is mandatory. Second, I'd like to offer you a job and third, I have converted the second large study across the hall from my study into what will be called the 'war room' so that you and I can discuss and track geo-political events around the world," Charles said.

"Charles, the answers to the first and third items are easy. I fully expected a pre-nuptial agreement and have no problem with one whatsoever. As to setting up a war room, I'd love it. I would be thankful for the opportunity to study with you. As far as a job, what do you have in mind?" I asked.

"I'm very concerned about the attempt on your life. I think if people knew that you worked for me it might ensure your safety. The job itself would entail your opinions about world leaders and events from a psychological perspective. Your advice is worth half a million to me."

"Wow, that's quite a sum," I said. "Every job I have held has always been helping people in one way or another, whether they be clients or patients. I have never worked where the sole object of my efforts is to make money. It would be quite a switch and one that I have to give a lot of thought to. I'll have to get back to you on this one. Give me a week to think about it," I told Charles.

"Take two weeks, if you need it," he said.

Interestingly enough, Pelosi, Sam, Elicia, Christianity and Islam went out of my mind. A half million dollars just to be a one man think tank intrigued me at a basic self centered level. Charles, Taz and I slowly walked back to the house. I played with Taz as if I had rediscovered a good friend. Money trumped all my concerns about America.

The thought of a half million-dollar salary cleared my head and for the rest of the day, I didn't think at all about my concerns that caused me such grief in the morning. Even my bio-terror nightmare was hard to remember. I peaked into the war room study and discovered that Charles had rigged out the room with maps and projectors. A very large table was centered in the middle of the room with a chair on each side. All my notes, drawings, maps and diagrams had been transferred from my small study to the war room in exactly the same manner that the material had been in. Charles passed by and asked, "So, what do you think?"

"Perfect," I answered. The pre-nuptial agreement was a no brainer for me as I fully expected it. I didn't feel entitled to one cent of Gabby's money either during marriage or upon divorce. I was, however, going to get an attorney to at least look at the document for bombshells. What started as a horrible morning transformed into a lovely afternoon. Gabby and I took an afternoon walk with TT on the beach heading towards Montauk. I think we walked for five miles. Upon our return, Charles had pre-dinner appetizers prepared and ice cold beer. I realized that I was an easy mark for money. The mention of money could turn my head in an instant. I wasn't a man of strong convictions. If I had felt so strongly about what Sam and his reborns were going to do to America, I would have been out there marching with the 400,000 that had invaded New York City to protest Sam's convention, gunshot wound notwithstanding. I was nothing more than a loudmouth standing on the sidelines bad mouthing Sam, complaining like a little "girlie-man." Maybe it was time to shut up or act upon the alleged depth of my convictions. Maybe I was a phony?

Dinner consisted of lobster bisque, crab cakes and strawberry cheesecake that Charles brought from Junior's in Brooklyn. We laughed as Charles rehashed a fishing story. After coffee, Charles grabbed my arm and told me to come with him. He led me out the front door to the awaiting limousine. He told the driver to go to "the club." "What's this all about Charles?" I asked.
"I told you early this morning that I was going to take you out this evening and so, here we are," he answered.
"What club?" I inquired.
"Oh, just a little weekly get together that many of my close old time Hamptonites attend after Labor day," he answered. Gabby got in the open door of the limo and sat across from us.
"You're coming too?" I asked.
"Wouldn't miss it for anything," she answered.
"What kind of club are we going to? Political? Social? Yacht? Religious?" I asked.
"Kind of like a neighborhood get together," Gabby answered.
"It's like a box of chocolates, you never know what you're going to get," Charles added. I smiled at the Forrest Gump reference.
"But, it's always friendly," Gabby assured me.
Gabby's assurances of friendliness made me uneasy.

## Chapter Two

The limo pulled into a driveway of an estate and drove a quarter of a mile towards the mini-castle located next to the ocean. We got out and headed towards a large barn situated a hundred yards from the main house. A bouncer type man greeted us at the door.

"Mr. Westerfield, Gabby, good evening," he said. There was a slight pause as the man wanted someone to identify me.

"Chuck, this is my future son-in-law, Dr. Stanley Warlib," said Charles.

Chuck and I exchanged pleasantries as he stared at my face to ensure that he would recognize me the next time I showed up. The barn was enormous. It had been used to house horses in another time and had been converted to a large hall. It had the appearance of a square dance hall, which Gabby confirmed. As Charles, Gabby and I made our way through the barn, everyone greeted us. I was introduced to those that did not know me. Susan and Alan, who I had met during August, came over and hugged Gabby and I. I started to feel at home. It reminded me of a reception before a wedding. There was mingling, drinking and chatting. There was a dais at the front of the barn with a speaking lectern. I could not get a handle on the crowd. The scene did not appear to be anything but social. A man appeared at the lectern and began to speak. Everyone took a seat. The conversations ended slowly and the barn became quiet. Chuck closed the door.

"Welcome. I hope all of you had a summer as wonderful as the summer that I have just had. I see some new faces here so I can only conclude that many of our children have divorced over the summer and have brought their next victims." Everyone in the barn laughed.

"As you know, this is an election year and I would prefer if everyone refrained from making any political speeches or announcements as I don't want our status to be questioned by the Internal Revenue Service."

Again, there was more laughter. 501(c) corporations, not for profit organizations, were being watched by the I.R.S. for engaging in recommending one political candidate over another. However, this was clearly a social gathering and the speaker was merely practicing his jokes on the crowd. It appeared that it was nothing more than a gathering of well-heeled local residents meeting to announce births, deaths, marriages and upcoming social events. The speaker finished his remarks and asked for those in the audience who wanted to make an announcement to raise their hands. Only four raised their hands and Charles remarked that it was going to be a short evening. "Thank God," Gabby responded. The first and second speakers told the audience about an upcoming birth and an appointment to a high level State Department position, respectively. Charles made his way to the lectern as the second speaker was concluding his remarks. Charles received a small applause as he approached the microphone. None of the other speakers had received any applause and it was a testament to his apparent popularity in the group.

"Good evening everyone. I have the pleasure of announcing the upcoming marriage of my beloved daughter Gabby to Dr. Stanley Warlib. He's the poor fellow seated next to Gabby. Notwithstanding his shortcomings, he's a good fisherman," said Charles.

There was polite laughter in the barn.

"Stand up Stan and let the people get a good look at you," he continued.

I stood up and slowly turned a full 360 degrees enabling everyone to get a long sustained look.

"Welcome," someone shouted from the back of the barn.

"Thank you," I responded. Charles continued his speech.

"My future son-in-law Stan is going to come up to the microphone and tell us all how Sam is using public assets, meaning our soldiers and tax money to promote purely private interests that benefit only a few. Come on up Stan," said Charles.

I sat at the table and glanced at Gabby and Mr. Westerfield. I wasn't happy and I could feel a slight twinge of anger start to overtake my body. I got up from the table and slowly, very slowly, walked to the dais. I couldn't figure out why Charles boxed me into a political speech when there was a clear prohibition against it. I felt like I had been set-up for a fall. Maybe it was a rite of passage to exhibit grace under fire with this crowd. Maybe it was just a simple way to humiliate me. I quickly abandoned these thoughts and tried to focus on what I was going to say. I felt an overwhelming need to perform in a manner consistent with the great Charles Westerfield tradition. I approached the microphone with dread, sweat; trepidation and some well justified anger.

"Hello, my name is Stanley Warlib," I said.

"*Dr.* Stanley Warlib," Gabby yelled out.

"I don't know why Charles Westerfield so artfully boxed me into a political speech. There appears to be a prohibition against political speeches and I wouldn't want to jeopardize the tax-exempt status of this wonderful assembly. I know how the well heeled *love* to pay taxes," I said.

Some people laughed. I took this small opportunity to survey the crowd and examine their attire. Specifically, I was looking for the ever-present American flag pin affixed to their lapels. There were several. I couldn't figure out if there were present any artsy East Hampton types, old money Southampton, nouveau riche Westhampton or just some plain old leftover potato farmers.

"Therefore, to assuage the I.R.S., I will refrain from making any speeches whatsoever and simply introduce myself in a little more detail," I said.

"The political speech ban rule is waived. Does anyone second the motion?" some guy asked. It seemed the entire group seconded the motion on the floor.

"Go ahead, tell us how Sam is using public assets for purely private purposes," someone yelled. The men in the audience leaned back in their chairs and crossed their arms and struck what appeared to be a judgmental pose. The women stared at me kindly as if they were offering support to some victim who was about to be skewered. It was my distinct impression that this was indeed a rite of passage, kind of like when the shit hits the fan, can I look sincerely into the camera and express some bullshit emotions and explanation for vile acts that either my companions or I committed.

"My belief, that Sam is using public assets, your money and your children's money to protect pipelines in the Caspian Sea region is, at the present time, merely conjecture and under study. However, next spring, after I have done a sufficient amount of research enabling me to connect the dots in a clear and succinct manner, I would be glad to return to this barn and present all of my circumstantial evidence to such a degree that no one could conclude otherwise. I will not have direct evidence to support such a conclusion, because, as you know, many people are better off when plans are undocumented. Plausible denial," I said.

I looked at the crowd and noticed that many of the men smiled. I continued, "therefore, I will change the subject of my speech although not the topic. It will remain political. The subject of my speech will be 'gas lighting.' The art of making someone believe something that's not true. Sometimes, to the extent that the person thinks he or she is crazy. We have all practiced gas lighting in some form or another. In business, for example, we may try to convince the gentlemen sitting across the table that we may have more oil reserves than we have. Some people might go so far so to produce written letters from engineers attesting to proven oil reserves. In car dealerships, salesmen often tell little white lies to customers to close a deal. The courts have differentiated between mere 'puffery' and outright fraud. Take, for example," at this point I paused and looked at the crowd and noticed that I had their attention and took out a napkin and spread it across the lectern, creating the appearance that I had prepared notes, and continued, "the intelligence on weapons of mass destruction that Sam proclaimed Iraq had. It was the sole basis for the invasion of Iraq and Sam overturned fifty years of foreign policy. We now exist, all of us, under a policy of pre-emptive attacks on foreign nations if we believe that such an attack is necessary. Well, if that's our policy, I'm sure all of you would agree that our Intel better be right and more important, that our interpretation of that Intel better be correct. The 9/11 Commission only examined the events leading up to that date, not the drumbeat for war on Iraq afterwards. Sam and his minions frightened all of us with talk of mushroom clouds and imminent attack. I ask you, each and everyone one of you, mere puffery or outright fraud? Did Sam gas light you into believing that Saddam Hussein posed an immediate and present danger? Prior to the war, Scott Ritter said Iraq didn't have W.M.D.'s. We called him a traitor. After the invasion, we found no chemical weapons. We found no biological weapons. We found no nuclear weapons. David Kay, our specialist, came back from Iraq and stated that we made a mistake. Iraq had no weapons. We attempted to bribe every Iraqi scientist with money and yet, not one scientist came forward to reveal the location or even proof of existence of weapons of mass destruction. After this messy episode, Sam and his boys said the entire episode was a direct result of C.I.A. groupthink. A massive intelligence failure and now we are guilty of massive groupthink. It's the fault of the C.I.A., not ours. I ask you, did Sam engage in mere puffery or outright fraud?"

I paused and asked for a glass of water and Gabby ran up to the dais and handed me one. Once again, I looked around the room and noticed no visible dissension or hostility. It appeared that everyone was interested in my speech.

"Before you consider an answer to that question, let me tell you a little history story. Twenty-nine years, on a long flight to Moscow, Gerald Ford, then head of the family, was en route to Moscow with his Secretary of State, Henry Kissinger, to engage the Soviet Union, subsequently called the Evil Empire, in an effort to conclude SALT II treaty talks and to further our foreign policy of détente. The war hawks were furious. Peace does not sell weapons. The Department of Defense needs a boogeyman, always did and always will. In an effort to scuttle the talks, someone leaked information to a young reporter named Robert Novak and the plane was turned around in mid air and returned to the United States. Because the assessment of our very own C.I.A. did not support the hawk's position, the Director of the C.I.A. proposed a novel idea. He called for a competitive assessment by an outside agency in juxtaposition to the C.I.A. The Secretary of Defense supported the idea. A Team A/Team B approach was instituted. Team A was the governments C.I.A. and Team B was composed of outside people. Team B assessed the Soviet Unions threat to the United States to a greater degree than our own C.I.A. The assessment formed the basis for the National Intelligence Estimate, the document that the head of our family receives. The result was the creation of the Evil Empire. Defense had a boogeyman and the greatest arms race known to man ensued. I am sure that if anyone present in this barn tonight sells arms they're happy. Twenty-nine years ago, the Secretary of Defense was Donald Rumsfeld. Twenty-nine years ago the Director of the C.I.A. was Sam's father. Twenty-nine years ago, Dick Cheney was assistant Chief of Staff to the head of the family. I question then, since the players today are the *same* as they were twenty-nine years ago, did they take a page out of history or is it mere coincidence?

It's easy to dismiss my entire viewpoint as partisan, or anti-American or just sheer nonsense and it's easy to dismiss because we are all basking in the swift victory of our military. Nothing feels better than winning, does it? Who are we going to demonize next? Iran? They are, after all, part of the Axis of Evil. They are part of our fight necessary for civilization to exist and part of our war on Islamic terrorists, or so says Sam. Many of you are thinking that it's a mere coincidence and that I bootstrapped myself into an argument. The smarter of you know fully well that if you have the same players and the same idea then Sam was advised by his colleagues to lift a page out of history and create an evil Iraq to justify his invasion. The inquisitive among you are probably wondering what group is the modern day Team B," I said.

I paused to take a drink of water and again glanced around the room. No one was squirming yet or coughing. I looked at my watch and noticed that ten minutes had passed. I thought that it would be appropriate to conclude my monologue in five minutes. Gabby appeared impressed. Charles didn't. Someone seated near the dais and off to the right shouted, "so, what's your point?"
"Good question," I said.
"Suppose, Sam and his administration decide to start a war with Iran and invade that country. Are you going to believe him just because he's head of the family or might you consider that he hyped the intelligence? It might not seem important since it's going to be just another cakewalk in a desert kingdom. An easy fight. Who cares if Sam or his intelligence is hyped or not? They're Islamic and we're in a war with extreme Islam. Look at this little boy seated at the table in front of me with his proud dad. Maybe he is three years old. To grow big and strong, he needs food. Food is human energy. Similarly, for a nation to grow, it needs food. It needs oil. Lack of energy resources limits a nations growth. When a truck that leaves New York to deliver goods to Chicago runs out of gas it stops. When a country runs out of oil it stops. I would venture to say that if oil stopped flowing, America would come to a standstill within ten days. Invading Iran will have serious, very serious consequences. The reality is as follows: Iran is China's leading

oil supplier. Since mid-2001, Iran has overtaken the Kingdom of Saudi Arabia and Oman to become China's leading supplier. Russia has had extensive ties with Iran for years and is currently building a nuclear reactor in Southern Iran for its energy needs. Iran has available military manpower of 20,937,348. Russia has available military manpower of 39,127,169 and China has an astounding 379,524,688 people available for military manpower. China and Russia have nuclear capabilities and the means of delivery. I don't think China would feel kindly disposed towards Sam if Sam decided to take away its largest gas pump. It would stop growing and might take steps necessary in conjunction with Russia to secure Iran's sovereignty. The next step should Sam seek an easy opponent would be Syria, however, if Sam heads East towards Iran, I would highly recommend that all of us be very, very careful in our analysis of Sam's claims. Heading East puts him in the arena with real heavyweights and international politics, especially when it involves oil, can be a sophisticated game, always more so than envisioned. For example, one of our strongest allies and supporter of the war in Iraq and against terrorism is Australia. Allegiance and money swim in the same river. The Chinese recently negotiated a deal with Woodside Energy of Australia worth $25,000,000,000 for a 25-year supply of liquid natural gas. Huge as this deal is, it comes hard on the heels of a deal valued at $30,000,000,000. When Sam and President Hu of China stood before the Australian parliament it was President Hu who received a warmer welcome. Once again, allegiance swims in the same waters as money. Thank you."

I concluded my speech and looked around the room as I drank some water from the glass. I was surveying the crowd's reaction. One man, who I could not see from where I was standing, said "blow it out your ass," quietly but loud enough for me to hear. Another man, obviously military, buzz cut and all, stood up with a clenched fist but was restrained by his wife. As I walked down the steps from the dais, I could see Charles and Gabby making their way towards me, however, three men were waiting at the bottom of the steps and blocked their access. Charles said that he would be waiting in the limo. Gabby lingered and talked to one of her girlfriends. Each man, one by one, introduced himself and handed me their card and requested that I call when I got a chance. One gentleman was well dressed and looked like Goldman Sachs partner material. The second guy looked like a liberal, lefty, ivory tower political wonk type and the third guy looked average. His card only had his name on it. M.B. Federov it read. I looked at the card and at him.

"Mikhail Boris Federov," he said. "That's my private number and I would like it if you should call me," he stated.

"What's your affiliation?" I asked.
"Call me and we discuss," he answered.

Walking with Gabby through the crowd that still remained, I received some pats on the pack. Near the door, one man stopped me and said "Charles cheated. He's not supposed to tell you in advance about being put on the spot. I mean you had sufficient time in which to prepare a speech. I saw you take out a piece of paper and lay it on the lectern," he said.

"Oh, you mean this napkin," I said and handed him the blank napkin. He opened the napkin and examined each side looking for words on paper. I could hear him say "wow, that's pretty good," as I walked past Chuck towards the limo.

For five minutes no one said a word. I didn't know whether Charles was pissed at me because he was embarrassed at my performance or because my speech showed a certain level of stupidity because it lacked details.

"Not bad, Stan, not bad at all," Charles said quietly.

"I threw you a fast curveball and you hit a double. Not out of the park mind you, but a solid hit nonetheless," he said.

"What would have made my speech a homerun?" I asked.

"Detail, Stan, detail," he answered.

"But this was a social gathering. I looked at my watch and ten minutes had gone by and I didn't want to bore everyone, so I decided to wrap it up," I said.

I didn't want to argue with Charles. I didn't agree with him either. Gabby leaned next to me and gave me a kiss on the cheek. Dad had spoken and I got a kiss from Gabby for hitting a double. I fantasized that had I knocked one out of the park I would have gotten laid in the back seat with Charles in attendance. Charles interrupted my fantasy. "Your speech about Iran was a little prophetic. I see Iran is making the newspapers these days. It's exactly the reason I offered you a job. Things are getting pretty hot internationally and you and the war room will aid us tremendously. So who or what is the modern day version of Team B?" asked Charles. I was sure Charles knew the answer and concluded that it was another little test that he was giving me post speech.

"The Office of Special Plans," I answered.

"And who are they?" he asked.

"When the State department and the C.I.A. couldn't make specific links with Saddam and 9/11 and al Qaeda, containment of Iraq was rejected as soft policy. Sam's Secretary of Defense Donald Rumsfeld set up the Office of Special Plans, which was staffed and overseen by handpicked associates of the Secretary, Wolfowitz, Cheney, Feith and Libby. Interestingly enough, Feith is the Undersecretary of Defense for Policy and at one time was a legal counsel for defense contractors. The God of these guys is Leo Strauss, the philosopher-king of the Neo-Cons. They believe that us commoners can't understand anything and that our beliefs and opinions must be shaped by the powerful and visionary. The bottom line; this group moved private unsupervised intelligence to Sam. I'm sure Sam is not that stupid that he wasn't aware of the bullshit that he received? After all, that kind of information fits neatly in his calling and mission from God. I'm sure he was a willing participant," I said.

Charles interrupted, "and that brings it back home to Lawrence A. Franklin one of Doug Feith's little toys who is currently being investigated as a spy for passing information to Israel, doesn't it, Stan?" Charles asked.

"It certainly does," I answered.

"I'm sure your saw the headline 'Pentagon Office in Spying Case was Focus of Iran Debate,' in The New York Times?" he asked.

"I sure did. I liked the part that stated that before the war with Iraq, Doug Feith established a small intelligence unit. Voila, Office of Special Plans. This is all political junkie bullshit. What's really going down is that Sam and his boys need a stable Middle East for oil and they're going to get it one way or another. Little Franklin passed on info to Israel about Sam's position on Iran because they wanted to know whether to bomb the shit out of Iran first or let Sam do it under his bullshit terror campaign. After all, Israel bombed Iran's nuclear plant twenty-three years ago and they'll bomb it again," I said.

"So the question then becomes at what point does Israel pull the trigger?" Charles asked. "Well, I think Sam's approach is destabilization of the ruling theocracy and there's no way Israel is going to wait for that destabilization process to take effect. But Sam's religious buddies are pissing off so many Muslims with their Christian crusade crap that even if they effect regime change these Muslims aren't going to do business with the Americans. I mean they're creating enemies of Christianity all over the Arab world," I answered.

"And so to secure Middle East oil you need what?" Charles asked.

"Occupation and military draft," I answered.

"Which still leaves Russia and China standing off on the sidelines deciding what to do," Charles said.

"Yeah, Russia and China, all 379,000,000 of those Chinese military men," I mused.

The limo pulled into the driveway and TazTwo came bounding around the house from the dune that he had been resting on. I got out of the limo as quickly as I could to beat Taz to the car, as I didn't want him to jump up and scratch the paint with his paw nails. "Thanks," Charles said. "I'm going to bed," he added.

Gabby and I decided to take a late night stroll on the beach. I felt great and was a million miles away from the nightmare less than twenty-four hours ago.

"Stan, it's time to turn off the brain. You have a woman here who needs tending to," Gabby said. Immediately, I stopped talking and gently pulled Gabby down to the sand. We were at the edge of the ocean's waves. I gently lifted her bottom off the sand and penetrated her. She must have been fantasizing about making love in the limousine because her vagina was soaked. As I lay on top of her I glanced around to see if anyone was present. I saw the silhouette of a person on one of the dunes off in the distance but that person was too far away to see anything.

## Chapter Three

"Good morning Charles," I said as I came into the kitchen. "Where's Gabby?" I asked. "Don't know. I think she's off clamming with Tazmobile," he answered. "Military draft and occupation," he said.
"I'm taking a vacation from politics for the day, Charles. It's a no political day, today," I told him.
"However, I got a personal question for you, if you don't mind?" I said.
"Sure, what is it," he responded.
"Exactly, why did you break off relations with your financial buddies?" I asked.
"I'll try to make it short. What you're witnessing are two perfect parallels lines. Sam's financial buddies want to take over the Middle East and its oil, including the Caucasus area and Sam's religious buddies want to kill the Muslims. They're an evil religion. Both are working hand in hand. At those points in time when there's conflict they try to resolve their differences amicably. Most of the time they do resolve their differences. On rare occasions, they can't resolve their differences. I broke because both groups are so invested in their own mind-set they can't get beyond themselves. They just don't see that there are a handful of powerful leaders who have their own agenda and their own spheres of influence. There will be a clash of interests because Sam and his buddies see what they're doing as a zero sum game. They win and their opponents lose. That's short-sighted and dangerous. It is a very, very dangerous game. So I broke from the group," Charles concluded.
"And you would like my psychological input in this great game we're witnessing?" I asked.
"People play games and you know people. At this point in time, it is invaluable to know people," Charles said.
"I understand," I responded.
Gabby came in from clamming and said "hello everybody, fresh clams for dinner tonight?" she asked.
"I thought I'd take the day off and go into the city. You know, see my office, make some calls, stuff like that," I said. Gabby and Charles glanced at each other. "Probably a good idea. You've been cooped up with us Westerfield's for a long time. Even I couldn't stand being cooped up with myself for as long as you have been holed up here. But, you're going by limo. There has been one attempt on your life and I don't want another," said Charles. Charles looked at Gabby.
"No problem, guys," said Gabby.

I knew that Charles knew that I was going to make calls to the three people that had given me their business cards the night before. I was sure that he would question me upon my return.

I was delighted to get away from the estate, Gabby and Charles included. It was delightful living there most of the time but on certain occasions it was intense. I was enjoying my freedom and especially enjoying the thought that Dr. Stanley Warlib had been offered a job for $500,000.00, was riding in a limo and speaking in a barn where the elite tread. Power and money were intoxicating. I could feel its pull on me. I knew that I didn't possess the strongest of convictions and could easily succumb to the allure of what was being placed before me. Easily placed before me. In the limo I looked out the window on several occasions and noticed people staring at me trying to figure out whether I was a celebrity or V.I.P. Their stares were an aphrodisiac. I pushed the button to lower the window that separated the driver from me and told him that the whole experience was pretty cool. "You'll get used to it," he told me. His name was Harry.

"Harry, take me to my office on 88th street," I said.

"Been there before, Dr. Warlib," he replied.

"I'll tell you what Harry. You call me Stan and I'll call you Harry," I said.

"Bad habit to get into Dr. Warlib. In these circles, it's expected that I address those in the back seat by their proper names. It's part of the deal. Don't be a novice, Dr. Warlib. Just get used to it," Harry said.

Seventy miles of people staring at me in the limousine blew my mind. I was a nobody that felt like a somebody and only because I was riding in the back of a limo with a chauffeur at the wheel. I realized how easy it was for the underlings in Sam's mission to get sucked into the allure of power by being a small cog in a greater calling. They could tell their grandchildren that if it wasn't for them and their efforts, Sam wouldn't be sitting on Iraqi oil and they would be speaking Chinese. It was all bullshit but it had a major impact on me. I was a whore and the only question was price. Harry double-parked next to the cars in front of my office. He got out and raced around the limo to open the door. Several people stopped and looked.

"Hey Warlib, how are you?" a neighbor shouted when he realized it was me.

"I'm fine and getting better," I said.

Several other neighbors gathered around and told me that they read about the shooting in the paper. They all wished me good-luck and took a second look at Harry and the limo. They were all glad that I was back. I was missed in the neighborhood and it felt good to be home.

"I'll wait outside Dr. Warlib," Harry advised me and added, "take your time, it's my job to wait."

"Thanks Harry," I responded.

I unlocked the door and stood for a brief moment staring at my apartment. At my feet was a mound of mail that I picked up and placed on the kitchen table. The apartment felt small compared to the large expanse of the Westerfield estate. I walked around the apartment and examined each room and sang an old show tune to myself, "getting to know you, getting to know all about you. Getting to like you, getting to hope you like me," I sang. I thought to myself that I was one sick fuck who just never grew up. I laughed anyway. I opened the fridge and grabbed a bottle of wine, stuck the mail under my arm and headed out to the backyard deck. It was junk mail and bills. "Doesn't anyone write letters anymore?" I asked myself. Interestingly enough, buried in the pile was a letter from my son Jordan. His mom, my ex of twenty years, had called him and told him that I had been shot. He wrote that he tried to call but the phone system in Mongolia left something to be desired. His contract of two years with the Japanese government had ended. Jordan was an ALT schoolteacher in a northern coastal town named Akita. He left Japan with a young lady named Maki heading back to the states by way of China, Mongolia, Russia and Europe. When I was shot, Jordan was somewhere on the outskirts of Shanghai and couldn't call me. His mom didn't know my whereabouts after I was shot and certainly didn't know anything about my current life style. Had she known about the estate and limo I would have caught verbal hell and an immediate demand for back alimony and child support. Jordan was fulfilling his life long dream of pretending to be Indiana Jones, horse back riding on the steppes of Mongolia. At this point in his life, he had been in every part of the world. I smiled as I recalled one incident in Nepal where he lost his Sherpa and had to sleep outdoors. The leeches got him. To prove his story, he lifted his shirt and showed me the numerous dark marks that the leeches left all over his stomach and back. Jordan had met Maki, a nurse, at a salsa social dance. I was surprised that she left her small town of Akita to travel the world with my son. It was certainly behavior out of the norm for a Japanese woman to leave her hometown and run off with a "gaijin." Nevertheless, the letter indicated that things were going fine and his Mongolian dream was just several days away. He wrote that Maki wasn't feeling well and I made a mental note to e-mail and ask him if it wasn't morning sickness. I could be a Grandpa-Stanley-San. It felt nice, just plain nice, sitting in the backyard, sipping wine and looking through my mail. "Nice," I defined as simple. The estate was complex and consisted of endless head games and an incredible use of brainpower. I didn't mind the game but I liked it at my pace and the ability to choose if and when I wanted to play. Accepting employment with Charles was going to remove my ability to choose when I wanted to play. The old codger loved the game with every fiber of his being but I didn't. Deciding whether to choose employment with Westerfield was going to be tough. I remembered that Harry was waiting outside. I went outside and yelled to Harry that I wasn't going to be too much longer. Harry advised me that that was his job and that I could take as long as I wanted. "Hmmm," I said to myself. Pretty cool having someone wait on you while you take as long as you want. I went back to the deck, poured another glass of wine and continued reading Jordan's letter. Maki was a javelin thrower at a professional level and her salsa group placed third in some kind of regional competition. I folded Jordan's letter and put it in my back pocket. It was always my practice to read Jordan's letters several times. After all, he was my baby boy. I wondered what he would think of Gabby, Charles and the whole Westerfield wonderland of money and power.

The name read Bruce Hemming, III and he was apparently a managing partner at a major wall-street firm. I was sure that he had given me his card only because I was going to be the son-in-law of the great Charles Westerfield. I called his office and re-introduced myself. We chatted politely. The bottom line was that he was simply networking. My name was added to his list. He wasn't added to my list and I tore up his card. The next guy was Timothy Bellbottoms, the lefty liberal sort of gentlemen.
"Hi, Mr. Bellbottoms, this is Dr. Stanley Warlib. We met last night at the barn. I gave a speech on Team A/Team B," I advised him.
"Oh yes, yes, I recall. Dr. Warlib. You know the first thing I did this morning was Google Team A/Team B and you were right. Quite a connection," he said.
"Well, what can I do for you? Why did you give me your card? Are you networking?" I asked.
"Well, I thought that we might get together for brunch sometime and talk," he said. "About what?" I asked.
"Things, you know. Politics, Sam, Team A/Team B, matters like that. I would like to introduce you to some of my friends who would be interested in what you have to say," said Mr. Bellbottoms.
"What kind of friends are we talking about Timothy?"
"My atheist anarchist friends," he answered.
"Really, how interesting. Do you mean anarchist from a pure political science standpoint or do you mean anarchists from a out in the street blowing up buildings standpoint?" I inquired.

"Both," Mr. Bellbottoms responded.

"O.K., brunch is on. I'll call you in several days for brunch the week-end after this one," I said.

"Fine, and thank you for calling."

That was an interesting call. Atheists and anarchists, a combination I wanted to know more about in the current political atmosphere. The third call was to Mikhail Boris Federov and this was the call that I was the most interested in making.

"Hello, Mr. Federov, how are you? This is Stanley Warlib."

"Oh, Dr. Warlib, so kind of you to call this quickly," he said.

"Last night you gave me your card so I assumed you wanted me to call. Did you want anything specifically or were you just networking?" I asked.

"No, I want something but it should not be discussed on the phone. Can we meet tonight?" he asked.

"I guess so. I was going to go back to Southampton but I can't envision lingering in the city would cause anyone a problem. Sure, we can meet tonight," I said.

"Fine, I'm going to take you to Odessa in Brighton Beach, Brooklyn. You'll have a good time, I promise you. I live at 860 United Nations Plaza. Meet me outside the building at 6:30 p.m.," Mikhail told me.

"Sure, no problem. Good-bye," I said and hung up the phone.

I went out front and walked over to the limousine and told Harry what the plans were. He told me that he was taking off and would return at 6:00 p.m. to pick me up. He assured me that Mr. Westerfield or Gabby didn't need him. I understood that these kinds of happenings were Harry's breaks. I was going to ask him what his salary was but decided not to. A two and one half hour break was pretty good. I decided to take a little stroll around the neighborhood. I felt good. Everyone who knew me came over for details about the shooting and told me they sorely missed me. Apparently, I had more of an impact on the hood than I realized. I made my way over to the Madison Avenue Bar and had a beer. The staff was happy to see me. The bartender told me that his income was off since I hadn't been in and he was real happy I was back in town. One guy came over and slapped me on the back exactly where my wound was. I saw stars. He apologized. I left the bar and walked up to Mykonos and peered into the diner. Angie was there and waived. As I walked through the door she put some plates down and ran over to hug me. "Doc, I was so worried about you. I'm so happy to see you. Are you o.k?" she asked. "Yes, Angie, I'm fine. I'm really all right. Everything is fine. You know, I had a dream about you last night," I told her.

"Tell me it wasn't a dirty dream," she said.

"Sorry Angie can't do that. It was a great filthy dirty sex dream with you and I as the star attractions. However, in the dream you were a doctoral student in sociology writing your thesis about the role of waitresses in society," I told her.

"Well, I'm not a student anymore and I do have a Doctorate degree. I'm a professional student that hates working. That's why I waitress," she said.

After that fascinating little personal tidbit, Angie picked up some plates and went to the kitchen. Spiro and Olympia were waiting at the register to greet me. I got a wonderful handshake from Spiro and a European type double kiss on each cheek from Olympia. I told Spiro that he should remove the television. He laughed. I left the diner and told Olympia to tell Angie that I wanted to talk to her.

"You're engaged, Dr. Warlib," Olympia emphatically reminded me.

I continued on my stroll in a big loop around the neighborhood and made it back to my apartment in time to shower, dress and meet Harry outside at 6:00 p.m. Harry rushed around the limo and opened the back seat door just as I arrived. Before he put the limousine in gear, he asked where we were going. I told him the address and he looked at me through the rear view mirror with a raised eyebrow. He arrived at 860 United Nations Plaza exactly at 6:30 p.m. and Mr. Federov was waiting outside talking to the doorman. He approached the limousine and Harry, as required, opened the door. "Enjoying the benefits of wealth, Dr. Warlib?" Mikhail asked.

"Enjoying and trying to get use to the benefits of wealth," I said. I told Harry where we were going and Mikhail gave him directions. Mikhail did not engage in substantive talk. It was only polite little chitchat. The window separating Harry from the back seat was open. I realized that the conversation might have been different had I closed the window. I was a novice but I swore to myself that I would learn quickly. Harry drove us over the Brooklyn Bridge and got on the Brooklyn Queens Expressway until it turned into Ocean Parkway. He headed straight down to Avenue Z, took a left to Coney Island Avenue, made a right and stopped just before Brighton Beach Avenue. Once again, Harry performed the ceremonious door opening sequence and Mikhail and I disappeared into Odessa. It was a place of moderate size with tables in front of a stage. The place was packed and many of the Russian patrons were half drunk. It seemed that every minute someone was saying salute and lifting a small shot glass containing Vodka. There were belly dancers on stage. To me the belly dancers looked Rubenesque, to Mikhail they looked voluptuous. The whole scene looked like an out of control vaudeville party. There were some heavyweight Russian Mafia types with bodyguards surrounding a table. Mikhail and I were seated at a table next to the stage. Two tables to the right was a stunning Russian woman, maybe 35 years old who had an absolutely gorgeous body. I have not seen a woman that beautiful in over twenty years. Mikhail whispered to the waiter to bring over a couple of shots. I was sure that he told the waiter to continue until one of us fell over. I couldn't keep my eyes off the Russian beauty. After four shots I finally asked Mikhail what exactly was it that he wanted. M.B. Federov wanted me to be something that was akin to a spy. He was willing to pay me $3,000,000.00 a year to have access to Charles Westerfield. He advised me that Russia was in the process of growing financially and that Vladimir Putin was extremely worried that Sam was going to upset that growth. I was to act as a voice of moderation in my geo-political discussions with Charles in the hope that Charles with his tremendous influence and power would somehow influence Sam and temper his actions. The Russian woman passed our table and slipped me her number. Mikhail told me that she was not only beautiful but also extremely dangerous to flirt with. It was Russian Mafia property. I slid the note across the table and told her that although I was flattered I was faithfully and happily engaged. Boris looked at me with a slight smile. The evening concluded. After Mikhail and I settled in the back seat of the limousine, Harry handed me the cell phone. "It's Mr. Westerfield," he said.

"Charles, how the hell are you?" I asked.

"Are you a fucking idiot?" he shouted.

"Why, what did I do?" I asked in return.

"I let you alone for twenty-four hours and you're hanging out in Odessa with a fucking K.G.B. agent. Are you an idiot? Can't you see the headlines: 'Westerfield and Future Son-in-Law Indicted for Espionage.' Jesus Christ, Stan, I didn't realize you were so stupid," he yelled.

I held the cell phone away from my ear and put it close to Mikhail's ear so that he could hear the tirade. Charles asked what I had to say for myself.

"Charles, a stunning Russian woman is sitting in a bar. In come a stockbroker, anarchist and Russian spy." I couldn't finish my joke, as Charles was hysterical on the other end of the line. It was a long time before Charles calmed down. I heard Charles repeat to Gabby what I had told him.

"When did you know?" Charles asked.

"Really, Charles, an atheist anarchist named Timothy Bellbottoms who looked like he couldn't beat up a two year old," I said.

"Come on home son," Charles told me.

"Charles, when will the loyalty tests stop?" I asked.

"Come on home son," he repeated.

# CHAPTER FOUR

I took my place at the kitchen table the following morning. "A no nightmare night?" Gabby asked.
"Yes, no nightmares. A great nights sleep. God, that Russian woman was just absolutely stunning," I said to Gabby.
"Don't push it, Stan," she responded.
Charles, Gabby and I settled in to read the morning paper. TazTwo sat at my feet, covering my toes.
"I have to start that war room today. There's too much important stuff happening in the world that I'm going to forget," I said to Charles. Charles lowered his paper and asked if I thought about his offer. I told him that I wanted to talk to a friend of mine first. He smiled and exclaimed that he could feel the price tag going up. He didn't say that the salary he offered was final. I realized that it was going to be a negotiating process. As I was reading an article, I blurted out in Elvis style "the superego has left the building." "Very funny Stan," Gabby said.
"What does that mean?" asked Charles.
"Well, I'm not a Freudian, however, in psychoanalytic terms it means that every person has a personality that consists of a superego, ego and id. The superego is a largely unconscious part of the personality, regarded as dominating the conscious ego and acts principally in the role of conscience and critic. The ego is the superficial part of the id developed in response to the physical and social environment. The id, Charles, the id is the concealed, inaccessible part of the psyche, seated in the unconscious, independent of a sense of reality, logic, and morality, but actuated by fundamental impulses towards fulfilling instinctual needs. Thank you Webster very much. In order words, the war between the blue states and the red states. In other words, the evangelical Christian crusade against evil. In other words." Charles interrupted me.
"I get the point, Stan," he said.
"If Freud were alive today he'd be happy. It's a classic example of his theory. The red states, flag waiving, god-fearing people are the id. They are acting independent of any sense of reality, logic and morality. The blue states are the ego and the superego that stands as our conscience and critic, has left the building letting the two sides fight. In the great sandbox of international friends and acquaintances, everyone has left the sandbox and Sam is alone beating himself up. It reminds of a scene from the end of the movie The Fight Club where you see Edwin Norton alone in the parking lot punching himself in the face."
"And dragging himself through that indoor garage," Gabby added.

"Great movie," Charles said.

"That's exactly why I offered you a job, Stan. I didn't quite like Gabby getting her masters in psychology but I'm beginning to see that your discipline might be a great predictor of individual behavior. What exactly would a guy like Putin of Russia do with Sam making inroads into his territory? Knowing is invaluable," he concluded.

Gabby, Charles and I resumed reading the paper and exchanged sections as necessary. Charles always grabbed the financial section first; I grabbed the main section for Op-Ed pieces and Gabby reached for Arts & Entertainment. It was an arrangement that worked flawlessly.

I told Gabby and Charles that I was going back to the city to wrap up some details. I realized that I had not checked my phone messages or called my clients. I owed them an explanation of what had happened, what was going on and what my intentions were. I was surprised that I neglected to do so. They were probably extremely worried and concerned about themselves and me. My failure to call was extremely negligent and unprofessional. However, after realizing this, I didn't feel that I was sufficiently upset. My attitude was rather cavalier. I felt that I took an exit ramp onto to another expressway that was fairly painless and very exciting. A big smile came over my face as I walked towards the limousine and saw Harry standing next to the open door.

"Good morning, Harry. How are you?" I asked.

"Just fine, Dr. Warlib. Where are we going to go today?" he asked.

"To my office and then downtown for lunch," I said.

"Seeing Bellbottoms and Boris for lunch?" he asked.

"Pretty funny," I said.

Speeding towards Manhattan on the Long Island Expressway, I wondered if Charles would let me get a vanity plate for the limousine that read "Warlib." I continued my new game of staring out the window and looking for someone that was staring at me in the limo. Sure enough, they were out there. I was listening to Crosby, Stills, Nash & Young when a thought shot dead center into my mind. Harry said Bellbottoms and Boris when I got in the car. How the hell he did know the name Bellbottoms. I had called Timothy from my backyard. There were only two explanations. Either Harry was in on the joke or Harry had some kind of listening device in the limousine that was capable of eavesdropping. I was going to ask Harry if he was in on the planning of Charles little joke and decided against it. Nevertheless, the entire episode took the fun out of the big shot ride I was enjoying. Harry pulled up to my apartment and opened my door.

"Harry, did you help Mr. Westerfield with his plan yesterday? I mean did you get together with Bellbottoms and Boris to organize that little farce?"
Harry looked at me and stared as if he was trying to determine whether I was angry about the charade.
"No, didn't know Bellbottoms or Boris. Don't blame me if you're angry with the boss," he said.
"Just asking Harry, just asking. I'm not mad at anyone. As a matter of fact, I haven't had this much fun since, well, since I was shot."

I walked up the steps to my apartment, glanced around as I slowly opened the door to check if anyone was watching Warlib the Big Shot. I grabbed the mail and sat at my desk.
"Reuben?" I asked.
"Whoever this is, I'll call you back," Reuben said.
"Reuben, it's Dr. Warlib," I said quickly.
"Doc! You mean my fucking Doc. My very own Stanley. How the hell are you, Doc. I was worried about you. I read in the paper that you were shot. Your girlfriend Gabby called everyone and told us that you would need a month off. I was kind of expecting your call this week," he said.
"First, how are you and how is everybody in the group that you have seen?" I asked. "Well, I'm o.k. And you know that the group doesn't hang out with cocaine Reuben. Doc, make it quick the oil pits are going crazy," he said.
"Let's have a quick early dinner at Puglia's at 5:00 today," I told him.
"No problem," he said and hung up.

I carefully listened to all the messages and took notes where appropriate. All messages started off with the obligatory "I hope your feeling better" and left messages of varying lengths but no patient seemed to be in any particular distress. I was relieved. I couldn't wait for the limo ride down to Puglia's restaurant just to see the face on Reuben and the faces on all the other patrons. Harry knew that I was excited and purposely pulled the limo up to Puglia's in the most conspicuous manner possible. He jumped out, ran around the limo with a particular degree of excessiveness and boldly opened the door. "Shall I wait here Dr. Warlib or shall I take my leave for awhile," he asked. I knew what Harry was doing and responded accordingly. "Harry, take your leave and be back in an hour," I said. "A little stuffy," Harry whispered in my ear. I saw Reuben seated in the outdoor section of the restaurant and wished I had a camera to record his expression. Everyone turned their head as I took my seat next to Reuben and Reuben himself puffed out a little. After all, since a very important person was sitting with him, he must,

by extension, be very important himself. He got up as I approached and threw his arms around me and said loudly,
"Dr. Warlib, how long has it been? I haven't seen you since Monte Carlo."
"Cool it Reuben," I said.

Reuben motioned for the waiter to bring over two shots of Grappa and whispered to the waiter "basement." Basement was a euphemism for home grown.

"Salute Doc, to your recovery," he toasted.

"Salute, Reuben," I said.

Reuben and I had a thirty-minute chitchat and then finally got down to the meat of why I was there.
"Reuben, I want your undivided attention," I said.
"I know, no cocaine breaks," he stated.
"First, I have been offered a job by Charles Westerfield for $500,000.00. He wants my psychological geo-political advice as an aid in making a decision as to where to put his money. I want to know what you think?" I asked.
"First, a half million is chump change on the street and if you accept that offer he'll know you're stupid and don't even value your own opinion. Start at $2,000,000.00 and don't go for a penny less than $1.4 million," he answered.
I thought for a minute and then blurted out, "that's about $50,000.00 a week. Holy shit." "Look cool, Doc. You just got out of a limo," he said.
"That's it, Reuben?" I asked.
"Yeah, that's it," he said.
"Just like that," I added.
"Just like that," he said.
"Alright, then the next thing is what am I going to do with my patients if I accept the job?" I asked.
"It's a no brainer, Doc. The neurotics will survive, notwithstanding your God like status. They're big babies anyway. Who gives a shit?" he said.
"You don't think there will be any problems?" I asked.
"None, Doc. None," he said.
"You're not really asking for my opinion about your practice, so what do you really want?" he asked.
"Well, let's assume I have somewhere between 1.5 and 2 million to invest and I want to hook up with you investing some of this money," I said.
"No problem, but that's a real long weekend type conversation," he told me.
"I'm sure. At the estate," I said.
"That would be nice," Reuben responded.

"Finally, I want to coordinate with you a little something that will require complete discretion," I told Reuben.

"Now you really have my undivided attention. A little skullduggery," he beamed.

"Yes and it will require you to keep your mouth shut and your eyes and ears open. I don't have too much space at the estate to maneuver freely. I think my moves and talks are monitored. I don't know for sure but that's the feeling I get. When I call you, I want you to find an audio/visual store out of state that can install a motion and sound activated recording system that can store data on disk. I need tiny cameras that cannot be seen and the installers will have no more than 4 hours to install. They can't park near the estate. Are you reading me?" I asked.

"Doc, this is fucking great. It's real 007 shit, you know. I'd be more than glad to do it. I'm coming in my fucking pants. It's a better rush than coke," he said.

"When I call you from the estate and you hear the code word 'pork bellies,' you'll know it's time to move. You have homework to do after we leave and get the equipment lined up. I'll pay a premium for the hush-hush stuff and speed for which I need it accomplished," I told him.

"Doc, what a fucking rush," he said.

"Are you with me?" I asked.

"One hundred per-cent," he answered.

"Now that I think about it, having you out at the estate might be a good idea. It will give Gabby and Charles a chance to meet and see you about. But no cocaine under any circumstances and having a deep concern for your problem, I'll keep our meeting short enough so you won't get out of control," I said.

Rueben brought up the fight that he had had with Sam in the one group therapy session that Sam attended. I laughed out loud at Rueben's caricature of Sam. I glanced at the limousine and noticed that Harry was on the phone. I also noticed all the people that looked at the limo looked at the gathering of people outside Puglia's in attempt to connect the limousine to a face. I realized that I was planning spy maneuvers with a cocaine addict.

"Rueben, I'm starting to feel that I'm getting a little carried away with all this 007 stuff. Here I am, sitting at Puglia's, planning a raid on my future father in law's estate with a cocaine addict. I don't know, I'm starting to feel foolish," I said.

Rueben stared at me.

"Cocaine addict! Is that what you think of me, Doc? That hurts," he said. He sat back in his chair and folded his arms. I could tell he was preparing a speech in his head. He sat and stared. I gave him a sufficient opportunity to gather his thoughts.

"So, Rueben, what gives?" I asked.

"I'm going to talk to you off the record so to speak. Not like you're my shrink and I'm your cocaine addicted little shit head patient."

I realized that Rueben had been severely offended. I started to apologize but he quickly continued.

"Not for nothing, Doc, but I'm going to talk to you like a friend. Yeah, I had a cocaine problem for a long time, which you know. But let me tell you something that you don't know. For the last year my cocaine problem has substantially subsided. If I was doing four grams a week I got down to one. The money I saved on the three grams, I put in a savings account. Little shit head Rueben has got a savings account. Not only that, like you always told me that a shrink can't get to a persons problems while he's on drugs, ever since the cocaine lessened its grip on me, I started to see a Rueben I used to know. And I like the Rueben that I'm seeing. And on top of all this stuff, I started to look at all the issues that pushed me to cocaine in the first place. The Rueben that I'm seeing I like. For the first time in ten years I like myself. As far as I'm concerned you helped me rediscover me. I found myself with your help and Rueben is going to be all right. In my neighborhood, what you did for me is worth gold. It's what friendships are made of. Let me tell you the bottom line, Doc. If we were in Nam, I'd pick you as the guy that I wanted in the foxhole with me. You watched my back. Do you know what I mean? I never thought of you as some scumbag shrink taking my money and passing on me. You helped me," Rueben said.

I sat riveted to my seat. Rueben was talking real shit, as the saying goes. He was talking from his heart about a bond between people that generally forms only in wartime under fire. I started to speak. Rueben interrupted me.

"And something else, Doc. Blood brothers don't watch each others back when things are going well, they're there when the shit hits the fan. And the shit has hit your fan. Three weeks ago someone put a bullet in your back. You got that. Someone shot you in the back. The Westerfield's were kind enough to take you in and nurse you back to health. You come here tonight in daddy's limousine and tell me he offered you a job for $500,000.00. It sounds to me like everything is going o.k. But no, you want to pull some 007 bullshit and spy on your fucking wife to be and future father-in-law. I've been in therapy. I know how it works. You're either pissed to the gills or paranoid, or both. The next question is, do you have reason to be so angry or so paranoid that it would cause you to enlist me in spy work because if you do, I'm there," Rueben said.

I explained to Rueben that I was starting to feel anger about getting shot in the back and Charles having boxed me into a speech that I felt was designed to embarrass me. I also told Rueben that I thought Charles was spying on me through Harry.

"Well, maybe you should let some time go by and see if more incidents develop to confirm your suspicions," said Rueben.

I was hammered by Rueben's sincerity and depth of feelings. I felt like the guy would take a bullet for me. This was a concept that was beyond my comprehension. "Let's put Operation Pork Belly on hold Rueben, and if need be, I'll resurrect it," I told Rueben.

"No problem, Doc," said Rueben.

I was blown away from this entire episode because I never experienced the depth of feelings and conviction that Rueben expressed. I didn't know whether or not I would ever take a bullet for anyone. I felt that if anyone ever hurt my son I would but I really didn't know if that belief was bullshit or real. Rueben felt entirely comfortable with our little chat and didn't look at me with any less respect. I was his shrink and I was his foxhole buddy. It was easy for him to continue to respect me as his shrink. Rueben and I continued drinking and wrapped up our meeting with Italian pastry and ice cream. The limousine didn't appear so large or so impressive. The feeling of having helped Rueben was worth a thousand limos and far exceeded any salary that Charles could offer. Maybe I wouldn't take the offer that Charles made.

"Need a lift home?" I asked.

"No, Doc, I'm fine," he said.

Rueben moved forward and grabbed my hand to shake it. He looked at me and said, "Semper Fi," the Marine phrase for Always Faithful. "Semper Paratus," I said. Rueben looked at me and I knew that he didn't know what the phrase meant. "Always prepared," I said. On the drive back to the estate I stared out the window and never spoke a word to Harry.

It was 7:00 p.m. when I arrived at the estate. Gabby and Charles had had dinner. Gabby told me that Charles was out in the back and that he wanted to talk me. I told Gabby very little about my dinner session with Rueben other than to indicate that it was nice seeing him again. She asked me if seeing him rekindled a desire to continue my practice. I told her that I didn't know.

"Stan, it's going to be a long night with daddy," Gabby warned me as I made my way to the deck.

"Charles, how are you?" I asked.

"I won't know until after our conversation," he said.

"So, how much has the price gone up since this morning?" he asked.

"Two million is what my price is," I told him.

"Were you two gentlemen having a business meeting or smoking dope?" he asked.

"My friend told me that $500,000.00 is chump change. That's what you give junior exec's when they're starting out," I said to Charles.

"But you are starting out," he added.

I stopped talking and walked up the dune and gazed out towards the ocean. There is no better smell than salt water. I sucked in a huge amount until my lungs no longer expanded. I turned around and looked at Charles.

"I really don't know why you want my advice Charles. I am a psychologist not a finance guy. I can't add anything to the base of your knowledge that you already don't know. Believing that I have something to offer you is just bullshit to me. It doesn't add up," I told Charles.

I decided to shuck off the self-important persona that I developed from hanging out with the rich people and riding in the limousine. This was serious and I was going to be myself. I was determined not to buy into my own bullshit.

"Stan, I've been thinking about what you said this morning. You know, the little psych joke about the superego leaving the building and that the id is fighting it out with the ego. There's a lot of truth to what you say, but I'm beginning to get the distinct impression that the ego took a stroll with the superego. The only one left is the id and that makes for an entirely different equation," he said.

"Yes, it certainly does. We have that hidden, concealed inaccessible part of the psyche, seated in the unconscious, actuated by fundamental impulses towards fulfilling instinctual needs," I advised Charles.

"But, there was something else, wasn't there?" asked Charles.

I thought Charles was trying to get at something to make a point but he wasn't. I reviewed the definition of id in my mind.

"Oh, yes," I said and added, "independent of logic, reality and a sense of morality. The world has a severe case of rampant id and I'm afraid it will be fatal. The winds of war are starting to stir."

I was beginning to see where Charles was going but he was going to help me along to get to his point faster.

"For last twenty years, money and the making of money has been largely unaffected by personalities or geo-political concerns. It used to be that money trembled in the wake of what was perceived to be harmful geo-political news. Today, money is money and analyzed on that basis. I didn't have to pay any attention to events, political or geo-political. On a scale of one to ten, outside human events was a zero. Today, I am of the opinion that current events play a four and rising.

The only thing I want to know is what will my money do, not what would Jesus do?" he said.

"And I'm interested in what would a psychopathic narcissist do," I added. Charles was becoming increasingly concerned that events propelled by personalities was a factor in making money. Charles couldn't figure out why any Iraqi would be motivated to blow up a pipeline. Oil is money and acting contrary to making money, like blowing up a pipeline didn't make sense; the act itself was independent of logic and a sense of reality, the reality of money. I had a comfortable feeling that I was, at this point in human evolution or devolution, a very necessary and important part of making things work. I could easily see why Charles needed me. I was going to add at least 40% to Charles equation of making money. I mused that my price should have been three million instead of two million dollars. I asked Charles if I could tell him about my nightmare to which he agreed.

"Missionaries, infected with Lassa, Junin, Marburg and Pneumonic Plague came over from Africa. It was estimated that 3,000,000 people would die. At a last supper type romance scene with some waitress, Sam appears out of nowhere and wants to know if I still don't believe in terrorists. I didn't believe in terrorists to the extent that Sam believed but I told him I changed my mind. I told Sam that he was joined at the hip in a historical moment in history with the terrorists. They both needed each other to exist and I believe that," I told Charles.

"A dance of the id," said Charles.

"That's right. A dance of monumental proportions that will forever change our lives and you can't make sense of the id that is divorced from a sense of logic, reality and morality. We're witnessing the most basic elemental dance of being propelled to fulfill instinctual needs. It's the dark ages all over again where simplistic slogans will motivate various groups to kill each other. It's just going to be another crusade," I said.

Gabby came out of the kitchen with a bottle of wine and some snacks.

"It will be a long evening just like I told you," she said as she quickly disappeared. After a fifteen-minute rest, Charles and I started up again.

"All you have to do is just look around you; The Towers in New York, the Iraq war and now the mess in Russia. We're approaching 1,000 dead young American men and woman and close to 7,000 severely injured and wounded. If you add the Iraqi dead and injured it's close to 60,000. For what! There's no fucking correlation between our safety and the invasion of Iraq. The whole march to war was built upon bullshit intelligence and in my opinion fraudulent intelligence. It was a song made up for the Dance of the Id. And take a look at what happened in

Russia for Christ's sake. Two jets exploded in mid air by terrorist bombs, a car bombing in Moscow two weeks ago and yesterday the unimaginable horrific ending to the school siege in Beslan. I mean, Charles, shooting little children in the back defies comprehension. It is just incomprehensible. What are they going to do next? Blow up a train like the terrorists did in Spain." My heart stopped beating and I threw up the food that I was swallowing.
"What's wrong Stan? Are you o.k?" Charles asked excitedly.
"My son. My son Jordan is in Irkutsk visiting Lake Baikal in Russia. He's taking the Trans-Siberian Railroad back to Moscow," I said choking on the words.
"Don't worry Stanley. He'll be all right. I'm sure of it," said Charles.

Money, id, geo-political bullshit and limousines no longer seemed a concern. My son and terrorists was the only thing that mattered right now. I thought about my conversation with Rueben only two hours ago about not having anyone in my life that I would take a bullet for. There was one. It was Jordan. I started to get angry about the theoretical possibility that someone might hurt my precious boy and I laid it on the doorsteps of Sam. I was furious at Sam. From my prospective, "bring em on," placed the only person that I truly loved in danger. I whipped around and faced Charles.
"And where the fuck was Jesus when 280 little girls and boys got shot in the back as their mothers and fathers wailed outside in helpless disbelief. I know we can't even comprehend the infinite wisdom of God and his master plan and his reason for letting this tragedy to occur. It is beyond my ability to fathom. Bullshit. Little babies are shot dead and that's it. Period. This event is reason enough to know that God doesn't exist. I swear if anything happens to my Jordan, there will be hell to pay. I'm not kidding. You know what's wrong with this fucking world? Psychopathic narcissists, a whole bunch of them, run the world. They don't give a shit. They don't get hurt. Their children are never put in harm's way. They just stand at some podium with Christian crosses on the front like Sam did and urge resolve in the face of terror. Stand strong as the young man you nurtured as a baby has his brains blown out. What fucking bullshit. It's the age-old question. What do you do with the bully on the block? At what fucking point do I stand up and fight and sink to his level? When he knocks down my fence? What he shoots my dog? When he beats up my kid? When he rapes my wife? Really, at what point do I stand up and fight," I said loudly.

Charles saw that I was extremely agitated just at the thought of harm coming to Jordan and decided to let me blow off some steam.
"You know what you do," I said to Charles.

"With all the advances in genetic engineering that have occurred, you devise a test to screen out those babies with an aggressive genetic gene and you kill them at birth. Pick up the little Damien's by the ankles and smash them against a wall cracking their heads open. The Nazi's wouldn't waste a bullet on little Jewish babies during the holocaust. They smashed their brains out on the walls of the delivery rooms," I roared. I saw Gabby peek out the back window and make a move towards the door. She stopped and stared, deciding whether to come out or not. I stopped talking and went back to the top of the dune. Charles turned around and waved her off.

"I'm supposed to help you with financial decisions?" I asked. "With what and whose information? The C.I.A., F.B.I., Defense Policy Board, D.I.A.? Information today is bogus. It's disinformation. It's hyped, false and misleading designed by madmen to fit their own specific agendas and you want me to make sense of it all?" I asked.

"For two million dollars, I would expect nothing less," said Charles. Those nine little words stopped me dead in my tracks.

"I'll be truthful with you Stan. The initial offer of $500,000.00 was merely to keep you around. Kind of like companion money to keep you close to Gabby and I. The more we talk the more I realize that your kind of input might be invaluable. It's certainly worth two million dollars. So, what's it going to be, Stanley? Do we have a deal or not?" Charles asked.

I was a whore; of course we had a deal. With Dr. Stanley Warlib it's only a question of price. I stood next to Charles staring at the sky. I was trying to divide two million bucks by fifty-two weeks to determine what my weekly pay would be, however, I couldn't get my mind off the number two million to do any division. I looked at Charles, grabbed his hand and told him that we had a deal. It was getting late and Charles suggested that we retire to the war room to continue our discussions. Gabby, having anticipated her father's action had two shot glasses filled with Glenfiddich. As I walked into the study, I told Charles that I hoped that the name "War Room" was not prophetic. He agreed. Passing through the door, I realized that two million dollars was about $40,000.00 a week. I wasn't impressed by the amount as much as I was impressed that is was weekly. "Holy shit," I kept on repeating to myself.

It was clear to me from the scotch that was provided that Charles was going to get his money's worth and I was going to start earning some of it right now. He pressed a button on a little pad that was on the large table in the center of the study and a large screen slowly came down from the ceiling covering the wall on which appeared a typical computer screen. He placed the cursor over the Internet icon and double clicked. He typed in an address that brought up the Castaneda-Map collection from the University of Texas library. Shortly, a world map appeared on the screen. Charles and I took seats in two large hand crafted club chairs made of expensive Italian leather. He handed me a Cuban cigar and we both lit up. It was quite a scene, one that I never experienced before. I felt important and powerful and now, rich. We stared at the world map for about ten minutes. Charles placed the cursor over North Ossetia in the Caucasus region to zoom in on the area in more detail. Both of us studied the map and respectively conjured up our own images of the unimaginable tragedy that had occurred. Today was a day of national mourning in Russia. CNN beamed images of men working tirelessly preparing a mass grave for the tiny victims of the latest terrorist attack. Charles touched a button and the world map reappeared. The conservative talk show radios were a buzz with the tragedy that befell Russia, reminding their listeners that this horror could happen in America and whether one had children or not it was terrifying. Then came the question: as the war on terror was too amorphous what should Americans call the "war?" The callers phoned in their collective answer. The war on Islamic Terror was the ubiquitous answer. It was to be a war on Islam and so commenced World War III. "So what do you think?" asked Charles. "I think it's getting late," I told him. It was 2:00 a.m. "For two mil I don't expect you to check your watch," he said. "Charles, do you mind if I check my e-mail?" I asked. I wanted to see if Jordan wrote me anything. I knew there were Internet cafes throughout the world and I desperately hoped that Jordan had found one.

> "Dear Daddio (you pointy headed cracker boy),
>
> How's life on the east coast? Hanging in there? I just got back from another four-day stint out near the Gobi Desert. Beautiful, desolate country. I got to ride the horses with one of the most famous training in all of Mongolia. I fulfilled my dream by flying at about 40 mph on horseback sailing across the Mongolian steppes. The stars at night were astonishing. It was like you couldn't fit one more star in the sky even if you tried. I have never seen the Milky Way so bright. I also got to ride on a camel, which had to be the funniest looking creature I've even seen up close. They look like old men and are very sensitive. They cry when they hear traditional Mongolian music. I'm back in Ulan Bator for three days until we head for Irkutsk and Russia. Russia is not seemingly like the best destination these

days. Really, I just want to check out Lake Baikal. Still a mystery how we get from Baikal to Italy. I'll keep you updated. See you in a few weeks.

Love Jordan."

"Sounds like a son with a head on his shoulders," said Charles.
"Yeah, but he's clearly worried about getting to Italy. He says it's still a mystery, so I guess he's skipping Russia," I said. Charles brought up another map on the screen that depicted Russia.
"I assume Jordan heard or read about the two Russian jets so he's not flying," said Charles.
"I think you're right and if he's not gonna train it, I'm hard pressed to figure out a way how he's getting back," I said.
"Horseback," said Charles. I laughed.
"Yeah, with Maki in tow," I responded.
"He'll be all right. I feel like he's my grandson and I like him already. Leeches in Nepal! Horseback riding on the Mongolian steppes! Kid has got a big pair of balls. He's my kind of kid," said Charles. "Mine too," I added.

I felt relieved and ready to look at the world map that Charles brought back up on the screen.
"This is what I think Charles, in the broadest possible strokes that I can paint. There's been a breach in the world and Sam caused it. He invaded Iraq for no reason and the rest of the world sat up and took notice. It's one thing to bargain your way into someone's home or even bribe your way in, but to invade your way in is a horror show. During this breach, all of the major players realized that life could go on without Sam and collectively concluded exactly what shrinks know; run from a guy with a personality disorder. People with personality disorders are bad news and nothing good will come out of any relationship with Sam. The more time goes by, the wider the breach becomes and the more Sam's friends know that life is a lot better without him. Notice that Sam is still fighting all alone in Iraq. No help and no money. Interestingly enough, into this breach came a big strong guy to court and that guy is China. The more Sam goes on his mission and calling from "beyond the stars," the more the world looks to China and China is a huge counter balance to Sam's aggression. Now, in this mess, you want me to figure out where to put money that will be safe, secure and earn you thirty per-cent," I said. "Exactly," said Charles.
"I'm too tired to start painting our picture with a finer brush. We've got the break-up of a polygamous marriage and all the wives have discovered that life is

better without hubby. Let's leave it at that for now," I said. It was 4:00 a.m. Gabby, who I thought had gone to bed, came over to hug me. She suggested a walk to which I agreed. Taz raced out the door in front of us as we headed west along the dunes. Two mansions down, Gabby told me to lie down for a back rub, to which I offered no refusal. As I lay on my stomach with my chin resting on my folded hands, I noticed the faint glow of a small orange dot that appeared and reappeared at regular intervals. I stared at the orange dot. "I think someone is watching us again," I told Gabby. "What makes you think that?" she asked. "I think someone is standing on the deck in front of that bungalow and smoking a cigarette. I can see the orange glow now and then as he takes a puff," I told her. "Maybe, he's the same guy who was watching us before, but he can't see anything we're doing or about to do," said Gabby. I turned over and thanked her. She pulled my pants halfway down and performed oral sex. It had been quite a day and quite a night, but I had my two million.

## CHAPTER FIVE

The next morning Charles wanted to go into the war room immediately after breakfast. I told him that I had to go into the city and call my patients. I needed to advise them of my career change. I advised Charles that it would take only the morning hours to complete the task and he advised me that he was knocking off about $8,000.00 for the day. That number chilled me to the bone. I couldn't get over it. That sounded better than the weekly number and I realized that compared to the real heavy weights, it was pocket change. Contemplating my money was mind-boggling. I wondered what I made each minute. Each second! The drive into the city was peaceful. I no longer looked out the window to see if anyone was trying to get a peek inside. The one line in Jordan's e-mail about getting to Italy from Lake Baikal in Russia occasionally haunted me. After settling in at my desk, I opened the mail, reviewed some notes and called my former patients. Three out of four already moved on. The balance had contacted other psychologists and was waiting for my approval. It was too easy. All asked how I was doing and wished me well. I called Rueben at the conclusion of my chores and told him that I wanted to go long on oil future contracts. He laughed for a long time. I invited Rueben out to Southampton for dinner the following day and explained to him that I was now ready to put my new found wealth to work. I wanted to use Rueben as my vehicle to conduct my trades. I arranged to meet Rueben downtown for a quick infused martini during his lunch break.
"So big shot, what's up? No more anger and paranoia?" he asked.
"Kind of left me. I heard from my son in Mongolia and he's doing fine. I was worried," I said.
"And the Westerfield's?" he asked.
"Just fine," I said.
"What couldn't you say on the phone, Doc?" Rueben asked.
"Rueben, do you know anyone that can get you a night scope. You know, those binoculars that our troops use to see in the dark. I think I got some pervert checking out Gabby and I. Every time we're doing our thing, this guy is out there watching," I told Rueben.
"Not paranoid now, are we?"
"No, Rueben, I mean it. Some fucking guy is jerking off watching Gabby and I do our thing."
"No problem, Doc. You didn't even have to ask me. You could have got one of those things yourself. All the stores sell them. All right, dinner and some night time binoculars. Long oil. Really! The oil market is going down and Doc's going

long. Be careful, you can lose big, fast. One last thing, what did you get from the old man," asked Rueben.

"Two million," I answered. Rueben and I shook hands good-bye.

Gabby was nowhere to be found when I got home. I checked Charles's private study and he wasn't there. I called out for Taz and he didn't come running either. Charles was taking a nap in the war room and awoke when he heard me fumble with the controls that we assembled on the table. I asked Charles where Gabby and Taz were and he told me that she was visiting some neighbors. I advised Charles that I had invited Rueben over for dinner and that we were going to talk about investments. Charles looked surprised but didn't say anything. I recalled that Charles once told me, "if you can't spend another person's money, don't count it." He probably couldn't care less what I did with the money I earned after I earned it. He only cared about moving his bags of money around the world to earn him thirty percent. I checked my e-mail and there was nothing from Jordan. From behind me, I heard Charles clear his throat. "Let's see where we are in this story. Polygamous Sam broke up with his wives and they found out that life is better without him. Into this separation, maybe trial separation, maybe not, comes a big handsome suitor named China and all the ex-wives are falling over themselves to get a piece of this big new guy on the block. Did I get it right," Charles asked.

"Perfect," I said.

"Secondary plot?" Charles asked.

"Ah, the secondary plot. This is the one I love. I just eat this one up. This is psychology in action," I told Charles.

"Play down the religious aspect Stanley," Charles advised me.

"You mean, in the story plot or how it effects investments?" I asked.

"The latter," he said.

"No way, Charles. Religion drives the script. Forget it, I'm not going to do it. It's the god damn meat in the meat loaf sandwich," I told him.

"You mean to actually tell me that you'll walk away from two million dollars over this?" he asked.

"Yes, that's exactly what I'm telling you. This entire historical episode is being propelled by religion and nobody gets it. Yes, I'd walk. That's your answer," I said. "Well, now we know there are two things you get passionate about. Jordan and your opinion," Charles said.

"Look, Charles let me explain it to you. It is not too often that a shrink gets to sit ringside during great historical dramas that are acted out over many years. I wasn't at ringside for Alexander the Great or Julius Caesar. But I'm at ringside for

Sam. It's a rare event. What makes a true Narcissist are his visions of grandiosity. Not little dreams like owning a home or making two million bucks but grand visions. Are you a true full blown Narcissist? No. Maybe a little narcissistic but not like the kind of grand Narcissists that history encounters every so often like Hitler, Julius Caesar, Alexander the Great and Genghis Khan. We are in the presence of another one of history's grand Narcissists and no one in his right mind can expect that investments will not be effected. They will. Look, every time Sam makes a speech to his family he uses the words calling and mission. Those are code words in the evangelical movement. At his convention, Sam said a 'calling from beyond the stars,' to carry forward freedom which is a euphemism for Christianity. Sam speaks to God and God speaks to Sam and God called upon Sam and gave Sam a mission. What people don't get is that this is real. Everything that Sam does is done in accordance with the evangelical interpretation of what would Jesus do. He is propelled by God to bring freedom to the world. Death is a real consequence of moving forward to complete God's mission. Resolve! Resolve! Resolve! Stay the course. We are doing the Lord's work. This isn't a joke. But no one wants to deal with it. You have a wacko running the country. Did you see Paul Krugman's article entitled 'A Mythic Reality.' Krugman wrote that the best thing he read was about war psychology. War, it stated, plays to some fundamental urges. The id, Charles, the id, the Dance of the Id. People get close but they just don't want to wrap their arms around the fact that a lunatic is running the asylum. This isn't politics as usual. This is the real deal. Get on board the soul train. Also in the New York Times, David Brooks wrote an article entitled 'Cult of Death.' His point was that the Russian massacres were so horrible that we don't want to get to near to reality. We don't call the people murderers. We call them insurgents, separatists and terrorists. It's the same thing with Sam. People can't believe what they're witnessing. They can't get their arms around what's happening. Could Sam really be on a messianic mission from God to rid the world from evil? It seems so ancient. Everything that Sam does, he does to save nothing less than civilization. So, I would quit. I'd walk from the money," I concluded.

"Maybe you have a point," said Charles.

"What do you mean maybe? Are we all suppose to walk around saying 'isn't that nice, Sam is on his messianic mission saving the world and civilization. That's so cute. Bullshit. Sam's calling was to lead his country on his mission. He can't lead anything but a Christian Nation and that's what is coming. You probably think Zell Miller was up there as a counterbalance to the Democrats Ron Reagan. He wasn't. Zell Miller was the closest thing to a Southern Baptist bible-thumping preacher you could get and he gave Sam political cover because he's a Democrat. It was a test to see how that kind of speech would go over. Sam wanted to know if it would frighten people. Bible thumping, good time religion, that's what coming." Charles sat silently and listened carefully.

"I'll make you a bet, Charles. I'll bet $40,000.00 that within 4 months after Sam is reappointed head of the family he appoints one or two of the following: (1) Asa Hutchinson (2) Senator Brownback (3) Bill Owens or (4) Rick Santorum."

"I'll take that bet. What's the point?" he asked.

"The point is that they are the first phalanx of Christian soldiers in taking back America for Christ. Their ranks will increase. So think Jesus when you think money. Think Jesus when you think geo-political and think Jesus right here in the United States," I said.

"Stanley, what gets you so riled up. When I see images on CNN of Sam or his opponent giving speeches, I just see American faces in the crowd. Apparently, you see something different and what you see just sets you off. I'm just trying to understand," said Charles. "It's what you don't see, Charles, that's freaks me out. Put it this way. Suppose with all your experience and wisdom you see your daughter invest one million dollars in an investment that you know through experience is not going to work out. You would probably get riled up. The further Gabby went with this investment the more riled up you would get and from the outside it would look like you're losing it. You're not though, are you? You see the inevitable consequences that are looming on the horizon. I see the same thing when it comes to issues of the mind. You see the surface and I see the inevitable consequences that are looming on the horizon. I have walked down every nook and cranny of the mind. Been there, done that, so to speak. I see the horizon and most people don't. They just can't get their arms around that good ole boy looking at them on the screen and believe he's a nut. Can't be! Isn't true! Dr. Warlib, you're crazy. Sam's family is about to commit a huge mistake in reelecting Sam as head of the family. They will play their part in history by affirming Sam for a second time. The last thing you want to do is affirm a Narcissist. It only emboldens their grandiosity. Think of it this way: If Sam thought he was Gods man on earth; affirmation can propel Sam to believe that he is God himself. The consequences are rarely benign. The consequences are generally fatal," I said. I looked at Charles and saw that he was contemplating what I had said. I realized that I could make headway by making analogies between money and psychology. I went for a walk on the beach and watched TazTwo negotiate the waves in attempting to retrieve a stick that I was throwing in. I walked about a mile in one direction and a mile in the other direction. Gabby jumped on my back and said, "guess who?" She appeared out of nowhere. I continued to walk with Gabby in place and asked her where she had been and she told me that she was visiting a friend. I was confused since I did not see her at all during my walk. I asked Gabby if her friend lived near the mansion and she didn't answer. Gabby appeared annoyed at my questioning and after asking me how it was going with her father, ended the conversation with as exasperated exclamation that she was just visiting a friend. "Geez Stan," she said. I reappeared in the War Room and sat down next to Charles. I decided to speak in a less aggravated tone.

"Look Charles, what we have going here is the Dance of the Id. Conscience, criticism, a healthy relationship to our surroundings is gone. In this dance, there is no right and wrong, just a tribal obsession worshiping the fulfillment of our basic aggression. This dance is only of death and destruction. Just today, Vladimir Putin stated that he will wage a war against terrorism in any part of the world, adopting a Sam invented pre-emptive policy. It's political cover to advance on provinces that Russia lost during its breakup. The provinces that have oil! In USA Today, in the 'Forum,' in bold type it said, 'Muslim leaders may face the world's wrath.' That's out and out Bible talk and the full article went on to mention Arabs, Muslims and Islam. Evangelical Sam is giving the war a face and it's Islam. A Biblical war between the prophets Jesus and Mohammed is commencing. What I find amusing is that it is only a prelude to the ultimate fight. A war of such monumental proportions that it will be called Armageddon and that is the clash between Sam's evangelical capitalist Christian America and atheistic communist China. A final battle to the death between Christ and the Anti-Christ!" I said.

"How do you stop the dance?" Charles asked.

"Easy, you get off the dance floor. Unfortunately, Sam's personality precludes such an action. The affirmation of his reelection will only make him increase the tempo and so the dance will go on at a frenzied pace," I said.

"What would you do?" he asked.

"I rather not get into it because my answer comes from the bowels of my id. However, I'll tell you and ask for your forgiveness in advance. For many years, my ego and superego had to be messaged into a dominant position to keep my aggressive id held at bay. I'll tell you. For starters, we eliminate newborns at birth or in the womb that tested positive for an aggressive gene thereby ridding the world of Type A personalities. Hopefully, in generations forward, we'll cultivate many Mother Teresa types who inherently seek peace over aggression. Next, I believe, as the Leo Straussian Neo-Cons believe that the masses are asses. However, where as they like to con the masses, I would liquidate the masses. I am an anarchist and believe that only a handful of very special people who intuitively know how to get along can live without law and governments. In my world, none of us need to be told what to do, as we instinctively know. This is my id talking and I have learned to bury the fantasy," I said. "You're no different than Sam. Sam gets you so riled up because you see yourself in Sam, except Sam's in power. I think you're jealous," said Charles.

"Sorry Charles, you are wrong. What gets me so riled up is that I know when my id is talking and my superego kicks the shit out of him. Sam and the rest of his army don't have a fucking clue what they're doing. That's what gets me so fucking upset and I'm helpless in this struggle. If you want a safe, secure return for your money you have to know Sam. When does this insanity stop! Don't you think that Arabs and Muslims all over the world are starting to get worried with a big bad Christian Sam beating the bushes enlisting his evangelical Christians for his crusade? He's only stirring the pot and feeding the Islamic extremists the sustenance they need to continue to grow. The Muslims are just as worried about Sam's intentions as we are about theirs and unfortunately, Sam and his Christian warriors are the same as the Taliban. Al Gore said pretty much the same thing in a recent article. Sam's brand of religion is the hellfire and brimstone variety that comes from an evil id. Like I said, a Dance of the Id," I concluded.

"What's the starting point in this war room Stanley?" asked Charles.

"Before, we put money in the game; let's figure out what the game is. Let's study for a while and take a cue from Warren Buffet and sit on cash. Right now, I'd go natural resources like lumber, oil and iron. I wouldn't put a dime in America. Sam is up to his eyeballs in debt, a ticking time bomb. The real estate market is suffering from the same affliction that enveloped the dot.com community. Irrational exuberance! a ticking time bomb. Greenspan has pumped more money into America, lowered interest rates to historical levels and Sam is still just barely hanging on, a ticking time bomb. Sam's workers are going backwards in money and spending more time doing it, a ticking time bomb. I don't think anything in Sam's country is a good investment. Long Oil!" I exclaimed and walked out signaling a break was in order.

Taz came running over when he heard me leave the war room. "Come on boy, we're going for a walk," I said. Taz ran over the dune to the beach and came to halt at the ocean's edge. He turned around and looked for me anticipating that a stick was going to be thrown into the waves. I obliged and waited for a large wave that TT crashed into swimming towards the stick. "Long Oil," I mused. I watched Taz as he swam back towards me and I thought that I was a big smuck. Long oil indeed! Exactly what I was doing I didn't know. All the changes had come so quick and I was starting to buy into my own bullshit. Limousines, estates, geo-political speeches, two million dollar salary and a future wife and father-in-law that I wanted to spy on. I didn't feel right. All I wanted to do was escape and that's precisely what I did. I marched into the war room and announced to Charles that I was taking a day off and go into the city. Before he could say anything, I told him to deduct eight thousand dollars from my salary. I told Charles to relay my plans to Gabby and when me indicated that he would get Harry, I waived him off.

## CHAPTER SIX

Starting up my car, I knew what I was going to do and headed into the city. I stopped by the apartment, checked the mail and messages, returned some calls and headed straight to Mykonos and Angelina. I needed to strut, flirt and screw and Angie had a bull's eye on her back. I looked through the window and immediately spotted Angie even though she had her back towards me. After having watched her butt swagger for several years, I could pick out her ass blindfolded. I sat down at a table and buried my face in The Times, hoping to surprise her.
"Aaaa, what's up Doc?" she asked.
"Can't get nothing by you, can I?" I answered with a question.
"If you were having your best day and I was in a coma, you still couldn't get anything by me, Doc. What brings you here? Shouldn't you be home playing house with Gabby trying to get her bare foot and pregnant," she said.
"No, I thought I'd come into the city and try to get you barefoot and pregnant. Well, at least naked. I couldn't get Gabby pregnant cause I'm shooting blanks anyway. So that applies to you too. So, how about naked? Come to think of it Angie, Gabby has been walking around barefoot. Barefoot and jeans is her attire and she looks terrific. Got a glow going and some chubby feet," I said.
"Maybe you had a live one among all those blanks," Angie said.
"I doubt it," I responded.
"Here, for lunch or polite little conversation?" she asked.
"I ran away from home and I'm unemployed. Remember Ferris Bueller's day off? This is Warlib's version of the movie," I said.
"Really, unemployed. Quit your practice?" she asked.
"Yes, I did," I told her.
"Really, I thought you were kidding. What are you going to do?" Angelina asked.
"I'm waiting for my new business cards to be printed. Stanley Warlib, Male Prostitute. Available anytime for a dime," I said. Angelina laughed and couldn't figure where I was going with our conversation. Neither could I, but I was angling to hit that mark on her back. I realized that I had been in the house too long. I go normal for a while and then huge compulsions overtake my personality and I willingly follow.
"So you really quit your job? And you're a male ho. I'd do a tumble but you aren't worth a dime. How about a mercy stumph for the Gipper?" she asked.
"Absolutely," I answered. "I'm not kidding Angie," I reminded her.
"Neither am I and I'll bring you oysters," she answered and walked to the kitchen. I didn't have a clue as to what had just transpired with Angelina and that

made me nervous. I think I was going to get laid. I couldn't believe it. Angie came back with Mousaka and oysters. I kidded her about being the poster boy for Viagra and she said, "Whatever turns you on." I made arrangements with Angelina to meet her at her house at 8:00 p.m. I called Rueben and reminded him about dinner and he screamed in the phone, "long oil." It was going to become a mantra for all manner of things. I took various paths through Central Park eluding whoever might have been following me on my way to West 81$^{st}$ and Columbus Avenue. Five minutes before arriving at Angie's, I popped a Cialis, instead of Viagra and hoped I would have to be admitted to the emergency room because my dick wouldn't go down for four hours. The commercial advised to seek medical attention and I envisioned that arriving at the emergency room with a hard on would be funny. Angie had some appetizers waiting and a bottle of red wine. She told me to sit and make myself comfortable, which I gladly did to hide the stiff I got when she opened the door. Angelina and I took a shower and then made love.

"Is that thing ever going to go down? Christ, I could use that to hang a towel on," she said.

"What the hell are we doing Angie?" I asked.

"Does it make a difference? We're having fun," she said. Angie was straightforward and that was disarming. I wanted a touch more of the "I'm her hero" stuff; however, I got use to the mutuality of our respective equality. Angelina was an interesting character. She had three degrees; the proof was mounted on a wall. Books were strewn around the apartment and I assumed that she read several at a time. Desktop computer, decent kitchen, a little messy all around, but perfectly comfortable. It felt like a guy's apartment and that made me feel at home. I wrapped a towel around me and stared at her book collection, something I did in all apartments. I always had a fascination with personal libraries. "Drop the towel," Angelina requested. "Twenty years ago, I wouldn't have even grabbed one," I told her. Her library was arranged alphabetically, which I found unusual. I was witnessing nothing more than the accumulation of books by a professional student. After starting at "A," I quickly moved through the alphabet and stopped occasionally. At the "D" authors, I backtracked to "B" and stared at a book.

"What struck your fancy?" Angie asked from the bed. She had a blanket covering her tits. She had no reason whatsoever to hide her breasts.

"Bakunin. Why does that name sound familiar?" I asked.

"What was your major as an undergraduate?" she asked. I told her that I had majored in Political Science and then went on to law school to obtain a Juris Doctorate.

"Then the name should sound familiar. Take a guess?" she said.

"This is a long shot but I'm thinking very late 19$^{th}$ century or early 20$^{th}$ century Anarchist," I answered.

"Very Good, Dr. Stanley Warlib," she said. I continued searching Angie's book collection and discovered many books about political science and in particular, Anarchism. I tried to get Angie to talk about the subject but she didn't reveal anything one way or another.

"Oh, Mr. Librarian, why don't you bring yourself and that stand up buddy of yours over here for round two and then maybe I'll tell you something," Angelina said. The whole scene was provocative and mysterious. Angelina and I had another round of sex, it wasn't love making and she reminded me several times that I was pushing too hard to get sex over with. She knew that I wanted to talk about Anarchism. She let me get away with the rush job this time but reminded that if there was a round three that I had better be into sex. "So, tell me about this Anarchism stuff?" Black shirts and burning Sam in effigy, that kind of stuff? Did you attend the rally in New York City?" I asked.

"No, not that kid stuff," she answered. I could tell that Angelina was engaged in a self-debate.

"Come on Angie, talk to me," I implored.

"Did you ever see the movie The Fight Club? Remember the first rules of The Fight Club? Just in case you forgot the first rules of The Fight Club is that you never, never mention The Fight Club," she said. A long pause ensued. "If I tell you about what I do and you follow up on it, what you do might be a reflection on me and I'll lose points," she said. I was totally mystified, bewildered and intrigued by our cryptic conversation. Angelina pressed hard on what I thought about Sam, his citizens, the world, politics, sociology, poor people and poor nations. She demanded honesty. I was concerned that honest answers would set me off on another soapbox tirade and I eyed Angelina for sex. It was clear that Angelina would not disclose anything unless she was convinced about something. Her reference to The Fight Club movie piqued my imagination. I gave Angelina truthful answers without the histrionics and that was sufficient to tip the scales in my favor enabling Angie to proceed. "Do you know anything about multi-player on line game playing?" she asked. I told her that I knew very little other than that it existed. "On the Internet there's a game. It's a game of anarchy and it's played worldwide. Obviously, it's anonymous. No one knows the real identity of the players. You log on to the game, create a character and give yourself a name. In the game you'll meet lots of people. When you're new, others will walk up to you

and ask you your name, who are you, what you're doing there and who told you about the game. They might act suspicious because you could be F.B.I.," she said.
"What's the point of the game?" I asked.
"Remember Ted Kaczynski the Unabomber. Well, think in terms of a million unknown Unabomber's out there in cyberspace creating havoc outside in the real world and coming on line and talking about it. A million single anonymous cells connected in cyberspace. Getting the picture?" she asked.
"Yeah, I can envision what you're talking about. Against whom or what is the anarchy directed?" I asked.
"One of the rules of the game is that no one can commit an act of anarchy against the little guy. You know what I mean? The average Joe, the poor guy or even the middle class. Only acts against the powers that be," she said.
"Suppose someone has a target that he is unsure of?" I asked.
"Well, in true democratic cyberspace, you'd bring up a target and a debate would ensue among the players about the target and a consensus achieved. There is no authority that determines right and wrong. A typical target that wouldn't get debated would be Washington, D.C., 'K' Street lobbyists," she said.
"Is this real or a cyberspace role playing game?" I asked.
"You never know, Doc. You just never know. In the paper this morning was a little blurb that Governors in four states received letters that were rigged to burn when the envelopes opened. The letters were sent to the Governors in Montana, Nebraska, Idaho and Utah. Tonight, some one may show up in cyberspace and claim credit. He may brag about it or he may not. Once you play the game you get to know the bull shitters. If enough people believe the character, he gets points. After a while, you get to know the real players. The main theme of the game is kind of like the French Revolution," she said.
"Guillotine the rich and powerful?" I asked.
"We all know who's fucking us," she answered.
What's your ranking?" I asked.
"Doc, I can't tell you that. You should know that," she answered.
"Is there a leader in this game?" I asked.
"Yes, in the game there is, but in real life there isn't. Single cell anarchists, remember Stanley," she said.
"What's the name of the leader?" I asked.
"You have to earn the right in the game to know the name and if that's the first question you ask, you will be voted out of the game. I've told you enough. Our conversation is over," she said.

"Where do I go online?" I asked. "I'm debating whether I made a mistake in telling you," she said. Can you handle a sexual round three?" Angelina asked. It was 6:00 a.m. and Angelina had to go to the diner. I kissed her at the door and asked her the name of the game.

"When you go online, hang out for a week and get a feel for the game. Don't freak anybody out and chat with the characters you meet. It's the same as real life, except it's cyberspace," she said.

"And the name, Angelina, the name?" I asked.

"The Multitude.org," she answered "and you didn't get it from me unless you prove yourself. I'll get points," she added.

# Chapter Seven

Prior to heading back to the estate, I went to my apartment to relax. There were sixteen messages on my machine, all from Gabby. The first five messages expressed concern; the next seven messages expressed anger and the remaining four messages screamed outrage. The sixteenth message Gabby told me to go fuck myself and added that I should consider staying in the city. I called Gabby five times but she hung up when she heard my voice. The sixth time, she went into a ranting rage and I was told to stay in the city. "Try single life," were her final words.

"Rueben, my friend, what's up?" I asked. "Doc, what the hell is happening?" he asked. I explained to Rueben what had happened over the course of the last twenty-four hours including Angelina and excluding The Multitude. Rueben was surprised and concerned. He wasn't talking fast or rushing me off the phone. He explained to me it was a post holiday slow period in the commodity pits. I figured that he wasn't doing much cocaine. Rueben suggested that he and I hook up for the evening to which I readily agreed. The rest of the day I sat on my deck staring out across the garden wishing that Taz Two was with me. I was relatively calm and that concerned me.

Rueben and I had dinner at a new "in" spot in Tribeca. After a considerable amount of discussion we decided to buy a bottle of Tequila and find someplace to drink. There were many hidden little parks in the City. They were more like secluded sitting areas nestled between tall high rises that the owners were required to build for public purposes. I remembered one that I was particularly fond of somewhere on the eastside of Manhattan between East 50$^{th}$ and East 57$^{th}$ streets and between Fifth and Park Avenues. Rueben and I took a cab uptown and slowly traversed the entire area, taking slugs of Tequila along the way until we came upon my favorite spot. By the time we found this little gem, Rueben and I were happily inebriated. There were two women sitting on a bench who quickly exited the area after they spotted the bottle. We had the area to ourselves. Against the wall was a waterfall that was architecturally lit coupled with the soft sound of falling water. A line of trees ran perpendicularly away from the waterfall. Rueben was surprised that such a public gem existed in the City and more surprised that he was unaware of it.

"Doc, you're out of control. I mean are you still employed with Westerfield?" he asked. "Beats the shit out of me," I said.

"Holy shit, two million out the window before you even got your hands on it," he said. "And the limousine, the estate, my dog and Gabby," I added.

"Man, when you do something, you do it big," said Rueben. Both of us sat in silence pondering the enormity and gravity of my actions.

"I mean, we're talking mega bust here, Doc. Did you call all your patients after Puglia's and close down your practice?" he asked. I slowly turned my head and half smiled. Both of us cracked up laughing. "I'm fucked," I said. I got up from the bench and danced around yelling, "I'm fucked. I am big-time fucked."

"Doc, what's going on with you?" he asked.

"I don't have a clue, old buddy. My brain is having a little problem. Houston, we got a brain problem. I'm seeing things Rueben," I said.

"Yeah, like what? Visions, gremlins, monsters! Tell me, Doc, we're buddies. No risk here," he said. At this point in time, Rueben and I were fairly well crocked. I put my arm around him and pulled him closer and pointed to the brick wall across from where we were seated. "You see that wall, Rueben? I'm going to paint a picture on that wall for you and you can see what I see. O.K. You ready dude, cause here we go. Take a look at that wall. Imagine a world map. See all those countries. A man's home is his castle and a nation's home is its sovereign borders. You got that Semper Fi, buddy. Well, I remember when Sam invaded Iraq with no international support from the major players that counted for shit. You know what I mean. And then I these fucking beaming generals on cable television claiming that when Iraq falls those fucking friends are just going to come running and begging to help Sam out after the shooting stops. Guess what? The shooting stopped over a year ago and there aren't any friends. So I start to think what the hell that really means and I stare at some wall like the one in front of you and out comes a vision. Sam took an axe and smashed it into the world's collective psyche. Now there's a big fucking space there that looks like a big V. Sam invaded a man's home. He walked in and took over. Visualize that one, buddy. He invaded a sovereign nation over bogus bullshit. Well, well, well, the boys are thinking. Sam violated the most sacrosanct dictum that the civilized world lives by. A man's home is his castle and a nation's home is its sovereign borders. If Sam could do it once, he could do it again. Got the picture. Isn't anybody liking Sam and the axe gone in so deep, the breach can't be repaired. Here's where the fun starts. Rueben, baby, you're with me. Now, all of Sam's former friends see him as a possible enemy. They don't want to help because they all want Sam to spend money and lose his soldiers thereby weakening Sam and maybe slowing down his forays into their neighborhoods. Remember when Saddam took a stroll into Kuwait. Saudi Arabia got so freaked out that they called and told Sam that he better do something about it. Well, Sam wants to protect his private gas station so he goes over and kicks some butt around but nobody minded that one because

Hussein did what? He violated the basic principle that a man's home is his castle. He didn't like Kuwait having all the oil so fuck them and I'm taking it. Now Sam turns around twelve years later and does the same thing. Now Sam is a psychopathic narcissist so I'm figuring out what the hell he's going to do next. Is he going to head east to Iran, another evildoer or head west to Syria, another cakewalk. A narcissist has to protect his image at all costs. He's the able bodied guy who enters a hundred yard dash in the Special Olympics. Only contests where he can't lose, you see. So one part of Sam, the narcissist part, wants to turn west to Syria, an easy mark. The psychopathic part of Sam knows that and is determined to head west to Iran. Now, this sick psychopathic nut starts to feed top-secret intelligence to the Israeli's about what Sam's narcissistic part is really going to do knowing full well that Israel will bomb the shit out of Iran if Iran crosses certain markers in the development of nuclear weapons. Now, what the hell happens? Iran is the private gas station of China and how do you think they're going to feel about that? If it's just a nuclear reactor and doesn't interrupt the operations of the gas station, China might let that one slide. Maybe not? However, all this time everybody is letting Sam go on and fight, thereby exhausting himself and depleting his assets. You can't get to the big evil kung fu master until you beat up a thousand little kung-fu masters. I watch the Kung-Fu movies and know this. It's probably in the Art of War too. If your potential opponent is occupied with other enemies, don't help him out. China stays out of the fray and watches Sam go up against a lot of little Islam Kung-Fu masters watching Sam weaken which is fine with all of Sam's former friends. In real time, take a look at what's happening in the Sudan. Within its sovereign borders, the Arab Sudanese don't like the black Sudanese. They kill a whole mess of them and then herd them into Darfur in the western region of Sudan. That's what everybody sees, but Doc here, sees something else. I watch the footage on BBC and see the Khartoum endorsed Janjuweed militia strolling leisurely outside the black Sudanese camps with a cocky smile and I wonder what the hell they're so cocky about. Sam is tied up doing his thing and the grand Kung-Fu Chinese master is looking for a couple of additional gas stations and buys Sudan as a back-up gas station to Iran. Grand Master Kung Fu decides he better protect his investment and puts about 4,000 little Kung-Fu guys in Sudan. Sam is practically begging the world to stop the genocide in Sudan and is going to the United Nations that Sam thinks is bullshit and is going to ask the U.N. Security council for sanctions against Sudan exporting oil. Well, 'fuck that,' Sudan says, because I got a lot of friends on the Security Council like China and Pakistan and that keeps the Janjuweed happy little guys riding their camels ready to kill any women or child strolling outside the camp to fetch firewood. But, Rueben, the real big problem is that axe that Sam slammed into the world's psyche. Suppose you're Saudi Arabia? You have to think that if Sam could do that to Iraq, Sam could do it to me. Sam isn't bargaining to get oil anymore; he's taking it. Now, if I'm a Saudi King, I'll keep Sam happy for now and flood the market with oil at a discount to support him but deep down, they know it might be time to shop for a new owner. A new, big Kung-Fu Master, who just so happens to be named China. All the time, I'm Sam's superego, his conscience and critic, and Sam has got me nailed on a cross like Jesus Christ in his brain and my mouth is taped. I can't say a fucking word. All I can do is watch," I said. I looked at Rueben and after intensely staring at each other for a minute he burst out laughing. "Doc, you got a huge problem. Dude, you need some hobbies. "Do you really see cartoon characters in your brain?" he asked. "Yeah. Sam is in his traditional red, white and blue outfit with a top hat. China looks like Jabba the Hut in a Kung-Fu outfit and the Muslims are dressed in their traditional garb. I input, like a computer, history, facts, maps and current events, spin them around and strain the whole thing out and the only thing that remains are the basics," I said. Rueben became serious.

"Doc, not for nothing, but you're making me nervous. You just lost a job with Westerfield for two million dollars and you're banging a waitress. You're engaged for Christ's sake," Rueben said.

"I didn't have a job and I didn't have a fiancée," I said.

"What do you mean?" asked Rueben.

"Never mind. We're not going down that road," I angrily told Rueben.

"Come on Doc. Semper Fi and all that stuff," Rueben said.

"Let it go and just go long oil," I told Rueben.

"Doc, did you talk to Mr. Westerfield the same way you talked to me?" asked Rueben. "Worse, I through in some religious junk which always gets me going," I told Rueben. "That's it. You definitely don't have a job. Look, these rich people play a different game. They're cool, calm and collected. They don't like or want histrionics. These guys can look you in the eye and in the calmest voice tell you a lie with all the sincerity that a mother would tell her young ones that she loves them. You don't have a job, that's for sure. Maybe, you still have a shot with Gabby?" said Rueben.

"Trust me buddy, it's over. I know." Rueben and I finished the bottle. Rueben asked if I needed assistance, however, I turned him down.

As I walked away from Doc, he was hunched over, looking like a broken man grumbling "long oil." I knew that Doc lost his girl and his job. I was worried that Doc lost his mind. Just as he was about to scale the Westerfield summit, the rope broke and my buddy was lying in a valley watching cartoon characters in his mind. I was deeply concerned for my friend and felt helpless. What does a patient of a shrink do when the shrink needs help? I called the Doc before heading off to work but he didn't answer the phone. After work I planned on taking a cab uptown and making an unannounced visit.

During a coffee break, I walked over to a friend in the commodity oil pits. "I got a friend that keeps on telling me to go long oil," I said. "The trend is not his friend," he replied. That meant the oil market is going down, not up. "My friend tells me that there isn't as much oil that the companies and governments claim and that the trend is just an election year gimmick to ensure that Sam gets reelected. He says the bottom line is about $39.00-$41.00 oil and then the markets are going back up," I said. "The trend is your friend," the oil trader repeated. I didn't pursue the topic but I did add oil to my laptop to watch and track the trend.

## CHAPTER EIGHT

I had fun with Rueben but the hangover wasn't worth it. I could smell the Tequila every time I burped. The only thing I could manage was a hot shower and going back to bed. I no longer knew whether it was age or a change in metabolism that made hangovers much worse at my current age. I wished that my dog Taz was with me, at least I would have a reason to get up and move. I was unemployed. The first time in over thirty years that I had no schoolwork to do or job to go to and I didn't give a shit. Several hours later I got up and still felt sick. However, I was well enough to get up and stay out of bed. After coffee and The New York Times, I felt invigorated. The java served as a jump-start to the day but the new poll results showing Sam ahead of his opponent in the upcoming election made my blood pressure rise. I still felt nailed to the inside of Sam's skull with duct tape on my mouth. None of the traditional media outlets assuaged my concern. They were limp dicked liberals and the Anarchists demonstrating in the streets of New York City could only muster burning an effigy. What the fuck happened to the Black Panthers, the Chicago Seven and the Sybianese Liberation Army. Those guys were armed and dangerous. Political correctness chopped the balls off of everyone. The only thing angry people could do today was wear a black shirt and burn effigies. These guys weren't going to tote guns and wreak havoc. The articles that I read in the New York Times were becoming a daily source of irritation and I realized that the next two months during the election season were going to be particularly troublesome. There was a message on my answering machine that I didn't want to listen to. I figured it was Gabby with additional bad news and I wasn't interested. Financially, if I made some adjustments I could last one and a half years. Since money had always been an issue with me, I thought that I might be in denial but the truth was that I didn't give a shit. I was starting to think and talk using foul language. The streets of Brooklyn were coming back and I felt at home. For a month at the estate, I spent time in my own study and the war room analyzing every bit of information that I could developing my theory that I was witnessing a land grab for oil and my former patient Sam was well suited to the task being a psychopathic narcissist. I decided to continue the war room in my office and felt renewed energy throughout my body. The shock, psychological and physical, disappeared from my mind and body. I realized that restarting the war room would only make me nuts. Fuck it! I took my coffee cup and stood outside my door on the stoop. The city was full of energy, both good and bad and I was glad to be back home. The women looked wonderful and I didn't even mind the suits as they walked by my stoop. I didn't even care about the people staring at me in my pajamas. Fuck them too! So Warlib is having a breakdown. No one is getting injured, not even me.

I thought about Doc throughout the day. He lost everything. Notwithstanding the insanity of the trading pits, the trading day dragged on endlessly.
"Mike, what do you think about long oil," I asked.
"Trend is your friend. It's going down," he said.
"I know about the Saudi promise and oil, but I got a friend who thinks that there isn't as much oil as everyone thinks and that the long term the trend is up," I said.
"Rueben, I'm a fucking trader not an investor. I think in terms of one day, one week, a month at the most. Investors think long term. It might be time for you to get out of the pits, Rue. You're not thinking like a trader anymore," Mike said. Maybe it was time to consider my future? I had saved enough money to retire. Maybe the pits were nothing more than a reflection of my coke addiction and that now that I was almost off coke the pits were making me nervous. "There's a time and place for everything," I thought and perhaps the commodity pits were no longer the place. Mike was right. Investors do not make good traders. Traders do not think long term.

All my notes, newspaper clippings and maps were at the estate. I had to reconstruct everything. My studies were in my mind, crystal clear and represented nothing more than a needless waste of time to duplicate them. I didn't get upset. The flashing light on my message machine disturbed me every time I passed it. I turned the machine over and moved on. After making my office a war room, I went on the Internet to check my e-mail. There were no e-mails from Jordan. At this point in time, Jordan was in Russia and I knew he was anxious. I visited my favorite sites on the Internet and prior to logging off; I got pissed at the plethora of overlapping pop-up ads that appeared on the screen. From my perspective, it was a monumental invasion of privacy of such aggravating proportions that they made me curse at the screen. What I hated the most were the ads that wouldn't close when you clicked on the close button. After getting rid of five ads, I noticed an ad for multi-player chess games and immediately thought of The Multitude.org. The game required me to download their software, which I did and pick a character and name, which I tried to do. The game must have had a million players because every name that I tried was in use. I got fed up and exited out of the game. I made a list of items that I needed to complete the war room, such as corkboard, pins and little "post-it" notes of different colors. The afternoon sped by unnoticed. I placed articles of interest that I printed out on my desk arranging them in order of importance and subject, oil, religion, election, Sam's opponent, etc. Someone knocked on my door and that made me realize that there was a world outside my door that I wasn't aware of and at that point in time, didn't want to intrude on my life. The knock either came from Gabby, Charles, a salesman, a former patient or an idiot lost on 88th street. I didn't answer it and patiently waited until I felt comfortable that whoever knocked on my door had left. After ten minutes, I felt relieved and took a break outside on the backyard deck. Staring at my backyard, I realized that I was hyped and should have been. My own self-analysis arrived at a conclusion that I was keeping busy to ward off any thoughts that my world had collapsed. Another part of me felt relieved because I knew that I just didn't belong in the Westerfield world. I couldn't fake the airs necessary on a sustained basis to keep me going in that world. Sooner or later, I would implode or just get fed up playing the role that I was not destined to play. Thinking of Sam, I realized that he was not my calling or my mission. An hour later I could hear another knock on my door that I disregarded. I didn't want to deal with anyone, in any fashion for any length of time. Within five minutes the phone rang and every ring sent my body into convulsions. I picked up the phone and did not recognize the number on the caller identification. I decided to answer it.

"Is this Stanley Warlib?" the caller asked.

"Yes," I said with regret.

"This is officer Bob Segow with the local precinct. We received a call from your neighbor who has been knocking on your door and is concerned," the officer said.

"Well, I'm o.k." I told the policeman.

"It's not you your neighbor was concerned about, it's the luggage on your stoop and the dog that goes with it. I'm outside your door now. Can you come outside?" the officer asked. I ran to the front door. I could hear Taz barking excitedly. Upon opening the door, TT flew in racing six feet past me and then turned around. Taz sat down and stared at me. "Come here boy," I said and with that he ran into me as I knelt down and hugged him. The officer handed me the luggage. "Didn't feel like answering the door. Just broke up with my fiancée," I told him.

"I totally understand Mr. Warlib. Looks like you have one very happy pup there. Girlfriend probably left the luggage and the dog," he said.

"More like Harry, her limousine driver, left the dog and the luggage," I said.

"Rich bitch, huh. High maintenance. You're better off," the officer said and went back to his patrol car. Taz ran around the apartment getting reacquainted with every room and then bounded down the deck steps to take a long leak caused from his excitement. Lifting his leg, he didn't take his eyes off me and after he

finished he flew up the steps and crashed into me. I remembered Sam's brother Bill stating that if you wanted a friend in Washington, get a dog. No truer words were ever uttered than those. After Taz calmed down, I opened the luggage and looked for a note. There wasn't any note or letter. However, I was surprised that all my notes and maps that I made in my study were neatly packaged in the suitcase.. All traces of my existence had been removed from the Westerfield estate. When it's over, it's over and a note might present itself as an invitation to respond. The Westerfield message was clear. I was figuratively dead. The doorbell rang and I assumed it was the officer.
"Rueben, what the hell are you doing here," I said.
"Came to visit. I wanted to make sure you were all right," he said.
"I'm fine, just fine. Come on in buddy," I said to Rueben. Rueben glanced around the "new" war room and asked what it was.
"Looking for words to put in the mouths of your cartoon characters?" he asked.
"Absolutely, Rue," I said. "What's with your office?" he asked.
"It's my war room," I answered.
"I don't know Doc, either you got the biggest case of denial going on or the best mechanisms to self correct," said Rueben.
"Who knows and who cares," I said. Rueben walked around and examined the apartment carefully. I recommended wine on the deck to which he gladly agreed.
"I asked around about going long on oil. Everybody's going the other way," said Rueben.
"Yeah, so what. It's election time and there are cracks showing up in the system. US Air filed for bankruptcy on Sunday. That's two major U.S. airlines in bankruptcy and a third is possible. There's lot of arm twisting going on and Sam needs lower oil, but if the fundamentals mandate long oil, there's no amount of arm twisting that's going to rule over supply and demand," I said. I could see Rueben didn't want the evening to descend into financial talk. I knew he was there to check on his buddy. Semper Fi in action. Rueben asked many questions all of which had at their core the query of whether his friend Doc was all right. I assured him that I was. I didn't have any food in the apartment. Rueben and I decided to have burgers at the Madison Avenue Bar. He to eat and I to look for Haven, a girl I had met on a previous occasion or Anarchist Angie. There were new faces but not the ones I wanted. I did make a mental note of the women that I wanted to meet at a later point in time. Rueben couldn't come to grips with my seemingly composed demeanor and behavior.
"Would it make you more comfortable if I was freaking out?" I asked.

"Probably, Doc," he answered. He wanted to know what I was going to do about a job. I told him that the next two months I was going to work in the war room and follow Sam and his cohorts on a daily basis.

"After Sam wins the election, I will let it go," I told Rueben. I could tell Rueben was concerned, as he wasn't getting what he wanted out of me. He didn't believe that someone could be that composed. He was right. If I needed to be in denial, I was going to permit myself to be in denial until such time as I could build support structures to replace the ones that Gabby and Charles had removed.

Arriving at the office the next day, I checked out the futures in oil. It's downward trend stabilized at $42.00 per barrel and I decided that I would take a shot with the Doc's advice and go long at some point above $40.00 per barrel. After watching my computer screen I decided to take a bet on long April contracts at $41.54. Within an hour after I bought the long oil contracts the ticker indicated that a major Iraqi oil pipeline was bombed and oil rose accordingly. I realized that the market was responding to the bombing news and not the overall fundamentals. Maybe out of loyalty or stupidity, I put $50,000.00 into the April contract. The next time I saw Doc, I was going to make him explain his adamancy in going long oil.

"Hello, is this Dr. P.?" I asked.

"Yes," the voice responded.

"My name is Rueben and I am a friend of Stanley Warlib. It took some time to get your number," I said.

"Yes," Dr. P. repeated. Dr. P. wasn't helping me in getting the conversation moving. He was being cautious.

"How can I help you?" he asked.

"Like I was saying, I'm a friend of Stan Warlib and I am concerned about him," I said. "Yes," he repeated again. Clearly, Dr. P. wasn't going to assist me.

"It's like this. Several days ago, Stan was on top of the world. He was getting married to a gorgeous younger woman, driving around in a big limo and had concluded negotiating with Charles Westerfield for a two million dollar salary. Within forty-eight hours, Doc is unemployed, not getting married and the limo is a memory. In addition, thinking that everything is solid, he closed his practice. So now, he doesn't have a fiancée, no job and no practice," I said.

"Yes," Dr. P. said.

"Look, I had enough of this 'yes' bullshit. I'm calling because I'm concerned and you ain't helping me at all," I said.

"Well, I don't know who you are," Dr. P. told me.

"I told you, I'm his good friend and I'm worried. You are his shrink?" I asked.

"Yes," he said. "Fuck you," I screamed and hung up the phone.

"Stan, this is Dr. P. Pick up the phone. Stan, pick up the phone. O.K., have it your way. Here's the message. I just received a call from a man named Rueben who claims that he is a friend of yours. He is worried about you and after speaking to Rueben; I'm worried about you. Stan, pick up the phone. Stan, this is serious, pick *up* the phone," Dr. P. demanded.

"Thank you, Stan. Now, what is going on?" Dr. P. asked.

"Nothing, Dr. P.," I responded.

"O.K., Stan, I'll try this again. You're not engaged, you're unemployed and you closed your practice all within 48 hours and you say 'nothing is going on.' I know you, Stan, this is not your typical modus operandi," said Dr. P.

"Nothing," I repeated again. I wasn't going to give Dr. P. any information. He asked about Rueben and I told him that Rueben was my Semper Fi buddy and part of the family. Dr. P. asked for Rueben's number and I gave it to him. Both of us continued our stilted conversation until I hung up.

"Rueben, this is Dr. P. I would like to ask you some questions. Is that alright," asked Dr. P.

"Of course," I answered.

"Answer yes or no where appropriate and give a narrative when called for," Dr. P. said. "Go," I requested.

"Is Stan a danger to himself?" "No."

"Is Stan a danger to others?" "No." "How would you describe his mood?"

"Agitated and aggravated."

"I would be too under the circumstances," said Dr. P.

"No. Not about losing the girl and the job, about the world and Sam," I explained. "Really. Is he manic?"

"What do you mean?" I asked.

"Is there an abnormally and persistently elevated, expansive or irritable mood?" asked Dr. P.

"He's not irritable, that's for sure. I would say his mood is elevated. Almost like he's having fun in an agitated kind of way," I told Dr. P.

"Decreased need for sleep?"

"Don't know."

"Pressure of speech?" "No."

"Flight of ideas?"

"Lots of ideas, but no, no flight."

"Increased involvement in goal directed activities."

"Definitely increased involvement in the analysis of world affairs and money, but to what goal, I don't know."
"Excessive involvement in pleasurable activities?"
"Absolutely not."
"How about inflated self-esteem or grandiosity?"
"Hard to answer. I don't think so," I said.
"General condition of apartment?" "Fine."
"General appearance?" "That's o.k."
"How about grandiosity again."
"Doc has uncritical self confidence. He's giving explanations about the world as if he were the Secretary of State," I said.
"I guess we can rule out depression," said Dr. P. I laughed.
"Would you describe his mood, euphoric, unusually good, cheerful or high?"
"Yes." "Would you say his mood has reached delusional proportions?" "No."
"Tell me what concerns you?" asked Dr. P.
"Doc, sees the world in cartoon characters. He puts a ton of information into his head, spins it around, spits out the bullshit and is left with the essence of what motivates people. Then he creates these cartoon characters and tries to determine what each would do according to their own interest. He sounds like he knows what he's talking about. I mean I can follow him. Then he tells me he's Sam's superego, his conscience and critic, except that Sam has got him nailed to the inside of his skull and his mouth is duct-taped shut," I told Dr. P.
"This imagery, do you think he believes it real or imagined?" asked Dr. P.
"No, Doc doesn't think it's real. He's just being very colorful and descriptive," I said.
"I see. I can't force Stan to come to my office or to check into a hospital. He's not a danger to himself or others. What baffles me is that Stan took off and blatantly went out for a night on the town. That's not the Stan I know. Something happened that motivated Stan to do that. When you see him next, see if you can find out if anything happened at the estate before he left for the city. The bottom line; it sounds to me like he's a frustrated Rush Limbaugh without the audience. This election is getting many people agitated and aggravated. I fear that this condition might last until November 2. Call me in a week if you have anything further to report. I'll try Stan again and if necessary, I'll visit him. Goodbye," said Dr. P.

## Chapter Nine

The biggest question I had was what was I going to do for the rest of the day. I wasn't going to call my former patients and beg them to come back. I didn't want to restart a practice. I had enough money to last at least a year. It was 10:00 a.m. and I was still lying in bed. Taz jumped up and lied across my body. He turned his head and stared at me. I realized that I wouldn't have lasted too long with the Westerfield's. I didn't belong in that world. Gabby and Charles knew it and I knew it. After showering, I got dressed, put Taz on a leash and headed towards the Mykonos diner. Before tying Taz to a parking meter, I checked to see whether Angelina was working. I wanted another piece of her. I was disappointed when I didn't spot her but felt a great relief when I saw her come out of the bathroom.

"Good morning Doc. Any more dreams about me?" she asked.

"Why dream Angie when I can have the real thing," I said.

"Pretty cocky. Tomorrow night, my place or yours, at 9:00 p.m.?" she asked.

"My place," I answered and wrote my address and number on a piece of paper. I never mentioned The Multitude.org. After breakfast, I took a long walk around Manhattan for a four-hour people-watching stroll. The City had game. It was alive. It pulsed and vibrated and I was just one of The Multitude.

I checked my e-mail. There was no message from Jordan and I became concerned. He was either in Irkutsk or on the Trans-Siberian Railroad heading towards Moscow. Vladimir Putin had just consolidated his power by removing elections from Russia's provinces and instituting an appointment system for each province leader. Putin was going to make the appointments. He instituted the move in response to the terror attacks that Russia had experienced over the last month. I was somewhat relieved but I knew I wouldn't feel comfortable until Jordan was back home. I checked my Internet favorites and then logged on to The Multitude.org. I tried fifty names for my character and none worked. I decided to try a name entirely opposite from the concept of anarchy and typed in FASCISTI, a member of the Fascist movement under Benito Mussolini. It worked. I hoped that the board members had a sense of humor. Instantly, I was in a make believe land with little characters roaming around bumping into each other. There were boxes that I could click on but I didn't. I just strolled.

HEADBANGER: What's your name? Are you new here?
FASCISTI: My name is Fascisti and yes, I am new here.
HEADBANGER: How did you know about the game?
FASCISTI: I stumbled onto it.

EAGLE: You're a smuck for coming on this board with a name like that.
FASCISTI: No sense of humor Eagle?
EAGLE: Not when it comes to fascism, moron.
FASCISTI: Why don't you put on a black tee shirt and go burn a urinal.
HEADBANGER: For a new guy, you're pretty aggressive.
FASCISTI: Go fuck yourself.

    I logged out of the game and realized I made a mistake. I should not have said anything about black tee shirts and burning urinals. I hoped Angelina wasn't playing and if she was, didn't notice my appearance. I felt too old to be playing anonymous multi-player Internet games. I checked The New York Times for articles about minor or major crimes against the rich and powerful and then went on line to see if anyone was bragging. I pissed away the rest of the day and played with Taz. My dog was one happy puppy.
"Doc, it's Rueben. Want to come out and play? I'm right outside your door," said Rueben.
"Rueben, get off your cell and come on in, the door is open," I said. I explained to Rueben that I had lit the bar-b-queue several minutes prior to his call and was about to prepare dinner. I had enough for two. Rueben went to the liquor store on Madison Avenue and bought a bottle of Tequila. I brought out some finger food as Rueben was opening the bottle. I explained to Rueben that we were going to drink the Tequila from the cap of the bottle, something I learned in Mulege, Mexico. It's the way to get a good, slow Baja buzz. He was surprised that I had a date with Angelina the following night. I felt as if Rueben and I were becoming good friends. I knew he would be faithful but I wasn't sure he liked me. I decided to let the relationship develop.
"Doc, what's your thinking about long oil?" he asked.
"Why, did you take a position?" I asked. "No, just trying to figure out why you're so adamant about long oil," said Rueben.
"Settle in, buddy, I'm going to tell you. At the beginning of the year, a major oil company came out and said it has substantially less oil reserves than they had previously declared. About three weeks ago, Sam said he has more oil reserves than he thought. The following week Sam comes out and says he got less oil reserves than he stated the prior week. I watch the oil market and notice how the price reacts. Now the cartoon guy comes into focus and I see a little character in a scuba suit being lowered into the great salt pit where Sam has his Strategic Petroleum Reserve. I start to think, exactly how do the oil guys calculate their reserves. They really can't, you see, and so they can manipulate the price anytime they want. Forget about that. I'm really thinking whether the world has a sufficient

supply of oil or doesn't have a sufficient amount of oil. No one is going to come out and say the world doesn't have enough oil because oil will go through the roof; so every one is flapping their lips that the world has enough oil. But, I'm still thinking about the question because my gut tells me something is going on and you can't believe the morons that are manipulating the market for short-term gains. My antennae are up. Either the world has enough oil to meet demand or it doesn't. I read an article in The New York Times entitled 'Oil Explorers Searching Ever More Remote Areas,' which starts to answer the question. The article is about Norway. It tells a tale about Statoil, Norway's leading energy company coming up dry on two wells that cost fifteen million each to drill. The explorers convinced management for one last try and the third well struck oil of 550 million barrels, enough to satisfy Britain's consumption for a year. However, this is a story that happened eleven years ago. In eleven years of hunting hardly any oil has been found. The same is true across much of the industrialized world. The article states that oil companies are running out of likely places to look and significant finds are becoming rarer. 'Hmmm,' I think to myself because I know that the media keeps on telling me that the world's oil demand is intensifying. Now I'm starting to get interested. Oil at $40-45 might justify looking for oil in new places but the oil companies are worried that the price of oil will drop and their investments won't be justified. There aren't enough long—term investments. This guy, Claude Mandil, executive director of the International Energy Agency, which represents twenty-six oil consuming nations, says 'we're ringing the alarm bell.' O.K., I say to myself, now it's starting to make sense, but my brain is swirling around looking for pieces to complete the puzzle. Statoil and others are spending nine billion searching for oil but are drilling fewer and fewer exploratory wells. Norway, a leading producer has leveled off at three million barrels. The bottom line is that finding sufficient quantities of oil are becoming harder and harder to find. With the most accessible areas picked clean, the oil companies have to go further and further a field or look more closely at sources of oil that were out of bounds for political reasons. A couple of days later, another article appeared entitled 'OPEC Finds Few Options to Put a Lid on Oil Prices.' I read and analyze the article. OPEC has one third of the world's oil production, half of oil exports and three-quarters of known reserves. However, OPEC can't control the oil prices anymore. Prices are moving independently from whatever OPEC decides. No one wants high prices because it kills the golden goose. Now, I'm thinking about the first article that stated that certain areas are off limits because of political reasons and I think of Iraq. Flashes of things I have either read or heard get thrown into the stew that's brewing in my brain. It is no longer occupied by the content of the articles that I just told you about. A flash of Newt Gingrich telling Tim Russert that those Muslims are sitting on two thirds of the world's known oil; a flash of Uncle Sam, in costume, looking at his Strategic Petroleum Reserve and his two producing areas; Alaska's North Slope and some rigs in the Gulf of Mexico; a flash of Frum and Perle, Sam's psychopathic neo-cons, writing in their new book about dominating the world and then the realization that Sam made the first move in a new game: if you can't find oil, take oil. Sam invades Iraq and I'm thinking, notwithstanding his protestations to the contrary, that it's about oil and then it goes further. Another flash of the Silk Road Strategy Act of 1999, introduced by Senator Brownback with former Secretary of State James Baker, declaring in essence that the Caucasus nations are now our best friends. It is believed that the region has six trillion dollars of oil and gas and Sam is making inroads. Then another flash about a rumor that Sam is building four main permanent bases in Iraq since he plans to stay there; a flash of Senator John McCain stating that in his opinion Sam will be in Iraq for ten to twenty years and I'm thinking he's protecting his oil interests and he's fucking with the Iraqi government until he gets the one he wants that will favor him with oil; flash, a rumor that Vladimir Putin offered to put in forty thousand troops if Sam got out of the Caucasus area; flash, Germany and France asking Iran to cooperate not because they agree with Sam but because Sam has demonstrated his willingness to invade sovereign nations; flash, the Arab nations requesting Syria to get their troops out of Lebanon, not because they think it's a good idea but because Sam is on the loose. Now, in this swirl of bullshit, I know Sam is thinking, in his psychopathic narcissist mind set, that he is one bad mother fucker, while the rest of the world wants to calm things down because the oil rich desert kingdoms need protection from people like Sam. Another flash. The insurgents are getting better organized in Iraq and the frequency and coordination of attacks is increasing. Underneath, the militants are thinking that they can take Sam in a fight and wouldn't that be great to get Sam the fuck out of the Middle East. Russia, having sustained damage from terrorist attacks, makes a move yesterday to strengthen its hand in the Caucasus area, the oil rich Caspian Sea, by stating that it's going to control its provinces and then another flash comes into my mind. The first thing out of the mouth of a terrorist captured in the Beslan school massacre states that his mission was to 'set fire to the Caucasus's.' Now, all this shit is floating around up there and I ask myself a simple question; Is all this crap going on because the world has a sufficient amount of oil or has an insufficient amount of oil. To me, the only logical answer to that question is that the madness the world is currently encountering is because there isn't enough oil and Sam has changed the equation of

obtaining oil by exploration and legal contracts with sovereign nations to invasion of sovereign nations. Finally, Osama bin Laden knows the West will collapse under the strain of high oil prices. No one thought that fully fueled airplanes could become weapons of mass destruction but 9/11 taught us otherwise. Now, listen to me, the price of oil has become a weapon and Osama is never going to let the price go down. High oil is a weapon. So, long oil," I concluded.
"Doc, you're either a madman or genius," said Rueben.
"Let me tell you something else. There's a tiny little country named Equatorial Guinea wedged between Gabon and Cameroon on the west coast of Africa. I mean, it's a little thing, but the guy running the show is depositing close to a billion a year in Riggs National Bank. Its army is nothing more than a band of hoods sufficient to control and intimidate his tiny country. What happens? Well, it appears that Margaret Thatcher's little boy decides that a band of about seventy mercenaries should be able to do the trick to take over Equatorial Guineas oil. They get caught and deny their intentions. What bullshit. You get my point though. It's just another blatant attempt by a white boy to invade a country and get its oil. Sam started the process; oil by invasion and others are going to follow his example. Remember what I told you before about Russia offering to send 40,000 troops to help Sam in Iraq in return for Sam getting the hell out of Russia's area. Sam is all over the place burrowing in, in places like Estonia, Latvia, Lithuania, Georgia, Azerbaijan, Turkmenistan, Uzbekistan and Kazakhstan, forming a pearl necklace around Russia. Putin floats a trial balloon by offering troops to help Sam in Iraq but since that goes nowhere, he institutes Plan B. He steps up to the plate and reorganizes the political landscape of Russia to exert control of its strategic oil provinces. He's making money hand over fist for mother Russia and he isn't going to stop. Words like 'freedom' and 'democracy' are euphemisms for oil and the war on 'terror' is political cover for re-exerting control and dominion over oil rich countries. The gloves are coming off between the world and Sam and the fun is just starting. No one wants Sam to win in Iraq and I'm sure behind the scenes there are a lot of actors supplying the insurgents to ensure that Sam suffers losses in his self inflicted quagmire. Not enough to kill Sam because they need his family's voracious appetite for consumer goods, just enough to weaken him to prevent any additional forays into the Caspian Sea area. Listen up now, you heard it here first; D A G E S T A N. It borders the Caspian Sea thereby giving Putin control with Iran of the western edge of the area except for Azerbaijan, which is leaning towards Sam. On the west, you have Kazakhstan and Turkmenistan controlling the eastern border of the Caspian Sea. Here's the rub of it all Rueben. Putin is telling Azerbaijan, Kazakhstan and Turkmenistan

that they're betting on the wrong dog. He's got a point doesn't he? All the time, the big Kung-Fu master is sitting in the background pleasantly smiling. What a fucking nightmare. If you remember nothing else, remember this: The nation that controls oil will write the history of the 21$^{st}$ century."

"How do you know this stuff?" Rueben asked.

"I told you Rue, I'm nailed inside the skull of Sam and I've got a ringside seat. I'm all eyes and no voice," I told Rueben. I had enough of my own bullshit, grabbed a Frisbee and tossed it into the garden. TazTwo went flying off the deck to retrieve the Frisbee and Rueben handed me a cap of Tequila. Rueben and I finished the evening telling jokes.

# Chapter Ten

I made my money in the commodity pits by going with the ebbs and flows of the market that I was playing. I was never interested in fundamentals or technical analysis. I traded the rhythm of the market. This was the first day that I bought The New York Times. Yesterday, I was long 25 April contracts of light sweet crude at $41.54. Each contract entitled me to purchase 1,000 barrels of light sweet crude at $41.54 a barrel. If the price went up I made the difference. The contract closed at $41.96 and I was up .42 cents a barrel. I controlled 25,000 barrels and so I made a quick $10,500.00. In my opinion, the price firmed because the insurgents blew up a pipeline in the northern Iraqi city of Bayji and Hurricane Ivan was threatening oilrigs in the Gulf of Mexico. The weathermen expected Ivan to hit Alabama early Thursday morning. I agreed with Doc from a long-range investor perspective, however, not from a trader's viewpoint. I was going to cash out at the end of the day. The risk of the market going against me could produce catastrophic losses and I was not going to take a chance. Prior to the opening of the bell, I leaned against a wall drinking coffee and read The New York Times. Many of the headlines just exploded off the page. I was sure that my conversations with Doc made the stories seem more important than they were. However, I started to think like Doc did and could see he made some sense. He just wasn't blowing smoke out of his ass. Wherever the oil, refineries and pipelines were, you would have flashpoints of the 21$^{st}$ century. The headlines that struck me were the following: (a) "Putin Backs Gazprom Bid To Buy Big Oil Company (1) OPEC To Put Formal Lifting Of Output On the Table and (c) U.S. Current Account Deficit Hits Record $166.2 Billion." No matter how hard the markets were trying to jawbone oil down and calm fears over supply, oil was holding and I could envision that Osama was weaponizing oil. If Doc's cartoon characters were right, attacks on oil pipelines and refineries would continue and escalate. Secretary of State Colin Powell was out there talking about Putin's backward move against freedom and democracy because of Putin's consolidation of power, but what could Colin do on behalf of Sam. Sam was stuck in the Iraqi shit hole spreading his troops thin and running up a huge tab on his broke country. Putin carefully planned his move on the Caucasus region and waited for the right time. Sam was unable to make an effective countermove. Sam's feet were stuck in the ever-hardening concrete of Iraq's sands. Putin was a brilliant tactician. In the western region of Sudan, Darfur, Sam was back-pedaling on a resolution boycotting Sudanese oil because Pakistan and China were large importers. Sam wanted to go it alone in the world and the world said o.k. Cocaine felt like a thing of the past. I had no urges at all. I diligently tracked Hurricane Ivan's path in the Gulf of Mexico. Doc was taking bits of information, stringing them together and putting his own spin on it. Doc's spin was worldwide in scope while everyone else was focusing his or her spin on the upcoming election. I was bored to death with both campaigns talking about a war that was waged thirty-five years ago. Maybe Doc was right? The real action lied beyond the shores of Sam's boundaries. The news ticker came across the top of my laptop stating that the United States crude oil stocks had a big drop and oil was on an upwards march. The price of oil touched a two-week high and I sat there counting my money. I felt that it was "home-run" time, where a trader puts down $10,000.00 in the morning and walks away that afternoon with $150,000.00. The allure of hitting a home run is stronger than any addiction on earth. It is a holy affirmation from on high that you are thinking right, or in this case, Doc was thinking right. The price started to drop after lunch and I assumed that the traders were taking profits. However, the trend continued and I sat transfixed at the computer watching my profits evaporate and then my money diminish. I fell into the novice trader trap of thinking that I was infallible. The best way to describe the mind-set is that I'm right and the collective market place is wrong. Doesn't the world know what I know? Oil is going up, you start to silently scream at the screen. "What morons" you say to yourself and by the end of the trading day, you're so angry at some unknown collective market place that you hold your position and take a loss. No discipline. All the trading rules get thrown out the window and you're now going to hold your position and show the marketplace that you're right. My contract settled at the end of the day at $41.25. I lost my profit of $10,500.00 and sat in the hole with an approximate loss of $7,500.00. I left the trading desk with that horrible feeling that maybe Hurricane Ivan would wipe out an oil refinery in Pascagoula, Mississippi or some oil rigs in the Gulf of Mexico. Betting for a tragedy to bail you out of a trade position is morally abhorrent and I waited anxiously for the CNN video footage of Hurricane Ivan the following morning.

Taz was sleeping next to me in the bed. The alarm clock went off at about 6:00 a.m. and I just lied in bed with my arms behind my neck. I watched Taz-Two twitch as he slept. My dog was having a dream. He was probably running on the beach catching a Frisbee. Bill Bennett's "Morning in America" show was on and he was interviewing some guy from Claremont Institute. It was their collective opinion that Sam had arrived at that point in time that he should use greater force in Iraq. It was time to kill greater numbers now in order to save larger numbers later. "Killing to save," what a strange idea that was, but completely comprehensible to the evangelical mind, I said to myself. However, the

Muslim banderillos were sticking the brave bull in the shoulder with barbed hooks weakening him. Sam's generals were probably advising him that his soldiers were going to die a slow death unless Sam takes off the gloves. Bennett's guest added that a complete show of force would set off alarm bells in Iran and Iran would collapse into complacency under Sam's overwhelming use of force. I recalled that several days ago, the Pentagon had asked Sam's congress to authorize a switch of three billion dollars from reconstruction to security. Knowing Sam, he was petrified that the facade of his image might develop cracks and he would do anything to protect his psyche. Killing tens of thousands of innocent Iraqi's were not as important as protecting his image at all costs. In Sam's head, his military could dominate the world so it might be time to exercise his military. "Come on Taz. It's time to get up," I said. Taz followed me out to the front door to get The Times and we headed back to the kitchen. As I waited for my coffee, I read the headlines of The Times and was extremely interested in the lead article entitled "U.S. Intelligence Shows Pessimism On Iraq's Future-Tone Differs From Public Statements." Of course, the tone differs from the public statements. Every narcissist protects his image. I wondered if Iran was on the phone with the Kung-Fu master asking whether they were ready to protect their gas station. I thought about the 4,000 Chinese troops in Sudan and wondered whether China had troops in Iran to protect their largest supplier of oil. I was going to check that out. Maybe the world is afraid of Sam? Maybe the psychopathic Neo-Cons were correct in their assessment that no one in the world would challenge Sam. The world was asking themselves the question that I always asked myself: At what point do you stand up to the bully? The article indicated that the National Intelligence Estimate, a highly classified document issued in July 2004, was pessimistic. Essentially, every scenario went from bad to worse. I concluded that a talking point memo went out to the talk show pundits to start talking about the necessity of a more aggressive stance in Iraq. "Taz, we have work to do," I said. Today, I was going to reconstruct the war room that Westerfield had constructed. I needed cork board for maps, easels to place the corkboards on and different colored pins to indicate oil fields, oil pipelines, routes of oil pipelines, proposed routes and little post-it notes to make notations. My office that formerly treated patients was going to be transformed into the inner sanctum of Sam's brain. Even though Sam had me nailed to a cross inside his skull, my office was going to be my mouth enabling me to speak out, even if Taz was the only one that would hear me. Two hours after breakfast, the easels and maps were up. I was prepared to delve into my first area of concern, "The New Europe." Sam's new foreign policy of pre-emption was clear. He changed fifty years of foreign policy that ensured that

Sam would only use his military might to defend himself to a policy of pre-emption. Sam would attack first and ask questions later. That policy depended on having a well thinking brain and excellent military intelligence, neither of which Sam had. I was fascinated by Sam's second change of policy. Going from the "Old Europe" to the "New Europe." Clearly, the Old Europe was France and Germany but who was the "New Europe." Sam abandoned centuries of friendship and alliance in favor of some new countries and I didn't know exactly who they were. I was determined to find out. I Googled "The New Europe" on my laptop and prepared to research when I heard a voice. I turned around. The radio or television wasn't on. Taz sat at my feet and looked up. I thought that it might have been the wheezing sound that came from my lungs from excessive smoking. There were many times I woke up at night thinking that someone was in the room making noise. In my half sleep, it sounded like talking or strange noises, but awakening more, I realized I was wheezing. I heard the noise again but it wasn't wheezing, it was definitely someone talking. Taz put his front paws on my lap and I motioned to him to get down and be silent. Someone was talking. "Sam, show resolve. Show resolve Sam for now is not the time to let up," the voice said. I was stunned. I was in Sam's head. Although I was nailed to the inside of his skull and had my mouth duct taped shut, my ears were open. I could hear. God was talking to Sam. I instantly settled down. I didn't want to miss a word. "Sam, you must show resolve. I have called upon you and given you the most important mission since I called upon Abraham to deliver the Ten Commandments. Do not abandon me. You must persevere and march forward. You are my Christian Warrior. Proceed on the path I have given to you. You must open up those countries that deny my people religious freedom so that they may accept my son Jesus as their savior. Sam show resolve," the voice finished. I couldn't believe what I had heard. I heard God talking to Sam. I was there, right inside Sam's damn head listening to God. I was hearing what Sam heard. I realized that if I told anyone what I had just experienced they would think that I was nuts. "Incredible," I thought to myself. I needed a double Dewar's to calm me down.

I started typing "The New Europe" and stopped. "Taz, what the hell am I doing this for. I know what's going. I'm acting like some college professor writing a thesis that's going to sit on a shelf collecting dust. This is stupid," I said. I pulled over a chair and told Taz to get up and sit on it. He obligingly honored my request. "Taz, this bullshit about the 'Old Europe' and the 'New Europe' started on January 22, 2003 when Donald Rumsfeld, Sam's Secretary of Defense, in response to a question, stated that France and Germany where the 'Old Europe.' Donald was interested in the 'New Europe,' countries that were waiting entry into the European Union and NATO. Who are they you ask? Well, countries like Poland, Hungary, Czech Republic, Slovakia, Slovenia, Latvia, Lithuania, Estonia, Cyprus and Malta. Some of these countries signed a letter supporting Sam's war against Iraq and that really pissed off the French President Jacques Chirac who said that those countries that signed the letter missed a great opportunity to "shut up." Chirac singled out Romania and Bulgaria; he stated, "Romania and Bulgaria were particularly irresponsible. If they wanted to diminish their chances of joining Europe they could not have found a better way." Taz look at the map. We're forsaking good old friends, France and Germany for Romania and Bulgaria. I mean, what the fuck is up what that. Taz, just study the map. Taz, Romania and Bulgaria border the Black Sea. There's a pipeline that is almost completed called the Baku-Tbilsi-Ceyhan pipeline. The main pipeline heads south towards the Turkish port of Ceyhan, however, a there's a spur that heads due west to the city port of Sup'sa in Georgia. You see that Taz. Here, use a magnifying glass. The main pipeline heads out to the Mediterranean Sea and can provide oil to points west, like America. The Black Sea port of Sup'sa in Georgia can transport oil by tanker to the port cities of Constanja in Romania, Varna and Burgas in Bulgaria. The 'New Europe' represents areas for pipelines to be built to provide oil to Europe by Sam and his buddies. However, Russia already has a series of pipelines and routes to provide oil and gas to Europe. So, you see Taz, this is all about the Caspian Sea oil fields and Sam and his buddies have to have friendly countries that will allow Sam to build oil and gas routes. Hence, Sam's interest in the 'New Europe.' However, these countries need military muscle to protect the areas and that's where Sam comes in. It's all about the Benjamins Taz; it's all about the Benjamins. Sam sends his army engineers into Romania and Bulgaria to assess their respective capabilities of handling Sam's military bases. I didn't know this but Sam has 700 military bases in 130 countries. How's that for an empire. The Russians are alarmed. On August 4, 2004, Konstantin Kosachyov, chairman of the State Duma International Commission told Ekho Moskvy Radio that 'our worries are founded.' Sam says that it is being done for the anti-terrorist fight and the bases will be targeted southward, but while the deployment of military bases in Hungary, Bulgaria and Romania is the southeastern movement, a military base in Poland is a movement to the east. Even before 9/11, Caspian Sea oil and gas and planned pipelines for delivery of those energy resources dictated a re-evaluation of Sam's strategic interests. Look here, Taz, there are two tiny disputed areas in Georgia, Abkhazia and Ajaria that are dangerously close to the Baku-Tblisi-Ceyhan pipeline and border the Black Sea. Watch those areas Taz. Take a look at the Republic of North Ossetia, a republic of Russia, where the Beslan massacre occurred and South Ossetia that juts into Georgia. The political cover for military advances into these areas is the war on terror. Both sides will use the war on terror to disrupt one side or the other in this great oil game. A Russian Delta Force blows up a terminal in the port of Sup'sa to slow down Sam's plans and then puts out disinformation claiming it's terrorists. Sam does the same. Taz, look over to the eastern shore of the Caspian Sea. There's Turkmenistan, Afghanistan and Pakistan, countries that are being lined up to supply oil and gas to the East.

I heard a faint knocking but didn't associate the sound with someone being at the door. The knock became louder and louder until I realized that someone was yelling and pounding on the door. I opened the door and found Angelina with a shoe in her hand, half-cocked, ready to bang on the door again.
"Stan, what the hell were you doing in here that you didn't hear me knock?" she asked. "Don't ask, Angelina. War room stuff. It's unimportant," I said.
"I might be interested," she responded. My dick went hard the moment I saw Angie. I grabbed her by the hand and led her to the bedroom. I can only describe what happened over the next seven hours in what would be considered guy talk: I screwed the shit of her. First, I nailed her on the bed. When she got up to wash her hands at the bathroom sink, I nailed her again. Looking in the refrigerator for something to eat provided an excellent opportunity to get Angie from behind. I could not stop myself and I screwed Angelina anywhere I could. "Well, well, well. If it isn't the Cialis Kid," she said. "Sorry Angie, no drugs tonight," I told her. "You're kidding. At your age! Stan. If you're telling the truth, I'm impressed. I'm really impressed," she said. I was prepared to continue but Angie had enough. It was 4:00 a.m. when Angelina left, hoping to grab two hours of sleep before appearing for work. Neither Angie nor I ever mentioned The Multitude.org. I didn't give her a chance and I wasn't interested. A deep tiredness overtook my body and I succumbed to a satisfying sleep. "Good night Taz," I said.

The phone rang three times in the morning. I didn't answer it. For a second I thought that it might be Gabby but I knew that she would never call. It wasn't any of my former clients. It was probably Dr. P. checking up on me. He was the last person that I wanted in my life. I could hear myself talking to Dr. P. about being nailed to the inside of Sam's skull listening in on a conversation that he was having with God. Oh, that would make his day. I started laughing and grabbed Taz around the head. It was roughhouse time and Taz responded accordingly. When Labrador Retrievers pretend to be angry it is pitiful. A lab is the last dog in the world that has any bite behind his bark. "Come on dummy," I said to Taz as I pulled his tail. Next up for the war room was Rumsfelds "Lily Pad" concept and the redeployment of Sam's troops. If I had no one to talk to, it might as well be Taz.

"Stan, buddy, what's up?" asked Rueben.

"Rueben, how the hell are you?" I asked.

"What are you doing tonight?" Rueben asked.

"Waiting for you," I said.

"You know Doc, after our conversation about oil being weaponized I started watching the oil market. The April light sweet crude contract closed at $41.68. I started watching it at $41.54. It's up .14 cents," said Rueben.

"I told you, long oil," I responded.

"Yeah, if I would have taken a position, I would be up $3,500.00. What are you doing tonight?" asked Rueben.

"Waiting for you. I'll see ya later and bring some wine," I told Rueben. I forgot what day it was. It was Thursday. I decided to clean up my act and take TazTwo for a stroll past Mykonos to see if Angelina was working. In the shower, I heard a voice, barely audible over the sound of the water streaming from the showerhead. I immediately turned off the water. I strained to hear the voice but it was so low I couldn't hear. I put my fingers in my ears. "Stan, you must help me. Sam is the anti-Christ. He is a wolf in sheep's clothing. My true son Jesus would never act in my name as Sam is doing. You must stop him. In my name I am calling upon you for this mission: You must do everything in your power to put an end to the evil that Sam has thrust upon the World. I stand for love, not war, and I will continue to send hurricane after hurricane upon Sam until he ceases," said the voice. My fingers remained in my ears for ten minutes. I waited patiently in case the voice wanted to speak to me again. It didn't. I stopped into Mykonos for breakfast and made arrangements with Angie for an afternoon delight. From 4:00 p.m. to 5:30, I screwed Angie with such ferocity; I thought that she would break in two. I think I frightened her.

Rueben knocked on the door at 6:00 p.m. and as I opened it he popped the cork off of a bottle of champagne. "We'll celebrating," he said. I asked Rueben what the celebration was all about but he wouldn't tell me until we toasted. "Here's to getting your voice back," he said as he raised his glass. "What the hell are you talking about?" I asked. "I gave you your voice back. You always tell me that you're nailed inside the skull of Sam and you can't talk cause Sam has got your mouth duct-taped shut. Well, I bought you air time on a radio station. It's a prime time spot on a minor station. You go on this coming Monday at 5:00 p.m.," Rueben said. I was shocked into silence. I could tell that my silence scared

Rueben into thinking that he made a mistake. After a minute of stunned disbelief I grabbed Rueben and started screaming.

"Are you fucking kidding me?" I asked.

"No, I wouldn't lie to you. You're my Semper Fi buddy. I thought you would like it," said Reuben.

"Like it, I love it. I can't believe it. I just can't believe it. I finally can tell people what's going on. I can't f u c k i n g believe it," I said. Rueben smiled. My mind raced at a thousand miles an hour.

"You mean this Monday?" I asked.

"Yes," he answered.

"At 5:00 p.m.?" I asked.

"Yes," answered Rueben. I ran into the war room and pushed aside the maps and sat down at the computer. Before, I could type anything Rueben interrupted me.

"Doc, you have to stop all this stuff. Look around, Doc. Maps, easels, post it notes. You're starting to look like that character that Russell Crowe played in that movie 'A Beautiful Mind,'" Rueben said.

"I'm not a paranoid schizophrenia, if that's what you're wondering," I said.

"Doc, I hope I didn't do a bad thing," Rueben said.

"Rueben, you have no idea what you did. Possibly the greatest gift that anyone could give, ever," I said.

"Doc, I just wanted to give you a voice, that's all," Rueben said and added, "not to give you more work."

"I need this Rueben. The world needs this. What I am supposed to do, spend the rest of my life screwing Angelina like a madman? Or talk to my dog because I have no one else to talk to? Or dwell on the video from Operation Pork Belly. Oh yeah, you remember Operation Pork Belly, don't you. Well, I'll tell you what was on the video. Gabby and her dad took a walk on the beach. In their absence, I reviewed the video. There wasn't much on it until the day I left. In Charles private study, I saw Charles and Sam. Charles was sitting in his chair at his desk and Sam was sitting across. They were smoking cigars and drinking scotch. On a couch were Gabby and that sniper bitch Elicia. Gabby was lying down on, her back to Elicia's belly and Elicia had her arms wrapped around Gabby and her hands were resting on her stomach. The audio was out. I couldn't hear anything they were saying, but it looked like one big love fest. They were all laughing and I know they were laughing about me. Stanley Warlib was a big fucking lollipop. An all day sucker. I was never so humiliated in my life. I went to the dune, stared at the ocean and realized there was only one thing I could do. Leave, and that's exactly what I did. Does that make me insane?" I asked.

"No. I probably would have punched the shit out of Charles and Gabby," said Rueben. "Exactly, and before any damage was done, I left," I told Rueben.
"Rueben, you're my Semper Fi buddy, right?" I asked.
"Yes," he answered.
"Don't get scared. You know how I always tell you I'm nailed inside the skull of Sam. He's got my mouth taped shut but he forgot about my ears. I heard God talk to him. I swear. I heard God. God told Sam to show resolve. This morning God spoke directly to me. I was taking a shower and God told me that I must expose Sam as a wolf in sheep's clothing. Sam is the Anti-Christ. God called upon me and gave me a mission and that mission is to expose Sam. Now you come along and tell me you bought radio time. If this isn't divine intervention than I don't know what is. It all fits," I said.
"Doc, why would God tell Sam one thing and tell you exactly the opposite?" Rueben asked. I became annoyed.
"What the fuck do I know; maybe God has a sense of humor, maybe God is psychotic or maybe God likes a lively debate. I'll ask him next time I hear from him, o.k." I yelled. Rueben was nervous but he managed to finish the evening without letting on that I freaked him out. I had four days to prepare for my debut and I started preparing when the door closed behind Rueben.

"Rueben, this is Dr. P. I received a call from my answering service. They told me you called with an emergency. Is it Stan?" asked Dr. P.
"I think I made a huge colossal mistake," I started to say, however, Dr. P. told me to calm down and compose myself.
"I had dinner with Stan several days ago and he freaked me out. Number one, he's screwing his brains out with a waitress named Angie and he told me that an eighteen-year-old porn stud would be proud of him. Number two, while he was nailed to the inside of Sam's skull he heard God talk to Sam. Number three, God spoke to him in the shower and gave him a mission to try to stop Sam and Number four, and he's just plain freaking me out," I told Dr. P.
"I see," said Dr. P. "Don't give me this 'I see' bullshit," I said angrily.
"I'm thinking Rueben. I'm thinking," said Dr. P.
"Oh and number five, he watched a secret video that he made of Charles study and saw Charles, Sam, Gabby and some girl named Elicia, all hanging together and laughing. Doc, thought that they were laughing about him," I said.
"Do you think he's a danger to himself or to others?" asked Dr. P.
"No," I answered.
"Rueben, you started off the conversation saying that you made a huge colossal mistake. Do you mind telling me what that is?" asked Dr. P.

"No. Not at all. Well, Doc is always saying that he has his mouth duct taped shut and that Sam is got him muzzled. I made extra money on Stan's advice and so I bought him airtime on a New York City radio station. I thought that it might do him some good. Now, I'm thinking that it's only going to make him worse. I think I screwed up big time," I told Dr. P. There were several minutes of silence. "Based upon our last conversation and this one, I believe that Stan might be experiencing two distinct episodes. It sounds likes he's having a Manic Episode and the start of a Delusional Episode, neither of which appear to be life threatening. I'm going to visit Stan on Sunday night and try to talk to him. In the interim, if you can get in touch with the station manager, you must cancel his Monday show. I feel strongly that it will only agitate him. Your radio station idea was not a bad one. Everyone has defense mechanisms. One defense mechanism is sublimation whereby you channel maladaptive feeling or impulses into socially acceptable behavior. Contact sports to channel angry impulses. Don't feel bad it was a good idea. Now, this extra money you made on Stan's advice, what's that all about?" asked Dr. P.

"Doc was always saying long oil, so I asked him what he meant. He told me that oil is only going up because, in his words, 'high oil prices has become a weapon of Osama bin Laden and the country that controls oil, will write the history of the 21$^{st}$ century. Doc went into a full explanation and made some sense. I went long oil and made some money," I told Dr. P.

"Do you think Stan is right?" asked Dr. P.

"I got the money to prove it. Oil closed at $42.80 and I bought in at $41.54. I am up $31,500.00 in a week," I said. After an exchange of some additional pleasantries, the conversation ended. I am always amazed by the lure that easy money has on people and Dr. P. wasn't excluded. I would bet that Dr. P. was on the phone with his stockbroker asking about "long oil."

The next four days I spent thinking and analyzing, Googling, devising and executing a marketing plan, banging Angelina, reading the Bible and I tried everything I could to talk to God. On Sunday, I avoided Rueben and refused to answer the door. I slipped a note through the mail slot telling Rueben that if he were a real Semper Fi buddy he wouldn't stop me. He would support me. I hid in the backyard and completely ignored Dr. P. I pretended that I wasn't home and I knew that Dr. P. knew it. Nothing was going to stand in the way of the mission that God had given me. I had one last thing to do before I went to sleep. I had to check my e-mail and see if Jordan had a chance to e-mail me from Russia. I was disappointed. I typed in The Multitude.org and appeared on the board. Within a

minute, a crowd of characters, all telling me to get off the board, surrounded me. The crowd of Avatars parted and another Avatar appeared before me.
KHAN: It appears your presence here always causes a disturbance.
FASCISTI: I guess so. Are you the leader?
KHAN: There are no leaders, on or off the board. Talk to me privately by instant messaging.
KHAN: What do you want?
FASCISTI: Your Help.
KHAN: For what?
FASCISTI: Tomorrow, I start my own talk show. I want a near riot. Half the people for me and half against me. I want you to call the television stations and get coverage.
KHAN: Are you ready to get off the board and take it to the street?
FASCISTI: Maybe. Sam's opponent is dead in the water. Sam is going to be reelected as head of the family.
KHAN: What's in it for me?
FASCISTI: Don't know. Will you help me?
KHAN: I'll see. What's the theme?
FASCISTI: Don't know yet.
KHAN: I'm an atheist.
FASCISTI: So am I.
KHAN: I see. I'll think about it.
FASCISTI: Thanks.
"Doc, what's up?"
"Nothing and everything Rueben. I am preparing for my show this afternoon. I thought that those ominous gray clouds left over from Hurricane Ivan would ruin my opening day, but no one rains on my parade. To make a beautiful day even brighter, Jordan e-mailed me from Moscow. Maki and Jordan are just fine. They're staying in Moscow for two days and then flying to Italy," I told Rueben.
"Hey Doc, not for nothing, but I think you're wired in to something. I don't know what you see upstairs in that head of yours but you're wired into something. You know all that long oil stuff you've been ranting about, well, I went long oil last week and by Friday, I sat on $31,500.00 in profit. Yesterday, I read in The New York Times an article entitled 'Yukos Cuts Oil Exports to China.' Today, Brent crude is up to $46.00 a barrel and my 25,000 barrels of April light sweet crude is up as well. You're wired Doc and you're onto something. What's next?" Rueben asked.

"Oh, so you don't think I'm nuts. Don't talk to Dr. P. He'll try to convince you that I'm nuts. Yukos is trying to get out of Putin's billion-dollar tax bill demand and so Yukos threatens that they can't pay the transit fees for 100,000 barrels to ship oil to China. Russia is one of China's largest suppliers. The most important thing between a producer and supplier is stability. Yukos, aware that Putin won't jeopardize his relationship with China, is thinking that Putin is going to run scared and loosen his claim on the Yukos oil company. It's a dumb move because Putin will only strengthen his grip. Nothing, absolutely nothing, will stand in Putin's way of exhibiting to China the stability of his beloved Mother Russia as China's main gas station. Yukos wrote its own obituary. It was one big dumb fucking move. Here's where it starts to get interesting. China just consolidated its power in the hands of one man. The old guy is out and a new guy named Hu is in. He controls the Communist Party, the military and something else, which I can't remember. Hu is an unknown on the geo-political scene. But, Sam in his infinite stupidity continues to stir the pot thinking he's a big bad bully. The International Atomic Energy people, the IAEA, is pressing Iran to cease developing their nuclear energy ambitions and Sam is pressing for a ban on oil exports from Sudan. Iran is a major exporter of oil to China and Sudan exports oil to China. I think behind the scenes, the Sudanese and the Iranians are on the phone saying to China, it's time to step up to the plate and exercise your power. If Sam came in and kicked the crap out of Iraq in 1990, at the request of Saudi Arabia because they felt threatened when Saddam went into Kuwait, now it's China's turn to show it's stuff. The questions being asked are will China stand up to Sam and protect its gas stations? The query takes on added importance now that Yukos has threatened to ship less oil," I told Rueben. "And?" asked Rueben. "And, all the time Osama bin Ladin is sitting in a cave someplace or some luxurious villa, sipping tea, laughing his ass off because high oil is weaponized. The cracks are starting to show up in Sam's marketplace. Third quarter pre-announcement warnings are starting to come in from Sam's corporate America that many companies are not going to meet their targets. Just this morning the market opened down fifty-four points and then sunk to minus sixty-eight and all the big wigs are saying soft patch. Short the S & P, Rueben. Now is the time for Russia and China to make a move. Sam and his buddy Ayad Allawi, the interim head of Iraq, are begging the world for support for the upcoming elections. They aren't going to get any. No one, absolutely no one, is going to help Sam. He violated the rule of sovereignty and invaded a country for its resources. China and Russia might throw down the gauntlet. China might move additional troops into Sudan to compliment the existing four thousand and may, just may, put troops into Iran to protect their interests there. You know, one time Putin wrote on a napkin that his interest lied with China and we'll see if he made the right choice. I think he did. You do this now when Sam is tied up in elections and the quagmire in Iraq and I don't think the world is going to let Sam suffer just because they're pissed, I think the world wants to see Sam injured enough to crack the façade of his psychopathic narcissistic delusions. In other words, you aren't the top dog anymore and get used to it. In addition, surreptitiously, probably Syria, Iran, Russia and China are sending in more sophisticated small weapons and fighters to coordinate the existing insurgents already there. I wouldn't be surprised if Sam found some weaponry that clearly indicated that China made a footprint in the sands of Iraq. Kind of like, "we're here." Sam would never let on to his family. What's he going to do then? Tell his family that the Russians and Chinese are helping to defeat him in Iraq! His family will demand an answer. He doesn't have any answers and he never had an exit strategy because Sam didn't plan on exiting. More war, more death, more pipelines blowing up and more long oil, dude," I told Rueben.

"So, what should I do?" asked Rueben.

"Well, let's see, you could take some profits at the end of the day, but I don't think the oil story is finished or you could short the S & P index. O.K., do this. Stay long oil one more day and then short the S & P.," I said.

"Thank you, Doc," said Rueben.

"Rueben, there's one more thing. The thing that I'm happiest about is that I read an article on the web that indicated that the British Ambassador to Italy said behind closed doors that Sam is the best recruiting tool for Osama bin Ladin. That's exactly what I told Charles Westerfield, so I know I'm not crazy. I'm dead on, brother," I said to Rueben.

# Chapter Eleven

It was 12:00 noon when I turned on the television to watch CNN. Of course, the ubiquitous breaking news banner was present. I switched to Fox and MSNBC and they too had breaking news. I stayed with MSNBC. A radio station received a terrorist bomb threat for its willingness to air a new show that afternoon. I knew immediately that KHAN was behind the threat. I switched back to CNN and Fox. There were television cameras everywhere and then the newscasters started to develop their story. The new show was by Dr. Stanley Warlib and the terrorist threat was probably aimed at Warlib's future father-in-law, internationally known investment banker, Charles Westerfield. Within five minutes there was an update. Mr. Westerfield had put out a statement that Dr. Stanley Warlib was no longer engaged to his daughter and that all connections with his family had been severed. This announcement only whetted the appetites of the news networks. I switched to ABC, CBS and NBC; however, they did not pick up on the story. I wondered whether the story would make the major networks evening news. The newscasters on all the channels mused whether there was enough room for another conservative talk show host or whether I would be a Dr. Phil psychology type show. In any event, all the stations stated that they would follow the story and keep their listeners updated. More important than anything else, the cable news stations posted the call letters of the radio station, the number on the dial and the time of the show. I felt compelled to thank KHAN on The Multitude.org. I didn't. I was going to leave the thanks for later on that night. After the bomb squad searched the building and found nothing, the radio station was given the all clear to proceed.

I met the station manager one hour before airtime and he explained the details of operation. The manager's name was Michael. I had no producer and no screener. We performed a microphone check and made adjustments for my voice. Two minutes prior to airtime, I sat alone behind a microphone and watched the clock on the wall. I stared at Rueben and Michael standing outside the window, their arms crossed, engaged in conversation.

"So Rueben, what's going to be?" asked Michael.
"Network," Rueben answered.
"Network. What the hell does that mean?" asked Michael.
"You know, the movie. I want you to go to the window, open it up and scream 'I'm made as hell and I'm not going to take it anymore,'" said Rueben.
"You mean, I got a madman in the booth," said Michael. Three, two, one.

"Good afternoon. This is Dr. Stanley Warlib. As many of you know, the radio station received a bomb threat this afternoon and the building has been declared safe and secure. You can reach me at 1-800-WARLIBS. I have no producer or screener. I apologize in advance for any sophomoric mistakes that I might make. Today, I'm going to talk about war. My war. As my name indicates, I am a warrior liberal and I am going to fight back against the war being waged against liberals. At the end of the show, I will ask you to join my group. You can go to www.warlib.org. I am not a soft-spoken, British sounding intellectual that will try to dazzle you with intellectual acuity. I am a Brooklyn born fighter and I am taking the gloves because when a group systematically, such as Christian evangelicals, comes after me with bad intentions, it's time to stand and fight. It's my answer to the age-old question: At what point do you stand up to the bully and fight? The time is now and the place is here. Join me in my fight. I know you're out there. Call 1-800-WARLIBS. Sam's opponent is going nowhere. It's time to fight. You know what I hate? I hate ball players that thank the Lord Jesus for hitting a home run. I hate boxers that cross themselves and if they win their fight, offer all praise to the Lord Jesus. I hate when people who didn't evacuate during Hurricane Ivan tell me that God and Jesus were their protectors so they didn't have to leave their home. We have an eight hundred gorilla sitting in our living room that no one wants to talk about. I'm going to talk about it, because it's an insidious noxious weed that's spreading in the beautiful garden once called America. My hands aren't tied and my mouth is not taped shut. When you lead with your chin you have to expect to take some punches. I have been told that Sam's opponent's war record is fair game because he said 'I'm here reporting for duty.' He made his Vietnam record an issue so it's fair game. Well, when you knock on my door and tell me that accepting your Lord Jesus is the only path to salvation, or point to the sky after hitting a home run, or tell me that you didn't knock out that guy in the boxing ring, Jesus did, you're fair game. Your religion is in play and you're fair game. Here's my advice: shut the hell up and pray.

I watched the Republican convention and I agreed with the pundit's analysis that it was nothing more than a show. The real party stood behind the scenes, out of view, like some mugger waiting to snare a mark. A Good Christian is the mark. If Jesus walked in love, why the hell are all of you so riled up? I can feel the hatred that emanates from your pores. You're so angry that you want to go to South Carolina and succeed from the nation. You lost your way and I'll tell you why later. On every conservative and religious talk show they remind their listeners that they are in a culture war. A very real war and make no mistake, that it is a war that threatens the very existence of civilization and America. Armageddon is shouted from the rooftops and since these dysfunctional listeners are prone to that type of stuff, they become true believers and see me as the enemy. There are only several things that stand in their way: (1) the liberals (2) black robed judges and (3) the secular federal government. These devils, hiding behind their religion are the real threat to America and yet, no one talks about it. It's a third rail that we can't discuss because we're attacking a man's religion. Screw that. They're coming after you and I and I'm fighting. How about you? 1-800-WARLIBS. During the Republican convention I was reading The New York Times and one article written by David D. Kirkpatrick entitled 'A Call to Win this Culture,' intrigued me. Senator Brownback of Kansas urged conservative Christian supporters to win the culture war. In a speech before an invitation only crowd held at the Waldorf Astoria hotel, Senator Brownback singled out subjects of special interest to conservative evangelical Protestants including abortion, same-sex marriage, the plight of Christians and other victims of violence in Sudan, human trafficking, events in Israel and a desire to roll back the Supreme Court's half-century-old interpretation of the separation of church and state. The article then goes on to state that Brownback 'feared for the Republic.' More apocalyptic evangelical bull talk that plays well with Christians. Ralph Reed a senior campaign adviser to Sam's campaign also spoke at the event. These evangelicals are dysfunctional and they are forever waiting for the rapture wherein God will come down and take them to heaven. I can't wait because I had enough of them right here on earth. 1-800-WARLIBS. Then I see the same obscure Senator Brownback prancing around the convention stage later on that night and I begin to wonder who this guy is, this far right evangelical wonder boy. Then I read another article by David Kirkpatrick in the August 28, 2004 edition of the New York Times entitled 'Club of the Most Powerful Gathers in Strictest Privacy.' The article informs me that there is some mystery group named Council for National Policy that meets three times a year in secrecy. It states that details of the club are closely guarded. Guests may attend only with the unanimous approval of the executive committee. A list of rules obtained by The New York Times states that 'the media should not know when or where we meet or who takes part in our programs, before or after a meeting.' Bill Frist, the Senate majority leader accepted the Council's Thomas Jefferson Award and said that 'the destiny of our nation is on the shoulders of the conservative movement.' Again, these guys are saving the world. My interest is starting to ignite. The article states some more facts and names, however, I, the original Warrior Liberal decide that I'm on to something. Who the hell is this Council of National Policy? I spent the last four days Googling myself to death and I'll give you the conclusion first and the supporting material later on. The Council of National Policy is a bunch of hard-core, unbridled capitalists that want to conquer the world that decided to wrap themselves within the evangelical movement. They protect themselves and their psychopathic aggression within the comfort of the flag, country, religion and God. These capitalists use Christian evangelicalism as a springboard for conquering nations and achieving their goals. Once the evangelicals capture the conscience of the people to be dominated, the capitalists move in and install their puppets. How many times have you heard Sam say the words freedom and democracy? The evangelical bigwigs have in their heart money. The capitalists have in their heart money. Someone figured out that it was the perfect marriage and they have been gaining in power ever since they walked down the aisle.

CALLER: Hi, Doctor Warlib. My name is Steven and I'm your first caller and first Warlib.

WARLIB: Why, thank you, Steven. You always remember your first, don't you? I won't forget you.

CALLER: I'll visit your website and hang-up as you should continue.

WARLIB: Thank you.

I saw the station manager gesturing with his hand that I should cut the talk show. He poked his head in the door and told me that the station received another bomb threat and the police had ordered the evacuation of the building. I asked the manager if he was annoyed and he advised me that bad publicity is the best kind you can get. I was putting the radio station on the map. Rueben, Michael and I took the elevator down to the ground floor and were not prepared for the mayhem that we encountered. There was a large demonstration outside the building of approximately 300 people. A boom box had been set up to listen to my broadcast. I noticed camera crews everywhere. CNN. ABC, FOX, MSNBC, CBS and NBC were in attendance. Someone had printed WARLIB tee shirts and handed them out. I heard shouts of "Shut up and pray," being screamed by one group. Another group was screaming "blasphemy." Several reporters shoved microphones into my face. "Dr. Warlib, don't you think it's disrespectful for you to say that Christianity is like a noxious weed ruining America?" one asked. "No," I answered. "Doctor Warlib, who is the Council of National Policy?" another asked. "Tune in tomorrow," I answered. Michael couldn't wait for tomorrow and told me that he would have a huge sign made up of the call letters of the station placed above the entrance of the building. Rueben pushed me to the street and jumped in a cab that was stopped at a red light. There were people in the cab who were shocked upon seeing new visitors. Rueben gave the passengers three twenty-dollar bills and requested their forgiveness for the intrusion.

They left the cab, said "no problem," and waved good-bye. "How did I do?" I asked Rueben. "You were just getting started, we'll find out on the news, I guess," he said. Rueben told the cab driver to go to my apartment. We picked up a bottle of Tequila on the way. Taz was waiting at the door. I was ecstatic. The day was perfect. Rueben, TazTwo and I marched out to the deck with a sense of triumph. We sat down, lifted our shot glasses and said "to life."

"What a day, doc. What a trip. Before we get into your shit, just let me tell you my shit. As you know, Yukos threatened to cut some oil to China and, listen to this, it was reported that Putin threatened to suspend oil supplies to Lithuania. Analysts said the China curbs were aimed to embarrass Putin less than a week before China's Prime Minister Wen Jiabao is due in Moscow. Oil closed up high. Long live long oil," said Rueben.

"There isn't any possibility that Putin is going to be embarrassed and Lithuania is another whole story. I think the Chinese are taking a look see at their gas station and more importantly talking about what they're going to do about Sam. Things are starting to heat up. Stay the course with long oil and short the S & P. I really think the Russian Bear and the Kung-Fu Master are going to take a stand while Sam is tied up. Watch Sudan, Iraq and Iran. Sam just hit the ball back into the court of Russia and China and I think they're going to swing the racket. The Council on National Policy has got all their little false prophets bogging down Sam's opponent with the Swift boat nonsense and the fake CBS documents. They don't want anyone looking at the mess in Iraq,"

"What's the subject for tomorrow?" asked Rueben.

"I'm going to finish with the Council on National Policy and call for a boycott on Focus on the Family and American Family Association. These two Christian groups are urging a boycott of Procter & Gamble. I'm going to demand that WARLIBS go out and buy every Procter & Gamble product that they need," I told Rueben. The phone rang. I told Rueben to be quiet. I could hear a voice leaving a message. It was Michael from the station. Several minutes later, the phone rang again and Rueben and I immediately went silent. We could hear the message: "Stan, this is Charles Westerfield. I strongly urge you to call me immediately."

"Seems I touched a nerve. Fuck him and his daughter," I said. Rueben asked if I needed time to prepare for tomorrow and I told him that I was prepared and ready to go. We completely forgot about the possibility of news coverage until Rueben mentioned the word TV and we both shot out of our chairs and raced towards the television. Every station had a clip of Rueben and I leaving the radio station with the interviewer asking me about the noxious weed statement with the chaotic crowd as a backdrop. Unbeknownst to me, the station was swamped with calls and repeated my show throughout the evening. Rueben asked me whether I was going to return Westerfield's call. I looked at him with a smirk. He knew the answer.

I stood on the board of The Multitude.org. No one came near me. All the Avatars stayed in a corner. One Avatar came over to me. Her name was Catherine. I thought that it might be Angelina, however, the Avatar made no response.
CATHERINE: Talk to me privately.
FASCISTI: All right.
CATHERINE: You didn't come through.
FASCISTI: I didn't have a chance. There was another bomb scare. Are you…?
CATHERINE: Don't use any names, ever. You have till tomorrow.
FASCISTI: You won't be disappointed.

I arrived at the radio station one hour before airtime. As I walked down the block, I noticed a huge mob, blocked from the entrance of the station by police barricades. There were hundreds of white tee shirts with the word WARLIB emblazoned on the back. The cable news networks were everywhere. I called Michael on his cell and asked him what I should do. He told me to walk up to the police and march right in. He told me that he had some surprises for me. As I neared the crowd, several people recognized me. The cameras swung quickly in my direction. I could hear equal shouts of "Go get em' Warlib" and "traitor." As I stood inside the barricade, a young man in a tee shirt with "Jesus Loves" imprinted on the back leaned over the barricade and swung his fist towards my head. He broke my nose. I grabbed him and punched him in the head as many times as I could and was stopped only by police interference. Entering the building, Michael told me that a still picture of the kid with the Jesus Loves tee shirt breaking my nose would make a great photo. During the night, Michael had upgraded the studio and added a producer and screener. He asked me what music I wanted as a lead-in to the show. I thought for a moment and told him that we would start out with Chicago's chant that the whole world is watching and then move to the beginning of a U-2 song. Michael explained some additional features that he added and installed. I could see that there were four calls waiting for me. A guy named Bobby, my new screener, told me that the first caller was Fred from Colorado Springs, Colorado, the epicenter of James Dobson Focus on the Family. I wanted to stir up the evangelicals and I had the feeling that that was exactly what I accomplished. I told Bobby that I was going to talk for a half-hour and finish my Council on National Policy stuff and requested Bobby to advise the callers that they had a chance to either call back or wait. I could see the producer outside the window hold up one hand and close one finger at a time: five, four, three, two, one.

"Good morning Warlibs. I sit here this morning with a broken, bloody nose. A young man with a tee shirt that had imprinted on the back "Jesus Loves" took a punch and connected. However, I can assure you that I got in a couple of good shots before the police broke the fight up. On the way in this morning, I read an article in The New York Times about a guy named Myron Beldock who is a foe of injustice and a champion of lost causes. Under his picture, it states: 'Power is easily misused by those in power. You either roll over or you fight back,' and that's what we're doing; we're fighting back against the wolf in sheep's clothing. O.K., the Council on National Policy is where we left off yesterday. Take out your pens and pencils and get a blank piece of paper and start writing down what I'm about to tell you. Tonight, go on the Internet and research the subject matter and tomorrow call in and my screener will pick out the best nugget of information on the evangelical infestation that is polluting our environment and you get an extended five minutes of airtime. Think of it this way; it's your Andy Warhol's fifteen minutes of fame. In 1981, the CNP was conceived by at least five fathers, including the Rev. Tim Lahaye, an evangelical preacher who was then head of the Moral Majority. Lahaye is co-author of the popular *Left Behind* series of books that predicts and subsequently depicts the Apocalypse. Nelson Bunker Hunt, billionaire son of billionaire oilman H.L.Hunt, who was connected to both the John Birch Society and to Ronald Reagan's political network. Then there was one time murder suspect T. Cullen Davis and wealthy John Bircher William Cies. Let's now back up a bit to the seventies because many of the far right wing conservative players were stirring in that era. The Council on National Policy was born when Ronald Reagan took office but its gestation period can be traced back to the sixties, when the American Right, looking for a little more piece of the pie, wanted to influence policy and there was no organization in place to do so. The religious right had many religious organizations but no political muscle. Present at the meeting to found The Religious Roundtable was Ed McAteer a retired sales marketing manager for Colgate-Palmolive Company. McAteer was director of the Christian Freedom Foundation, an organization devoted to training evangelicals for places of leadership in government. After the Christian Freedom Foundation, McAteer served as national field director of Howard Phillips Conservative Caucus. Bill Bright, the founder of Campus Crusade for Christ, was closely allied with the Christian Freedom Foundation, which was heavily funded by Amway billionaire Richard Devos. Devos took over the Christian Freedom Foundation in 1975. Bill Bright was a fancy food salesman and there is some speculation that

Bright thought that the gospel could be marketed in the same manner as any other product. The goals were to bring the policies of the evangelical far right and laissez faire capitalism around the globe, especially the United States. The Religious Roundtable brought together the top leadership of the religious right and acted as a clearing house for large organizations such as the Christian Broadcasting Network, Billy Graham Evangelical Association, Moral Majority, Christian Voice, Church League of America, National Religious Broadcasters, Campus Crusade for Christ, Plymouth Rock Foundation, the National Association of Evangelicals, Gideon Bible, Wycliffe Bible Associates and Intercessors of America. The average Joe of Christian evangelical fundamentalism is dysfunctional and is highly suggestible to fear. The secret to fundraising is to try to make these average fundamentalists angry and stir up hostilities. The shriller you are, the easier it is to raise funds. That's the nature of the beast. That's why Sam is always saving civilization and protecting the world from homosexuals and evildoers. This crap sells and the religious power elite knows it. On Sunday, I was listening to Christian radio and the guy being interviewed stated that three nuclear warheads were found in Iraq and then criticized the liberal press for failing to report it. However, that stupidity spreads like wildfire over the airwaves to these gullible evangelicals. They are the greatest track of virgin timber on the political landscape. Now, remember these names Phillips, Viguerie and Weyrich. Viguerie was the master of direct mail solicitations making winners of all the right wing evangelical organizations. Direct mail brought in millions of dollars claiming, in essence, the end of the world if the average Joe didn't act. Paul Weyrich was the founder of The Heritage Foundation and Free Congress Foundation and employed Fabianist, British race scientist Roger Pearson of the World Anti-Communist League, the multinational network of Nazi war criminals, Latin American death squad leaders and North American neo-fascists. Bill Bright was the founder of Campus Crusade for Christ. I hope you're getting all this. Now, let's back up even further and get at the genesis of this vast right wing conspiracy. Nelson Rockefeller, the scion of the liberal Standard Oil family wanted to conquer and expand his vast empire in South America and in particular, the Amazon jungle because of it's vast natural resources. At the same time, William Cameron Townsend, founder of the ultra-conservative Wycliffe Bible Translators, had his missionaries pacify native populations in frontiers rich in oil and minerals. Seeking to hasten the prophesied Second Coming, Townsend pursued a fanatical effort to reach every Bible less tribe with the word, even to the point of saving their souls by destroying their culture and allaying with the dictators who oppressed them. Wycliffe Bible Associates was a lay ministry that was created to support the work of the Wycliffe

Bible Translators, an evangelical organization that raised funds and recruited missionaries to do the work of the Summer Institute of Linguistics. Ed McAteer was a member of the board of Wycliffe Bible Associates. Rockefeller and Townsend discovered the unholy, but profitable alliance of capitalism and religion. These two guys contributed more than any other Americans to the conquest of Latin America. Their systematic campaign of colonization was a chilling foretaste of American intervention in the third world that has become common today. We take for granted the repeated forays in the name of freedom and democracy and the securing of valuable resources. Ed McAteer was instrumental in bringing together wealthy liberal and conservative patrons to fund and direct the Wycliffe organization that, in the name of Jesus, was assisting Rockefeller in the conquest of Latin America. McAteer, the former Colgate Palmolive salesman was the real organizing force behind the politicized Fundamentalist movement. He substituted Christ for soap and was a major force of Wycliffe Associates, a powerhouse of resources for the Summer Institute of Linguistics with construction skills, money and promotion. McAteer applied his advertising and public relations skills to organizing a base of support for Ronald Reagan and turned his attention to American politics. The board of directors and early membership reads like a Who's Who in the future Council of National Policy. The Council is the vast right wing conspiracy. The wealthy have used many methods to accumulate wealth, but it was not until the mid 1970's that these methods coalesced into a superbly organized, cohesive and efficient machine. The Council on National Policy is that machine that blends many parts into a cohesive capitalistic aggressor wrapped within the arms of God and Jesus. Sam is the first-born of that machine. Notice the language of mission and calling. The euphemism of freedom and democracy for the naked aggression of Sam's conquest for natural resources! The children of The Council have grown up. Rick Santorum, the Senator of Pennsylvania and Tom Delay in the house are but two of the devil's spawn. Look at the Senatorial race in Oklahoma! Dr. Tom Coburn, a creature of the evangelical right won the Republican nomination over his moderate opponent. He is a darling of the extreme right. He is vehemently opposed to gay rights and embryonic stem cell research. There is a rebellion on the right that's spawning these creatures of hell to go against moderate Republicans. Their ugly heads have emerged in Senate races in Alaska, Colorado, Pennsylvania and South Carolina. Dr. Coburn has cast his fight in terms of good vs. evil and he favors the death penalty for abortionists. This is the soul of the Council on National Policy; ugly, mean, vindictive and death merchants, all sold to a dysfunctional base of evangelical Christians that fervently believe that the world is coming to an end. The his-

tory of this vast right wing conspiracy is so complex that we'll have to continue it another time. First caller, Robin from Queens:
ROBIN: Thank you, Dr. Warlib. I agree with you. What do you want me to do?
WARLIB: Off the top of my head. Whenever you see a boxer or ballplayer or artist thank Jesus or God, scream out 'Play, don't praise.' Second, and this is current, Dr. James Dobson of Focus on the Family and Donald Wildmon of American Family Association just urged a boycott of Proctor and Gamble's two premier products, Tide and Crest, because these God's Bullies are trying to place on the ballot in Ohio a measure to amend the Ohio Constitution to ban same-sex marriage. Dobson reaches nine million radio listeners. He's got power. Now here this: I want all the Warlibs out there to support Proctor and Gamble and buy their products. Increase their sales. Support P & G, Tide and Crest! Silence equals death.
GEORGE: May you rot in hell for your disrespect. Everything you say is not true. My hair is on fire you bastard.
WARLIB: Look George, you're a piece of meat in the hands of Satan. Do you have anything specific you want to say?
GEORGE: I'm so upset I can't talk.
WARLIB: Next caller, Harry from Suffolk County.
HARRY: You're nothing more than some fudge-packing, communist, atheist faggot, you vermin. Die, you bastard!
WARLIB: I've been waiting for a moron like you. No, I'm not gay. Yes, I am an atheist. No, I'm not a communist. You left out asking if I were an anarchist and the answer is yes. I am an anarchist. Now, I know you little conservative pea-brains out there think that I mean chaos. That's the simplistic definition for you morons. You guys believe in less government and the libertarians believe in less government than you guys believe. Well, I'm even further right than that. I believe in no government. You Christians want to replace government with a theocracy, which has a demonstrable history of death, destruction, colonization and suppression. I don't want that. Anarchism merely is the political theory that all forms of government are incompatible with individual and social liberty and should be abolished. However, this lack of government takes a special individual to live in and that's not people like you. A state of anarchy is filled with nice people not people filled with hatred like you. The Democrats and Republicans are nothing more than gangs stealing your money to line their pockets. Get rid of them, all of them. However, to get there, we have to go through some chaos. I envision a million single cell amoeba only interconnected by their desire to abolish the illegal slavery that the ruling elite, religious and financial, has subjugated

the citizens of America to. Go out and create acts of chaos, whatever you're capable of doing. Stalk the 'K' Street Washington, D.C., power brokers. You got the picture. Take back your country before it's too late. Now, I want to talk to you evangelical Christians out there. The scriptures contain many warnings about false prophets and their miracle working powers. In the New Testament, Matthew 7:15 states: 'Beware of false prophets, which come to you in sheep's clothing, but inwardly they are ravening wolves.' Matthew 24:24 states: 'for there shall arise false Christ's, and false prophets, and shall shew great signs and wonders; insomuch that, if it were possible, they shall deceive the very elect.' 2 Peter 2:1 states: 'But there were false prophets also among the people, even as there shall be false teachers among you, who privily shall bring in damnable heresies, even denying the Lord that bought them; and bring upon themselves swift destruction' and 1 John 4:1 states: 'Beloved, believe not every spirit, but try the spirits whether they are of God: because many false prophets are gone out into the world.' The Book of Revelation discloses a False Prophet that is in a class of his own. This False Prophet will arise in the last days when the Beast comes on stage. The False Prophet that is in a class of his own is the Lying Spirit. The Lying Spirit has perfected the art of lying and deception. Who are these False Prophets? The false prophets are Rush Limbaugh, Michael Medved, Laura Ingraham, Michael Savage, Sean Hannity and others conservative radio talk show hosts. These False Prophets come to deceive you and stand guard protecting the ultimate false Prophet, the Lying Spirit, Sam and the Council on National Policy. Why aren't I deceived? I am not deceived because God called upon me and gave me a mission. He was pissed to the gills about these False Prophets and the Lying Spirit: conservative pundits, Sam and the Council on National Relations. God has anointed me 'the very elect' who cannot be deceived and commanded me to go on this mission of truth to turn you away from these false prophets. Jesus never intended to fill your hearts with rage and hatred. Jesus walked in love not rage. These False Prophets are filling your hearts with hatred. My producer is indicating that I'm running out of time. Here is your homework for tonight. Research on the Internet all the names of organizations and individuals that I have mentioned today. Start to connect the dots. In particular, research The National Center for Privatization and The Mont Perelin Society. The latest list of the Council on National Policy is on my website, www.warlib.org. Peace out, brothers in Anarchy.

A—Ambassador S. L. Abbott, Larry Abraham, Jack Abramoff, M. Douglas Adkins, Howard Ahmanson, Jr., Dr. Frank Aker, Honorable Barbara Alby, John

Alderson, Gary Aldrich, Richard V. Allen, Daniel B. Allison II, Thomas R. Anderson, Senator John K. Andrews, Jr., Dr. John F. Ankerberg, Philip F. Anschutz, Hon. Richard K. Armey, Ben Armstrong, Thomas K. Armstrong, Sen. William L. Armstrong, Dr. Larry P. Arnn, John M. Ashbrook, Edward G. Atsinger III

B—Dr. Theodore Baehr, Cy Bahakel, Sr, Carole Baker, Dick Baker, Terry C. Balderson, Howard A. Ball, William H. Ball Jr., Dr. David Balsiger, A. Clifford Barker, Herbert Barness, Tommy Barnett, David H. Barron, Rep. William G. Batchelder III, Hon. Gary Bauer

Be—Patricia Beck, John D. Beckett, Melvin Behnke, Jeffrey Bell, Carlos Benitez, Mark A. Benson, Ray Berryman, Paul Bigham, Dr. Robert J Billings, William Billings, Morton Blackwell, Neal B. Blair, James K. Blinn, Thomas A. Bolan, John R. Bolton, Pat Boone, T. J. Bosgra, Richard Bott, Rich Bott, Dr. James C. Bowers, Lynn Francis Bouchey, L. Brent Bozell, III

Br Dr. David W. Breese, Dr. William "Bill" R. Bright, Floyd Brown, Robert K. Brown, Samuel A. Brunelli, Charles H. Brunie, Anita Bryant, Allen Burkett, Larry Burkett, Honorable Dan Burton, Sandra Butler

C—Hon. Howard "Bo" Callaway, Jameson Campaigne, Jr., Ken Campbell, Jim Carden, Charles S. Carriker, Margo Carlisle, Alan Carlson, John W. Chalfant, Margaret "Peggy" Cies Michael S. Coffman, Ph.D John Commuta Guy M. Condon Robert L. Cone Peter C. Cook Holland (Holly) Coors Jeffrey Coors Joseph Coors Mrs. Judy M. Cresanta T. Kenneth Cribb Jr. Mary C. Crowley Les Csorba James C. Czirr

D—Beverly Danielson Sen. William Dannemeyer Rt. Rev. Dr. C. Truman Davis Cullen Davis Karen Davis Arnaud de Borchgrave Don DeFore Rich DeVos Richard M. DeVos Jr. James E. DeYoung, Jr. Richard B. Dingham Dr. James Dobson John Dodd John Doggett John T. (Terry) Dolan Elaine Donnelly Ann Drexel Arthur M. Dula Robert P. Dugan Pierre S. du Pont Richard Dunham W. Clark Durant III Alan P. Dye

E—John P. East Jack Eckerd Thomas F. Ellis Stuart Epperson Michael Etchison M. Stanton Evans

F—Dr. Jerry Falwell, Joseph F. Farah Michael P. Farris Dr. Edwin J. Feulner, Jr William A. Fields Father Charles Fiore Robert Fischer Peter T.

Flaherty Donald Lambert Folkers Richard A. Ford Clarke D. Forsythe Peter C. Foy Ann Frazier Tracy Freeny Foster S. Friess Corinne S. Fuller

G—Willard Garvey Peter B. Gemma Jr. Kevin Gentry George F. Gilder Dr. Duane Gish Thomas Glessner Ronald P. Godwin Stephen Goodrick Alan Gottlieb Robbie Gowdey

Gr—J. Peter Grace Lt. General Daniel O. Graham Anthony Grampsas Robert Grant Jim Groen Dr. Haldeman 'Hal" W. Guffey Darryl E. Gustafson

H—Rev. Ben Haden Billy Hale Colin A. Hanna Samuel A. Hardage Sara Divito Hardman Benjamin Hart Anthony Harrigan Kevin J. "Seamus" Hasson H. Preston Hawkins Richard Headrick Donna Hearne Charles C. Heath Randall Hekman Jesse Helms Harry V. Helton Carl Herbster Thomas D. Hess Rev. E.V. Hill James "Jimmy" Martin Hill Jr. Joseph K. Hilyard Roland Hinz

Ho—Hon. Donald Paul Hodel Rev. Melvin Hodges William J. "Bill" Hofer Douglas F. Hofmeister Gary Hofmeister Neal Hogan Lou Holbrook Robert P. Holding III George Holland John Holt Donald R. Howard Dr. John A. Howard Ernest B. Hueter Joan Hueter Max Hugel Robbie Hughes Herbert William Hunt Mary Reilly Hunt Nelson Bunker Hunt

I-J-K—Reed Irvine Hon. Ernest J. Istook, Jr. Lorena Jaeb E. Peb Jackson Kay Cole James Gary Jarmin Terry J. Jeffers Dr. Mildred Faye Jefferson James M. Jenkins Rep. Louis (Woody) Jenkins Margaret Jenkins Willa A. Johnson Bob Jones III Rep. Hal Jones W. Daniel Jordan Michael Joyce James F. Justiss Howard Kaloogian William Kanaga Dr. C. L. "Casey" Kay Barbara Keating-Edh David Keene Rep. Jack Kemp

Ken—Dr. D. James Kennedy William R. Kennedy Alan Keyes William A. Keyes Paul A. Kienel Cliff Kincaid Jerry Kirk Larry Klayman Brig. General Albion W. Knight Dr. Robert H. Krieble

L—Beverly LaHaye Lee LaHaye Dr. Timothy LaHaye Reed Larson Jerome M. Ledzinski Dr. Ernest W. Lefever Lewis E. "Lew" Lehrman John Lenczowski Andrew W. Lester Mark R. Levin Dr. Earl Little John Lofton Hon. Trent Lott Edward Lozick

M~Mca—Mark R. Maddoux Marlin Maddoux Marion (Mac) Magruder Carolyn Malenick Peter Marshall, Jr. Connaught (Connie) Marshner James L. Martin Christopher "Kit" Mason Richard Mason James Mather Pat Matrisciana Paul Maurer Donald S. McAlvany Ed McAteer

Mc—Thomas E. McCabe Bryan McCanless Richard F. McCarthy, Jr Norman P. McClelland James A. McClure Timothy McConville James D. McCotter Tidal W. McCoy Larry P. McDonald Roy McKasson Emanuel McLittle Hon. Edwin Meese III Major F. Andy Messing, Jr. Eugene Meyer Rev. Austin Miles James C. Miller III Tom Minnery Charles W. Missler

Mo—Terry E. Moffitt Barbara Monteith Dr. Stanley Monteith Charles Moore Dr. Raymond Moore Sam Moore Thomas Slick Moorman Dr. Henry M. Morris Rev. Duane R. Motley William D. Mounger

N~Pa—Senator Don Nickles David A. Noebel Grover Norquist Dr. Gary North Lt. Col. Oliver North George D. O'Neill, Jr. J. Stanley Oakes Jr. Phillip Olsen William J. Olson Ted Pantaleo J. A. "Jay" Parker Thomas G. Parker Colleen G. Parro G.N. Parrot Carmen Pate Dr. Paige Patterson Maj. General George S. Patton III

Pe~Q—Tony Perkins Robert J. Perry Howard Phillips Thomas L. Phillips Burton Yale Pines Robert M. Pittenger Theda Oates Plimpton Larry W. Poland William M. Polk Robert Poole Jim Powers Lawrence D. "Larry" Pratt Judge Paul Pressler Paul Pressler IV James S. Price Edgar Prince Elsa Prince Coy C. Privette Penny Pullen

R—Raymond V. Raehn Ralph E. Reed, Jr. Gerald P. Regier Thomas L. Rhodes Dr. Charles E. Rice H.L. "Bill" Richardson Richard A. Riddle Elizabeth Ridenour Lawson Ridgeway Stephen D. Ridley Isom J. Rigell Dr. Paul Craig Roberts Dr. "M.G." Pat Robertson Ronald E. Robinson James Robison George C. Roche III Thomas A. Roe Kathleen Teague [Rothschild] Howard J. Ruff Rev. R. J. Rushdoony William A. Rusher

S—Guy Sanders, Jr. William E. Saracino Richard M. Scaife Terence Scanlon Rich Scarborough Frederic (Rich) Schatz Blaine Scheideman Phyllis Schlafly Otto Scott John Scribante Lynda H. Scribante Alan Sears Ronald L. Seeley Harry G. A. Seggerman Jay A. Sekulow Duncan Sellars Hans F. Sennholz Beurt SerVaas

Sh—Frank Shakespeare Dal Shealy Richard Shoff Terry Siemans William E. Simon Major General John K. Singlaub "Father" Rev. Robert Sirico Dr. W. Cleon Skousen Mark Skousen Baker Armstrong Smith E. Roy Smith Henry J. "Bud" Smith Jim R. Smith Dr. Lowell Smith Malcolm E. Smith Jr. Victor P. Smith

Sn—Geraldine (Gerry) Snyder Thomas R. Spencer, Jr. LaNeil Wright Spivy Ted Squires Scott Stanley, Jr. Darla St. Martin Mathew D. Staver, Esq. Allen Stevens Donald R. Stewart Steve Stockman Robert Stoddard John Stoos John A. Stormer W. Robert Stover Jay Strack George W. Strake, Jr Kathleen Sullivan Lt. General Gordon Sumner Jr. John H. Sununu Gaylord K. Swim

T~V—John G. Talcott Jr. Dr. Lewis Tambs Hon. Helen Marie Taylor James "Jim" B. Taylor Stacy Taylor Dr. Edward Teller Robert L. Thoburn Bill Tierney Robert G. Tilton Herbert W. Titus Steven A.F. Trevino Patrick A. Trueman Timothy E. Twardowski Sherman E. Unkefer III Rev. Nathaniel A. Urshan Jon Basil Utley Harry Valentine Mike Valerio Guy Vander Jagt Balint Vazsonyi Richard Viguerie Christine Vollmer Barbara Vucanovich

W—Gray Wakefield Peter E. Waldron Robert Walker Henry L. Walther James G. Watt Anthony Wauteriek Winston O. Weaver Robert T. Weiner P. Craig Welch Jr. Judi Westberg-Warren Diana Weyrich Paul Weyrich Dr. Jack Wheeler James Whelan Somers H. White John W. Whitehead Faith Ryan Whittlesey

Wi-Z—Rev. Donald Wildmon Tim Wildmon Alvin Williams Dr. John Wilke James M. Wilson Thomas S. Winter Richard B. Wirthlin George Witwer Robert Wolgemuth Robert Wood Rev. Jim Woodall Carter Wrenn Carl Young Charles B. Young David Zanotti Billy Zeoli

The station manager advised me that there was a near riot-taking place outside the building. He was concerned for my safety and led me to a little used emergency doorway that led to another street. He had to disconnect the automatic alarm on the door. I immediately called Rueben and told him to come over. He told me that his April light sweet crude contracts closed higher on Monday. He was going to hold his position until Tuesday night. He listened to my show in his office, notwithstanding several of his associates demanding that he turn me off and put on Rush Limbaugh. He told me that overall, I was being well received. I was the new kid on the block. The publicity catapulted me to the number one position in the New York market. Michael called me and discussed syndication. I gave him the name of my attorney. In addition, Michael received funds from anonymous sources for my show to continue the following week after the money Rueben gave him ran out. Things were definitely going my way. I decided to call Mr. Westerfield when I got home. I made a note to look into the availability of a website to be named www.VastRightWingConspiracy.Com, that people could go to and add information about the Council on National Policy. I remembered that the wife of Sam's brother Bill stated that there was a vast right wing conspiracy and that the book on this subject had not yet been written. I decided to let the world do my research and publish a book. I was going to take her advice. Why not? Rueben was waiting at the door with a bottle of Tequila, the drinking of which was becoming an institutionalized ritual between Rueben and I. After several busted nose jokes and four shots of Tequila, Rueben told me that oil closed on Monday at $43.26 a barrel. He was up $43,000.00. He felt compelled to tell me that that was over $7,000.00 a day for six trading days. I asked him about the close on Tuesday however, he just smiled. "Long oil. Oil has been weaponized," he said. I knew he made more money. I'd find out Wednesday morning. Rueben and I decided to go out to the Madison Avenue Bar for more shots and hamburgers.

# Chapter Twelve

"Doc, remember me?" a woman asked.

"Of course I do. Your name is Haven, the closest thing to Heaven," I said.

"What a memory," she said. "This is my friend Amy. May we sit down with you guys?" she asked.

"Absolutely. This is my best friend Rueben," I said. We all exchanged hello's and then Haven and Amy proceeded to tell Rueben and I that I had become quite a celebrity. She told me that there was a large picture of me getting a broken nose by some guy wearing a tee shirt with "Jesus Loves" on the back. The image was all over the city with the call letters of the radio station. Obviously, it was the brainchild of the station manager. Against the backdrop of Rueben's $43,000.00, my radio show, lovely Haven and Amy, Sam was standing before the United Nations talking about freedom and democracy to a mild, polite applause. The collective body knew only one thing: Sam invaded a sovereign nation for spurious reasons. At the same time that Sam was speaking, Iran told the world to go screw themselves on nuclear inspections and vowed to proceed on in the development of their nuclear reactors. I envisioned that the Kung Fu master returned Iran's call and said go ahead, I'd protect you. What a screwed up dangerous world.

"Let's go everybody. We are going to my favorite tango place," I told the group. No one objected. Walking towards the exit door, Rueben grabbed my arm and confided in me that he didn't close out his position in long oil. He smiled and said, "I'm still long oil and it closed at $43.75 a barrel. I'm up $55,250.00. And another thing Doc, I shorted the S & P. I'm with you all the way. You're my financial Buddha."

I was exhausted when I got home from dancing. The strain of being "on" and "keyed" into events was beginning to take a toll. I wasn't excited about the radio show that was scheduled for Wednesday. I was sad. I saw things throughout the day that clearly indicated the winds of war were blowing. I decided to be honest with my listeners about my overwhelming concern for the safety of the United States and the absolute absurdity of the path that sick psychopathic narcissist Sam was walking down. I was truly worried and Rueben's profit only fed into my fears that I was correct. The money proved it. I called Michael and requested a back door entrance to avoid the crowd. Three, two and one:

WARLIB: Today, I'm tired and a little hung over from dancing the Tango with my friend Rueben. I hope that all of you have been doing your homework. Instead of getting on my soapbox, today, I'll take calls. First caller is David from Philadelphia.

DAVID: Mr. Warlib, I'm a salesman from Philadelphia and I was up in New York over the last two days and I listened to your show. I am appalled at your description of the Christian evangelical movement and find it extremely offensive that you, an admitted atheist and anarchist, quote Holy Scripture.
WARLIB: Are you upset because I said I was one of the "special elect" and that God has chosen me to unmask the wolves in sheep clothing and the Lying Spirit.
DAVID: I'm mad because you don't know what you're talking about. You made factual allegations and then made conclusions, that don't follow.
WARLIB: Because I didn't have a smoking gun?
DAVID: You're like Michael Moore and his Fahrenheit 9/11 movies. A couple of facts and then you spin your conclusions. You just make it up.
WARLIB: So you want direct evidence, like a written letter, or some fax or a tape of some conversation stating that I am Sam and I am invading Afghanistan because of some pipeline that might be built. Is that what you want?
DAVID: That would be closer to the truth then the lies that you propagate on radio.
WARLIB: So I'm a liar. I guess you have never heard of circumstantial evidence. A smoking gun is rare. Most cases in court are built on circumstantial evidence. Circumstantial evidence is evidence consisting of circumstances, which furnish a reasonable ground for believing or deciding the existence of a certain fact. For example, let's take two rooms next to each other, connected by an open door. In one room you have a group of Nazis discussing their hatred of Jews and how they wanted to kill them. The group has guns. In the other room you have a group of twenty dead Jews. Dead by bullets! Could an average man make a reasonable inference of the fact that the Nazis in the connecting room killed the dead Jews? I think it would be fair for an average man to make that reasonable inference. A jury might want to know more but the inference is reasonable. It's called circumstantial evidence. If I say that the Council on National Policy is the Lying Spirit, the master of lies and deception it is because I infer that fact from circumstantial evidence. I'm allowed and entitled.
DAVID: I understand what you're saying but your facts are sketchy and your conclusions are false. You have been put here to lie and deceive.
WARLIB: Can I assume that you are an evangelical Christian?
DAVID: Yes, I am.
WARLIB: Are you in New York?
DAVID: No, I took off from work and I am sitting in my car on the other side of the Lincoln Tunnel listening to your show. You are evil!

WARLIB: All right, is that all you have to say. I've been very patient and let you go on, and if you're not finished, feel free to continue. I can't believe you drove all the way from Philadelphia just to listen to me. Did someone send you up here?

DAVID: No. No one sent me here. I was just very upset about the evil lies that you were spreading on the radio. I couldn't believe that you would make such an attack.

WARLIB: David, do you listen to conservative talk show radio in Philadelphia?

DAVID: Yes, I listen to NEWSTALK RADIO. 990 AM on the dial. It's a better show than yours. They have Bill Bennett, Laura Ingraham, Dennis Praeger, Michael Medved, Hugh Hewitt, Michael Savage, Michael Gallagher and Jerry Doyle.

WARLIB: That is certainly a cast of conservatives. I've followed the career of Laura Ingraham and she has become much more strident and extremely conservative. She was, at one time, what I would describe as a moderate conservative.

DAVID: It's a great show. These guys know what they're talking about.

WARLIB: Do you listen to Christian radio?

DAVID: Yes, I do. I listen to WFIL, 560 AM out of Philadelphia.

WARLIB: That's interesting. I'm going to permit myself several minutes at this point. David you may hang up or listen. David listens to two radio stations in Philadelphia, one Christian and one conservative talk show radio with the speakers David mentioned. I was in South Jersey and listened to TALKRADIO 990. I listened for several hours. I noticed that all the hosts had the same strident stance on all the issues. It was the kind of stance that you would find on Christian talk radio. I was very interested in Laura Ingraham having followed her career. She was at one time what I would describe as a moderate republican and not the nasty bitch ultra-right winger that she sounded like on the 990 station. I'm sure; many conservatives in the Philadelphia area thought they were listening to the regular conservative Rush type show. However, I heard one commercial and one announcement. The commercial was from Dr. James Dobson, the leader of Focus on the Family and the announcement was for an October demonstration in Washington D.C., protesting same sex marriage. I thought that this was all strange because it wasn't the kind of thing that conservative talk radio usually airs. It is usually the province of Christian talk radio. I decided to do some research and when I got home I hit the Internet and did some Googling. My research, and these are *facts*, showed that the same company owned WFIL, the Christian talk station and NEWSTALK radio. That was interesting I thought. Both stations were owned by Salem Communications Corp, a devout evangelical

Christian radio empire. I researched the officers of Salem and read that a Mr. Epperson and a Mr. Atsinger were CEO and President, respectively. Those names looked familiar. I went to my list of members of the Council on National Policy and there were Mr. Epperson and Mr. Atsinger, including Dr. James Dobson. NEWSTALK was a wolf in sheep's clothing snaring the unsaved conservatives. The reason Laura Ingraham went from moderate to ultra right-winger became apparent. She needed a job and sold her soul to the devil. Now, I think we should know exactly what the Council on National Policy has in mind. Mind manipulation is in play to turn the Liberals into traitors in the public's mind. The penalty for treason is death. That is why I am a warrior liberal. They're coming after me, I know it and you should know it too. Sean Hannity's book has the words evil and liberal in the title. You must start to see what they're doing. This grand Lying Spirit figured that if they could con the evangelical Christians with their non-sense than they can con the American public. That's why I called them weeds. Noxious weeds taking over the beautiful landscape of America!

However, I'm sad to today. I'm tired and sad. Two Mondays ago, I told my friend to buy oil future contracts because oil was going up. As of yesterday, he made $55,250.00 in seven trading days. Unfortunately, I saw the rise in oil for all the wrong reasons. He made money not because I saw a rosy scenario but because I saw a frightening vision in my mind. I have seen another frightening vision that I would like to share with you. I apologize in advance if I frighten you. I don't mean to. Go back in time to 1990-91 when Sam invaded Iraq. It is well known that Saudi Arabia was extremely agitated and feared for its own oil fields, which were nothing more than Sam's private gas station. I could almost hear the King on the phone saying to Sam, 'so, what are you going to do. It's time to stand up and protect my kingdom. Sam did exactly that. Oil is the lifeblood of any nation and Sam protected his blood supply. Sam is currently in Iraq again, except this time he's there to expand his blood supply. He violated the first rule of sovereign nations. He invaded a country for its natural resources. However, Sam during his 'shock & awe' demonstration of military power against a nation that was unable to defend itself really demonstrated the limitation of his power. One question on everyone's mind was where would Sam turn next, to Syria or to Iran? Syria, lying to the east presented no threat, however, Iran, is part of the original Axis of Evil and is allegedly developing a nuclear program that could be turned into a program to develop a nuclear weapon. Several months ago, the Federal Bureau of Investigation commenced an investigation into the inquiry of whether some of Sam's underlings passed secret information to the Israeli's to help decipher Sam's intentions. It was well known that Israel might attack Iran if it passed certain markers in its' development of its nuclear program. Syria withdrew 3,000 troops from Lebanon allegedly at Sam's request. Libya decided to cease its efforts of developing weapons of mass destruction. Sam, enveloped in his narcissistic mind-set, interpreted those events as signs that the Middle East countries feared him and his powerful army. However, during this time, Iran became China's largest supplier of oil. Russia was assisting Iran in building nuclear reactors and was also supplying large quantities of oil to Russia. Sam has mounted a monumental effort to stop Iran in the development of its nuclear program. I have been waiting for a sign and yesterday I saw it. Just as Saudi Arabia called upon Sam to protect its major gas station, Iran called upon China to protect its major gas station. I can envision the call from the President of Iran to the head of China, 'so, what are you going to do?' Iran received a call back several days ago. Iran told Sam and the world to go screw themselves. It claimed that they were proceeding with its peaceful nuclear program and that it wasn't going to worry about Sam's paranoia. Sam pulled that crap once with Iraq and they weren't going to pull it with Iran. The President of Iran stated this during a military parade in Tehran as he watched missiles pass by him on trucks. The sign that I had been waiting for arrived. Draped on the missiles, in big bold English letters, large enough so that no one could mistake Iran's declaration were the words, 'crush America' and 'wipe Israel off the map.' This was my sign that China stood up to the plate and said I'll protect my gas station. Now, picture yourself five miles above Iraq and get out of the mind set that Sam is the most powerful man in the world. Look down and watch what is going on and look at it from the perspective that the hunter is now the hunted. The attacks against Sam are increasing on a daily basis. The coordination and sophistication of the attacks exhibit a degree of planning that previously wasn't present. Syria might have withdrawn its' troops to enclose Sam on his western flank. China is protecting Iran on Iraq's eastern flank. Sam's military bases in Iraq's desert make an easy target. The line in the sand has been drawn. Sam will not advance any further. In the dark of night, six squadrons of Russian MIG's head southeast from Moscow. They immediately take out all of Sam's helicopters and jet's and continue on into the Mediterranean Sea to blast Sam's aircraft carriers. Sam's tanks and armored personnel carriers become easy targets in the light of day. Sam's troops can only find safety by mingling with the Iraqi population, however, after kicking in doors and abusing the Iraqi's they find hostile warriors hunting them down in the streets. What will Sam do? Sam is in a catatonic state too mentally disabled to order an effective defense. And my question to you is: are you really prepared to fight China and Russia? Do you know their military capabilities? Both countries have Intercontinental Nuclear Missiles.

Years ago, there was a concept that the world lived by. It was called MAD, mutually assured destruction. No reasonable, normal superpower would push the bottom and destroy the world. This equation for mankind's survival no longer applies. I am scared when one finger on the button belongs to an evangelical Christian that would like nothing more than to advance the Apocalypse and Armageddon to usher in 1,000 years of the reign of Christ. MAD only works with sane superpowers. This is Dr. Stanley Warlib. Good Night.

My producer and screener were silent. I remembered telling Mr. Westerfield a lesson I learned watching the current political campaign was that a paranoid personality trumps a histrionic personality every time. I was trumping the paranoid personality with the ultimate tool, today's reality. Rueben called immediately after the show and told me that April light sweet crude oil closed at $44.39 a barrel and that he was up $71,250.00. In addition, his March 2005 S & P Composite Index contracts that he shorted closed down 14.50. I didn't ask Rueben how much he made on that trade and declined his invitation for dinner. I told Rueben that he was making money for all the wrong reasons. He was betting on disaster and winning. He asked me for additional investment advice and I told him to consider long gold. He thanked me and hung-up.

FASCISTI: Is Catherine here?
HITLER: Let's talk privately. I'm Catherine.
FASCISTI: Do you always change your name?
HITLER: This board is real life. Did you read the article in The New York Times today? It's about the government monitoring the Internet. It's full time, all the time. I suggest you change your name and don't use your home computer. You're doing well. Good night.

# Chapter Thirteen

The next several days my show focused on the results of the homework that my listeners were requested to do. Coors of Coors beer fame was in a tight Senate race in Colorado and one caller pointed out that Holland, Jeffrey and Joseph Coors were members of the Council on National Policy. Another caller pointed out that Richard Viguerie, a columnist for USA Today was also on the list of the Council. I suggested that my listeners find connections between Reverend Sun Myung Moon and the Council. My listeners were going wild. I explained that in taking back America for Christ there must be a period of indoctrination and that we are we in that period now. Demonize and marginalize the liberals, attack the courts and create fear in the country. I further explained that during the period of indoctrination code words are used, such as "black robed judges." My listening audience was starting to catch on. They were beginning to see the light and I could hear in their voices the paranoia start to leave. They understood the game and my own multitude of Warlibs were gaining strength. By Friday night I was completely exhausted and decided that I needed a break. I was going back to the mountains, a place of solace and comfort that always nourished me in times of need. Saturday morning I packed a small backpack with a "Go-Lite" tent and a backpacking stove. TazTwo and I headed to the Berkshire Mountains.

Taz and I strolled aimlessly for hours. The leaves had not yet made their colorful fall appearance, although there was a leaf or two that started to exhibit their fall dress. Occasionally, Taz took off after a chip monk, squirrel or rabbit. I could never see what he chased. It all happened so fast. We went off trail and started bushwhacking. I was lost within thirty minutes and did not know north, west, east or south. I intentionally left my compass home. Three hours later I discovered a small, high mountain gem of a lake about 3 acres big and set up camp nestled between two large Maple trees at the lake's edge. Making camp required a minimum of effort, except for digging a deep fire-pit and lining it with stone. The only chore left was to gather firewood and I decided that late afternoon would be a perfect time for that chore. Fishing was in order. It was my sincere wish that no fish would take my bait. It was enough to have the line in the lake. For the next three hours I did nothing but stare at the lake and empty my brain of all the bullshit that had accumulated. At some points during meditation I laughed at my own shenanigans. Stanley Warlib a talk show host revealing False Prophets and Lying Spirits. What a joke I had become. Every time I had any thought that broke my tranquility, I ejected it from my mind and returned to the water, the air and the trees. It was the first time in five weeks that I felt myself.

"Stanley Warlib, long oil," really and then I catapulted that thought out of my head. It took one and one-half hours to completely come to rest when no thoughts entered at all. I became one with nature and it felt wonderful.

My tranquility was interrupted by several quick nudges in my armpit. I looked down and it was a black female Labrador retriever. I grabbed the dog by the head. "What's up girl?" I asked. Taz quickly ran out from the tent and both dogs started sniffing each other's private parts, a practice I wished humans would employ. The bar scene would be so much simpler. I looked around but spotted no one. Taz and his new friend chased each other around the campsite but did not go further out than twenty-five feet. I knew that they would not stray outside of Taz's comfort zone. Several times I looked through the woods but saw no one among the trees. Taz and his new friend played for two hours before both of them fell asleep in my tent. Sunset fell upon the lake and I gathered wood to start a fire. Both Taz and his new girlfriend followed after me, each with a stick in their mouths. I made a fire and all of us sat around. I filled Taz's bowl with extra water and fed the dogs. Nighttime came quickly. "Excuse me," a gentle voice whispered. "I've been waiting for someone to light a fire. I knew that I would find Tina when I found a fire. She's such a grubber," a woman said. I could not see the woman standing a mere eight feet from me. She was waiting for an invitation to enter which completely went over my head. She wasn't going to invade my space unless invited. "Well?" she asked.
"Oh, I'm so sorry. I completely forgot. Please join me. Your dog is named Tina?" I asked.
"Yes," the woman said.
"She's been a pleasure. Tina has been hanging out with her new boyfriend Taz all day," I said. Out of the shadows of the surrounding trees emerged my female visitor. The glow of the fire revealed a pair of hiking boots. I'm a sucker for a woman in hiking boots. Next, the glow revealed a pair of long legs contained within a pair of Wrangler jeans. Whoever this woman was, I was immediately intrigued. I couldn't see her face as it was ensconced in the darkness above me.
"May I sit?" she asked.
"Of course, please, take a seat," I answered. She slowly descended into the light of the campfire and revealed her face. She had deep sky blue eyes. Her brown hair was pulled back in a ponytail. She was the epitome of understated elegance.
"What's your name?" I asked.
"Izzy," she answered.
"Is that short for something?" I asked.
"Isabella," she answered.

"Well, Izzy, what brings you up here?" I asked.

"That's a question I should be asking you. I've come here for years and have never met anyone. Are you lost?" Izzy asked.

"Yes, I'm lost and I'm running away. I've had enough of everything and everybody," I answered. I couldn't take my eyes off Isabella. She was stunning; the kind of good looks that interrupts normal speech and leaves one staring at the beauty in front of you. I couldn't talk and didn't. Taz sat next to me. Tina sat next to Isabella. I didn't feel awkward at all. We sat quietly and looked at the fire. Isabella asked me for white gas for her Whisper-Lite camp stove, which I freely offered. Izzy petted Taz and left. The next several hours I fantasized about Isabella and wondered whether I would ever see her again. I fell asleep by the fire.

"Good morning. Would you like some coffee? I would have said 'good morning some name' but you never told me your name," said Isabella.

"Stan. My name is Stan. What time is it?" I asked.

"It's 8:00 in the morning. I've been waiting and watching you from across the lake. You must have needed the sleep," she said.

"Yeah, I guess I really did. I was exhausted. Let me wake up and I'll join you for coffee," I told Isabella. I made a simple breakfast for Isabella and we fed the dogs. After breakfast, Isabella suggested a hike. We spent the next six hours meandering around the area. Izzy pointed out her house that was built on a ridge overlooking the lake. Isabella was a yoga instructor and she explained that she worked out of a studio in her home. Her clients were local and international. The international students stayed in her home. Isabella was beautiful and centered. I did not answer her query about my occupation. She told me that whatever it was that I did, it was making me uptight and out of balance. "Completely out of balance" she advised me. Izzy told me that if my appearance suggested that I was out of balance she was sure that internally I was in bad shape. I maintained my silence concerning my current state of life and left her wondering rather than knowing. The lake that I was camping at was her lake. It was on her property, however, she had no intention of kicking me out. I did explain to Isabella that I felt like I was in a hurricane and was being battered about in a storm. She explained to me that hurricanes could be fun if one is centered in the eye of the hurricane. Being centered, Isabella explained to me, is central to having good mental and physical health. She didn't sound like a New Age nut; otherwise, I would have cut her short. I spent several hours asking her questions to which she responded politely. She knew I was seeking an answer on how to center myself, however, Isabella quietly answered all my questions leading me to answers on my own. I created a hurricane and I was trying to get out of the outer and inner storm bands and reach the calm of the center. I realized I didn't have to go back to the mess that I created in the city, but I needed to complete my mission. I needed to scratch my way into the eye of the hurricane for safety. At the end of our walk, I concluded that having information and having command of that information would center me. Knowing my shit was the bridge to the eye of the storm. Izzy passed by her house and picked up two bottles of red wine and streaks for dinner. What I found interesting was that not much was said about anything between us. The energy flowed easily between us. I realized that Izzy was more together than I was. She was centered and I made up my mind to get centered. "Know my shit" was my new mantra. We stayed in her backyard, cooked dinner, chatted, listened to music and watched the sun go down. Without preaching at me, Isabella centered me. She walked me back to my campground and suggested that I needed to be centered physically as well. I assumed that "physically centered" meant sex. It meant rubbing my back first and then sex. Izzy explained to me that she thought that I would have fast sex with her and so decided to relax me first. Hence the back rub. It was a wonderful suggestion. We spent the whole night together and quietly watched the sun come up over the lake. Taz ran after a chip monk and accidentally got caught up in the fishing line hanging from the pole. The line slid across my forearm and the fishing hook dug itself into my flesh. The hook was set deep. I couldn't push it through my skin. A knife was necessary to cut a slit in my arm to dislodge the hook. It was bloody. Izzy performed emergency first aid, kissed me on the cheek and asked that I come visit her next weekend.

When I arrived at Doc's Monday morning, the door was partially opened. "Doc, you in there? Yo, Doc, are you in there?" I shouted. I smelled something burning and decided that between the open door and the odor, there was a problem. I looked for Doc in his office and on the deck. He wasn't there. I ran to his bedroom and froze in the doorway. The room was splattered with blood. Doc had erected a tent on the floor next to his bed. In front of his bed was a pile of wood that he took from the backyard. It was smoldering. Doc was inside the tent dry humping a pillow. It was clear that he thought he was making love to someone. I didn't know exactly what I should do. I never came across what appeared to me to be an active delusion, but there it was in front of me. I thought first of calling the police, next the fire department and last, Doc's shrink. Instead, I ran into the kitchen for water and poured it on the fire. I looked in the tent and Doc was still humping away. It took three pitchers of water to completely put out the fire. Calling the police and fire departments were out. I dialed Doc's shrink and waited for him to answer. Just as Dr. P. answered the phone, Doc stuck his head out of the tent and stared at me. I could tell he didn't know where he was. "Dr.

P., this is Rueben, I'll call you back later," I said and hung up the phone. I told Doc to come out of the tent, which he complied with. He stood quietly in the middle of the room and looked around, pausing at each scene. The blood, tent, fishing rod, campfire, camp stove and Taz. Doc looked at his arm in disbelief. I took Doc into the bathroom and washed the blood off his arm. The cut was not as bad as the scene implied. Doc looked in the bathroom mirror, turned towards me slowly and said, "I hope you're still long oil and gold and short the S & P." I didn't know what to do. I simply didn't know what to do. I could only respond simply, "yes." When Doc came out of the bathroom he looked around, started to clean up, put the tent away and swept up the charcoals from the floor. He slid a small area rug over the burnt area and quietly walked into the kitchen, prepared coffee and breakfast and asked me "what's up." Stunned, I answered, "nothing." Doc and I had breakfast and he advised me to stay long oil and gold and maintain my position shorting the S & P. We finished our conversation and Doc explained to me that he had to prepare for his talk show and walked me to the door. "Call me later Rueben," he said as I walked down the stoops of his brownstone. Arriving at the trading floor fifteen minutes before the bell, I scoured the paper for tidbits of information that confirmed Doc's theories. Articles confirming Doc's description of current events exploded off the page: In Nigeria, delta rebels threatened to attack oil wells; a Senior Iraqi oil official, Sana Toma Suleiman was shot and killed in the Northern city of Mosul; China decided to help Russia pay shipping charges in advance for crude oil from Yukos and Putin stated that Russia could be a bidder for Yukos oil assets. In addition, in recognition of China's growing economic power, China would meet with the Group of Seven industrialized nations. Doc was right; high oil prices were a weapon and in advance of the elections, sabotage and assassinations would be the norm.

## CHAPTER FOURTEEN

I sat in my office and centered myself. I decided upon a theme for the day, gathered information, closed my eyes and visualized the show. I became secure and centered. At 2:00 o' clock I took Taz for a walk and stopped by Mykonos for lunch. Without asking me, Angelina brought over Mousaka, smiled and said "hello." Under the plate, folded into a little square were two articles. I finished eating lunch, left ten dollars on the table, picked up the little squares and left the restaurant. Walking down the block, I unfolded the articles and read the headlines. Both articles were from the New York Times, one entitled "Web War-Online and Even Near Home, a New front Is Opening in the Global Terror Battle," and the other entitled "Online Remarks by Heckler Are Examined by Secret Service." It was clear that Angie was reminding me that F.B.I. agents might be present on TheMultitude.org. The "Online Remarks" article caused me to pause. A woman, Sue Niederer, the mother of a soldier killed in Iraq, made comments on the Web site counterpunch.org writing a post that stated that she "wanted to rip Sam's head off" and "shoot him in the groined area." The article further stated that it was federal crime to threaten Sam and accordingly, Special Agent Tony Colgary of the Secret Service in Trenton, New Jersey confirmed that an investigation was under way. I was concerned because I recalled during one session with Dr. P., several remarks that could be interpreted as a threat. It was a fantasy that I told to my shrink. Our conversation was protected by privilege but law doesn't matter when it comes to Sam. However, the article started me thinking and I began wondering exactly what I said to Dr. P. and whether Sam had secretly recorded my sessions with Dr. P. I decided to call Dr. P. later and ask him to review his notes and tapes of our sessions. I was curious. I expected an investigation as a ploy to stop my talk show but I wasn't concerned. I was centered. I touched base with the station manager. He told me that a crowd was forming outside the building. I decided that I wasn't going to use the back entrance and walked calmly through the crowd, shaking hands with some people and fending off insults from others. I knew my shit, I was centered and I was ready to go.

Five, four, three, two and one: "Good afternoon, this is Dr. Stanley Warlib and I hope everyone had a wonderful week-end. The weather was gorgeous in the Northeast and unfortunately Florida was hit again with another hurricane, this one Hurricane Jeanne. I wish all Floridians good health and safety. Last week, I told you about the connection between the conservative radio talk show station in Philadelphia and Salem Communications, a Christian right wing conservative corporation. I showed you the connection between the ownership of Salem by Mr. Epperson and a Mr. Atsinger, CEO and President and their membership in Council on National Policy. This weekend I got to thinking about all those right wing conservative books that are written and published that bash liberals and discuss impending terror attacks. These two areas are specifically designed to scare you and then point a finger towards a domestic group that is part of the problem in an effort to seduce you into believing that eradicating liberals will better protect you from terror. These areas are relentlessly addressed over and over until they become part of your conscience. Permit me, at this point, to name some of the authors and titles of the books that I am discussing. First, let's tackle the terror issue. Here are some authors and titles:

| Author | Title |
|---|---|
| Shyam Bhatia | Brighter Than the Baghdad Sun-Saddam Hussein's Nuclear Threat to the United States |
| Bill Gertz | The China Threat-The Plan to Defeat America |
| Bill Sammon | Fighting Back: The War on Terror |
| Michelle Malkin | Invasion: How America Still Welcomes Terrorists, Criminals and other Foreign Menaces to Our Shores. |
| Robert Spencer | Onward Muslim Soldiers: How Jihad Still Threatens America and the West |

Liberals

| | |
|---|---|
| Mona Charen | Useful Idiots: How Liberals Got it Wrong in the Cold War and Still Blame America First |
| Michael Rose | Goodbye, Good Men: How Liberals Brought Corruption into the Catholic Church |
| Jed Babbin | Inside the Asylum: Why the United Nations & Old Europe are Worse Than You Think |

| | |
|---|---|
| Robert 'Buzz' Patterson | Reckless Disregard: How Liberal Democrats Undermine our Military, Endanger our Soldiers and Jeopardize our Security |
| Ann Coulter | Treason! |
| Sean Hannity | Deliver Us from Evil…Liberalism |

Regnery Press, a wholly owned subsidiary of Eagle Publishing, publishes many of these books. For example, hot off the press is "Unfit for Command," by the swift boat Vietnam era soldiers. Interestingly enough, the Chairman of Eagle Publishing is Thomas L. Philips, a member of the Council on National Policy. It appears to me that there really is a 'vast, right wing conspiracy' and from a media standpoint, print and radio, it goes back to the Council on National Policy. So, now we have radio stations owned by a man that is a member of the Council on National Policy and a publisher of extreme right wing conservative books that is a member of the Council on National Relations. The point being is that they are implanting into your psyche a very simple equation: liberal=evil+treason=death. I am being set-up for internment in a camp. After all, the conservative right wing thinks that is a pretty good idea. The sad part of all this is that by the time you turn around, you don't know what happened. Like a Pavlov dog, you hear liberal and you think evil, you think treason and eventually you think death. It's all so easy with a dependent, histrionic and paranoid personality culture. You guys out there are not even listening. It's mind control. How do you take back America for Christ without mind control? Everyday, on the radio, tens of millions of listeners are pounded with the mind message of terror, terror, terror and then liberal, liberal, and more liberal. We're being set up, do you understand that. I wouldn't doubt that every conservative radio talk show host logs on to a internet site giving them talking points for the day. It's all coordinated. Get it! And who would coordinate all this bullshit? Why, the Council on National Policy, of course! That is why it is so important to know who and what these guys are all about. We know two things: (1) they are demonizing liberals and (2) freaking you out with the terror game. Unfortunately, they lost out on the terror game because it is no longer to scare you, Sam really brought you a problem with his stupidity and visions of grandiosity. The tirade against the liberals will only get worse.

They are emboldened by our liberal silence and their tactics are going national in scope. Tactics no longer exist on a sub-level because without opposition and with your mushy brains susceptible to control they have come out of the woodwork. Not only that, they have millions of people who agree with them. Yeah, if it weren't for those fucking liberals we wouldn't be in this problem. What's national in scope? Several days ago, I noticed a small article entitled 'A Ban On The Bible?' the guts of which stated that the Republican National Committee sent out a mailer to the voters of West Virginia that the Bible would be banned and that men will marry men if liberals win in November. Usually, this kind of stupid shit is done sub-level, below the radar screens. However, because they are getting away with this kind of brazen stupidity and fear mongering, this approach has been raised to a national level. Several days after this little blurb appeared, a fuller article appeared in The New York Times entitled 'Republicans Admit Mailing Campaign Literature Saying Liberals Will Ban the Bible,' wherein the Republican Party admitted mass mailing to residents of two states warning that 'liberals' seek to ban the Bible. It was an effort to mobilize religious voters. An editorial in The Charleston Gazette of West Virginia on September 22, 2004, asked 'Holy Moley! Who concocts this Gibberish?' That's exactly what it is, gibberish. However, the masters of the evangelical conservative Christian movement decided that if they could sell the gibberish to their evangelical screwballs they could go after their next constituency; the conservatives. So what happens? You get a million conservatives listening to conservative radio talk shows, which are really Christian radio talk shows, owned by Salem Communication, whose owners sit on the Council on National Policy. It is a coordinated campaign designed by this group to ensnare ever increasing unsuspecting citizens. How about Sam's second in command suggesting that his opponent is unpatriotic because he opposes Sam's position on Iraq. This is low-level political discourse, however, it doesn't prick enough people's ears to alienate them. The public is becoming indoctrinated with hate and blame, which is what they have been doing to reborn Christians for years.

WARLIB: Deborah from San Francisco. How are you?

DEBORAH: I'm fine Dr. Warlib, but I'm a little pissed at you.

WARLIB: Why?

DEBORAH: Because of your statement about mushy brains! I like your program. Lots of people like your program and we don't have "mushy brains." We're becoming an army of Warrior Liberals, Warlibs. Perhaps, you haven't check your website lately, www.warlib.org. There's a ton of activity. Anyway, several friends and I got to wonder about Sam's push for privatizing social security. It sounds appealing to us young folks. In addition, my friends and I decided that we would tackle the 'G's' of the membership list of the Council on National Policy.

WARLIB: O.K., tell us what you found.

DEBORAH: We got to thinking about privatization and started doing research. We came across an organization named The National Center for Privatization. Willard Garvey founded this organization in 1983 with another Wichita, Kansas businessman. In 1986, the Board of Directors included Garvey and Robert D. Love, a founding member of National Council of The John Birch Society. The purpose of the National Center for Privatization was to 'educate Americans about the then new concept of privatization.' I think Garvey and his partners felt that government services could be performed more efficiently and effectively within the private sector. The objective was to eliminate government waste, reduce taxes, and government control of citizens.

WARLIB: Sounds innocent, doesn't it?

DEBORAH: Yes, benign. On April 6, 1984, Willard Garvey, wrote President Reagan a letter, which I will read shortly. This letter was used as promotional material at a conference named International Conference on Family Choice/Educational Vouchers. The letter reads as follows:

6 April 1984

President Ronald Reagan
Executive Office of the President
The White House
1600 Pennsylvania Avenue
Washington, D.C. 20500

Re: Privatization

President Reagan, congratulations on rejecting the political system negatives. Now why not adopt the all positive system-privatization? Hold a White House Conference on Privatization and appoint a Presidential Task Force on privatization.

Privatization is documented in the enclosed paper from the Heritage Foundation and dates back at least to Adam Smith, Plato, Aristotle and Jesus.

Privatization's more recent advocates include most of the non-profit sector-and the entire profit sector. To name a few, Peter Drucker, Milton Friedman, Heritage Foundation, Reason Foundation, Pacific Institute, Manhattan Institute, National Legal Center for the Public Interest...churches, labor unions, etc.

Privatization is now "an idea whose time has come" The knowledge, communication, and computer industry can make political representatives obsolete!

Privatization might well be the theme for the 200$^{th}$ anniversary of the Constitution. Privatization is essential for national salvation.

To restore privatization is the National Center for Privatization's purpose. May we help you?

With best wishes,

Willard W. Garvey

WWG:ks

Encl: Heritage Foundation paper
National Center for Privatization brochure

That's the end of the letter. However, it's like I said, a copy of this letter was enclosed as media promotional material for the International Conference on Family Choice. Guest speakers at the conference were James Dobson, Tim LaHaye and Phyllis Schlafly. Here's my point: Willard Garvey is a member of the Council on National Policy, James Dobson is a member of the Council as well as Tim Lahaye and Phyllis Schlafly.
WARLIB: What you're seeing today was conceived years ago and I think the point is nothing less than no government and no taxes will do. The question is: To be replaced with what? I appreciate all this Deborah. Is this information posted on the website.
DEBORAH: Yes, and a lot more.
WARLIB: Thank you Warlibs. I'm starting to feel good.
I feel renewed and centered, ladies and gentlemen. However, as I said, the big question is replacing the government with what?
WARLIB: Next caller, Fran from Chicago.
FRAN: In my opinion, they want to replace the government with allegiance to the corporation or a theocracy.
WARLIB: Fran, good point. When I do in depth research into the underbelly of evangelical conservative Christianity it appears to be nothing more than

unchained capitalism sold with good traditional Christian values. It's all about the Benjamins and the evangelical leaders have been fleecing their flock forever. When I hear talk about faith-based initiatives, well, that's like giving a bank robber the keys to the vault. It's scary. Fran, I hate to cut you short, but my producer is signaling commercial break. Thank you for calling and please call back.

Michael, the station manager poked his head into the studio and told me that it was a good show and that a major sponsor was considering coming on board. "I'm back and thank you for listening today. Tune in tomorrow because I'll be talking about the gays and lesbians. Please tell your gay friends to tune in. However, before I leave you, I want to tell you guys about a little episode that I had the other day. While I was thinking about the show, I kept on repeating to myself, 'Take Back America for Christ,' 'Take Back America for Christ,' and wondered how exactly does one move a country in an entirely different direction. It doesn't happen willy-nilly. It can only be accomplished by design and dedication and I think the Council on National Policy conceives the design and their good Christian warriors provide the manpower and dedication. Nevertheless, it's an interesting question to toy with: How do you capture the conscience, heart and soul of a large nation? As I pondered this question, I was staring at the books in my library and kept on going back to one. I didn't want to dwell on the book that my eyes kept on bringing me back to, because it was too sick to even consider. The book was 'The Rise and Fall of the Third Reich,' by William L. Shirer. Adolph Hitler employed a process of turning his nation in a direction that fit his grandiose vision. Could the Council on National Policy possibly employ a process that closely mirrors the process that Adolph Hitler employed? The answer is easy: mind control. Let me read to you two passages from the book: On page 268, it states:

> 'There is no independence of law against National Socialism. Say to yourselves at every decision, which you make: How would the Fuehrer decide in my place? In every decision ask yourselves: 'Is this decision compatible with the National Socialist conscience of the German people?' Then you will have a firm iron foundation which, allied with the unity of the National Socialist People's State and with your recognition of the eternal nature of the will of Adolph Hitler, will endow your own sphere of decision with the authority of the Third Reich, and this for all time.'

Now, for example, replace 'How would the Fuehrer decide in my place' with the following: 'What would Jesus do?' It's scary, isn't it? Move on to page 264 and see if this sounds familiar describing conditions during 1936:

'Finally, the take-home pay of the German shrank. Besides stiff income taxes, compulsory contributions to sickness, unemployment and disability insurance, and Labor Front dues, the manual worker-like everyone else in Nazi Germany-was constantly pressured to make increasingly large gifts to an assortment of Nazi charities…'

Good night, this is Dr. Stanley Warlib.

## CHAPTER FIFTEEN

"Dr. P., this is Rueben. Doc's friend," I said.

"Yes, Rueben, how are you and how is my favorite former patient, Stanley Warlib?" Dr. P. asked. I explained to Dr. P. in detail what I discovered in the morning. I further explained to Dr. P. that I had no clue about what to do. I didn't want to call the police or fire department because I thought that would mean involuntary incarceration in some mental hospital.

"Well, Rueben, what you described can be classified as a psychotic episode. It's rare. A psychotic episode can last a day or a month and when it goes it over. However, I am concerned about the campfire in his room. That kind of thing endangers Stanley as well as others. Is there anything else?" Dr. P. asked.

"Yes and I can't fucking believe that Stanley is plugged into the great financial Buddha in the sky. The guy is psychic! He's insanely correct about the financial market. I mean, how can a guy who we think is going bonkers be so god damn correct about money. Maybe he's not crazy and that's where I get confused. He's humping pillows in a psychotic episode and calling the markets dead on. Doc tells me go long gold and oil and short the S & P and I'm up $125,000.00 in two weeks," I said.

Dr. P. and I agreed that we would watch Stanley closely and keep in touch with each other weekly. Dr. P. was going to make a house call by the end of the week.

FASCISTI: I'm looking for someone.
BENITO: It's me you're looking for. Talk privately.
FASCISTI: How am I doing?
BENITO: Fine, I've been listening. However, there is only one conclusion that you will reach. All roads lead to single cell action. Good-Bye.

"Doc, how the hell are you. I listened to your show today. Scary stuff. I just can't figure out how you think," said Rueben on his Monday night visit. I knew he was checking up on me and I knew he wanted to talk about the markets, which was fine with me.

"I was screwing some girl named Isabella in my tent on a camping trip in the Berkshire Mountains." Rueben was visibly taken aback.

"It's o.k., no problem," said Rueben. He did not want to talk about the incident. Strange behavior frightens people. Rueben followed me into the kitchen where I grabbed a bottle of red wine and we continued on out to the deck. "Let's get buzzed, Rueben. I need a good buzz," I said. Rueben had no problem with my suggestion and we gulped down two glasses of wine and opened the second bottle. "So, you want to know what the great Warlib sees in his minds eye, do you?

All the little cartoon characters are having a great time up in the old skull. It's party time and everybody is scrambling all around, moving the pawns and placing the bets. It's a huge fucking party Rueben. I've been invited and I'll tell you some real good shit. I mean real good shit," I said. Rueben leaned forward. "Fuck them all," I said. Rueben burst out laughing.

"Yeah, fuck them all," I repeated half-drunk.

"I mean, Israel is buying 5,000 bombs and 500 bunker buster bombs and Iran is sticking out its' middle finger, screaming fuck you. Everybody got their back up against the wall with their middle finger held high in the air and they're all screaming 'fuck you.' 'Fuck me, well, fuck you.' 'Oh yeah, well, fuck me fucking you.' Everybody is having a fuck you party. Isn't any cooperation anymore dude. Kofi, the U.N. dude, claims that the Iraq war is illegal a couple of days before Sam gives his speech and then right after the speech, holds a press conference, reminding Sam about the rule of law. 'Fuck you.' Got it Rueben. That's what is going on. But, I know that you want to know about money. Right. Right. I told you that high oil is a weapon. Right now, there's a small group of Niger Delta rebels that's threatening to commence a full-scale war on October 1, 2004. These rebels are going to close the place down. Nigeria is the seventh largest exporter of oil and the fifth largest supplier to good old Uncle Sam. High oil is a weapon against the United States. The chief of the rebel group is Moujahid Dokubo-Asari and he says that 'we will start a full scale armed struggle.' Are you with me Rueben? Oh, who cares, just listen. Lean and mean Osama bin Ladin is sitting with his head lieutenant in some cave sipping Arabian tea and planning. They got everybody thinking about physical terror attacks, which Sam has under his control from a domestic standpoint. Osama, being the shrewd little devil that he is, has something else in mind and that is financial terror attacks. Create conditions and bring Sam down financially to his knees. Sam, the biggest debtor of all, can't sustain high oil prices. Car sales go down, people get laid off and airlines file for bankruptcy. 'Why not?' the man in the turban asks, finance the little Niger Delta rebels and stir up the pot some more. Get oil higher. You see what I mean. Osama is getting the tall building swaying because it is structurally weak. You might get a play out of Venezuela. Keep your eye on that one. Terror bombs you can diminish, but financial instability you can't. You see, Rueben? The building starts swaying and there's no real effective defense against the financial turmoil. The market is built on perception and if the world perceives that the tall building of Sam is starting to sway, well, that's a big fucking problem. Interest rates aren't going anywhere because the economy hit a soft patch. The world supported the dollar because everyone thought that Sam was raising rates. When you're a debtor nation, you have to pay more interest so your financial instruments are more attractive. If Sam doesn't want to raise rates and he keeps swaying, it's a big, big, fucking problem. And so, young man, sitting at the feet of the great financial Buddha, SHORT the fucking dollar," I said. I intentionally fell off my chair and onto the deck, pretending to have fainted. I scared the shit out of Rueben.

"Doc, Doc, you o.k. Wake up!" screamed Rueben. Lying on my back, I opened one eye and stared at Rueben.

"Are you fucking nuts? You scared the shit of me," said Rueben.

"Isn't that what they do in the movies after all the oracles give their visions. They collapse dummy. Rueben you're losing your sense of humor. Lighten up dude," I said. Rueben and I finished the night laughing our asses off. Leaving my apartment, Rueben looked at me and asked if I would be all right alone. "Rueben, I'm going off to the Berkshire Mountains to find Isabella, except this time, we'll screw in the house. I'll leave the campfire and fishing rod at home." At the bottom of the steps, Rueben stopped and chatted with a man in a limousine. From the street, Reuben called out, "Hey, Doc you have a visitor." When I arrived at my front door, I stood at the top of the steps, looked at the limousine, turned around and went into my office. I reappeared at the door seconds later, bounded down the steps and cheerfully greeted Mr. Westerfield.

"Having fun Stanley?" asked Mr. Westerfield.

"Yes, as a matter of fact, I am," I answered.

"Get in the car," Mr. Westerfield demanded. I sat next to Mr. Westerfield and we stared at each other. I wanted to laugh out loud, however, I refrained.

"Aren't you scared?" Mr. Westerfield asked.

"No, not at all," I answered and asked Mr. Westerfield the same question.

"Why, should I be?" Charles asked. Charles looked out the window towards two black suited Secret Service types standing next to the limousine. Harry, the driver, put his hand in his vest pocket. I knew that Harry carried a gun and I was sure that the two goons outside the limousine were packing as well.

"Trying to scare me Charles?" I asked.

"You're skating on thin ice, Stanley," said Charles.

"Maybe, you're the one that should be frightened. If either Harry or those two goons make a move, you're a dead man," I said. Charles laughed.

"You're such a naïve little puppy," said Charles.

"Really. Naïve puppy," I responded. I put my hand in my coat and pointed the gun that I had placed there towards Charles.

"Is that a gun?" Charles asked.

"Aren't you the one who taught me to trust no one, watch my back and cover my ass? You don't think I would get into this car without protection and I can assure you that it really is a gun and I will use it," I told Charles.

"And what about those two gentlemen outside?" Charles asked. I lowered the window and raised my arm. Within ten seconds a crowd of ten people surrounded the men. Two members of the crowd were professional bodyguards that Michael, the station manager, provided. These guys were the largest, nastiest men I ever met. They didn't believe in posturing or negotiation. Their mind-set was one of dynamic threat removal. I didn't know them but I believed they were professional wrestlers at one point in time. The balance of the group was Warlibs. The two bodyguards slammed the two secret service type guys against the limousine with such force that they dented the side of the car. After they looked at me, I nodded for them to lighten up.

"Playing a real dangerous game, Stanley," Charles said.

"That's your problem, I'm not playing a game. I'm deadly serious. Tune in Thursday to my show; I have a little surprise for you," I told Charles.

"Well, I have a little surprise for you, Stanley. Gabby is pregnant. You're going to be a father," said Charles.

"Great, call me when my child is born. I'll come pick the baby up and serve Gabby with custody papers. There's no way you rats will ever raise a child of mine," I told Charles. "Apparently, our respective positions, are not compatible," said Charles. I left the limousine and headed back into the apartment. I patted my two monsters of the shoulder and invited them and the Warlibs in for drink and food. I had the beginnings of my own private army.

Five, four, three, two and one:

"Good afternoon, this is Dr. Stanley Warlib and we have a lot on our plate this afternoon. Alan from New York City, what's on your mind?

ALAN: Following up on our assignment about the Council on National Policy. On September 25, 2004, The New York Times had an article entitled "New Pet Cause for the Very Rich: Swaying the Election. The article writes about the 527 committees that have sprung up as a result of the McCain-Feingold bill. These 527 committees appeal to individual large donors, who donate in the millions. On the Republican side is the Progress for America Fund that received five million from Alex G. Spanos, a California real estate developer and owner of the San Diego Chargers; two and one half million from T. Boone Pickens and Richard M. DeVos, Sr., co-founder of Amway and owner of the Orlando Magic who gave two million. Here's the kicker, Richard M. DeVos is a member of the Council on National Policy. George Soros, a philanthropist and financier gave more than fifteen million to the Democratic 527 committees.

WARLIB: Great find! Let's add DeVos to our list and since the name of George Soros came up, permit me to expand upon my observation that the Republicans are going national and not sub-level. On Fox news, the Speaker of the House, Dennis Hastert, stated on national television that he believed that Soros made his money from selling drugs. In addition, Hastert and Sam's assistant flat out implied that a vote for Sam's opponent is a vote for terror. The underlying premise is clear: if you're not with me, you're against me, and since I'm with God I can't be wrong. Ergo, you must be wrong and are evil and a traitor. It is a simplistic equation that works well in the evangelical movement. Don't you guys get it! This is real. You may think that they are a bunch of Neanderthal screwballs but they're deadly and have power. They have so much power and arrogant confidence that their agenda is national in scope. It's above board and out in the sunlight. However, no one is screaming about the absolute horror about what these nuts are saying and doing. Everyday, I check World Net Daily, the evangelical conservative online newsletter to see what they're stirring about. Some guy wrote a book called 'America-A Call to Greatness.' Let me read one glowing review. 'The author has faithfully strived to demonstrate the incontrovertible fact that God is sovereign over all nations and all peoples. Without a renewed acknowledgement of accountability to our Creator, America will perish.' Howard Phillips, Chairman of the Conservative Caucus, Inc., and a member of the *Council on National Policy* wrote that review. The author of the book is John W. Chalfant, also a member of the *Council on National Policy*. Do you guys get it! They're national. They're not just some nut jobs trying to get some bucks by freaking out evangelical Christians. They're out to control the nation in accordance with their vision. What is that vision? My research into the book reveals the following and I'll read this direct from the World Net Daily.

## "Christian revival in U.S.—can it really happen? 'A Call to Greatness' provides major blueprint for restoring faith of Founders

While many Christian voices are calling urgently for a major national revival, author John Chalfant not only agrees, but also has offered up a stunning blueprint to help get the job done.

The United States is losing its greatness, says Chalfant, because Christian clergy have abandoned "the militant, power-filled, full-dimensional" faith of America's founders.

Indeed, in "America: A Call to Greatness," Chalfant asserts Christian citizens have allowed their traditional worldview to become corrupted by what he calls "abandonment clergy."

Many Christian leaders have compromised with a secular worldview that never could have created the Declaration of Independence, Constitution or Bill of Rights, claims Chalfant, a member of the influential Council for National Policy.

Without Christianity, he said, there would be no God-given unalienable right of the individual to life, liberty and the pursuit of happiness.

The problem America faces, he says, boils down to God's warning in Leviticus 26 that those who forget the creator and reject his commandments will be ruled by their enemies, "they that hate you."

Those words were echoed by William Penn, founder of Pennsylvania, when he famously said, "Those who will not be governed by God will be ruled by tyrants."

"We are in a war for our God-given nation and freedoms, and the workers of iniquity are winning," Chalfant says.

But he has not given up hope—far from it—insisting Christians still have at their disposal "the superior, available power and strength to take it all back."

"The hour is late, but the bell has not yet tolled for America," writes Chalfant, whose book offers a major action plan for restoration.

Christians need to realize, he says, "that they have the primary responsibility for reclaiming our nation's Christian heritage because it is Christianity upon which the Declaration of Independence and the Constitution were founded."

He points out that while non-Christians in America certainly are not obligated to adopt or convert to the Christian faith, it is "the duty of every American citizen to defend the Constitution and the Judeo-Christian pillars of law and liberty which grant us such freedoms."

"Every citizen who is a beneficiary of America's freedoms, especially the freedom to worship as he or she pleases, or not to worship at all, has a duty to defend the Judeo-Christian pillars and laws of our nation that make such freedom possible," he adds.

"In no sense is this duty a compromise with one's own religious convictions. In America this duty simply guarantees a person's right to worship as he pleases without fear of persecution."

## 'Author of freedom'

Chalfant says he committed the rest of his life "to the service of Jesus Christ and America's freedoms" after hearing a speech by the political hero of his youth, Richard Arens, staff director of the House Committee on Un-American Activities, who produced a research series on Soviet world expansion.

The Arens speech began, "Two thousand years ago there was One who spoke these words: 'No man can serve two masters,'" comparing Jesus Christ, the "author of freedom," to Karl Marx, the "destroyer of freedom."

Chalfant began his new career by organizing and directing the award-winning Delaware "Freedom on the Offense" program, recognized by the late FBI director J. Edgar Hoover and others.

Over the next three decades, he helped assist and fund the many Christian pro-defense leaders with whom he developed a relationship. Among his projects was a video marketing campaign, "SALT Syndrome," by the American Security Council, which President-elect Ronald Reagan later wrote was a major factor in his election victory.

The founder of a commercial real estate company in Florida, Chalfant also was invited to join the Council for National Policy, a group of influential leaders committed to Christian principles.

The first edition of his book, published with the title "Abandonment Theology: The Clergy and the Decline of American Christianity," was hailed by many state and national lawmakers. It has become a text for political campaigns, Christian and conservative organizations and has earned the endorsement of clergy across denominational lines.

## Militant faith

His book presents the "militant Christian faith" of the Founding Fathers "and the godly heritage they gave us, how we have abandoned that faith and commitment and what will be necessary for us to save our country from free-falling into tyranny and slavery."

Abandonment theology, he says, has laid the foundation for the "prevailing posture of non-resistance to overspreading evil."

The widespread retreat from Christian duty has opened the country to atheistic, humanistic, evolutionary and cult-based evils that undermine the founding principles of America and threaten our nation, Chalfant says.

He describes "Abandonment Theology" as:

> A faith which deceptively pawns itself off as Christianity by operating in the name of Christ, but which produces fruits destructive to America's God-given freedoms. It comprises what is left today of the militant, power-filled, full-dimensional Christian faith of America's Founders after decades of erosion, watering down and trivializing of God's action mandates by America's Abandonment Clergy. It is a "feel good" theology that patronizes Jesus Christ and thereby gains legitimacy, while at the same time produces disobedience to the commands of God and desertion of Christian duty.

## Evil's influences

His updated volume addresses contemporary political issues such as national defense, Islamic terrorism, public education and "reparations."

He summarizes areas in which evil has gained influence because of "abandonment clergy" and their followers:

- **Works:** Neutralized the will of many Christians to stand and fight for their liberties by convincing them that "works" are not important.
- **Government:** Inverted the meaning of Romans 13:1-2 to discourage Christian involvement and exercise of their sacred duties in the affairs of government.
- **Outlawed God in the public schools:** Abraham Lincoln agreed with our Founding Fathers that America's future security rested in teaching children the highest biblical and moral principles.
- **Two-way "wall of separation:"** The fabrication of a two-way wall between church and state made it illegal for the church to intrude in the affairs of the state.
- **Love:** Trivializing of the faith by inverting "Love" from an action mandate for obedience to the Commandments to a sentiment primarily of charity and tolerance.
- **"End-times, last days:"** Overuse of eschatology (the study of future events), biblical prophecy and apparent signs of the times generates futility and despair with an attitude of "Why bother?" and an abdication of duty.
- **Homosexuality:** This practice is condemned by God as "abomination" and "unclean" (transmitters for death-dealing diseases such as AIDS). It is "against nature," and is not genetic or an "alternate lifestyle."
- **Women (wives, mothers, sisters, and daughters) in combat:** It is an inversion of the natural role for which God created women and contributes to the destruction of a nation through downgrading and demoralizing its military combat forces.
- **Abortion:** This murder of infants would be expected in the Nazi death camps but not in Christian America, especially not under the banner of the mother's "choice." Her choice should be made before conception when there is only one life involved, not afterward when there are two.
- **"Peace, peace; when there is no peace:"** Years of disarming, neutralizing propaganda takes the fight out of Christians. The claim ignores "fallen human nature" and God's mandates for vigilance by selling the false doc-

trine of "peace" or "peace in our time" or "peaceful co-existence" (with evil governments) as if peace were nothing more than the absence of battlefield conflict.

In response, Chalfant lays out a comprehensive 18-point action plan. But the very first task, he says, is "to go to our knees in prayer and ask God to help us put the shattered pieces of our Christian worldview back together so we can clearly see the whole picture and the positive role that we as individuals can play in the areas of our calling."

This is serious stuff. This is the America that Sam envisions. Let me read from page 244 of The Rise and Fall of the Third Reich:

'Every morning the editors of the Berlin daily newspapers and the correspondents of those published elsewhere in the Reich gathered at the Propaganda Ministry to be told by Dr. Goebbels or one of his aides what news to print and suppress, how to write the news and headline it, what campaigns to call off or institute and what editorials were desired for the day. In case of any misunderstanding a daily written directive was furnished along with the oral instructions. For the smaller out-of-town papers and periodicals the directives were dispatched by telegram or by mail.

All of you have heard about 'talking point memos.' Well, here it is, as far back as 1933. You must understand that this is very, very real. The Republican conservative evangelical Christians are the true face of the Republican Party. I hate to beat this to death; however, here's another article from the World Net Daily concerning a Congressional race.

## CANDIDATE NAMES FUNDAMENTALIST ISLAM AS ENEMY
## MUSLIM GROUPS PROTEST HIS CONTENTION TERRORIST ACTS NOT ABERRATION

Muslim groups are protesting the comments of a Republican candidate for Congress who contends terrorist acts are not "aberrational behavior" by a few extremists but part of the expansionist aims of fundamentalist Islam.

Kurt Eckhardt, who is challenging three-term Rep. Jan Schakowsky, told World-NetDaily he won't retract statements to the Daily Herald newspaper of suburban Chicago.

"There's not a chance I will do that," he said in an interview with WND.

Eckhardt told the editorial board of the Daily Herald Monday he has distrusted Islam "for years" and supports the monitoring of mosques by the federal government.

Muslim groups responded immediately, calling Eckhardt's characterization of Islam inaccurate and dangerous, the paper reported.

"This feeds the cycle of misunderstanding, feeds the cycle of prejudice, feeds the cycle of hate crimes," said Yaser Tabbara, executive director of the Chicago chapter of the Council on American-Islamic Relations.

Tabbara's group, which touts itself as the leading Islamic civil rights group on the continent, is a spin-off of the Islamic Association For Palestine, labeled a "front group" for Hamas by two former heads of the FBI's counterterrorism section.

But Tabbara told the Daily Herald, "We are unequivocally opposed to terrorism. Our religion does not condone it in any way."

Eckhardt asserts secular democracies must be prepared to take pre-emptive action against the threat of fundamentalist Islamic expansion.

"No other issue matters if we're dead," he told the newspaper's editorial board.

Eckhardt, who was persuaded by Republicans to challenge Schakowsky for the 9th District seat in suburban Chicago, insisted terrorist acts by Muslims are not an aberration.

"Where is the voice of reason in the Islamic community?" he said.

His Democratic opponent believes, however, that terrorism and calls for violence are "not at all" inherent in Islam.

"Going in with the suspicion that every mosque is somehow a breeding ground for terrorism defies all the information," Schakowsky said.

Counterterrorism analysts say Islamic mosques, schools, associations, chaplains and clergy in the U.S. have been disproportionately funded by the radical Wahhabi stream of Islam promoted worldwide by Saudi Arabia.

## Rapid expansion

Explaining his remarks, Eckhardt told WND he was not referring to every Islamic nation or Muslim in the world but responding to the accusation from the left that America's foreign policy is the lightning rod for terrorism.

"The Muslim community and the press are hestitant to acknowledge that this has become a global issue," he said. "We are seeing the rapid expansion of globalist Islam in Russia, Africa, Southeast Asia and even in parts of Europe, and that has nothing to do with a free Palestine or American troops in Afghanistan or Iraq."

Eckhardt said his intent was to emphasize that the insurgency is widespread outside the Middle East, and "I am mindful we have to be on guard militarily."

He also acknowledged he's mindful of the fact that the Bush administration is careful to speak of a "war on terror" and brand Islam as a "religion of peace."

"I don't want to tell the administration how to run their war," he said. "I think at the end of the day they are going to get the job done."

But he said he was "surprised that they weren't more strident politically in naming the enemy."

"President Bush's polls were highest when he said, 'Either you are with us or against us,'" Eckhardt argued. "I think Americans respond well to that kind of bluntness."

Eckhardt is a sizeable underdog in the congressional race, but he says, if anything, his remarks about Islam will help his chances, noting he has received only positive feedback from voters in a district he describes as "very Jewish."

On his campaign website, Eckhardt describes himself as a "follower of the principles of Ronald Reagan," believing "in a less obtrusive government at home coupled with a strong national defense against both terror and rogue nuclear nations.""

What will happen to liberals, those evil traitors of the new state Christian state? Well, for one thing, we'll probably be labeled as enemies of the state, enemy combatants or persons of interest. Next we'll all go to Special Military Tribunals for prosecution. These courts have been set up. Next, we'll be interned in a camp and when they finally complete the process of indoctrination, we'll be liquidated. I know, I know, you can't believe that this can happen in America, but it can and the process proceeds apace. Reelecting Sam will be an affirmation that he is the chosen one and that his buddies on the Council on National Policy are ordained by God to complete the mission. Sounds like a bad play, unfortunately it's all too real. Just yesterday I received a visit from someone who advised me that I was skating on thin ice. I told him, in no uncertain terms, that the counter war to his culture war has commenced. I advise you to approach this battle the same way that these Fascists approach their war on us, with dedication and ferocity. However, I will not leave you without ammunition. It's time to stop trying to catch them in lies and play these little 'gotcha' games. Sam will win in November and if you all think that a woman in 2008 will be elected, you're wrong. By that time, the process of total indoctrination will be complete and all will be lost. Next caller, Dennis from Oklahoma:

DENNIS: Dr. Warlib, you are a pervert and a traitor. Why have you been spreading lies about good, no great, God fearing evangelical Christians?

WARLIB: Have I? Are you an evangelical Christian?

DENNIS: Yes, I am, and you sir, are an abomination.

WARLIB: Interesting choice of word. Let me ask you Dennis, you would kill a gay man?

DENNIS: Well, let's see.

WARLIB: Come on Dennis, it's an easy yes or no question. Remember the Bible though. Thou shall not kill. It a commandment of God! Would you kill a homosexual, yes or no?

DENNIS: I am a good evangelical Christian. The answer is no. I would not kill a homosexual man.

WARLIB: Well then, Dennis you are *NOT* a good *evangelical* Christian. I guess you haven't gotten the talking points memo. The Bible, Leviticus 18:22, states:

You shall not lie with a male as a woman; it is an abomination. Leviticus 20:13, states: If a man lies with a male as a woman, both of them have committed an abomination; they shall be put to death, their blood is upon them. That's what you real good evangelical Christian's really believe. Fuck this. Let's take the gloves off, you moron. I'm hanging up on this jerk. I will not debate these people. The time for arguing right or wrong is over. I'm right and they're wrong. 'Hang chi-chi gal wid a long piece of rope. Mek me see di han a go up, mek me see di han'a go up.' How about this one from 'Weh Yuh No Fi Do: batty man fi dead.' You must think I'm crazy. What the hell am I talking about? These are lyrics from Jamaican artist Beenie Man. He recently appeared at Hammerstein Ballroom where there was an exuberant crowd of thousands, waving whatever he told them to wave. This is from Dancehall music, the vicious side of Reggae music, advocating the hanging and killing of homosexuals. It seems that this music was based on an incident in Jamaica wherein people quoting scripture murdered a homosexual. But, I don't have to go to Jamaica for this kind of bullshit. Let's stay right here in America in Baton Rogue, Louisiana. Jimmy Swaggert is back. In front of a congregation he said:

"I get amazed, I can't look at it but about 10 seconds, at these politicians dancing around this, dancing around this, I'm trying to find a correct name for it, this utter absolute, asinine, idiotic stupidity of men marrying men." (shouts from crowd)

"I've never seen a man in my life I wanted to marry." (shouts, applause) "And I'm gonna be blunt and plain, if one ever looks at me like that I'm gonna kill him and tell God he died." (laughter, applause) "In case anybody doesn't know, God calls it an abomnation (sic). It's an abomnation (sic)! It's an abomnation (sic)!" (applause)

"These ridiculous, utterly absurd district attorneys and judges and state congress and 'well, we don't know'...they ought to, they ought to, they ought to have to marry a pig and live with them forever." (laughter) "I'm not knocking the poor homosexual, I'm not. They need salvation just like anybody else. I'm knocking our pitiful, pathetic lawmakers. And I thank God that President Sam has stated," (applause) "we need a Constitutional amendment that states that marriage is between a man and a woman." (applause)

There will be no homosexuals, lesbians or blacks in God's next kingdom. We all must band together. This is Dr. Stanley Warlib and before I sign off, I'll read from page 269 of The Rise and fall of the Third Reich:

> One of the worst examples of this, from the Nazi point of view, was the decision of the Reichsgericht, Germany's Supreme Court, to acquit on the basis of evidence three of the four communist defendants in the Reichstag fire trial in March 1934. This so incensed Hitler and Goering that within a month, on April 24, 1934, the right to try cases of treason, which heretofore had been under the exclusive jurisdiction of the Supreme Court, was taken away from that august body and transferred to a new court, the People's Court and soon became the most dreaded tribunal in the land.

It's coming. This is Dr. Stanley Warlib, leading the fight against the Christian Capitalist New World Order saying, good night! The station manager admonished me about four letter words and reminded me of the fine that the FCC recently leveled against a television station. I told him that I would clean it up and he smiled. Two men approached and it was clear that they meant business. I was handed a search warrant to search my apartment. They were from the United States Attorney General's office and I was now "a person of interest." CNN, FOX and MSNBC, having been tipped in advance, covered my exit from the building. The propaganda machine was in full swing and the Council on National Policy was coming to get me. I had other things in mind and decided to visit Anarchist Angie. I really wanted fantastic Isabella, however, Angie had to do.

## Chapter Sixteen

"Rueben, how the hell are you?" I asked.

"What are you doing for dinner?" asked Rueben.

"Well, I'm waiting for the Federales to finish searching my apartment and then I'm going over to Angelina, if she's home. I'm sure you heard that I'm a person of interest. These guys are tearing my apartment apart and they have dismantled the war room. All my maps and notes have been confiscated. I'm sure they're thinking I'm planning a worldwide take-over with my Warlibs. It's just plain harassment. By the way, how are you doing with your positions?" I asked.

"Doc, it's like I told you, you're my financial Guru. Oil up, gold way up, long euro up and I'm making money shorting the S & P futures," Rueben answered.

"Great, don't shake out on the dips, things are going to get hotter with the elections coming up," I told Rueben. The Federal agents destroyed my apartment. I expected that. I called Angelina and she was extremely happy, almost giddy, at my suggestion of getting together.

"Stan, come on in," Angie said. Angelina was in the kitchen preparing dinner. I looked over her shoulder and eyed homemade sushi and pork dumplings. She advised me to make myself at home and open up a bottle of white wine, which I did. A small dining room table was set with candles and fine old grandma type Lenox dinner plates.

"Angie, what's the occasion?" I asked.

"You're becoming royalty, Stan," she shouted from the kitchen and added, "I treat my special guests with extra care. Stan, you forgot two of the most obvious members on your list," she said.

"Really, who are they?" I asked.

"Well, there are actually three. Alan Keyes was a 2000 presidential candidate and the right wing screwball Gary Bauer was a presidential candidate. They're on the Council on National Policy and in 1996 there was Vice-Presidential candidate Jack Kemp running with Robert Dole. He's on the Council as well," said Angie.

The sexual frenzy that engulfed our first two encounters was no longer present. It was more intimate, two fiends smoozing and talking politics.

"Stan, TheMultitude.org received a 'National Security Letter' demanding the names of the Avatars. Your private instant messaging will never be known but your handle FASCISTI might be disclosed," she said.

"How do you know that? I thought that the recipient of that kind of letter could not tell anyone that it was received. It's against the law," I told Angie.

"The Webmaster is a friend of mine," Angie told me. Angie came over to the table, poured a glass of wine and handed me a key with a note.

"It's a key to a safe-house and the address. If necessary, someone will be there to assist you in whatever you need, just in case the Feds close you down. We have electronic pros that can provide the necessary expertise in keeping the show going even if you aren't in the studio," she said.

"Do you know something that I don't know?" I asked.

"Stan, it's the natural progression of what is going to happen to you. You don't think they are going to let you continue, do you?" she asked.

"I guess not," I answered. The rest of the night, Angelina and I spent a wonderful evening together without sex. It was nice. I was gaining status with the Anarchists.

Five, four, three, two and one:

WARLIB: Good afternoon. By now, I'm sure most of you know that the Federal Government considers me a person of interest. Well, so do I. I am interesting. Exactly what they're looking for I don't know and I'm sure they don't either. I guess my ratings are going up. First caller, Tonya, from Long Island;

TONYA: Dr. Warlib, my comment is about one of the recent polls by Gallup. They recently offered a poll stating that Sam is thirteen points ahead of his opponent. This spread was far and away larger than all other polls. However, George Gallup, Sr., is a devout evangelical Christian and recently stated that 'the most profound purpose of polls is to see how people are responding to God.' Gallup's name is not on the list of Council members.

WARLIB: Nevertheless, your point is well taken. Would these evangelical Christian's concoct a poll that specifically enhances Sam's lead? Why, of course. Gallup, Sr., should be on the Council on National Policy. Thank you Tonya. Next caller is Michael from Colorado.

MICHAEL: My comment is about privatization, you know, that Willard Garvey guy and his National Center for Privatization, getting rid of the government and replacing it with private enterprises. There is this guy named Daya Singh Khalsa, a co-founder of Akal Security, which is run by a religious group in Espanola, New Mexico. My research indicates the following: Akal Security has a contract with the United States Marshal Service for $854,000,000.00, making it the nation's largest provider of guards for federal courts in 9 of the 12 judicial districts. A contract with the United States army for $250,000,000.00 providing security at the military bases of Fort Lewis, Fort Hood, Fort Riley, Fort Campbell and Fort Stewart and Army weapons depots at Sunny Point, North Carolina, Blue Grass, Kentucky and Anniston, Alabama. In addition, a contract with the Federal Protection Service, Great Lakes Region, for $100,000,000.00, that covers the protection of 150 Federal office buildings and offices in Minnesota, Wisconsin, Illinois and Indiana. I think if anything goes wrong, the government can deny any liability.

WARLIB: Good point. I'm going to come back to that later as I want to tie that into something else. Next caller, James from upstate New York,

JAMES: Dr. Warlib, first let me thank you for taking my call.

WARLIB: James, this isn't conservative talk radio. You, and everyone else, please don't thank me. Just go ahead, without thanking me.

JAMES: Here's a good one. It's all starting to come together for me. I see where you're going and I am on board, heart and soul. A Senate committee opened hearings on Wednesday in an attempt to untangle the financial relationship between two powerful Washington insiders, Jack Abramoff, a Republican lobbyist and Michael Scanlon, a public relations specialist and a former aide to Representative Tom Delay of Texas. These guys sold themselves to six Indian tribes as powerful influential Washington operatives whose experience and relationships would reap great benefits to their tribes. Right now, these men are under investigation by the Justice Department, other federal agencies and Congress. By the time Abramoff and Scanlon were done, the tribes were out $66,000,000.00. In addition, they were required to make huge donations to groups controlled by these men, such as Americans for Tax Reform. Abramoff appeared before the investigating committee but Scanlon did not. Abramoff took the fifth. What really got me though, were the e-mails between these two guys referring to the tribal leaders as 'morons,' 'idiots,' 'monkeys' and 'troglodytes.' The tribes got nothing but bullshit for their money. Now, HERE IS THE KICKER, Jack Abramoff is on the Council on National Policy and there is a man named Terence Scanlon on the Council and one other thing, there is a guy named Rich Scarborough on the Council. Do you know if Terence Scanlon is related to Michael Scanlon and is Rich Scarborough related to Joe Scarborough of 'Scarborough Country' on MSNBC?

WARLIB: Thank you so much James. I don't know if Terence Scanlon is related to Michael Scanlon the man under investigation or whether Joe is related to Rich Scarborough. All you Warlibs out there do your research. I'll bet dollar to donuts that they're related. These are the kind of people that make up the Council on National Policy. They found virgin ground in the evangelical Christians who are susceptible to anything. I want all of you to think about this: when you hear privatization and faith based initiatives hold on to your wallets. Can you imagine your tax dollars going out the door and in the pockets of all the faith-based programs that the Council members might have set up? The Council controls Sam. Sam controls the Treasury. Sam advocates faith-based programs. The Council has many faith-based programs. Wow.

Right now, I'm not going to take any calls. I want to talk psychology. That's my field, as many of you know. The Council on National Policy members are psychopathic narcissistic snake oil salesman. They are very manipulative and extremely dangerous. Religion is a big seller and they wrap their naked capitalistic greed within God. The reason why it works so well is because the evangelical Christians and conservatives have two personality traits running in their psyche that make them susceptible to the con job. For example, the evangelical Christians believe in something called the Rapture. At a certain point in time, God will come down and snatch them up to heaven. Can you picture that? Can you imagine that? They really believe it. I'm not kidding. When this show ends I want you to dwell on the Rapture and try to imagine what kind of person would believe such a thing. If you can imagine that, than you can easily imagine that these evangelicals would really believe that civilization would end if two men got married, or Y2K was a sign from God signaling the end of the world and Jerry Falwell claiming that 9/11 was God's retribution for America's evil ways. They really,

really, believe this shit. I quoted you the Bible and it's claim in Leviticus that homosexuality is an abomination and that homosexuals must be put to death. These people believe in the literal interpretation of the Bible and that it is the written word of God. Not following the Bible is not following God. I hope you're getting this. This is all made possible by two personality traits. One trait is a paranoid personality trait and the other is a histrionic personality trait. I'm going to read to you from the Diagnostic Service Manual, commonly referred to as the DSM, *my* Bible, the signs of paranoid and histrionic personality disorders. In so far as a histrionic personality, it states:

### Diagnostic criteria for 301.50 Histrionic Personality Disorder

A pervasive pattern of excessive emotionality and attention seeking, beginning by early adulthood and a verity of contexts, as indicated by five (or more) of the following:

(1) is uncomfortable in situations in which he or she is not the center of attention.

(2) interaction with others is often characterized by inappropriate sexually seductive or provocative behavior.

(3) displays rapidly shifting and shallow expression of emotions.

(4) consistently uses physical appearance to draw attention to self

(5) has a style of speech that is excessively impressionistic and lacking in detail

(6) shows, self-dramatization, theatricality, and exaggerated expression of emotion

(7) is suggestible, i.e., easily influenced by others or circumstances.

(8) considers relationships to be more intimate than they actually are.

### Diagnostic Features

> The essential feature of Histrionic Personality Disorder is pervasive and excessive emotionality and attention seeking behavior. This pattern begins by early

adulthood and is present in a variety of contexts. Individuals with Histrionic Personality Disorder are uncomfortable with or feel unappreciated when they are not the center of attention. Often lively and dramatic, they tend to draw attention to themselves and may initially charm new acquaintances by their enthusiasm, apparent openness, or flirtatiousness' qualities wear thin, however, as these individuals continually demand to be the center of attention. They commandeer the role of life of the party. If they are not the center of attention they may do something dramatic (e.g., make up stories, create a scene) to draw the focus of attention to themselves...Emotional expression may be shallow and rapidly shifting...They are overly concerned with impressing others by their appearance and expend an excessive amount of time, energy, and money on clothes and grooming. They may fish for compliments regarding appearance and be easily and excessively upset by a critical comment about how they look or by a photograph that they regard as unflattering.

These individuals have a style of speech that is excessively impressionistic and lacking in detail. Strong opinions are expressed with dramatic flair, but underlying reasons are usually vague and diffuse, without supporting facts and details. For example, an individual with Histrionic Personality Disorder may comment that a certain individual is a wonderful human being, but be unable to provide any specific examples of good qualities to support this position. However, their emotions often seem to be turned on and off too quickly to be deeply felt, which may lead others to accuse the individual of faking these feelings. *Individuals with Histrionic Personality Disorder have a high degree of suggestibility. Their opinions and feelings are easily influenced by others and by current fads. They may be overly trusting, especially of strong authority figures whom they see as magically solving their problems. They have a tendency to play hunches and to adopt convictions quickly.....* (Emphasis supplied)

In the section of associated features and disorders it states that people with Histrionic Personality Disorder also crave novelty, stimulation, and excitement and have a tendency to become bored with their usual routine. These individuals are often intolerant of, or frustrated by, situations that involve delayed gratification, and their actions are often directed at obtaining immediate satisfaction.

Although they often initiate a job or project with great enthusiasm, their interest may lag quickly.

## *Diagnostic criteria for 301.1 Paranoid Personality Disorder*

A. A pervasive distrust and suspiciousness of others such that their motives are interpreted as malevolent, beginning by early adulthood and present in a variety of contexts, as indicated by four or more of the following:

(1) suspects, without sufficient basis, that others are exploiting, harming or deceiving him or her.

(2) is preoccupied with unjustified doubts about the loyalty or trustworthiness of friends or associates.

(3) is reluctant to confide in others because of unwarranted fear that the information will be used maliciously against him or her.

(4) reads hidden demeaning or threatening meanings into benign remarks or events.

(5) persistently bears grudges, i.e., is unforgiving of insults, injuries, or slights.

(6) perceives attacks on his or her character or reputation that are not apparent to others and is quick to react angrily or to counterattack.

(7) has recurrent suspicions, without justification, regarding fidelity of spouse or sexual partner.

B. Does not occur exclusively during the course of Schizophrenia, a Mood Disorder with Psychotic Features, or another Psychotic Disorder and is not due to the direct physiological effects of a general medical condition.

Tonight, at the end of the show I want you to think about the psychology of the evangelical Christian and the conservative right. The Council marginalizes the liberals by making their base and conservatives paranoid and due to their histrionic nature they overly trust, especially of strong authority figures that they see as magically solving their problems. I learned a very important lesson several months ago and that is that a paranoid personality trumps a histrionic personality every time. You cannot argue with these people because they truly believe you are evil and a traitor. To beat them you have to make them more paranoid than the

Council on National Policy and you have to do this within their mindset. You have to speak their language. Think about it because tomorrow the revolution starts. It's head banging time. Before I sign off and wish you all good evening, this is from page 247 of The Rise And Fall Of The Third Reich:

"I myself was to experience how easily one is taken in by a lying and censored press and radio in a totalitarian state. Though unlike most Germans I had daily access to foreign newspapers, especially those of London, Paris and Zurich, which arrived the day after publication, and though I listened regularly to the BBC and other foreign broadcasts, my job necessitated the spending of many hours a day combing the German press, checking the German radio, conferring with Nazi officials and going to party meetings. It was surprising and sometimes consternating to find that notwithstanding the opportunities I had to learn the facts and despite one's inherent distrust of what one learned from Nazi sources, a steady diet over the years of falsifications and distortions made a certain impression on one's mind and often misled it. No one who has not lived for years in a totalitarian land can possibly conceive how difficult it is to escape the dread consequences of a regime's calculated and incessant propaganda. Often in a German home or office or sometimes in a casual conversation with a stranger in a restaurant, a beer hall, a café, I would meet with the most outlandish assertions from seemingly educated and intelligent persons. It was obvious that they were parroting some piece of nonsense they had heard on the radio or read in the newspapers. Sometimes one was tempted to say as much, but on such occasions one was met with such a stare of incredulity, such a shock of silence, as if one had blasphemed that Almighty, that one realized how useless it was to even try to make contact with a mind which had become warped and for whom the facts of life had become what Hitler and Goebbels, with their cynical disregard for truth, said they were."

# Chapter Seventeen

Five, four, three, two and one:

Good afternoon, this is Dr. Stanley Warlib and I hope everyone watched the debates last night between Sam and his opponent. I hope you studied the elements of the histrionic and paranoid personality disorders. The main characteristic of the Histrionic person is that he or she has a high degree of suggestibility. Their opinions and feelings are easily influenced by others and by current fads. They overly trust, especially of strong authority figures that they see as magically solving their problems. If Rush Limbaugh says something is true, it must be true. All those ditto heads out there are a perfect example of people with elements of a Histrionic personality. The essential feature of a Paranoid personality is a pattern of pervasive distrust and suspiciousness of others such that their motives are interpreted as malevolent. Liberals are the problem. What the Jews were to the Nazis, Liberals are to the Evangelical Conservative Christian. You are evil! We, us Warlibs, are going to use these traits against them. You can't stay in your cocoons any longer. You must come out and fight because there will be no tomorrow if Sam gets reelected and we must prepare battle plans in accordance with the two character traits that I have mentioned. Let me give you an example of what conservative talk radio did right after the debate. First, they went to where ever they go to get their talking points and then dispensed all over the airwaves that Sam's opponent stated that he wanted unilateral nuclear disarmament and during wartime, that position is suicide. Totally untrue, however, it works. Sam's opponent didn't say that Sam should disarm unilaterally. A gullible mind made more paranoid by false facts. See how it works. It's all psychological operations but us liberals have to sink down to their level and I know that's not a place you all feel comfortable. I have ideas do you have any?

Getting back to some previous items. I hope you are going out and buying products made by Proctor and Gamble. We must counter every move of the Evangelical Conservative Christian Right. Last night, I decided to promote a boycott of Coor's beer, however, others beat me to it. However, let's take the boycott to a national level. I told you that Joe Coors was a member of the Council on National Relations. Let's really get into this subject. William Coors, one of the Coor's people, claimed in a statement he made to black and Mexican-American businessmen in 1984 that 'if they thought that it was unfair that their ancestors were dragged herein chains against their will...I would urge those of you who feel that way to go back to where your ancestors came from, and you will find out that probably the greatest favor that anybody did you was to drag your ancestors over here in chains, and I mean it.' Later in the speech, in reference to Africa, Coor's said, 'they lack the intellectual capacity to succeed, and it's taking them down the tubes. You take a country like Rhodesia, where the economy was absolutely booming under white management. Now, black management is in Zimbabwe, and the economy is a disaster, in spite of the fact that there is probably ten times the motivation on the part of the citizens to make it succeed. Lack of intellectual capacity-that has got to be there.' The Coors family gave money to pro-South African apartheid groups. There are even allegations against Adolph Coors Sr.'s family friend and lawyer who owned Castle Rock, a large rock outcropping in Colorado that he lent it to the KKK for a cross burning. As if this wasn't enough, Joseph Coors helped establish the Heritage Foundation together with Paul Weyrich, a far right wing strategist. Joseph Coors chose Roger Pearson, an outspoken anti-Semite and pro-Nazi, as co-editor of the Heritage Foundation publication 'Policy Review.' Pearson is the author of a racist book called 'Race and Civilization,' which used pseudo science to falsely assert the biological inferiority of black people. Paul Weyrich has many ties to Nazi collaborators and neo-fascist organizations. The Heritage Foundation is the most influential conservative right wing think tank. On the Board of Trustees was a man named Jack Eckerd, a member f the Council on National Relations. Also on the Board of Trustees is Richard M. Scaife, Larry P. Arnn, Holland H. Holly Coors and Edwin Feulner, all members of the Council on National Relations. Would it be fair to conclude that this Council is against affirmative action and hates blacks? Paul Weyrich is considered by conservative powers as the most powerful man in American Politics.

Just as I mentioned Paul Weyrich, there was a loud explosion, the building shook, the lights went out and I was off the air. The station manager rushed into the studio and asked if I was all right. I assured him that I was but he had a concerned look on his face. I asked him what was wrong, however he refused to talk. He hurried out of the studio and went outside. There was devastation in the street. A lone white man in his thirties attempted to get into the building and was stopped by the police. He blew himself up. Three policemen lay dead with five others who stood next to the police. From the epicenter outward the damaged lessened. Beyond the dead, lied the severely injured. Beyond that group, lay the less injured. There was blood everywhere. The ambulances arrived within minutes and the E.M.T.'s and paramedics set up a triage. In all, over one hundred people were injured including the dead. The television cameras were everywhere and I knew that the bombing and I would become major news.

"Dr. Warlib, I think we have to consider cutting you off," said Michael. The station manager was visibly sickened. I had not yet seen the carnage that was outside the doors. "What do you mean you 'think' you may have to cut me off? Haven't you been listening to what I've been saying. This is a fucking war. You're watching your god damn ratings and the money coming in and I'm watching my country going down the tubes and you 'think' you may have to cut me off. Fuck you, you punk piece of shit. You're either with me or against me. I want this show to go national. Hold tight and firm. There are always casualties in war. You better stop thinking and better start knowing by tonight," I told Michael. I left the building through the back door. There were fifteen young men waiting for me including my bodyguards. I called Rueben but he didn't answer. The sounds of additional ambulances and people wailing from the pain could be heard on the other side of the block. My war had begun. I realized that there was no way out of this dark alley except to proceed to the light. I was in this war to go the distance and I realized that I couldn't expect everyone to walk with me. There would be dropouts and casualties. Michael was going to be a dropout. I couldn't blame him. As we approached the corner, one young man pushed me into a cab just as the light turned green. The rest of the group just stood there, frozen in place. The two bodyguards grabbed several kids and questioned them. It was a surrealistic scene from the rear window of the cab. Everyone in New York City was running towards the radio station building and I was fading into the obscurity of millions of people. The City was the best place to hide. The young man who sat next to me didn't say a word. He followed a specific plan. We took a cab, rode a bus, a train and then another cab ride. In the last cab he gave me a hat, fake sunglasses and a wig. At a light, he gave a twenty-dollar bill, jumped out of the cab and said "good luck." The cab driver looked in his rear view mirror and asked "whereto?" I decided to get out. I was above Central Park on 112$^{th}$ street, off of Fifth Avenue. I didn't know what to do.

"Doc, this is Rueben, where the hell are you?" he asked.

"I'm in the city, I don't want to tell you where. I'm all right," I told Rueben.

"I saw on cable the explosion and the bodies. I thought you were dead," said Rueben. "Not yet, but I guess labeling me a 'person of interest,' is not enough. They want my head. I have to get off. I'll call you later, and remember Semper Fi," I said to Rueben. "Don't worry Doc, always faithful, don't worry. By the way, oil closed over $50.00," said Rueben.

"And don't you worry about the stock market. It always goes down after Sam speaks. The powers that be wanted to reverse a trend and show support. Monday, the market will resume downward, see ya," I said. I called Rueben again and asked him to get Taz and take him to his house. He told me he would. I stood in the middle of the street, bewildered as to what to do next. I could go home, Angie's house, Rueben's house, my son Jordan's house or the safe house that Angelina told me about. I didn't want to go home or get Jordan involved. I didn't know where Rueben lived. Angie was a possibility and the safe house was only a thought.

"Michael, this is Warlib. Did you make up your mind about the show?" I asked.

"I didn't have to, we're closed down. The building is a crime scene investigation. I wouldn't come back here if I were you," he said.

"I don't intend to. Not tomorrow anyway. Would you like a tape of my show?" I asked. "What kind of smuck are you. There are dead cops and people in the street you idiot and all you want to know is about sending me a tape for the show. There are freaking body parts hanging on the building you moron," said Michael. I hung up. I took a bus down Fifth Avenue, got off at 90$^{th}$ Street and walked over to the Mykonos Diner. I walked over to the take out counter and ordered coffee. I had my head down to avoid eye contact with anyone. Angie handed me the coffee and placed packets of sugar, Sweet & Low and several napkins in the bag. She didn't say a word to me or even acknowledge my presence. I knew that she passed me a note with the napkins. The note read that the safe house was the only viable place to go to and that she would be there after work. The safe house was located in a warehouse near the Brooklyn Navy Yard. The area was composed mainly of artists that had been forced out of the Soho and Tribeca areas of New York City. A strange looking man would not draw any attention. The stranger and more "artsy" I looked, the better. I decided after walking the area to grow a real beard, mustache and don a new look. Fake thick-rimmed glasses and painters pants, splattered with oil paint would complete my new image.

The safe house was located on the fifth floor of the warehouse and had an old freight elevator for transport. Upon opening the vertical wooden gate of the elevator, a large metal door was the only entrance to the loft. It was a typical loft layout. All open except for a small bathroom. The kitchen was incorporated in the open space. A small cot was in one corner and a wireless laptop sat upon a small movable desk. There was a small pile of magazines on a table and an ultra slick plasma television was set into an exposed brick wall. Upon eyeing the television, I immediately turned on CNN to watch the news. The explosion, dead bodies, injured and Dr. Stanley Warlib were the only news available. I made the headlines in a big way. No one knew the identity of the suicide bomber. The only thing that was known was that he was white. The paranoia of foreign terrorism led all pundits and newsmen in the direction of Osama bin Ladin and Islamic

extremists. Everyone grieved for the policemen and their families. My whereabouts were a major concern, however, it did not dominate the essential thrust of the news. The first question that had to be discussed was the possibility of Islamic terrorists. My name was mentioned several times but not within the context of anyone or group trying to harm a radio talk show host. The focus of attention was Islamic terror. Several bottles of red wine sat upon a counter in the kitchen and I helped myself. Not knowing what my next move was, I settled into the sofa, watched CNN and drank wine. I heard the key in the door, looked up and watched as Angelina entered the loft. She was calm, relaxed and strode in with an air of confidence. I got Angie a glass of wine and both of us settled in to watch the continuing non-stop coverage of the news. She advised watching FOX, as that was the most right wing cable news station on the air. The slant of FOX was entirely different than the other cable stations. They were leading the bombing episode towards one inevitable conclusion. It had to be foreign terrorists. It was clear that FOX wanted no one to make the connection between the content of my show and the fact that the Council might have anything to do with it. Every other cable news show was busy gathering facts. Only FOX was drawing conclusions. Angie and I watched quietly for hours. Neither of us uttered a word. CNN interviewed Michael, the station manager to get his slant on what had happened. He was asked if the stations airing capability had been destroyed and admitted that it had not been harmed in any way. The next question was the obvious one; would the Dr. Stanley Warlib show continue the next day? Michael stated that it was possible but that he believed I had been kidnapped and tried desperately to locate my whereabouts to no avail. Angie and I looked at each other and smiled. Both of us intuitively knew that there was a play somewhere within Michael's allegation that I had been kidnapped. We both started laughing. I spilled my wine on the sofa. In true Greek fashion, Angelina threw her glass against the brick wall next to the television.
"What do you have in mind Angie?" I asked.
"What do *you* have in mind?" she responded.
"I don't know, but there's a play there, I'm sure of it," I told her. Angelina and I bandied about different scenarios for five hours until we decided upon one idea. We were going to make a tape of me sitting on a floor, blindfolded, with three men dressed as Islamic terrorists, reading from a prepared statement that I was going to be killed within three days. They explained that I was an operative of the Council on National Policy and that it was the Councils intentions to take over the oilfields of Islam and foster hatred of all Muslims as the Council believed that Islam was a bastard religion. They wanted five million dollars for my safe return.

CNN reported that the F.B.I. recovered a hand of the suicide bomber and that the hand was sent to a lab for fingerprints and blood analysis to see if a match could be found. Angelina and I decided that this opportunity was too important to screw up. We went to sleep.

## Chapter Eighteen

We set the alarm for 11:00 a.m. and took a shower together. We decided that the key to this entire plan lie within a short statement that I would be forced to read. My job was to prepare a short speech and Angie went to Atlantic Avenue to get three Middle Eastern men to act as terrorists. She was prepared to offer $1,000.00 to each man for three minutes of work. As they would be masked there would be no element of risk to them. The most important thing was to prevent them from knowing where the safe house was. I felt secure in letting Angelina take care of the details, whatever they might be. I sat at the laptop and prepared a hostage speech trying to incorporate and implicate as many names of the Council as I could. The idea was to get the entire world to focus on the vast right wing conspiracy. Angelina and I wanted to get the cable news networks to do investigative journalism. It was a great opportunity that I wasn't going to blow. In addition, other schemes started to formulate in my mind. I was creating my own news. The most difficult writing is synopsis writing. I had to ensnare as many people and organizations in the shortest amount of time. At least one hundred drafts were written and deleted. Angelina came back and told me that arrangements had been made for a video. I told her that I was having trouble writing a short piece that sounded realistic. I continued to work on my "forced speech" until Angie came over and told me to wrap it up. I had ten minutes to decide on what to say. We had to leave to go to a studio for filming. "Get moving Warlib," she shouted. Five minutes passed and I typed a short paragraph, which was nothing more than ten sentences from various ideas that I had written. Angie and I left the loft and headed up the East River Drive to the Bronx. She wanted to film as far away from the safe house as possible. We drove to another warehouse in the south Bronx and met the three actor terrorists at the front door. We all shook hands. These young men couldn't care less what we were doing. Angie and I were two crazy Americans with money. Whatever we wanted was fine with them, especially since they were going to be in full terrorist garb and unrecognizable. Angelina set up two video cameras, one for digital and one for VHS format. The young Arab men brought with them ski masks, two rifles and a large banner that was taped to a wall. Angie explained to me that she was going to play a terrorist role and that at the end of my speech, she was going to turn me around, slit my shirt open with a razor and pretend to slash my back several times with the razor. She had pig's blood in a little bag that she would release with each slash. The young Arab men and Angelina took their places in front of the banner and I was placed on the floor in front of them blindfolded. The cameras started to roll.

One Arab man in the center, the pretend leader, got into his part and said something in Arabic, which I didn't understand. He was shouting and raising his voice in anger. I was sure that CNN would explain to me what the kid was saying when I saw my own tape on cable news. At the end of the speech, a different Arab kid came over to me and pushed me with the rifle.

"My name is Dr. Stanley Warlib. The terrorists behind me think that I am part of a plot to destroy Islam. They believe that Sam does not run America. They believe that there is a shadow government. They believe that James Dobson, Tim LeHaye, Paul Weyrich, Coors, Richard Scaife, Richard Viguerie and the new Messiah Sun Myung Moon run America. To our Christian brothers who walk in peace and love with Jesus, please go to the web sites of watch.pair. Com, seekgod.com and cephasministry.com. Please, please help me." At the conclusion, Angie came over kicked me in the side, which caused me to topple over. She pulled me up by the hair with my back facing the camera. She slit my shirt open and with the blade secured between her thumb and pointer finger pretended to slash my back six times. With each slash she let pig blood loose. On the second slash she leaned over and whispered in my ear to scream in pain. I complied. At the end of the scene I lied on the floor in blood. Angie stopped the recording and we all looked at each other. Angelina hooked up the digital video camera to a laptop and all of us stood around the screen. After the initial screening, we all looked at each other in disbelief. It was a very realistic video.
"Next time, don't kick me so hard," I said to Angelina.
"Baby," she said. "Is that the best you could come up with?" she asked.
"Those names are the biggest. They'll lead to others," I told her.
"Poor Stanley, very poor," said Angelina. The young men left immediately after the video and told Angie that they were available anytime. Angie and I headed back to the loft. Angie wanted to review the video a hundred times before releasing it. If necessary, she was going to edit it on her laptop. Arriving at the loft, I discovered an entire new wardrobe had been left on the sofa. It looked as if someone had fun at a second hand store. Angie spent the entire afternoon, reviewing the video as I scanned the news for further developments. Every time I envisioned the airing of the video, I smiled with gratitude at grabbing the opportunity to make things happen. Every channel focused on my possible abduction or kidnapping and not on the content of my show. Prior to this event, I had notoriety, however, it was localized and stayed mainly within the liberal community.
"Stanley, what the hell were those websites watch.pair, seekgod and cephasministries that you mentioned in the video?" asked Angie. She wanted to edit them

out. I looked at the video and that line looked out of place. I told Angie that I wasn't averse to deleting the line if the deletion wouldn't compromise the video. "Angie, those two web-sites are run by dedicated Christians who are more than suspicious of the Council. They view the Council as wolves in sheep clothing and false prophets. Their research is nothing short of astounding," I said.
"So, you want people to visit the web-sites, is that it?" she asked.
"Yes, that's exactly it," I answered.
"Stan, will people be drawn to those websites if they Google the names that you mentioned?" she asked.
"Yes, absolutely," I answered.
"They're out," she said. Angie edited the video and burned a hundred copies. The video lasted 32 seconds and wasn't gory. It was a perfect video sound bite with just enough blood to allow the video to be seen in its entirety. I was convinced that it would be aired around the world. Angelina decided to have ten copies of the video hand delivered to news organizations in New York, 20 copies to be sent overnight to various organizations and the balance were to be mailed by regular post.
"Angie, what do you think of my pleading at the end?" I asked.
"It was perfect Stan, just perfect," she answered. The coverage had an obvious dramatic progression. The question around the world, thanks to the light speed of modern technology was whether Islamic terrorists struck again in the heart on New York City and was Dr. Stanley Warlib the first American to be abducted on home soil by terrorists. To say that the media ran with this story was an understatement. The horror of being abducted by extremists in America was the best dramatic story for a paranoid nation. The story had legs. Angie and I discussed the timing of the release and decided that the best course of action was to first place phone calls to CNN and MSNBC claiming that Dr. Warlib was, indeed, a prisoner of some obscure Islamic terrorist cell located in New York City. Neither Angelina nor I had any idea of the magnitude that this fictitious event would command of the media. It would be in retrospect that we grasped its significance. Angelina went downstairs and took a cab to Manhattan and placed a call to the local site of CNN. In her best Arabic imitation, she told the man at the news desk that Dr. Warlib was a hostage and would be beheaded. By the time she arrived at the loft, CNN had aired a breaking news segment about the call and my abduction. At this point in time, the media aired only suppositions and opinions offered by their respective pundits. Fiction was about to become reality. I had only one concern. If the media didn't take the bait or follow up on the leads, my best shot was over. It would be a dead balloon that wouldn't stop the evangelical

Christian conservative movement from taking back America for Christ and bringing the glory of the Kingdom of God to America. I decided that since it was a fortuitous event from the get-go, to proceed anyway. If this didn't work there would be other opportunities. At the minimum, it would inform millions of people that I didn't reach with my radio show. CNN interviewed the station manager a second time. However, this time Michael just wanted his Stanley Warlib found safe and back on the air. The punk probably received a million calls from advertisers filling his corporate coffers. He needed me and I didn't need him. Money makes fast friends.

I sat at the laptop cruising the headlines on Google news. The market was up for a second straight day. I was sure Rueben was starting to question my judgment. The conservatives were going nuts because new polls indicated that Sam's opponent was dead even in the polls or slightly ahead. The evangelical conservative Christians were beside themselves promoting the absolute end of America if Sam's opponent got elected. Laura Ingraham of conservative talk radio was ragging on Oprah Winfrey and four of the Hollywood types that she had as guests. I could hear the hysteria starting to form.

"Angie, I think if Sam goes down in the polls he's going to pull some shit, like have some operatives blow something up. These guys will stop at nothing I tell you, absolutely nothing. Nothing will stand in the way of the Kingdom of Christ coming back to America," I told Angie.

"I agree," Angelina yelled back. Angie was thirty feet away making coffee in the kitchen. I stopped Googling and looked at Angelina. I wondered what she was all about. She had a certain ease about her that was fascinating. Nothing threw her. We went from insane sex to fake videos and nothing threw her. Angie brought coffee over to the laptop and sat on my lap.

"How about some nooky?" she asked.

"Give me a couple of minutes," I said.

"What are you researching?" she asked.

"When you send the video to CNN, I can't wait until they read the name of Paul Weyrich. This guy is considered the architect and mainstay of the conservative revolution. He's calling for 'reclaiming the culture' and for a 'second revolution,'" I told Angie. "Yeah, o.k. but what is that website on the screen?" she asked. It's one of those true Christian web sites that I visit periodically to get information and check up on what the sheep in wolves clothing are doing. Let me read you this one long statement from the website," I said. Angelina got up from my lap and went over to the sofa. "All right, you can read this one statement but then it's time for some love," she said. "No problem," I said to Angelina and started to read:

### Fascist Connection

"Paul Weyrich is a co-founder of the Free Congress Foundation. A look at the inflammatory, extremist rhetoric with racial and Inquisitorial overtones on the Free Congress Foundation web site should alarm Christians as to Weyrich real intent:

### The Next Revolution

'Are we are on the verge of a second American Revolution? In the old Soviet Union, the government seemed all-powerful-until one day it fell.'

'Next Revolution is one of the most radical-and most-popular-programs on America's voice. Each week, hosts Bill Lind and Brad Keena say what most people are thinking but are often afraid to say: that the cultural Marxism of Political Correctness is destroying our country, that multicultural nations break apart in civil war and that uncontrolled immigration and rising crime are turning America into a Third World nation. They ask the forbidden questions: is real reform still possible, or will a new Revolution be necessary to restore America's traditional-and very successful culture? Is the United States government still a legitimate government? Is 'racism' the real problem or do cries of racism arise as a result of bad behavior by minority groups?'

Since posting our expose, the promotional for The Next Revolution has been removed on the new Free Congress Foundation web site. On the home page, About FCF states, 'Each week, you can join us for Next Revolution, the show dedicated to fighting multi-culturalism and political correctness.' However, the program is not listed and no information given on the TV programs page to which the visitor is referred.

After I finished reading the article to Angie, she raised one eyebrow and said, "you promised." We made love on the sofa, but I was too jacked up to be into it and she knew it. It wasn't bad sex but it wasn't good sex. I think Angie expected a marathon, which I knew wasn't going to happen. I apologized over and over, while Angelina said "next time," over and over. I felt as if I was a man with a mission and couldn't get my head into anything else. Angie was about to drop off a video to CNN, which I thought would change the world and she wanted to make love. My brain was pre-occupied.

Angelina left the loft to go to a messenger service to hand deliver the hostage videos that we had made. My possible abduction was still front page and I was sure that the video was going to be played a thousand times. I couldn't wait for the listening audience to research the names that I had mentioned. It was going to be a blast. I recalled seeing an article about a conservative film festival that had opened. The evangelical Christian conservatives owned the radio airwaves with their propaganda and now they were going after film. The film festival was set up by Jim and Ellen Hubbard and promoted by KLIF AM radio and sponsored by WorldNetDaily.com, their propaganda Internet news dispenser. I had heard the name mentioned many times. The radio station was owned by Salem Communications that was owned by Epperson and Atsinger, who both sat on the Council on National Policy. WorldNetDaily.com exclusively sponsored it and the question I asked myself was who owned WorldNetDaily.com. Research indicated that WorldNetDaily.com was a spin off from a non-profit Western Journalism Foundation that retained control of 60% of WorldNetDaily.com and that the balance was owned by 75 secret investors. The question then became who owned or controlled Western Journalism and that was a man named Joseph Farah. I checked the names on my Council list and Joseph Farah was listed as a member, another member of the Council on National Policy that created a seamless web of interlocking organizations supporting and organizing the Council's policy. These guys were the equivalent of the Japanese Koretzu. What a fucking mess this was. Every path led to the Council and the Council was taking Hitler's path. Instead of the glorification of the Nazi state it was the glorification of the Kingdom of God and that was a much easier sell. Who could be against God? Only an atheist like me, I thought. I checked CNN and MSNBC. There was no coverage of Stanley Warlib. Angelina came back from her task and gave me a kiss on the cheek. She looked at me and I could tell she was wondering if we wouldn't have a go at making love again. After researching the WorldNetDaily.com part of the puzzle I felt that I had put enough of the puzzle together for the day. I did not disappoint Angelina nor did she disappoint me. Two hours later, we emerged from our passion drenched in sweat and utterly exhausted. Both of us completely ignored the cable news networks and the possibility that they might be airing the hostage video.

CNN had received the video. We don't know how many times it had been aired but I was hoping that there were a million Warlibs out there researching the names contained in the video. What happened next was unexpected, however, I should have considered the possibility. The announcer put his finger to his ear, the breaking news banner appeared and the announcer spoke. Six foreign Islamic extremists had blown up a gas tanker in the Gulf of Mexico. The Coast Guard was in hot pursuit and the extremists were on the run. "Fuck, Angie, we've been trumped. I should have known that they would get me off the news. Fuck, Fuck and double fuck," I said. Throughout the night, every news channel covered the terrorist gas tanker explosion and my hostage taking was off the radar screen. Once again, I had no voice. I was nailed to the inside of Sam's skull with a duct-taped mouth. I was depressed. I waved Angelina off every time she advanced towards me. I sat alone on the windowsill staring at the lights on the Brooklyn Bridge. Angie went to sleep at 1:00 a.m. The lights formed a necklace on the bridge that blurred into one bright line, burning its image in my mind, until the window was filled with bright light.

"Sam, you're making my angry. You will incur my wrath. I have given you four hurricanes, three earthquakes and a volcano eruption within one month. You must win reelection to bring the glory and the Kingdom of God to America," the voice said. I was listening to God speak to Sam once again. I couldn't believe it. It became clear that if Sam lost the next two debates and substantially lost ground in the polls, an attack was possible to divert attention. I was renewed with energy to complete my task. As I prepared to leave the window seat, a flash of bright light appeared and a force pushed me back down. I could feel the presence of a forceful hand on my shoulder.

"And you...you must stop Sam at all costs. Do not fail me in my time of need," the voice said. The voice was sending mixed messages. Sam must win and I must defeat him. I walked over to the bed that Angie slept in and got on top of her. Angelina opened her eyes, smiled and said quietly, "hmmm."

By morning, the Dr. Warlib hostage terror tape was not on any channel. Neither cable nor broadcast news mentioned anything about Dr. Warlib. I called the station several times. A tape recording announced that the station was closed for several days and would re-open shortly.

"What's next?" Angie asked.

"I have no idea Angelina. I'll continue calling the station and I'll try getting in touch with Rueben. Do you have any ideas?" I asked.

"Yeah, I do. Go on the Internet and go to a liberal chat room and start your program on that medium," she said.

"That's not a bad idea, Angie. Not a bad idea at all," I said.

"Don't do it from here. Put on a disguise and go the library," she said.

"Of course," I answered. I prepared information for my chat room dialogue, got into a disguise and left for the library. I searched the Internet for a liberal chat room and found one. I introduced myself to the group and requested that they e-mail their friends immediately to gather a larger audience. Several of the chat room members didn't believe that it was I and I did everything to convince the skeptics that I was who I claimed to be. Most, if not all of the chat room members had been listeners of my show. I hit the refresh button every minute and followed the number of chat room members who entered the room. Within ten minutes, over nine thousand people had entered the room.

"Good afternoon, this is Dr. Stanley Warlib. I cannot speak to you from my radio station as it has been bombed. By now, I am sure many of you know the story. I have been kidnapped and Islamic terrorists are holding me. However, they have permitted me to use the Internet connection that they have. Apparently," I said when another chat room guest cut me short and wrote, "this is all bullshit, terrorists letting you use the Internet, come on Dr. Warlib, or who ever this is. Really, I'm not a moron," the anonymous writer wrote. I froze up, thought for a minute and abandoned the board. Even I wouldn't believe the bullshit that I just wrote. Either, extremists were holding me or not. I stopped writing and read the subsequent posts. No damage was done, as it was the collective opinion of the chat room that I was an imposter trying to gain fame by faking an impersonation. Angie's idea seemed like a good one at the time, unfortunately it didn't work out that way. Upon arriving at the loft, I spotted Angie sitting at the laptop and she shrugged her shoulders. "Nothing ventured, nothing gained," she said. "I agree," I told her. I decided to call Michael at the radio station.

"Michael, this is Stan Warlib," I said.

"Warlib, where the hell have you been? You have a show to do," said Michael. The station had received thousands of calls from listeners demanding a return of the radio program and fifty calls from corporate sponsors, especially gay and lesbian corporate sponsors. It appeared that the body parts that hung outside Michael's building which upset him was trumped by the pure greed of money. The green-eyed monster had captured Michael. I explained to Michael that I escaped from my captors somewhere in the Bronx.

"That should play well on CNN. I'll arrange an interview," he said.

"No problem," I answered. Angie gave me an o.k. sign with her fingers. The safe house was no longer needed and I told Angie that I would be sleeping at my apartment. She agreed and our Bonnie & Clyde Anarchist routine came to an end but not without a whole lot of sex.

## CHAPTER NINETEEN

Five, four, three, two and one: Good afternoon everyone, this is Dr. Stanley Warlib. I would appreciate calls that did not bring up my capture and abduction. We have work to do. I escaped last night during a lull. The razor slashes on my back are healing. This program last left off talking about Paul Weyrich, Coors and some others. I want to pick up on those names, as I never completed my monologue. I am going to read to you information I found on the Internet. The first is about Paul Weyrich. The second is about Roger Pearson.

"Paul Weyrich is considered by conservative Powers That Be as the most powerful man in American politics today. Weyrich allegedly founded the immensely influential conservative think tank, Heritage Foundation, in 1973 with funding from Joseph Coors of the Coors beer empire and Richard Mellon-Scaife, heir of the Carnegie-Mellon fortune.

Over the past 25 years, private foundations such as Pew Charitable Trust, which also funded many GOALS 2000 initiatives, have also funded Heritage. William Greider's bestseller, *Who Will Tell the People: The Betrayal of American Democracy* reveals other benefactors: "Not withstanding its role as 'populist' spokesman, Weyrich's organization, for instance, has received grants from Amoco, General Motors, Chase Manhattan Bank [David Rockefeller] and right-wing foundations like Olin and Bradley."

Paul Weyrich served as President of Heritage Foundation until 1974 when he founded the Committee for the Survival of a Free Congress (which he heads today as the Free Congress Foundation). Heritage Foundation guided the Reagan administration during its period of transition and Joe Coors served in the President's "Kitchen Cabinet." During its first year, the Reagan administration adopted fully two-thirds of the recommendations of Heritage's *Mandate for Leadership: Policy Management in a Conservative Administration*.

John Saloma's *Ominous Politics* refers to Heritage as a "shadow government" noting that "[Heritage President] (Edwin) Feulner also served on the Reagan transition executive committee (fourteen other Heritage staff and board members also had transition appointments), but declined to join the administration."

A 1995 Wall Street Journal article observed the formidable influence of the Heritage Foundation on government policies since the Reagan era:

"WASHINGTON—With the Republicans' rise to control Congress, think-tank power in the nation's capital has shifted to the right. And no policy shop has more clout than the conservative Heritage Foundation.

"When GOP congressional staffers met in June with conservative leaders to help map current legislative efforts to cut federal funding for left-leaning advocacy groups, the closed-door meeting took place at Heritage headquarters. The group's involvement wasn't unusual. 'Heritage is without question the most far-reaching conservative organization in the country in the war of ideas.' House Speaker Newt Gingrich said early this year.

"Think tanks have long churned out studies that have wound up in official policy proposals. During Democratic times of power, the more liberal Brookings Institution has been a leading player here. Now, the 21-year-old Heritage Foundation, which rose to prominence in the Reagan years, is taking academic involvement to a new level.

"Over the first 100 days of the current GOP Congress, Heritage scholars testified before lawmakers 40 times—more than any other organization, Hill staffers say. Congressional members and staff credit its scholars as key architects of the House-passed welfare-overhaul plan and with inspiring some provisions in the GOP balanced-budget plan. 'They talk to me sometimes 12 times a week,' said Heritage budget analyst Scott Hodge earlier this year, explaining his ties to the staff of the House Budget Committee. 'We—I mean House members—are putting together a final list of cuts.'"

### Fascist Connection

Paul Weyrich—considered the architect and mainstay of the conservative revolution—calls for "reclaiming the culture" and a "second American Revolution." A look at the inflammatory, extremist rhetoric with racial and Inquisitorial overtones on the <u>Free Congress Foundation</u> web site should alarm Christians as to Weyrich's real intent:

### THE NEXT REVOLUTION

"Are we on the verge of a second American Revolution? In the old Soviet Union, the government seemed all-powerful—until one day it fell.

"Next Revolution is one of the most radical—and most popular—programs on America's Voice. Each week, hosts Bill Lind and Brad Keena say what people are thinking but are often afraid to say: that the cultural Marxism of Political Correctness is destroying our country, that "multicultural" nations break apart in civil war, and that uncontrolled immigration and rising crime are turning America into a Third World nation. They ask the "forbidden" questions: is real reform still possible, or will a new Revolution be necessary to restore America's traditional—and very successful—culture? Is the United States Government still a legitimate government? Is "racism" the real problem or do cries of racism arise as a result of bad behavior by minority groups?"

## VICTORIA

"Can America in fact go the way of Bosnia? Is 'Civil War II' part of our future? Is that what it will take to rescue our culture? Bill Lind is now working to answer these questions in a book-length version of Victoria—a novel in the form of a 'future memoir' that will rock and shock the 'Politically Correct' Establishment…

"She was not a particularly bad bishop. She was, in fact, quite typical of Episcopal bishops of the first quarter of the 21st-century—agnostic, compulsively political and radical, and given to placing a small idol of Isis on the altar when she said the Communion service. By 2037, when she was tried, convicted and burned for heresy, she had outlived her era. By that time only a handful of Episcopalians still recognized female clergy, and it would have been easy enough to let the old fool rant out her final years in obscurity. But we are a people who do our duty.

"I well remember the crowd that gathered for the execution—solemn, but not sad, relieved that at last, after so many years of humiliation, the majority had taken back the culture. Civilization had recovered its nerve. The flames that soared above the lawn before the Maine statehouse that August afternoon were, as the bishopess herself might have said, liberating."

[Note: Since posting our expose, the promotional for *The Next Revolution* has been removed on the new Free Congress Foundation web site. On the home page, About FCF states, "Each week, you can join us for "Next Revolution," the show dedicated to fighting multi-culturalism and political correctness." However, the program is not listed and no information given on the TV Programs page to which the visitor is referred.]

Paul Weyrich is a Melkite Greek Catholic whose personal background abounds with ties to Nazi collaborators and neo-fascist organizations. These well-documented facts do not seem to concern the U.S. Government, whose agencies have also been infiltrated by post World War II Nazi émigrés. [For documentation of the CIA-Nazi connection, please see the Watch Unto Prayer report .

In the 1970s, Weyrich and Coors made appointments and set up political contacts on Capitol Hill for Franz Joseph Strauss, Bavarian head of state who helped émigré Nazi collaborators. Another fascist, Roger Pearson, writer and organizer for the Nazi Northern League of northern Europe, joined the editorial board of *Policy Review*, the monthly Heritage publication in 1977. *The Coors Connection* notes in a caption under an illustration of Pearson's *Eugenics And Race*: "Dr. Roger Pearson's racialist theories are circulated worldwide by neo-Nazi and white supremacist organizations."

Pearson was brought to the U.S. in 1965 by Willis Carto, founder of the neo-fascist Institute for Historical Review (which denies the Holocaust) and the anti-Semitic Liberty Lobby, which publishes the weekly Spotlight newspaper. Pearson left Heritage after a Washington Post expose of the racist/fascist orientation of the World Anti-Communist League. Pearson chaired the American branch, the Council on American Affairs from 1975-80, as well as the WACL from 1978-79. The following brief mention of Roger Pearson on the British Eugenics Society web site is an indicator of his abiding contribution to pure racial breeding:

> "Hans K. Gunther, a Nazi anthropologist and eugenicist...was assisted by Roger Pearson of the Eugenics Society, an important figure on the racist journal, Mankind Quarterly...Mankind Quarterly is a racist journal still pumping out venom in 1994, still influenced by Roger Pearson. Josef Mengele's co-researcher at Auschwitz, Von Verschuer, was on the editorial advisory board of this journal before his death in 1970."

Paul Weyrich also sponsored and currently works closely with Laszlo Pasztor, a convicted Austrian Nazi-collaborator whose Coalitions of the Americas is housed as a subsidiary in the Free Congress Foundation, the political arm of Heritage Foundation. Martin Lee's book, *The Beast Reawakens*, refers to Pasztor as Weyrich's right hand man:

> "In addition to homegrown agitators who dredged up anti-Semitic motifs that harkened back to the 1930s, some countries had to contend with groups that were led or supported by pro fascist exiles who repatriated from the West where they had carried on as vocal anti-Communists during the Cold War, often with CIA support. The Free Congress Foundation, founded by American far right strategist Paul Weyrich, became active in eastern European politics after the Cold War. Figuring prominently in this effort was Weyrich's right-hand man, Laszlo Pasztor, a former leader of the pro-Nazi

Arrow Cross organization in Hungary, which had collaborated with Hitler's Reich. After serving two years in prison for his Arrow Cross activities, Pasztor found his way to the United States, where he was instrumental in establishing the ethnic-outreach arm of the Republican national Committee."

A recent SCOOP newsletter from the Heritage related National Center for Public Policy Research mentions foreign and defense policy meetings chaired by Laszlo Pasztor. NCPPR is a conservative communications and research foundation which also sponsors Wednesday luncheons frequently chaired by Weyrich and Pasztor."

I want you to think about what I have just read to you and I would like to thank the internet website for their research. Moving along let me read to you an article that appeared in the Wall Street Journal about Roger Pearson. This is a good one.

## RACIAL PURIST USES REAGAN PLUG

By Rich Jaroslovsky
Wall Street Journal
Sept. 28, 1984

**WASHINGTON**—Roger Pearson, a publisher of politically conservative academic journals here, has something other publishers would envy; a glowing letter of praise from Ronald Reagan.

Plenty of well-known conservatives have written for Mr. Pearson's publications, but his kudos from the most famous conservative of all stands out. Mr. Pearson has used reproductions of his 1982 letter—praising "your substantial contributions to promoting and upholding those ideals and principles he (sic!) values at home and abroad"—in bulk mailings to solicit sales and subscriptions.

Those who have received copies of the presidential letter might be surprised to learn that Mr. Pearson, a British-born anthropologist, has spent much of his career advancing the theory that the "purity" of the white race is endangered by "inferior" genetic stock. He has warned that people of European descent may be "annihilated as a species" unless they act to reserve their "racial identity," and he currently receives funds from a controversial foundation dedicated to "racial betterment."

The 57-year-old Mr. Pearson even draws harsh attacks from other elements of the hard right, members of which fear he may discredit their goals. He resigned from the World Anti-Communist League, a federation he once headed, after some of its chapters charged that he encouraged the membership of European and Latin American groups with Nazi or neo-Nazi ties. Former Maj. John Singlaub, who now heads the league's U.S. affiliate, calls Mr. Pearson an "embarrassment" who is "not at all welcome in any activity" of the group.

"The White House ought to repudiate this bird," says Justin Finger, civil-rights director of the Anti-Defamation League of B'nai B'rith, the Jewish organization. Mr. Finger complained to the White House when he learned of the letter this summer, but he says he hasn't received any response.

## Composed by Pearson Associate

Though the letter bore Mr. Reagan's signature, it was actually composed by a Pearson associate who had joined the White House staff. There isn't any evidence that the president knows Mr. Pearson, and Mr. Reagan's public statements on race don't bear any resemblance to Mr. Pearson's writings. But the incident shows how a highly ideological presidency—conservative or liberal—can be used by well-connected outside activities (sic!) to gain respectability.

What's more, the White House isn't disavowing the letter, or repudiating Mr. Pearson, although it wants him to stop using the letter to sell subscriptions to two journals he currently publishes, the Mankind Quarterly and The Journal of Social, Political and Economic Studies. Anson Franklin, an assistant presidential press secretary, says: "The president has long-held views opposing racial discrimination in any form, and he would never condone anything to the contrary. But that's a general statement; I'm not addressing Dr. Pearson specifically."

The White House says the letter was written after Mr. Pearson sent to the president a copy of his journals that didn't espouse his controversial racial views. Not all such gifts are answered so glowingly, but in this case Mr. Pearson had a champion in Robert Schuettinger, then a mid-level White House official and currently in the Defense Department.

Mr. Schuettinger says he has known Mr. Pearson for several years and is on the editorial board of one of Mr. Pearson's publications. He concedes he wasn't aware of all of Mr. Pearson's past activities but says "there is absolutely no valid…to accuse him of racism," though Mr. Pearson may have been "a little naive" in his associations.

In two lengthy interviews, the affable Mr. Pearson largely refuses to comment on the record about his activities, though he doesn't dispute the central elements of this account of them. But he insists, "I'm not ashamed of anything I've said or written."

## 'Breeding Ideal Types'

Among those writings is an old article calling for the use of artificial insemination to preserve "pure healthy stock" and allow "breeding back the 'ideal' types." The 1958 article, in a magazine Mr. Pearson founded called Northern World, also warned of a "terrible outcome" should such a program of genetic selection "fall into the hands of the cosmopolites or one-worlders, or any who wish to see our race and our heritage destroyed.

Other Pearson writings appeared in Western Destiny, a magazine published by the far right, anti-Semitic Liberty Lobby. Mr. Pearson edited Western Destiny briefly in the mid-1960s and wrote several books on race and eugenics that were issued by Liberty Lobby's publishing arm. These pamphlets are still sold by the National Socialist White People's Party, the Arlington, Va.-based American Nazi group; Mr. Pearson says he doesn't have any connection that group.

After breaking with Liberty Lobby Leader Willis Carto in a personal dispute, Mr. Pearson began moving more into the conservative mainstream, holding academic posts at several small colleges and authorizing (sic! authoring?) an anthropology textbook. In 1977, he was on the original board of editors of Policy Review, a journal published by the Heritage Foundation, a mainstream conservative think tank. Knowledgeable sources say he was asked to resign when Heritage officials learned of his background.

Mr. Pearson currently runs a tax-exempt organization called the Council on Social and Economic Studies out of a three-room suite in a downtown Washington apartment building. Besides his publishing income, he acknowledges that he also receives money from the Pioneer Fund, a controversial New York-based trust fund dedicated to "racial betterment." The fund also has supported the work of psychologist William Shockley, who holds views on race and heredity similar to Mr. Pearson's.

Mr. Pearson's current publications, which generally downplay his racial views, boast contributions from some eminently respectable conservative political figures. Spokesmen for several of Mr. Pearson's contributors say they weren't aware of his background when they submitted articles.

"Generally, the conservatives are so concerned with conspiracies on the left that they don't realize when they may be part of a conspiracy on the right," asserts John Rees, a contributing editor of the John Birch Society's magazine and a harsh critic of Mr. Pearson.

You have to wonder exactly where the Council on National Policy is going, don't you? Is this the Nazi regime resurrected? After all, Coors, Pearson and Weyrich are bedfellows. I don't know what to make out of all this. First caller is, Roberta from Brooklyn, New York:

ROBERTA: Dr. Warlib, good afternoon and I'm glad you're feeling fine. I have been connecting the names of the people and organizations that you have mentioned and I would like to post it on your website. It's all starting to come together.

WARLIB: Thank you Roberta for your diligence in keeping track of this hornet's nest. Your efforts are most welcome and I would ask all of you out there to start doing research and write me e-mails. This is a national liberal effort. You are all W A R L I BS. Roberta; send us your chart, as an e-mail attachment and I'll put it on our web site and thanks for calling. Next caller is Steve from Cleveland.

STEVE: Doc, I'm real happy to hear you once again and to hear that you are all right. I have been doing my research and I'm coming up with a Sun Myung Moon connection. The connection is real heavy and you don't read about this in the paper or hear about it on the national media.

WARLIB: Steve, you're exactly right. I too have been finding connections but let's leave that for another time. Please, I'm not putting you off; however, let's leave it for another occasion. I want everyone to check out how many authors in the stable of Regnery Press has formally worked for the Washington Times, the conservative newspaper in Washington, D.C. owned by Moon's Unification Church. In addition, I want everyone to start researching the connections between Sam's faith based initiatives that Sam set up by Executive order and the number of Moonie organizations that are receiving money from OUR federal government. Remember that's your tax dollars that are being spent. We will pick up these topics next week. In the interim, please check out the connections and let's go after them. That's all the time we have. Good night.

Michael grabbed me when I exited the studio. He shook my hand and apologized for being so nasty. Syndication rights to my show were underway and he had 50 stations lined up throughout the United States. Michael was making millions and I decided to negotiate for a new contract. "Another time," said Michael. "Next week," I demanded and Michael agreed. There was a crowd outside the building. I shook as many hands as I could as I made my way to the street. One sign caught my eye. It read: "Warlib is a fraud. No abduction. No wounds." I arrived at my apartment by cab and waiting for me was Angelina and Rueben. Taz ran towards me when he noticed me exiting from the cab.

I explained to Angelina that Rueben was my Semper Fi buddy and that there were no secrets between us. "Except the Multitude," I whispered in her ear as we entered my apartment. Rueben went immediately to the kitchen and started to prepare dinner. He called everyone over for a shot of Tequila. As we raised our glasses he said, "to long oil." Angie said "to life," and I said to "talk radio." We all laughed. Rueben started the grill. I pulled Angelina aside and kissed her. I hoped that she was not another Elicia. We formed a bond in our war and I felt that Angie was the real deal. After several hours, all of us were drunk and telling stories. Angie and I did not tell Rueben about our terrorist make believe adventure. I told Rueben to maintain his position in long oil and not to worry about the stock market. It was fourth quarter window dressing and that Wall Street felt compelled to pump up the market for Sam. The street had a vested interest in keeping Sam in office. I told Rueben that I wanted to talk to Angelina privately. He assumed that I was going to get a quickie and I left him alone with that assumption. I pulled Angelina to the bathroom and gave her a razor blade. I instructed her to make slashes across my back with the blade and asked her not to go too deep to require stitches. Angelina made three perfect slashes and the fourth one went too deep. Blood was everywhere. I didn't want to go to the hospital. Angelina had to ask Rueben for assistance. A decision was made to do the stitching at home and Rueben called a doctor friend and asked for sutures, no questions asked. By the time Rueben arrived, Angie had controlled the bleeding from the three slashes and held the fourth slash closed with her hands as best as she could. Angelina grabbed the thread from Rueben, threaded the needle that his doctor friend gave him and proceeded to stitch me up. I was never so thankful for Tequila as during those five minutes. The pain was bearable although I winced with each stitch. "Rueben, I know this episode is going to force you to call Dr. P., but do whatever you feel a need to do," I told him. Rueben knew that the video was faked. He felt a certain bond between Angelina and himself because of her dedication and no questions asked policy with me. After she stitched me up, Angelina was in the Semper Fi buddy club. Always faithful and no questions asked! Michael called and advised me that he arranged an interview with CNN for the Cross Fire show. He told me that we made it to the big time. I became the station's most prized asset. The interview was scheduled in the New York office of CNN after my afternoon show. The evening ended. I needed strong pain medication to go to sleep. Angie curled up within the fetal position that I created for her and I held her tight within my arms. Exactly what her game was I didn't know.

Three, two and one:
"Good afternoon, this is Dr. Stanley Warlib. I'm not going to take too many calls today as I want to raise another issue with my listeners. Once I feel we're all on the same page, we'll open up the lines for callers. The question today is, how does Sam and his buddies make money? I have been thinking about this issue for a long time and I think I came up with their modus operandi and what's really interesting is that it is perfectly legal. It is a beautiful seamless transfer of money from you the taxpayer to the government and then back to his military and religious buddies. It works perfectly and it's costing you billions of dollars. I don't have all the details, however, I do have the framework and I need your help in flushing out the details. Hold on, my producer is giving me a message. He says that I should finish our plan for attack, the psychological operations that I discussed the other day. Good point. In the tumult, the bombing and my capture, I completely forgot about the subject matter of the last show. Let's follow that up today. If you remember, I told you that a histrionic person is highly suggestible and a paranoid person is suspicious. We must separate the head, the Council on National Policy from the body, the vast collective of evangelical Christians. Instead of making the body afraid of liberals, we must make them afraid of the Council. The best way to do this is to make the Council appear as a wolf in sheep's clothing and towards that end we must direct all our Christian friends towards web sites that have been actively trying to expose the Council as a wolf. In addition, me must campaign outside evangelical organizations and churches handing out leaflets advising the parishioners of the dangers involved in following the members of the Council such as Dr. James Dobson, Dr. Jerry Falwell, Tim Lahaye and D. James Kennedy. There are others as well. I have given you the list, research the names and find out who their following is. We must produce commercials for radio and television advising the Christian base of what their leaders are up to, especially their connections with Reverend Sun Myung Moon. He has

declared himself the new Messiah. I hate to steer you in this direction because you'll encounter conspiracy theories all over the place. However, that's the nature of the beast and there is a vast network which has been trying for years to expose the Council and Reverend Sun Myung Moon. You must know your enemy no matter how distasteful or beneath you, you think this is. You can be liberal and you can also be dead. Here's the bottom line, the Council is nothing more than a Fascist organization masquerading as good Christians. They're selling snake oil. When the Italians voted for Benito Mussolini they thought they were getting Santa Claus, instead they got a dictator. Do you know what fascism means? The dictionary definition is as follows: Any authoritarian, anti-democratic, anti-communist system of government in which economic control by the state, militaristic nationalism, propaganda, and the crushing of opposition by means of secret police emphasize the supremacy of the state over the individual. Hitler followed the same principles in developing the National Socialist Party. In this case, the supremacy of the state is the Kingdom of God. Tell the base that God is punishing them for following the Council by showing them signs such as hurricanes, earthquakes and volcanic eruptions. Then we attack the Council for their connections to Reverend Sun Myung Moon. We go full bore after them. No holds barred. Whatever dirt exists, we throw it at them. We support whatever organizations they seek to boycott. We go after moderate Republicans who are threatened by the extreme right wing of the party. There is enough evidence to crush these guys. You must support liberal radio, people like me, thank you very much, and other strident liberals who are willing to take off the gloves. We need a full-blown attack machine. If Sam gets reelected, his second term will be devastating. The right wing conservatives, who aren't evangelical Christians must be made to see that their collective paranoia is unwarranted and that the core of their histrionic personality, the "me" core is jeopardized. Teach them that their jobs, security, homes, pensions and their children's future hang in the balance if they elect Sam. If we can't neutralize their paranoia we make it worse. Following Sam will put their lives in jeopardy, literally, by having to fight the twin monsters of Russia and China. I hate to do this to you people listening, however, we don't have time. It is only three weeks before the election and I can assure you that if the economic numbers deteriorate and Sam does not do well in the debates, resulting in a losing bid for reelection, the group behind Sam will think nothing about planning some interesting episodes in America. They will not lose under any circumstances, any circumstances. After the show, please go to www.seekgod.ca, a true believer web site and read the article entitled Moon Takes over Council. I must use their tireless efforts in research in educating you to the real agenda that the Council has. We must separate the base from the head and this is one way to do it.

I apologize in advance to all those who will wade through the material presented on www.seekgod.ca, however, it is necessary. Welcome to the New World Order and every other conspiracy you can think of. After you have read the material, ask yourself what the hell Reverend Sun Myung Moon was doing in the Senate building coroneted as the Messiah. A congressman even handed him his crown for Christ's sake. Next week, I want you to call and propose your psy-op plan based upon what we have spoken about today. This must be done. Let me leave you with this tidbit from the debate between Sam and his opponent:

OPPONENT: And I think a critical component of success in Iraq is being able to convince the Iraqis and the Arab world that the United States doesn't have long-term designs on it.

As I understand it, we're building some 14 military bases there now, and some people say they've got a rather permanent concept to them.

When you guard the oil ministry, but you don't guard the nuclear facilities, the message to a lot of people is maybe, "Wow, maybe they're interested in our oil."

This is from page 259 of The Rise and Fall of The Third Reich:

> 'But the real basis of Germany's recovery was rearmament, to which the Nazi regime directed the energies of business and labor-as well the generals-from 1934 on. The whole German economy came to be known in Nazi parlance as *Wehrwirtschaft*, or war economy, and it was deliberately designed to function not in time of war but during the peace that led to war.'

And from page 276

> 'Now he turned-in fact, he already had turned-to the two chief passions of his life: the shaping of Germany's foreign policy toward war and conquest and the creation of a mighty military machine which would enable him to achieve his goal.'

Good night, this is Dr. Stanley Warlib, peace.

# Chapter Twenty

On the way out of the studio, Michael informed me that he hired two additional bodyguards for my protection. I reminded him of the syndication rights to my show and that a new contract was in order. He nodded his head and told me that a new contract would be on my desk by tomorrow. Walking towards the exit of the building, I noticed two huge men and realized that they were my new bodyguards. I had an army of four. The television cameras were present, although not as many as there had been before. There were demonstrators on both sides. Several Warlibs or Anarchists, I don't know which group, were handing out leaflets to the evangelical Christians and talking to them about the wolves in sheep clothing idea. Some Christian's were openly hostile. Other Christian's listened intently. It was actually a peaceful exchange between the two. They were bonding as brothers in peace. Another Warlib had a huge sign with the websites that I mentioned on my show. I hoped that the websites appreciated the plug. Rueben called my cell phone and before he could speak I told him that I knew that gold was up, the market was down, oil broke through $51.00 a barrel and that the dollar was down. Rueben was ecstatic. Pushing through the crowd, I arrived at the curb and discovered Westerfield's long black limousine waiting for me. He got out of the car and stood next to me. This time, I was one step ahead of him. He pulled out a check for $10,000,000.00. "Why don't you stop this game and take the money, Stanley?" he asked. He was looking directly into my eyes. As he uttered the next sentence, he slapped me on my back. Notwithstanding the pain, I didn't wince. He was checking to see if I had wounds on my back. I told Westerfield that I wasn't interested and he slapped me on the back again, this time looking at my body language. Again, I showed no visible signs of pain. As I walked away from Mr. Westerfield, I noticed that he was on his cell phone. I knew whom he was calling.

Arriving at the New York office of CNN, I went immediately to the make up room. On the set, Cross Fire had pulled in one of its big right wing guns. I was prepared for an attack. I took the self-inflicted wounds just for this moment. Immediately after the introductions, the big gun got in my face and stated that he wouldn't sit on the same set with an evil traitor. He continued along the same lines and called me a total fraud. Then he looked directly in the camera and said, "I know for a fact that Dr. Stanley Warlib doesn't have any wounds." I sat silently and did not respond. When I captured everyone's attention and felt that the audience was enraptured, I slowly stood up, unbuttoned my shirt, turned my back slowly towards the camera and took my shirt off. Unexpectedly, the female camerawoman gasped which the audience heard. It was an ugly image seen by millions and duplicated by every other cable station. Exasperated, the big gun sat silently and I went on the attack in a calm voice. It was a victory. Throughout the interview, I sat without my shirt until the station break. The director demanded that I put my shirt back on, which I did. However, I remained on the attack for the balance of the show.

My four bodyguards took their posts at the foot of the steps leading down from my brownstone. Reaching the top of the stairs, I turned and invited them in. For security reasons, they declined. Angelina and Rueben were waiting for me. It appeared that both wanted to celebrate. The Tequila was out, chips and salsa were on the table and hip-hop music was blasting from the stereo. Jay-Z was on. I asked Rueben what was happening down in the oil pits. "Doc, I don't know how to thank you. My contract is up almost $10.00 a barrel. I have twenty-five contracts, each contract controlling one thousand barrels of oil. That's 25,000 barrels, Doc, and at $10.00 a barrel, I'm up a quarter of million dollars. Throw in gold, long euro and shorting the S & P and I'm close to $300,000.00. You're a genius," said Rueben.

"And you Angie, what are you so hyped up about?" I asked.

"Cause, I love you Doc," she said.

"Well, love and money, it is time to celebrate," I said. Angie, Rueben and I danced to Jay-Z, slugging capfuls of Tequila every ten minutes. At ten o' clock, all of us went out to the deck. Rueben started the grill. Angie and I sat down at the table and continued drinking. When the chicken was finished, Rueben brought over a large plate of wings. "So, Doc, what's this shit about Sun Myung Moon and the Council?" he asked.

"I don't want to get into it. Go to the website that I mentioned on the show," I told Rueben.

"No, Doc, really, what is that stuff about Reverend Moon being coroneted in the Senate building? I want to know too?" asked Angelina.

"Well, its' long and complicated and I don't think I even understand it, but it's true," I said.

"Doc, can I make any money from this?" asked Rueben.

"No, Rueben, no money making moves on this one," I told him.

"Come on Doc, tell me," demanded Angelina.

"All right, I'll start at the beginning. Jump in and ask questions any time you guys want. On March 23, 2004, Reverend Sun Young Moon was coroneted the next Messiah in the Dirksen Senate Office Building of the United States. A bipartisan group of congressmen attended the coronation. In attendance at the coronation was Representative Curt Weldon, a Republican from Pennsylvania, Representative Chris Cannon, a Republican from Utah, Representative Roscoe Bartlett, a Republican from Maryland and Republican strategist Charlie Black. Black's public relations firm represents Ahmed Chalabi's Iraqi National Congress. In addition, liberal House Democrats Sanford Bishop, a Democrat from Georgia and Representative Harold Ford, a Democrat from Tennessee were in attendance. On the host committee was Senator Lindsey Graham, a Republican from South Carolina," I told Angie and Rueben.

"No shit, you've got to be kidding," Angelina said. "No, I'm not kidding, I swear it. No one covered the coronation except Sun Myung Moons Washington Times. Even they skipped the Messiah part. However, here is the scene: First, a Jewish Rabbi is blowing a ram's horn. Moon is seen sitting at a table in a tuxedo, eating all this crap up. Moon starts to clap. Then the scene turns solemn. Some Congressman, people believe it is Representative Danny K. Davis, with his head down with all due reverence, brings a crown, that sits on top of a velvet pillow to Moon who is standing with his wife. Moon and his wife are wearing imperial robes," I said.

"I don't believe you. You're making this stuff up," said Rueben.

"No, I'm not Rueben. This is real stuff. I couldn't make this crap up. Do you know who Moon is?" I asked.

"He's the Moonie guy, you know, mass marriages, that kind of stuff," said Rueben. "Reverend Sun Myung Moon has been in America thirty four years. He first came to prominence during something called Koreagate in 1975-76. He threw money around the halls of Congress and bought influence. He was indicted and spent time in jail for tax evasion. Today, he is a billionaire and has continued to throw money around. He has an empire that is so vast that there are some groups who just try to track his various social, religious, military, political and business interests. He has various interests all over the world. He is no lightweight trust me. He spent the last three decades solidifying his power and position in the elite power circles of America. He actively cultivated the conservative religious right that now has so much power. Some of the evangelical players on the Council on National Relations have ties to Moon and his Unification Church. After he was convicted he made it his quest to make his enemies bow to him, and he has. Moon has made outrageous statements that Jesus, Confucius and Buddha endorsed him. In 2002, Moon took out an ad stating that the prophet Muhammad led three cries of victory. He also claimed that from beyond the grave, Hitler and Stalin called him none other than humanity's Savior, Messiah, Returning Lord and True Parent," I told Angie and Rueben.

"Yeah, but he's a nut job," said Angelina.

"True, but a billionaire nut job with a lot of influence in Washington, D.C. and he bought the Council on National Policy, that has a lot of very powerful folks on it. They're all connected. Moon supported all these right wing organizations a long time ago. They have been sleeping in bed for three decades," I told both my guests.

"Go on," implored Rueben.

"Essentially, Moon's position is that Jesus failed and that he is the Messiah to clean up this mess. In Moon's speeches, a 'peace kingdom' is envisioned and homosexuals, whom he calls 'dung-eating dogs,' will be a thing of the past. In January of 2004 he said that 'gays will be eliminated, the three Israelis will unite and if not they will be burned. We do not know what kind of world God will bring, but this is what happens. It will be greater than the communist purge but at God's orders. Moon is open about replacing democracy and the U.S. Constitution by religious government. It's called Godism. Moon claims that the separation of church and state is the work of Satan. He stated that 'the church and state must become one as Cain and Abel.' Moon has the Council on National Policy in his pocket. They can't turn against him now because he'll expose all the connections that they have to him," I said. Angie got up to go to the bathroom. Rueben remarked how nice her butt was as she walked away and I told him that was exactly what I thought three years ago when I first saw her rear-end at Mykonos.

"Rueben, this really is a vast Evangelical Christian-Sun Myung Moon, conservative right wing conspiracy," I said. Rueben couldn't believe what he was hearing. He kept on suggesting that the whole group was just a bunch of ill informed whackos. I told Rueben that that wasn't true. This group is well connected, powerful, and moneyed and has a clear dedicated mission to turn America on its head. Rueben wouldn't and couldn't accept my position.

"A conspiracy to run America? I just don't believe it," said Rueben.

"Rueben, do some research. It's all out there. I can't spoon feed this shit to you or to my listeners. There are just too many connections," I told Rueben. I continued, "a former Congressman, I think his name was Woody Jenkins stated that 'I predict that one day before the end of this century the Council on National Policy will be so influential that no President, regardless of party or philosophy, will be able to ignore us or our concerns or shut us out of the highest levels of government.' This is very, very real Rueben," I said. Angelina came back from the bathroom with another bottle of Tequila. She asked if she missed anything and Rueben and I shook our heads indicating that she did not. "Rueben, there are many connections between Sun Myung Moon and the Council on National Policy. Bill Bright recommended that Sun Myung Moon head up the Unification Church in America. Bill Bright is a member of the Council. Jerry Falwell, a Council member accepted 2.5 million dollars to save his Liberty University in 1994. The money was funneled through Women's Federation for World Peace, a Moonie organization, chaired by Beverly LaHaye, a council member. Gary Bauer, the founder of Family Research Council accepted $150,000.00 from Reverend Sun Myung Moon. The list goes on and on. You have to do the research. I've done it. It's your turn. And how can this group become so powerful, you might ask? Because, Americans are just plain fucking stupid! If Sam says up is down, 50% of Americans will believe that up is down and anyone who questions it is somehow evil. The Council on National Policy and Reverend Sun Myung Moon's Unification Church follow the same methods that work on dumb people, mind control through propaganda. It's as simple as that," I said.

"Doc if you believe that, why don't you embrace Anarchy?" asked Angie.

"I'm not ready to start blowing things up," I told her.

"You're a cute, useless pussy," she said "and I love you," she added.

"Look guys, the left and right are full of shit, you know it and I know it. The only thing that's left is to blow the whole fucking place up," said Angie.

"Both the left and right are full of crap and that's exactly what the Council on National Relations believes, that's why they want to replace it with a theocracy based upon the Bible," I said.

"I'm staying out of this conversation. I'm a money man," said Rueben. "But, it's still hard to believe," Rueben added.

"Rueben, Hitler had a depression that he could blame on the Jews and America's depression will be blamed on the liberals. They're head bashing the liberals' 24/7/ 365. Liberal has become a bad word," I said.

"Whoa, Doc, wait a minute. A depression?" asked Rueben. "Yeah, you heard me, a depression. I've been thinking about this. America's debt totals seventy-four trillion dollars. There's no way we can repay that. Greenspan can't raise interest rates to attract foreign dollars and the tax base is not sufficient to pay back the debt, so what can we do? I think it's going to be a deflationary depression, which is the worst kind of depression to have. Everything starts to spiral down. No one can afford anything and people start holding on to their money, the little that they have left. It's a mindset and when the depression comes, America repudiates its debt, blames it on the liberals and wipes out Social Security, Medicare, Medicaid and every other social program that it has and it replaces it with faith based voluntary giving under Biblical directions," I said.

"You have got to be kidding," said Rueben.

"Like the quarter million dollars that you're sitting on," I responded.

"That's scary shit," said Rueben.

"Blow it up," said Angie several times. I knew Rueben was thinking about what financial play he could make with the information he had.

"Rueben, before the smoke starts to come out of your ears, I'll tell you the way to go financially. Always hold gold and silver and remember in a deflationary depression, cash is K I N G," I said.

"Wait a minute, Doc. If America repudiates it's debt, then the dollar is worthless," said Rueben.

"That's right, however, before America does that and you'll see it coming, you take your cash and buy all those assets that will be on the market for pennies on the dollar. You get rid of your cash that way and then you have hard assets. Corporations are already repudiating their debt in bankruptcy. Take a look at all the airlines asking the courts to get them out of their pension obligations. America is not far behind. There will be panic, strikes and mass disruption. By that time, you'll have a national identification card in the form of your driver's license and the Patriot Act will be peering into the lives of the most agitated, like Angelina and I," I said.

"Doc, you're dark and gloomy," said Rueben.

"Yes, however, this time it's real," I told Rueben.

Angelina, Rueben and I spent the entire night together and watched the sun rise from Strawberry Field in Central Park. Angie and Rueben were tired. I wasn't. At 5:30 a.m., both my friends took their leave. Taz and I took a walk to the Hudson River on the West Side and sat on a bench, watching the small boats go by. "Don't give up!" I heard a voice whisper. I knew it was God, but I didn't know to whom he was talking. "Are you talking to Sam or me?" I asked. "I'm talking to you Stan. Don't give up," God repeated. I continued staring at the small sailboats going down the Hudson River, avoiding the voice in my head. Several minutes elapsed and I heard nothing. As I pushed down with my palms on the bench to get up, the voice said "Don't get up."

"All right, I had enough. Why don't you go talk to Sam," I told God.

"Because I want to talk to you," said God.

"Then, start talking, you're wasting my time," I said to God and then continued.

"You have to be wondering why the hell you ever invented the human species. Assuming you created all the animals on the planet, why you continued and created humans, in your image, no less, has to be bewildering."

"Just don't give up," God repeated. I bounded off the bench and started walking down the block. God's words kept on repeating in my head over and over, becoming louder and louder. At Broadway and 86th Street, I couldn't take it any longer and started screaming for God to leave me alone. The people surrounding at the corner gave me a wide berth. Someone called a policeman who took me to the wall of an apartment building and demanded that I calm down. After five minutes of questioning, to which I gave coherent answers, he stepped aside and told me to get my act together. "You're Dr. Stanley Warlib, aren't you?" he asked.

"Yes, I am," I told the officer.

"I ought to lock you up just on general principles. All those lies that you have been spreading on the airwaves. You deserve a couple of years in jail," he said.

"You mean the police are against me! Why am I not surprised," I said.

"Go on, get the hell out of here before I change my mind," he said. The cop gave me the jitters and I decided that it was not in my interest to linger longer than necessary. It was only 11:30 a.m. and I didn't know what to do. I decided to go to the Mykonos Diner for lunch.

"How you doing Angie?" I asked.

"I'm dead tired. Should I meet you after the show tonight?" she asked.

"Of course. How about a mellow evening?" I said to Angelina.

"Just you and I," said Angie.

"Just you and I," I repeated.

"O.K., honey, I'll be there. By the way, my boss doesn't want you in here anymore. He doesn't like you. He thinks you're attacking America," said Angie.

"Whatever. Tell Spiro this is my last meal in his god damn diner," I said to Angie. "What's the show about this afternoon?" she asked.

"I don't know, I'll find something to talk about. But, it's the last show for a couple of days. I need a break. Got any little Anarchists that can fill in for me?" I asked. Angelina laughed and went to the kitchen to get my lunch. She shook her butt with such an exaggeration that I thought she would fall. She did knock over several coffee cups at one table. She turned and winked at me.

There were only twenty people standing at the barricades when I arrived at the station. Only one cable television camera was present. I expected more after my

CNN performance the other night. I couldn't understand why the streets weren't overflowing with people. I didn't take the lack of crowds and cameras as a sign that my popularity was waning. It was too soon.

Five, four, three, two and one:

WARLIB: Good afternoon, this is Dr. Stanley Warlib and I don't have a fucking clue why I'm here. I mean I just went blank. I know, I'm supposed to say something, but I just don't know what to say. I've been told that the biggest mistake you can make is having dead airtime and I just went blank two minutes into the show. I think I should take some calls," I looked down at the board and there were no flashing lights. The producer shrugged his shoulders. The screener looked at me dumbfounded. Well, since there are no calls, I guess I'll just have to keep on talking. Ladies and gentlemen, there are several men outside the window, they look like government men, pointing towards me," I said. The door to the booth opened. Michael and two men grabbed me by my shirt and started yanking at me arm. "Will you get this lunatic out of here," said Michael.

"Michael, what's the problem?" I asked.

"Come on, you're outta here. I had enough of you," said Michael.

"Did someone get to you?" I asked. Both men pulled me down the hall as I was trying to talk to Michael.

"Take him out the back entrance," Michael yelled to the men. One man held the door open as the other pushed me through. I went tumbling into a garbage can, bewildered and bruised on my forehead. Something just happened and I didn't know exactly what the episode was all about. "I was taking a couple of days off anyway," I said out loud. I called Rueben. He didn't answer. Lying in the alleyway, I spotted Westerfield's limousine. Harry got out of the limousine and came walking towards me. He grabbed me under the arms, lifted me, and told me that Mr. Westerfield wanted to talk to me. I hesitated but Harry pulled me along. As I approached, the tinted window on the limousine lowered and Charles appeared.

"You did a real stupid thing Stan. Christians are noxious weeds! Really, I don't know if I can get you out of this one. Get in," said Charles. Mesmerized, I approached the car as Harry opened the door. Inside, sitting next to Charles was Gabby. I sat down opposite Charles and Gabby and stared at her stomach.

"You are pregnant!" I said.

"Yes, I am pregnant," she repeated.

"I think you should come back to Southhampton with us," said Charles.

"Are you crazy. You're my enemy. There's no way I'm going back to the estate," I told Charles.

"I'm not you're enemy Stan, I'm your future father-in-law and this is Gabby, your future wife," said Charles.

"Don't talk to me as if I'm an idiot. I know who you are and you people are my enemies," I said.

"Stan, we're not your enemies," Charles repeated. Gabby leaned over and placed her hand on mine. She looked me in the eyes and whispered, "sweetheart, we're not your enemy. Please come home," she said.

"Stan, I don't know what happened, however, one day you left the estate and never returned. All of us have been unable to understand anything that has happened. You had one appearance on a radio show and then when you left the show someone hit you on the head with a bat. You were admitted to a hospital, were in a coma and then left the hospital. No one has been able to find you. I sent Harry out everyday, scouring the city looking for you. Gabby has been near hysteria and she can't take medication because of the pregnancy. We don't know what's going on with you. Why don't you just come back to the estate," said Charles.

"I don't believe this shit. That's not what happened. I have had a radio show everyday. I've been on CNN. I have fucking razor blade slash marks on my back," I said. I ripped my shirt off and turned around. "See, see those slashes on my back," I said. I turned my head completely around and looked at Charles and Gabby. I saw their blank faces. They looked scared. I had seen that look before in other persons who had encountered someone who's crazy. I rushed out of the limousine and stood with my back to an open window on the limousine. "Raise, the freaking window, now. Raise it," I screamed. Charles pushed the button to raise the window and I looked at my reflection at it came into view. There were no scars. None. I dropped to my knees and cried. Harry picked me up and gently placed me in the limousine and rode off to Charles estate. I sat for two hours with my hands covering my face. I was too embarrassed to say anything and too bewildered to understand what was happening. Gabby and Charles left me alone.

# Chapter Twenty-One

In the morning, breakfast was unusually quiet. Charles read The New York Times. Gabby was cooking bacon. I made myself a cup of coffee and sat down next to Charles. He lowered his paper and said "Good morning."

How are you today?" he asked.

"I don't know. I think I'm fine. I'm a little shocked. It seems my reality and everyone else's appears to be at odds," I said.

"There's no need to talk about this stuff now. Why don't you just take a couple of days and settle down and then maybe you'll be able to sort things out," said Charles. I wanted to touch Gabby but I couldn't. I wanted to grab her around the waist and give her a kiss. It just wasn't possible. These people were my enemies. Charles and Sam. Gabby and Elicia. I saw it on video. Or did I? "I'm going for a walk. Come on Taz," I said out loud. As I walked out the back door, I peered into the war room. It was exactly the same as I left it. The maps, computer, viewing screen, my notes, everything was exactly as I had left it. Charles did not move a thing. Standing at the top of the dune, I gazed at the ocean trying to figure out what the hell had happened. Maybe I had a psychotic episode? I had to find out what was real and what was not. I called Rueben on his cell phone.

"Rueben, what's up, its Doc," I said.

"Doc, how the hell are you?" asked Rueben.

"Rue, just answer me some questions," I said.

"All right, Doc, no problem," answered Rueben.

"Did I have a radio talk show?" I asked.

"Well, I wouldn't call it a talk show. I bought you one hour of airtime as a gift. You said some pretty nasty things and the manager yanked the plug on you ten minutes before you were scheduled to end," said Rueben.

"You mean I didn't get national coverage. There were no demonstrations in the streets. Rock throwing, that kind of thing?" I asked.

"No, Doc, none of that. Just one time on some obscure station is all there was. Are you all right, Doc?" asked Rueben.

"Yeah, I'm o.k. How about you and Angelina slicing up my back with a razor blade? You were there, right?" I asked.

"No, Doc, I wasn't there and now you're starting to freak me out," said Rueben.

"How about this. Me telling you about the cartoons in my head in the city when we were drinking Tequila. You know, the Kung-Fu Grand Master. Long Oil, that stuff?" I asked Rueben.

"Yes, that happened," answered Rueben.

"How about you getting a video and arranging to have it installed in the estate?"

"Yes, that happened," answered Rueben. "And I showed you the video, right?" I asked. "No Doc, you told me about a video but you didn't show me one," answered Rueben. "Doc, are you all right. I don't know what you're talking about. We've seen each other about once a week and you have been giving me financial advice of all things. I have been following it and I've made a lot of money. That's about it. Who is Angelina?" asked Rueben. "Never mind, I'll get back to you. I'm all right. Just let me get back to you," I told Rueben. I continued walking down the beach for miles trying to sort things out. It was clear to me that some things that had occurred were true and that some were delusions. I had to visit Angelina. She was part of the puzzle and I needed to see her. I started feeling less disoriented, however, it was becoming clear to me that something very psychotic had happened. I felt like calling Dr. P. I needed him. When I got back to the estate, I logged onto the Internet and typed in www.warlib.org. There wasn't a web site. I typed in www.themultitude.org and it didn't exist. The name was reserved by someone but there was no website. As I typed, I realized that the video was the key. The video was back in my apartment. I needed to go back to the city, see Angelina and look for the video. I went into the kitchen and sat down next to Charles and Gabby. I kissed Gabby on the cheek. She smiled. Charles asked if the walk did me some good and I told him that it had.

"I think I had a brief psychotic episode," I told Gabby and Charles. They looked at me and waited for me to continue.

"I don't know too much about them other than that they are uncommon," I told Charles and Gabby.

"Maybe, it was brought on as a result of you being shot," said Charles. Gabby was strangely silent. This woman showed no affection or caring towards me. Perhaps she was frightened because I was the father of the little baby inside her. I didn't know, but it added an element of paranoia. None of us acted normal. Charles and Gabby talked and looked at me as if I was going to go off my rocker another time and they were just waiting for something or someone to trigger it. There was nothing, except the passage of time that would relax Charles and Gabby. Another thing I needed in the City was my Diagnostic Service Manual. I needed to do self-analysis. My condition could be many things ranging from a brief psychotic episode to a psychotic disorder not otherwise specified with a host of diagnoses in between. The best course of action was to try to resume a normal routine within the confines of the estate. I looked at Gabby and smiled. She half smiled back and winked. I started laughing. Charles put down his paper and remarked that that was exactly what the household needed, a little laughter. Gabby took hold of my hand and placed it on her stomach. I felt either an elbow or toe slide across her belly. "Can you see it move?" I asked. "You bet, you have got yourself a live one Stan," she said. That was the most conversation that Gabby and I had in a long time. My hand on her stomach, together with her hand on top of mine, made me feel connected. I sat back in my seat and looked lovingly at Gabby trying to mask the fact that I was reviewing the video in my mind of her and Elicia snuggled up together and laughing. Was this woman really a two timing lesbian bitch? I just kept on smiling. I could very well be in the belly of the beast. I started to recall little bits and pieces such as my bodyguards and Charles offering me $10,000,000.00. I didn't want to ask as I thought it might frighten them or at least take us all back to a place that reminded them that I was ill. The only thing I recalled from my school days about a Brief Psychotic Disorder was that the episode was at least one day and less than thirty days and that functioning returned to normal levels. I needed to speak to Angelina and look for that disk. In my head, I didn't believe that these two people were innocent parties. What I knew for sure was that I was unemployed, I closed my practice, I gave Rueben financial advice, he followed it, I think I screwed Angelina at least once or twice, there was no Warlib or Multitude website and I was sitting in front of either the grandest game players in the world or sincere people. I didn't know and at this point I didn't care. Whatever semblance I had of a normal life was a memory and a memory that I could no longer recall. Somehow, I had fallen into the devil's abyss and didn't give a shit. I felt secure for my life and decided to play out whatever movie I was in with the Westerfield's. I decided to jump into their lives once again and stir things up. I leaned over the table and gave Gabby a huge kiss. I lingered until she opened her mouth. She was receptive and responded. She threw her arms around me and whispered in my ear, "I missed you Stan." If Gabby and Charles were screwing with me I was in trouble. I operated on two levels. One, I was involved with the people sitting at the table and the other was trying to figure out if Gabby and Charles did not have sincere motivations, exactly why I was back as the estate. What did Gabby want and what did Charles want. I couldn't remember what I said on my one and only radio show. Maybe I said something in that show that concerned Charles? Maybe Gabby was just feeling motherly at the moment? I added another item to retrieve from the City, a copy of the tape of the radio show if it existed. I didn't feel comfortable at all.

"I think I need to go into the city," I told Charles and Gabby.

"Don't go Stan," said Gabby.

"Wait a couple of days Stan. Take a break for a while and then go in. I'll have Harry drive you there," said Charles.

"I feel awkward. It feels that you and Gabby are watching my every move wondering if I'm nuts or something," I said.

"Honey, it's not like that at all, honest. We love you; we just don't know what to do. You're right, it's kind of strange," said Gabby.

"A little rest will help," added Charles. I dropped the subject and asked what I could do to make me feel more at home. Gabby suggested a walk on the beach with Taz and her dad. We bundled up and walked over the dunes to the shoreline. I grabbed a shell and skipped it over the water. "Not bad Stan. That was three skips," said Gabby. I eyed the cottage that I thought I saw a figure smoking in the shadows. It was boarded up. Charles explained that the remains of the last two hurricanes required the cottage to be boarded. He told me that no one lived there. As we were walking, I realized that I could check for the audio/visual equipment that I had installed. If it wasn't there, then Charles discovered it. If it was still there, then either Charles hadn't found it or found it and decided to leave it alone leading me to believe that he didn't find it. This was going to be the great mind game, except they had an advantage. They cared and I didn't. I didn't like Charles and I didn't like Gabby. The bonds were broken and it didn't matter whether I had a Brief Psychotic Disorder or not. There was no love anymore. I wanted battle. However, I was fully prepared to be as phony as necessary. Looking at Gabby made me horny. Tonight, I was getting laid with a preggie. From the moment I thought of sex, I was hard until I got back to the estate. Gabby was tired and went upstairs to sleep. Charles invited me in to the war room and poured a scotch. Harry had lit the fireplace and Charles and I settled into the club chairs. I knew that Charles wanted to ask me questions and I wanted to ask Charles questions. Both of us sat there until I decided to talk first.

"Charles, you remember the Moonies from the seventies? You know, the cult run by Reverend Sun Myung Moon," I asked.

"I remember Reverend Moon. Influence peddling all over Congress handing out money like it was going out of style. He was convicted wasn't he?" asked Charles.

"Yes, he was convicted and after serving his term he built the Washington Times," I said. "What about him?" asked Charles.

"Oh, I don't know, there seems to be some connection between Moon and Sam and I thought you would know about it," I said.

"No, I don't know too much about that stuff. I pay attention more to money matters than domestic matters," said Charles.

"Well, it seems Sam's father accepted $100,000.00 back in 1996 as a speaker's fee at one of Moons functions. Then Sam's dad went on to praise Moons paper, the Washington Times, as the greatest paper in Washington, D.C." I said.

"So, what's the point?" asked Charles. I could see that Charles was visibly uncomfortable pursuing this line of conversation. He attempted to cut it short.

"You know, during my absence, I was giving financial advice to my friend Rueben and he acted on it," I said.

"Really, what did you tell him to invest in?" asked Charles. "I told him to go long oil, long gold, short the S & P and go long euro," I said.

"And how did Rueben do?" asked Charles. "He's up $250,000.00," I said.

"Now, if you told me that information and I invested two million on that advice, I would be at ten million. Now you know why I wanted you on the payroll. That was good advice," said Charles.

"Getting back to Sam, you know he started his faith based initiative by Executive Order and it seems that the Moonies and Reverend Moon are up to their necks in government money," I told Charles.

"Really," Charles said again and added, "So what's your point." It was clear that Charles was not interested. In talking to Charles, I realized that during my absence I must have spent many hours researching in my own war room. I wasn't going to get any insight or tidbits from Charles.

"Seems like all roads lead to the Council on National Policy," I said to Charles.

"Really," said Charles.

"Have you heard of them?" I asked.

"It's a familiar sounding name, maybe I read about the Council or some organization with a similar name," said Charles.

"Ever hear of the Constitution Party?" I asked Charles.

"Yes, it's a national party that has a candidate running for President," said Charles.

"It used to be the US Taxpayers party that was started by a Council member, his name was Phillips. Well, it seems that Phillips ran for President of the United States with his running mate Brig. General Albion Knight as Vice President. Knight is also a Council member. Ever read the party platform Charles?" I asked.

"Stan, what is all this bullshit? You're irritating me. It should be obvious that I don't want to walk down this road," said Charles.

"There's been a melding of evangelical Christians, the Moonies and the Conservatives and I think they're trying to set up a fascist state and the state will be the Kingdom of God," I told Charles.

"Kid, you're getting carried away. This is America. The United States of America! That kind of stuff doesn't happen and cannot happen in America," said Charles.

I was egging Charles on and I could see in his eyes that he was annoyed. I knew that he knew more than he was letting on, however, I didn't pursue the matter further. I was sure that my first radio show must have mentioned the Council, however, I couldn't recall whether it did or not.

"Maybe, we should start the war room up again. You always liked that," said Charles. "No problem, if we include the Council on National Policy as well. I mean I know what they're up to and I want you to know as well. The war room must have two parts, domestic and money," I said.

"I'm not interested in this damn Council and I won't proceed on that basis. You're making me angry," said Charles.

"Then I'm not interested Charles. It's the Council *and* money or nothing," I said.

"Then it's nothing. It was a mistake picking you up in the alley like some stinking little rat. I should have left you there to fend for yourself," said Charles. Charles picked up his cell phone and called Harry.

"Harry, take Dr. Warlib back to the City, now. Right now," said Charles loudly.

"I'm not letting this go Charles, I swear it," I said.

"You're a dead man walking Stan. You're a dead man walking," said Charles. Gabby came down the stairs and looked at me. She didn't ask where I was going. She didn't say good-bye. I sat in the limousine and closed the window between Harry and I. Taz sat next to me staring out the window.

When I arrived at my apartment, I thanked Harry for the ride. He advised me to take it easy and said "good luck." I ran up the steps, opened the door and immediately looked for the video. I couldn't find it. The war room that I set up in my office was still intact. I recalled that several government men served me with a search warrant and confiscated my materials. That didn't happen. It was another delusion of my unknown ailment. Taz ran out to the back of the deck and I followed. The table had empty bottles of Tequila strewn about and empty pizza boxes were stacked neatly on top of each other. It appeared that someone made an attempt to clean up. I continued searching for the videodisk, ripping apart the apartment to no avail. Several hours later, I stood in the kitchen and surveyed the mess that I had made. The audio/visual machine was real; Rueben confirmed that the machine had been installed. I knew that the disk existed and I was determined to find it. My phone rang. "Hello, this is Stan, who's this?" I asked. No one answered. "Who is this," I shouted. Again, no one answered. "Screw off," I said and hung up the phone. I walked into my office, stared at the materials placed all over the room and fell asleep out of exhaustion.

# Chapter Twenty-Two

The next morning, Taz nudged me with his nose. I looked at Taz and petted him on the head. The clock on my desk indicated that it was 10:00 a.m. I was surprised that Taz lasted that long without peeing on the floor. I got up, opened the door to the back yard and Taz ran out. I made coffee and sat at the kitchen counter. If there was only one radio show on an obscure station, then no one heard what I had to say. Once again, I was nailed to the inside of Sam's skull with my mouth duct taped shut. I understood why God told me not to give up. I hadn't even started. In the absence of media access, I didn't have a chance to get my message out. It was my destiny to be nailed to the inside of Sam's skull. I grabbed a piece of paper and decided to make a list of things that I had to do. First, I decided to call Dr. P. and schedule an appointment. I needed help. Second, I was going to go to the Mykonos Diner and see Angelina. Third, I was determined to find the videodisk and fourth, I needed a plan to get out the information that I acquired by research. I knew the last one was going to be impossible. I had to try.

I called Dr. P. and scheduled an appointment for 4:00 p.m. After calling Dr. P. I cleaned the apartment and started a more thorough approach to find the videodisk. I started with the bathroom and did not find the disk. At noon, I went over to the diner and sat at my favorite seat.

"Hey, Doc, how the hell have you been?" asked Angelina.

"I've been well, Angie. How about you?" I asked.

"I'm a little angry with you," she said.

"Why?" I asked.

"Well, you come over two times and we have incredible sex and then you didn't call me. I thought you liked me," she said.

"I do like you. Outside of sex, there were no trips to Brooklyn or The Bronx?" I asked. "Doc, are you o.k. What are you talking about? I told you about a website, but that's all. Are you all right?" asked Angelina.

"Sex, a website, no Brooklyn or The Bronx, right?" I asked.

"Right," said Angelina. I made arrangements to see Angelina later that night at her apartment. After lunch, I went back to my office and continued looking for the videodisk to no avail. Realizing that my appointment with Dr. P. was only two hours away, I started to get nervous. I felt in control but it was obvious that some kind of episode had occurred and I needed to see Dr. P.

The door was opened to Dr. P.'s private office when I arrived. I looked in and saw Dr. P. sitting at his desk. He waived me in.

"How are you Stan?" he asked.

"I'm all right, I guess," I answered. Dr. P. and I sat in silence for several minutes and I knew he would continue to let me sit in silence for the entire fifty minutes if I choose to do so.

"I think I had some kind of psychotic episode," I told Dr. P.

"Why don't you let me make the diagnosis," he responded.

"Look, I had some things happen that really didn't happen," I said.

"Like what?" asked Dr. P.

"Like, I believed I had a radio talk show and I didn't. I believed that everyday I went to the station to do my show and I didn't. I believed that there were demonstrations, bombings, and cable television coverage and there wasn't. I believed that people were killed by a bomb blast and it didn't happen," I said.

"Do you know where you actually were if you weren't at this radio station?" asked Dr. P.

"I don't know. I guess I was at home. I really don't know,' I said.

"Anything else?" asked Dr. P.

"Yes, lots of goings on. I believed that I had to live at a safe house in Brooklyn with a woman named Angelina. I believed that I went to a warehouse in the Bronx to film a video depicting my possible beheading," I told Dr. P.

"Anything else?" asked Dr. P. again.

"Isn't that enough," I said loudly.

"None of this was true?"

"No, none of it was true. I had one radio talk show session given to me as a gift from Rueben. It was on an obscure station. No one heard it. There is a woman named Angelina and we made love twice. We weren't in a safe house and we didn't film a video in The Bronx," I said.

"If nothing else Stanley, you have a vivid imagination," said Dr. P. I knew that Dr. P. was trying to make me feel secure. A little humor added to my sense of well-being.

"And what exactly do these events have in common?" asked Dr. P.

"I was trying to alert the country that there is a vast right wing conspiracy in the United States. There has been a melding of evangelical Christians, the Moonies and Conservatives to bring about a fascist state right here in the United States. God called upon me and gave me this mission," I said.

"Have you spoken to God?" asked Dr. P.

"Yes, I know it sounds ridiculous, but I spoke to God," I said.

"Don't you find that peculiar Stanley. Why would God speak to an atheist?" asked Dr. P. "Because I'm the only one left listening and watching what's really going on," I said. "How many times have you spoken to God?"

"I don't know, maybe three. It used to be that I was nailed to the inside of Sam's skull and Sam had my mouth duct taped shut. I could hear God speak to Sam but couldn't respond and then just this morning, God spoke to me directly and told me not to give up," I told Dr. P.

"Give up what Stanley?" asked Dr. P.

"Give up exposing the vast right wing conspiracy, that's what," I said. I sat back in my chair and stared at Dr. P. Several minutes went by. Dr. P. stared at me.

"You think I'm a nut job, don't you? You don't think there is a vast right wing conspiracy. I'm a nut who received special orders from God to blow the conspiracy out of the water. Well, guess what? I can prove it," I said defiantly to Dr. P.

"Stanley, I'm just listening. I'm trying to get my arms around your issues. I'm not sitting in judgment, I'm just listening," said Dr. P.

"If Sam gets reelected we're all in trouble. The next four years are going to make the last four seem like paradise. They will consolidate their power and position and this country cannot afford another four years of propaganda and war. We're learning to love the fascist state and that state is going to be the Kingdom of God. Standing up, arms raised, swaying back and forth, tears running down our cheeks because the Heavenly Father loves us while our lives go to shit. We will all have National Identification cards, pledging allegiance to the State under the penalties of treason. It's coming, I tell you, it's coming," I said.

"Stan, you know there can be bizarre delusions and non-bizarre delusions. You are having non-bizarre delusions. For example, the delusion that someone might be following you is a delusion that is non-bizarre. Someone might be following you and that's not impossible. However, alien creatures performing massive surgery without leaving scars is a bizarre delusion. Your variety is a non-bizarre delusion," said Dr. P.

"Don't give me a psychology lesson, I know what the difference is between bizarre and non-bizarre delusions. The simple truth is that you don't believe me that there is a vast right wing conspiracy," I said.

"Is this vast right wing conspiracy after you?" asked Dr. P.

"Is this the 'is Dr. Stanley Warlib paranoid' line of questioning?" I asked.

"Stan, don't get defensive. I'm just trying to help," said Dr. P.

"Is there any reason to believe that you are a danger to yourself or others?" asked Dr. P. "Only in my delusions," I told Dr. P.

"Several weeks ago, I received a call from your friend Rueben. He told me that he found you alone in your bedroom humping a pillow. However, what concerned me more was the fire you started in your bedroom. That could have killed you and others in your brownstone," said Dr. P.

"Well, I guess your right. You're not thinking about an admission to a hospital, are you?" I asked.

"No, I'm just trying to gather enough information to make a determination as to your ability or lack thereof of protecting yourself and others around you," said Dr. P. Again, there was silence. I sat in silence for five minutes looking down at me knees. I was trying to determine whether Dr. P. was angling to get me to voluntarily admit myself to some psychiatric clinic for observation.

"I'm not going to do it," I said.

"Do what?" asked Dr. P.

"Voluntarily admit myself," I answered.

"Stanley, you have been in a constant on-going delusion. I think it might be beneficial. You haven't hurt yourself or others yet, however, the possibility is certainly there," said Dr. P.

"You don't want to know about the conspiracy?" I asked.

"Stan, right now, I think twenty-four hour observation for three days might be appropriate at this point. We can talk about the conspiracy when you get out. It's voluntary and it's only three days. Think about it?" asked Dr. P. Both of sat quietly as I let sink in the reality of self-admission.

"I have to think about that," I told Dr. P.

"Until you make a decision, I want to schedule daily appointments at 4:00 p.m. How are your finances?" asked Dr. P.

"I can afford it, if that's what you're asking," I told Dr. P. The session ended.

## CHAPTER TWENTY-THREE

I arrived at Angelina's at 6:30 p.m. The door was open. Angie was in the bathroom putting on make-up. I walked over to the bookshelf and looked for her book on Bakunin. It was there. At least the book was not part of my delusion.

"Make yourself at home," Angelina called out from the bathroom.

"No problem," I called back.

I watched Angelina from the couch. A nearby bottle of red wine was uncorked with wine glasses placed next to it. The door to the bathroom was one third open and I could see a slice of Angelina through the opening. She was naked. Women have no idea how attractive they are when they go about their activities naked, unaware that a man is watching. When Angie pressed up against the sink I could see the slope of her back as it made its way to her ass. When she stood back from the sink to get a larger view of her make-up, I could see the pubic hair on her front. She repeated this process ten times, back and forth, views of pubic to the gentle slope of her made me nuts.

"I'll be out in a minute," she said.

"Take your time Angie, I'm enjoying the view," I said.

"You're a pervert, Doc."

To my chagrin, Angelina finished putting on her make-up and emerged from the bathroom fully dressed. She wanted to make love as our first act of getting together again and suggested that I take off her clothes. I asked her why she didn't come out of the bathroom naked and she told me that she gets turned on when a man take off her clothes. I asked Angelina whether I had left anything in her apartment. She said no. I thought that the video might have been left in Angie's apartment. I wanted music to accompany the removal of Angie's clothes and asked her if she had any.

"Oh yes, you did leave something. The last time you were here, you left a small case of compact disks. I listened to all of them. I liked Grover Washington and John Klemmer. I couldn't play one disk. It had hand written on it 'Van Morrison-Remix' but I couldn't get it to play."

"Really. Let me see that disk. Do you have a computer here?" I asked.

I clicked on a program allowing me to see streaming video and placed the disk into a bay. The disk began to play. Appearing on the computer screen was Mr. Westerfield's study. I stopped the video and explained to Angelina that I needed privacy and that after reviewing it alone I would let her see it. I put Grover Washington into her stereo and pulled her onto the couch as the music came on. In conjunction with the mood of the music and in rhythm with the beat I slowly removed her clothes. Angelina had a just-got–out-of-the-shower baby smell about her. We made love.

"Angie, my shrink thinks that I should commit myself for psychiatric evaluation for three days."

"Why?" asked Angelina.

"It seems that I have been living in a delusional world for the last couple of weeks. I had my own radio talk show. You and I were urban terrorists making fake videos in The Bronx and living in a safe house in Brooklyn. My talk show was so popular it was going to be syndicated. In addition, there were daily demonstrations and explosions outside the radio station. And guess what? They were all hallucinations. None of it existed. I lived in a counter delusional world. I was in my house and believed that I was somewhere else."

"And you're debating whether you should check yourself in for observation?" Angie asked incredulously.

"Yes, I'm debating whether to check myself in. That's a big step. Psychiatric evaluations, group therapy and individual therapy for seventy-two hours and I don't think I need it."

Angelina pulled me close and told me that she would not abandon me. She promised to come visit me everyday for three days and check me in and out. I would not be alone. Angelina convinced me that living in a delusional world for the length of time that I had mandated self-admission. Reluctantly, I agreed. I called Rueben from Angie's apartment and told him what I intended to do and he also promised to visit me everyday until I was discharged.

# Chapter Twenty-Four

"Dr. Warlib, my name is Dr. Stephan Hatfriend and I'm here to make an initial evaluation and set up a schedule for you for the next three days. As you know, there will be group therapy and individual therapy sessions. Tell me what brought you here? Why did you voluntarily admit yourself for observation?" asked Dr. Hatfriend.

"What kind of name is Hatfriend?" I asked.

"It's German. My grandfather's name was Hittelfreunde. The English translation is Hatfriend. Please answer my question, Dr. Warlib," said Dr. Hatfriend.

"I admitted myself for observation because all my friends think it's a good idea. I have been living in a delusional world for several weeks and everyone thinks that I should admit myself and before you ask whether I think it's a good idea, let me say that I don't know. It might be and then again, it might not be. You know, delusional people can be quite functional and still delusional."

"What's your delusion?" asked Dr. Hatfriend.

"My delusion? My delusion? I'm living in a country where a vast right wing fascist conspiracy is taking place. That's what my delusion is Doctor and guys like you have no freaking clue what's going on."

Dr. Hatfriend sat back in his chair, trying to determine where the visible anger came from and my accusation against him. I could see that he was groping for a next question.

"Think of it this way Dr. Hatfriend. Suppose you were a young investigative reporter in Germany in 1921 and you saw Adolph Hitler speaking before a crowd and stirring them up. Then you watched his movements and speeches for the next several years as he gained in power and you knew that he had bad intentions. Then you started telling everyone that Hitler was a fascist with bad motives. However, everyone was seduced by the rhetoric and you slowly became a lone voice in an insane country and everyone started looking at you like you're the nut. That's what it feels like to me. Everybody is looking at me like I'm the nut, but they don't realize what's going on. Some people are just starting to scratch around the edges without getting into the meat. I tell you an evangelical Fascist state is upon us in the name of the Kingdom of God and it has come about through a thirty-year conspiracy by a bunch of right wing nuts. Would you like to tell me why Reverend Sun Myung Moon was declared the Messiah in the halls of the Senate Building of the United freaking States of America?" I asked.

"Do you believe that Reverend Moon is the Messiah and that he was coronated in the Senate building of the United States?"

"Yes, I do believe that." I paused and then added, "No I don't believe that the Reverend is the Messiah, but I do believe that he was coronated in the Senate of the United States."

"I see," said Dr. Hatfriend and asked, "Is that part of your delusion?"

"You don't get it, do you? I'm telling you, Reverend Moon was declared by Congressman and Senators, the Messiah in the Senate building. I'm not going any further until you Goggle this issue. I demand that you type in Sun Myung Moon-Senate-Messiah," I told Dr. Hatfriend.

Dr. Hatfriend typed in what I told him to and clicked on an article. After he finished reading one article, he clicked on another article and then another. Several times he turned and looked at me, without an expression on his face. I saw an eyebrow go up at one point.

"I guess you read about a famous Senator. Senator Lindsey Graham on the Honor Committee at the coronation of Moon as the Messiah. Probably wondering what the hell this is all about. Maybe, I'm not freaking crazy, am I? It's against the Constitution you know," I said.

Dr. Hatfriend was visibly confused. I knew that he didn't know what to ask me next. He decided to go back to basics.

"Tell me about your delusions?" he asked.

"I told you, I'm not telling you about me personal delusions until I tell you about the vast right wing conspiracy. Someone has got to listen and it might as well be you. Listen, I've been tracking this bullshit for quite some time and you have got to pay attention. This is real and the beauty of the whole thing is that the country doesn't even know it's being indoctrinated into the fascist state because it is being sold as religion. These guys have a long history using cults as a vehicle for indoctrination. I'm going to give you the short version because time is running short.

Once Sam gets reelected the next four years will be like nothing you have seen before. On Christian television stations they're already celebrating victory and their victory will be your demise. You better bow down and ask forgiveness and ask the Lord Jesus Christ for salvation because if you don't you will be branded an enemy combatant of the state and thrown into a deep hole that no attorney, family or friend will be able to get you out of. The sad part of it all is that you think I'm kidding. Here's the deal. After researching various sources, I decided that the best thing that represents this vast right wing conspiracy, the closest thing to what they want is the Constitution Party of the United States. It is the fifth recognized party by the Federal Elections Commission. Who are they? In 1992 a coalition of independent parties united to form the U.S. Taxpayers party. In 1992, Howard Phillips was the party's presidential candidate. Howard Phillips is a member of the Council on National Policy. His Vice Presidential running was Albion Knight, Jr., and a member of the Council on National Policy. In the 2000 elections, the Constitution Party achieved presidential ballot access in 41 states and qualified write-in candidate status in seven other states, totaling in all 48 states. They identify, train and prepare candidates for future elections. The Constitution Party champions the principle of government laid down by our Founding Fathers in the Declaration of Independence and the United States Constitution. Sounds harmless enough, doesn't it. But what does that mean? On their web site they claim that they are the only party, which is completely pro-life, anti-homosexual rights, pro-American sovereignty, anti-globalist, anti-free trade, anti-deindustrialization, anti-unchecked immigration, pro-second amendment, and against the constantly increasing expansion of unlawful police laws, in favor of a strong national defense and opposed to unconstitutional interventionism. Again, that sounds like a party with a point of view. I disagree with them on some issues and agree with them on others. However, here's where the mind control fascist bullshit takes over. Here's the preamble to the Constitution Party and I've memorized it and branded it in my mind. The preamble states as follows:

'The Constitution Party gratefully acknowledges the blessing of our Lord and Savior Jesus Christ as Creator, Preserver and Ruler of the Universe and of these United States. We hereby appeal top Him for his mercy, aid, comfort, guidance and the protection of His Providence as we work to restore and preserve these United States.

This great nation was founded, not by religionists, but by Christians; not on religions but on the Gospel of Jesus Christ. For this very reason peoples of other faiths have been and are afforded asylum, prosperity, and freedom of worship here.

The goal of the Constitution Party is to restore American jurisprudence to its Biblical foundations and to limit the federal government to its Constitutional boundaries.

The Constitution of the United States provides that 'no religious test shall ever be required as a qualification to any office or public trust under the United States.' The Constitution Party supports the original intent of this language. Therefore, the Constitution Party calls on all those who love liberty and value their inherent rights to join with us in the pursuit of these goals and in the restoration of these founding principles.

The U.S. Constitution established a Republic rooted in Biblical law, administered by representatives who are constitutionally elected by the citizens. In such a Republic all Life, Liberty and Property are protected because law rules. We affirm the principles of inherent individual rights upon which these United States of America were founded.' You got that Dr. Hatfriend. These people want to replace the Constitution with the Bible. The United States is the Kingdom of God. They have split the Kingdom into two. The Kingdom of God in heaven and the Kingdom of God on earth and they're doing it now because they sincerely believe victory is at hand. Listen to all the conservative and Christian radio talk shows. They're celebrating. And did you notice that their Preamble states Life, Liberty and Property and not the Pursuit of Happiness. This is a fascist state. To the extent that you don't believe that America is a Christian Nation then you are a heretic and you know what happened to heretics. They get burned at the stake. It doesn't stop there. You should read the platform of the Constitution Party. I'm going to give you some examples.

**'Sanctity of Life**-The pre-born child, whose life begins at fertilization, is a human being created in God's image. The first duty of the law is to prevent the shedding of innocent blood. It is, therefore, the duty of all civil governments to secure and to safeguard the lives of the pre-born.'

**Aids**-HIV/AIDS is a contagious disease which is dangerous to public health. It should not be treated as a civil rights issue. Under no circumstances should the federal government continue to subsidize activities which have the effect of encouraging perverted or promiscuous sexual conduct. Criminal penalties should apply to those whose willful acts of omission or commission place members of the public at risk of contracting HIV/AIDS.

**Education**—All teaching is related to basic assumptions about God and man. Education as a whole, therefore, cannot be separated from religious faith. The law of our Creator assigns the authority and responsibility of educating children to their parents. Education should be free from all federal government subsidies, including vouchers, tax incentives, and loans, except with respect to veterans.

Because the federal government has absolutely no jurisdiction concerning the education of our children, the United States Department of Education should be abolished; all federal legislation related to education should be repealed.

**Energy**-We call attention to the continuing need of the United States for a sufficient supply of energy for national security.

Private property rights should be respected, and the federal government should not interfere with the development of potential energy sources, including natural gas, hydroelectric power, solar energy, wind generators, and nuclear energy.

We call for abolishing the Department of Energy.

**The Judiciary**-The United States Constitution does not provide for lifetime appointment of federal judges, but only for a term of office during good behavior. We support Congressional enforcement of the Constitution rule of good behavior and to restrain judicial activism by properly removing offending judges through the process of impeachment provided for in Article I, section 2 and 3 of the Constitution. Furthermore, Congress must exert the power it possesses to prohibit all federal courts from hearing cases which Congress deems to be outside federal jurisdiction pursuant to Article III, section 2 of the Constitution.

We particularly support all legislation which would remove from Federal appellate review jurisdiction matters involving acknowledgement of God as the sovereign source of law, liberty or government.

We commend Former Chief Justice Roy Moore of the Alabama Supreme Court for his defense of the display of the Ten Commandments, and condemn those who persecuted him and removed him from office for his morally and legally just stand.'

Maybe you don't know what all this crap means, but it has particular significance. There are only three things that stand between these Fascists and them bringing the Kingdom of God to America: Black robed Judges, the Constitution and Liberals and that is what they have been attacking relentlessly day and night and it all goes back to the Council. When these fascists control Congress they will start to impeach any sitting Judge who places the law over the Bible. They will start to legislate removing entire areas of social order from Judicial review. In the end, the Courts will only serve as a reinforcement of Biblical Law. I'll continue.

**Social Security**-The Constitution grants no authority to the federal government to administer a Social Security system. The Constitution Party advocates phasing out the entire Social Security program, while continuing to meet the obligations already incurred under the system.

**Taxes**-We propose legislation to abolish the Internal Revenue Service.

**Terrorism and Personal Liberty**-America is engaged in an undeclared war with an ill defined enemy (terrorism), a war which threatens to be never ending, and which is being used to vastly expand government power, particularly that of the executive branch, at the expense of the individual liberties of the American people.

The 'war on terrorism' is serving as an excuse for the government to spend beyond its income, expand the Federal bureaucracy, and socialize the nation through taxpayer bailouts of the airlines, subsidies to the giant insurance corporations, and other Federal programs.

We deplore and vigorously oppose legislation and executive action, that deprive the people of their rights secured under the Fourth and Fifth Amendments under the guise of 'combating terrorism' or 'protecting national security.' Examples of such legislation are the National Security Act, the USA PATRIOT ACT, and the proposed Domestic Securities Enhancement Act," I said. Dr. Hatfriend cut me short and started to ask me a question.

"It sounds to me that they want to limit the Federal Government. Where's the conspiracy?" asked Dr. Hatfriend.

"The conspiracy is replacing the federal government with the Kingdom of God. I have been trying to follow this movement and all I can say is that it is a work in progress. There seem to be some conflict with Sam and the Council on National Relations. However, they both agree on one thing: taking back America for Christ and they're everywhere. There were two articles in The New York Times the other day. One was about a rally against gay marriage that drew thousands to the Capitol. They quoted Dr. James Dobson, a member of Council on National Policy. Another article was about liberal Christians mobilizing to react to the religious right. A guy named Tony Perkins was quoted as saying that 'their activism is too weak to slow the evangelical movement.' Tony Perkins is President of the Family Research Council, a Christian conservative group and a member of the Council on National Policy. Everything points to the Council and everything points to a fascist state that masquerades under the auspices of God and Jesus. The Christian cultists are highly suggestive and they're expanding their circle to conservatives. I know what they're up to. Now, I'm starting to see this new movement spreading among the evangelical Christians. They are getting involved in politics. Any clergyman who does not actively instigate his flock to get involved in politics is part of abandonment theology. John Chalfant, a member of the Council on National Policy recently wrote a book entitled 'America-A Call To Greatness.' He writes that Christians need to realize that they have the primary responsibility for reclaiming the nations Christian heritage because it is Christianity upon which the Declaration of Independence and the Constitution were founded. Does that sound familiar? D. James Kennedy, a Council member and Howard Phillips, endorses the book; remember him, a Council member and running for President with the Constitution Party. I'm telling you it's a conspiracy. I can't even begin to tell you about Reverend Moon's association with all the Council members because it's so freaking hard to figure out. They're all happy though," I said.

"And what is wrong with living a good Christian life," said Dr. Hatfriend. I sat straight up in my chair. That's not the kind of question a psychologist normally asks. I looked straight into the eyes of Dr. Hatfriend. He started to smile. I knew that Dr. Hatfriend was one of them, a true believer. I did what was probably the dumbest thing that I ever did in my life. I grabbed Dr. Hatfriend by the collar and tie and pulled him across the desk and then slammed his head down. He must have had an emergency call button because within ten seconds security guards came rushing in and grabbed me around the neck and twisted my arms behind my back and pushed me out of the room. I knew what came next, isolation and a small notation in his file that I was delusional and a threat to the public and myself. With that simple act, my voluntary admission became incarceration. I didn't help myself either by resisting constraint or screaming "freaking fascists" as the guards led me down the hall. I wrote my own death warrant. The guards pushed me into a cell and held me down as the aide in attendance shot me up with a sedative. What was worse was that the fascist Dr. Hatfriend was going to be my therapist for the balance of my incarceration. Either I capitulated and accepted the Lord Jesus as my Savior, an impossible act, or I would rot in isolation. I knew that there would be a review of my case before a board and that Dr. P. would call and ask about me. It was only a matter of time before I would get a chance to speak again or someone would come to see me. After all, Angelina and Rueben promised to check up on me everyday. I knew that they would be turned away at the front desk. The only information that would be provided to them was that I had an "episode."

"Can I help you?" asked the nurse at the front desk.

"I'm here to see my father. I believe you have a Dr. Stanley Warlib staying here," said Jordan.

"Your father is presently unavailable for visitors," said the nurse.

"What's the problem?' asked Jordan.

"He had an episode which required some restraint. He's resting now. Come back tomorrow. I'm sure you'll be able to see him then," said the nurse.

"Excuse me. Are you Jordan? My name is Rueben. I'm a good friend of your father. I promised to visit him everyday while he was in here. Come with me. I don't think you're going to get anywhere with that receptionist. I don't know what happened but we'll find out tomorrow," I said.

"Miss, may I please have the room number of Dr. Stanley Warlib."

"And who are you?" asked the nurse.

"My name is Angelina. I'm a friend of Dr. Warlib."

I pulled Angelina aside and introduced myself and Jordan. We stood in the vestibule of the receptionist's area, bound by our allegiance to Stanley.

"Angie, I'm taking you and Jordan out to dinner," I said.

"I don't know who you people are," said Jordan.

"Apparently, we are all very good friends of your father," said Angelina.

Over dinner, Angelina, Jordan and I got to know each other. All three of us probed each other for genuineness concerning our main issue: loyalty to Stanley Warlib. Jordan was visibly upset. He only wanted to see his father. He explained to Angelina and I that he had been traveling from Japan to America and that upon arrival in the States he couldn't locate his father. He became increasingly upset until this morning when he broke into his father's apartment and found his address book. He finally spoke to Dr. P. who advised him that his father voluntarily admitted himself for observation. Angelina explained that she had known Stanley for three years and that they recently became lovers. I explained that I was Stanley's former patient and Semper Fi friend and that I was a loyal and dedicated buddy to Stanley. All of us shook hands and hugged at the end of the evening and promised to return to the hospital the next day for answers.

# Chapter Twenty-Five

I lied in my bed and looked at the ceiling. The room was barren. I had no thoughts of suicide and all objects that I could use to inflict injury upon others and myself had been removed. I was slightly dazed from the sedative that the nurse had given me. There was no doubt in my mind that Angelina and Rueben had come to see me and was refused admittance. The next day, I was told that I had a visitor and the guards took me to a room that had a table and two chairs. I expected Angelina to walk in. Sitting alone, I had the unsettling thought that Mr. Westerfield, Sam and Gabby were going to do everything in their power to keep me locked up. Not only was I fighting Dr. Hatfriend but also I was fighting against the big heavyweights. So far, I did no damage but I was sure that Mr. Westerfield felt safer with me in incarceration than out on the streets. I couldn't spread my counter propaganda against their movement. The door opened and a guard led in Jordan. I started to cry.

"Dad, what the fuck is going on. I come home and you're locked up," said Jordan

"I was delusional for about three weeks, so my shrink suggested that I voluntarily admit myself for observation. Unfortunately, I smashed the admitting shrink's head on his desk. That was a big freaking mistake. They will probably keep me in here for a long time. You know, as a danger to the rest of society," I said.

"Dad, be cool for the next two days and I'll make sure you get out. Unless, of course, you want to get out now," said Jordan.

"You're not thinking about doing something stupid, are you?" I asked.

"If you can be cool for the next two days, I'll make the shrink an offer he can't refuse," said Jordan. "Trust me, you'll get out," Jordan continued.

Jordan and I continued talking for the next twenty-five minutes. He told me about Maki and his adventures in China, Mongolia, Russia and Italy. He didn't want Maki to see his dad locked up in a looney bin so he left her home. I told him to move into my apartment and look after Taz. He couldn't believe that I bought another dog and named him TazTwo. He always felt that Taz was sacrosanct and no other dog should be named Taz. I took Jordan's advice and stayed quiet and cooperative for the balance of my voluntary admission. When the time came to dismiss myself I was full of anxiety. However, the process went smoothly.

Leaving the hospital, Dr. Hatfriend smiled and said "another time, my friend, another time." Apparently, Jordan made good on his promise. Jordan, Angelina and Rueben were waiting outside in a cab.

"Hey dad, we're in here," he screamed from the cab window. Rueben got out and gave me a big hug. Angelina kissed me on the lips and whispered, "I missed you big guy." Jordan told me that it was clear to him that I needed supervision and that he felt obligated to stay in America just to keep me out of trouble. Taz was in the back seat and jumped with approval. Jordan took me up on my suggestion and moved into my bedroom with his girlfriend. Maki was back at the apartment making a traditional Japanese dinner, complete with Sake. I was happy. My friends came through, especially Jordan. I wanted to ask Jordan exactly what he did to get me out; however, I thought that should be a private conversation. Maki was waiting at the door for my arrival. She gave me a hug and tears welled up in her eyes. Apparently, being Poppa-San to her boyfriend was a huge honor and therefore, respect followed. It was an honor to meet me. Honoring your elders, what a wonderful Japanese tradition. My crew followed me into the apartment. Angelina put on disco dance music, Rueben grabbed the sake, Jordan passed out the traditional Japanese wooden cups and Maki poured the wine. "To life," Angelina howled out with enthusiasm. Everyone, yelled out "to life," and the party started. Maki made beautiful hand rolled sushi and served it on a huge platter. Jordan and Angelina seemed particularly friendly. Rueben was just happy to have his financial guru out and home. Oil had busted through $55.00 a barrel and his euro position was in the money. Gold was up and the market was down. Rueben was making money on all fronts. Angelina saved an article from The Sunday New York Times Magazine section entitled "What makes Sam's presidency so radical-even to some Republicans-is his preternatural, faith-infused certainty in uncertain times," written by Ron Suskind. I thanked Angie for saving the article but told her that I probably knew everything in the article even before I read it. People just weren't getting what was going on and all they had to do was watch and read what the evangelical Christians, Moonies and Conservatives were talking about. They no longer were hidden, except for their association with Reverend Moon; they were out there starting to strut their stuff. They were having a bigger celebration than my group.

Angelina and Jordan were talking in a corner of the deck. Maki sat next to me at the table, waiting to fulfill any request that I might have and Rueben wanted to talk finances. I eyed Angelina and my son. Their chumminess was starting to get to me. Actually, I was pissed off. I couldn't understand the connection. I couldn't imagine my son hitting on my woman, but there he was, talking up a storm and being charming. Rueben and I talked finances, however, my eye drifted off to Angie and Jordan every minute.

"Jordan and Angie, get over here and join the crowd," I yelled. Jordan and Angelina came over to the table. Maki gave Angie her chair and Angelina sat next to me. Jordan took a place across the table and sat next to Rueben. I waited for the conversation level to rise until I spoke to Angelina in a quiet voice.

"What the hell are you doing with my son?" I asked Angie.

"Nothing, Stanley, I'm being polite. What's your problem?" she asked.

"You guys look a little too chummy for me. Is Jordan hitting on you?" I asked.

"Stanley, you're getting carried away. He's just being nice to your girlfriend, that's all," said Angelina.

"You don't know Jordan, do you," I asked.

"No, I don't know Jordan. Look Stanley, the way to a man's heart is through his stomach and being nice to his kid. So Maki is taking care of your stomach and I'm taking care of your kid. Got it!" said Angelina.

"Everyone, I want to make a toast to my financial guru and my Semper Fi buddy, Dr. Stanley Warlib," said Rueben. Everyone raised a glass and toasted to my good health. I felt loved.

"Rueben, Angelina, Jordan and Maki, I have something to say. As you know, for the last three or four weeks I have been out of sorts. At this point in time, I don't know whether this get together is a delusional dream or is real. So excuse me for this request, but I want one of you to make a little cut in my arm. I want to see if I wake-up in the morning with the cut that one of you make tonight," I said. Without hesitation, Jordan leaned over the table, opened a small pocketknife that hung from his key-chain and cut a two-inch slit on my forearm. We all watched as the blood flowed down my arm to my fingertips. Maki went to the bathroom and retrieved ointment and a band-aid.

"I hope I wake up with this tomorrow morning. It would be nice to know whether this is real or not. By the way Jordan, exactly what did you say to Dr.

Hatfriend to get me out? I was sure that I made the biggest mistake of my life. I didn't think I would ever get out," I said to the group.

"I didn't say anything. I just showed him a picture of his wife picking up his kids from school. That's all. Just a picture," said Jordan. Rueben and I looked at each other. The implied threat from Jordan's action did not bother Jordan, Maki or Angelina.

"Since when did you get so tough?" I asked Jordan.

"I'm not tough dad. It's just that you talk too much, that's all. Less talk and more action! I got you out, didn't I?" said Jordan. The group was silent. Everyone waited for anyone to say something. Finally, Rueben spoke up.

"I want everyone to know that in three weeks I have made over $400,000.00 following Stan's advice. As far as I'm concerned, a genius is entitled to whatever delusions he wants to have. The proof is in the pudding. I want my friend, Dr. Stan, to tell us what he sees now. It's two weeks before the election and the race is in a dead heat. I think it's important to know," he said to everyone.

"I'm leaving. My dad is going to get on his soapbox and start an hour-long harangue and I'm not in the mood. I've been listening to his shit for twenty-five years. I've had enough," said Jordan. My son didn't say what he said with a nasty tone of voice. It was the truth. Having been a single dad since he was two, he was my only ear in the world and I bombarded him with my tirades on a daily basis. Just as I finished the thought, I realized that Jordan was more like me than I knew. The apple rarely falls far from the tree and Jordan loved me. Jordan must have picked up what I believed and espoused over the course of twenty-five years. I ordered Jordan to sit down. He complied. Jordan understood that I rarely demanded anything from him but when I did, he knew it was important. The ensemble went silent and looked at me to begin.

"What I see is the most horrible consequences for America if Sam gets reelected. There will be significant disasters in foreign policy and a course of action at home that only can be described as the beginnings of a Fascist state. For my friend Rueben, I advise you to remain on the track that I have placed you because you will only make more money as the reality of Sam getting reelected starts to sink in, in foreign circles. The dollar will continue to sink against the euro and gold, as a haven, will rise. The stock market will continue to go down and oil will become a strategic weapon. From outside our borders, allies and financial terrorists will cease to view America as a bastion of democratic freedom and more as a Fascist State and America as a Fascist state is at the heart of the problem. Many of you don't know what Fascism is and have never lived under the umbrella of Fascism. It is an ugly, horrible existence, the kind of political system that brings about wars and mass deaths at home as the Fascist state purges its enemies. Examples are Francisco Franco, the leader of Spain in 1936, Benito Mussolini in Italy, Stalin in Russia and of course, Adolph Hitler. These people were horrible, horrible men that sought to control their nations through Fascism and blessed war as a moral necessity. Perhaps, the thought of concentration camps for liberals and even their own that don't tow the party line doesn't frighten you because you can't envision it taking place in America, but it can. These things can happen because one of the pillars of Fascism is propaganda, every hour, every day, every month and year after year until your moral compass no longer sends a signal to the brain that something is wrong. Listen to what you hear. The evils under American Fascism are black robed non-strict constructionist judges, liberals and the Federal government. You hear it everyday, incessantly, inexorably corrupting your mind until you no longer shudder at the implanted thought that liberals are evil traitors. Fascism is an authoritarian, anti-democratic, anti-communist system of government in which economic control by the state, militaristic nationalism, propaganda and the crushing of opposition by means of secret police emphasize the supremacy of the state over the individual. No, no, that can't happen here in America you say to yourself, but you're wrong. It can happen, it is happening and it will continue to happen because none of you is watching what is going on. I read the October 17, 2004, The New York Times article by Ron Suskind entitled 'What makes Sam's Presidency so Radical.' Mr. Suskind is just beginning to see the track that Sam is on. If he gets reelected it's too late. In the beginning of the article he says that 'if Sam wins, there will be a civil war in the Republican Party starting November 3.' Further on, Mr. Suskind states that 'He truly believes he's on a mission from God.' Well, well, well, I have been saying that for two years now and some people are just starting to catch on. The reason that I got shot was because I tried to expose Sam in a book I wrote entitled 'Sam, God's Man on Earth-The Man, The Mission and the Victories. Mr. Suskind, a little further in his article states that 'The nation's founders, smarting still from the punitive pieties of Europe's state religions, were adamant about erecting a wall between organized religion and political authority. But suddenly, that seems like a long time ago. Sam-both captive and creator of this moment-has steadily, inexorably, changed the office itself. He has created the faith-based presidency. The faith based presidency is a with-us-or-against us model that has been enormously effective at, among other things, keepings the workings and the temperament of the Sam White House a kind of state secret.'

I diagnosed Sam as a delusional psychopathic narcissist years ago. Listen, this battle among the Republicans comes down to this. As far as I can tell, there are three battlefields brewing. The battlefield takes place within the Council on National Policy. First, there is the libertarian conservative Republicans that want less government without the religious trappings. This is the only non-Fascist movement within the Council's ranks. Second, you have the Constitutional Party type of Fascists that want to place the Bible and God first and then the constitution second. However, these people are like religious libertarians because they don't want forays into international wars and they are against the Patriot Act. Essentially, less government, a little religion and no foreign policy and then there is Sam. Sam believes in a full-blown Fascist state replacing the United States government with the Kingdom of God, replacing the Constitution with the Bible, rewarding his friends who spread the Gospel with faith-based initiative awards and then making wars to spread liberty and freedom though out the world, which is a euphemism for spreading the word of God and the Kingdom of Christ and therein lies his down fall. Sam is not strong enough to complete his mission. Unfortunately, many people will suffer at home and abroad. At home, Sam is outsourcing domestic security services to corporations. This will be Sam's secret police.

Mr. Suskind points out a very important matter in his article. He wrote that 'The aide said that guys like me were 'in what we call the reality-based community,' which he defined as people who believe that solutions emerge from your judicious study of discernible reality…That's not the way the world really works anymore…We're an empire now, and when we act, we create our own reality. And while you're studying that reality-judiciously, as you will-we'll act again, creating other new realities, which you can study too, and that's how things will sort out. We're history's actors…and you, all of you, will be left to study what we do.' What struck me was the line about history's actors. I recalled reading something similar and then I remembered what I was thinking about," I said. I told Jordan to get The Rise and Fall of the Third Reich. Angelina and Reuben looked content. Maki was respectful, although she understood only a third of what I said. Jordan was relieved to leave the table. No one spoke. Everyone seemed intrigued. I was sure that it was not so much my speech as my references to history and current events. Jordan came back from my office and handed me the book, which I thumbed through until I found the pages that I was looking for.

"Here, right here, on page 98, let me begin. 'On Fichte's death in 1814, he was succeeded by Georg Wilhelm Friedrich Hegel at the University of Berlin. This is the subtle and penetrating mind whose dialectics inspired Marx and Lenin and thus contributed to the founding of Communism and whose ringing glorification of the State as supreme in human life paved the way for the Second and Third Reichs of Bismarck and Hitler. To Hegel the State is all, or almost all. Among other things, he says, it is the highest revelation of world spirit, it is the moral universe, it is the actuality of the ethical idea...ethical mind...knowing and thinking itself, the State has the supreme right against the individual, whose supreme duty is to be a member of the State...for the right of the world spirit is above all special privileges...

And the happiness of the individual on earth? Hegel replies that world history is no empire of happiness. The periods of happiness, he declares, are the empty pages of history because they are periods of agreement, without conflict. War is the great purifier. In Hegel's view, it makes for the ethical health of peoples corrupted by a long peace, as the blowing of the winds preserves the sea from the foulness which would be the result of a prolonged calm.

No traditional conception of morals and ethics must disturb either the supreme State or the heroes who lead it. World history occupies a higher ground...Moral claims which are irrelevant must not be brought into collision with world-historical deeds and their accomplishments. The litany of private virtues-modesty, humility, philanthropy and forbearance-must not be raised against them...So mighty a form, the State must trample down many an innocent flower-crush to pieces many an object in its path.

Hegel foresees such a State for Germany when she has recovered her God-given genius. He predicts that Germany's hour will come and that its mission will be to regenerate the world. As one reads Hegel one realizes how much inspiration Hitler, like Marx, drew from him, even if it was second hand. Above all else, Hegel in his theory of heroes, those great agents who are fated by a mysterious Providence to carry out the will of the world spirit, seems to have inspired Hitler..." I read. The table was silent, except for Jordan. I could see he was fidgety and wanted me to end my monologue.

"So, what's it going to be Doc?" asked Rueben.

"I've been watching carefully Rueben and I think based upon everything I know and the current moves by Sam he's in the full embrace of a total Fascist state which will masquerade itself under the guise of Christianity. In the Suskind article he states that Sam will immediately proceed with further enhancing his faith based initiatives. I was listening to D. James Kennedy, a Council member and Minister of Coral Ministries, a very powerful Ministry, that he was seeking money from his flock to open a new Ministry to lobby for Christian laws to govern the United States. He is going to K Street in Washington D.C., to become a lobbyist. In the 108th Congress, 1st session a bill was introduced, H.R. 235 to amend the Internal Revenue Code of 1986 to protect the religious exercise and free speech rights of churches and other houses of worship. It is called the Houses of Worship Free Speech Restoration Act. Prior to this act, the Internal Revenue Code prevented tax-deductible organizations from entering into politics. If they did, they would lose their tax-exempt status. This bill allows them to enter into politics without losing their status. D. James Kennedy is in the process of seeking donations for a Christian lobbying arm of his ministry. In conjunction with that move, John Chalfant, a Council member recently wrote 'America-A Call to Greatness,' where in he states that 'Christians need to realize that they have the primary responsibility for reclaiming our nation's Christian heritage because it is Christianity upon which the Declaration of Independence and the Constitution were founded.' Unfortunately, this third belief system in the Council is the strongest and most vocal. These guys are the real Calvinists of the group. A Calvinist is the system of or doctrines of John Calvin, who emphasized the depravity and helplessness of man, the Sovereignty of God, and predestination and characterized by an austere moral code. You're either with these guys or against them. It's that simple and unfortunately they can't let people like us exist because we're like a virus to them that might infect others. As the Suskind article pointed out, forget the facts and just believe. A non-believer is a heretic and heretics get burned at the stake. This kind of shit can happen here and it will. All those stupid little conservatives who think that this is a game, those little knit-wit Rushies are going to get a big surprise if they don't bow down and accept the authority of the Kingdom of Christ and Jesus as their Lord and Savior. I can hear them now. Oh, I didn't know this is what they meant. I was just kinda kicking the liberals and shit like that. Duh!" I said. I looked around and once again, I had everyone's attention, except my sons.

"Let's party," Jordan shouted. It took fifteen minutes to get back in the festive mood after my sobering portrayal of what was going to happen in the United

States. I looked at my arm. The bandage that Maki placed on my arm was still there. Jordan immediately struck up another conversation with Angelina. When she caught me staring at her, she shrugged her shoulders. Jordan turned his head and shrugged his shoulders as well. "We like each other," he yelled from across the deck. I put on Salsa music and danced with Maki, having remembered that Jordan told me she was a great Salsa dancer. Indeed, she was. Angelina looked at me in awe. She was surprised that I was a great dancer. Finally, Angie was swayed to come my way after spending the entire night with Jordan. The evening wound down as my guests departed. First Rueben and then Angelina left. Maki retired to the kitchen to clean up. I sat alone with Jordan in the garden. Taz sat next to Jordan.

"So, dad, I leave you alone for a couple of years and you go kind of nuts?" said Jordan.

"Jordan, am I having a hallucination talking to you? Are you really you and is this bandage on my arm really real?" I asked.

"Yes dad, everything is real right now. You are you and I am I. The bandage is real. I got you out of your voluntary hospitalization by threatening Dr. Hatfriend. You'll be fine now, don't worry," said Jordan.

"I'm not worried, I don't know what's real and what's not anymore," I said.

"Did you ever?" asked Jordan and continued "you've always been a little wacky you know," said Jordan.

"Well, if you're real and I'm real, then come over here and give me a big god damn hug," I said. Jordan got up from the chair, walked slowly towards me and gave me a huge hug. I spotted Maki through the window and saw a tear drop from her eye. While we embraced, I whispered into Jordan's ear, "I like that woman, Jordan. I really like her," I said.

"Weren't you the one who always told me to stay away from American women? By the way, Angelina is pretty nice. Easy to talk to, great butt, good head," said Jordan.

"Are you sure you never met Angelina before?" I asked.

"Dad, I promise you, I have never met Angelina in my life," answered Jordan.

"Dad, sit down. Tell me what the hell is going on here. Do you really believe all that bull you were telling everyone? Did Rueben really make all that money that he claims he made?" asked Jordan.

"Jordan, Rueben really did make all that money and it was based upon my advice. He'll top half-a-million within thirty days. I'm just keyed into what's going on. Remember Little League, when you were a pitcher and you told me you were in the zone. Well, I'm in the zone. I treated Sam for eight or nine sessions and he's a delusional psychopathic narcissist. He really believes that he's God's man on earth and once you make that analysis, it's a great predictor of what's to come. It's not hard to figure out what's going on. Sometimes, I just can't believe what I'm researching. There really *is* a vast fascist right wing conspiracy and it's the ugly kind. Reelecting Sam as President again will only reaffirm his delusion that he's God's man and make this vast right wing more strident. We're screwed. I mean we're really screwed," I said.

"Who's screwed dad," asked Jordan.

"Homosexuals, liberals, lesbians and blacks. Everybody is screwed. A fascist state cannot exist with dissenters. It's mind control and anybody who threatens to turn the mind away from the State or cast doubt upon the State is an enemy. It doesn't make a difference which people they fry. The Christian right will fry the gays and the blacks and the true Fascists will fry everybody else. Mind control is a dangerous thing to play with and from these Nazi's perspective it's a beautiful thing. Constant propaganda inculcates in a person's mind that the belief system that is being promoted is his or her own. We're fucked," I said.

"Dad, you need a break. I don't think you're having fun anymore. What happened with Gabby? I thought you guys were getting married?" said Jordan. I got up from my chair, told Jordan to follow me and went into my office. I loaded the videodisk into a bay of my computer and told Jordan to watch.

"That's not good," said Jordan. "Is Gabby gay?" asked Jordan.

"I don't know, but the bottom line is exactly what you said. It's not good," I said.

Jordan and I were tired. Maki had been looking over our shoulder and nodded in agreement that "it wasn't good." I gave Jordan and Maki my bedroom and set up a cot in my office. I couldn't wait for tomorrow. I wanted to see if the bandage was still there. Maybe my life was just a continuing delusion.

# Chapter Twenty-Six

Instead of letting TazTwo out back in the yard, I decided to take a walk down my block. Standing in front of my stoop as Taz urinated on the tree, a neighbor walked over and said hello. She told me that she hadn't seen me around lately and I told her I was out of town. She wanted to know where the limousine was. I explained to her that my relationship with Gabby didn't work out and as a result the limousine vanished.

"Dr. Warlib, what happened to you arm?" the old woman asked.

"My son accidentally cut me and bless you for noticing. Thank you so much," I barked and walked away with a huge smile on my face. Today, at least, I wasn't delusional. I picked up The New York Times at a corner stall on Madison Avenue and walked towards the Mykonos Diner. Angelina was at her station and waved when she saw me. She beckoned me to come in.

"Where are the kids?" asked Angelina.

"Sleeping. Do you know my son?" I asked.

"No, I told you last night I never met him. Move on Stanley, it's wearing thin," said Angelina. I ordered two scrambled eggs, home fries and sausage. I watched Angelina walk back to the kitchen. She turned and smiled and gave me another exaggerated butt swagger. I was beginning to like her.

"Angie, are you my girlfriend?" I asked.

"I hope so Stan. I really like you," she said.

I finished breakfast and told Angelina to come over for dinner after work. She smiled agreeably at the suggestion and mouthed seven o' clock. I nodded in agreement. Walking out, I kissed her on the cheek and said, "see ya later sweetie." Angie pinched my butt and laughed.

Arriving at my apartment, I found Maki and Jordan fast asleep. They were exhausted from their trip back to America. I decided to skip CNN, talk radio, the war room maps and all my notes. I fixed a cup of coffee and played with Taz on the back deck. My dog was so goofy in all his shenanigans that I couldn't contain my laughter.

"You seem pretty happy today," said Jordan.

"Absolutely, today is a great day. A wonderful beautiful day," I told Jordan.

"I thought I would find you in you office pouring over your maps and notes," said Jordan.

"Not today. Today is a day for you, Maki and Taz and later my girlfriend with the butt coming over for dinner," I told Jordan.

"Ya know dad. You should stay away from Sam and all that material you have been working on. You're a much different person when you don't have your head involved with that stuff," said Jordan.

"I think you're right Jordan. Maybe I will let it go. It does have an effect on me," I told Jordan.

"Hello, this is Stan," I said.

"Stanley, you should have called me when you got out," said Dr. P.

"Everything went all right. We had a big party last night, me, Rueben, Angelina, Maki and my son Jordan," I told Dr. P.

"Well, that's nice. I think you should continue to come everyday at 4:00 p.m. and there will be no charge," said Dr. P.

"No charge. Am I your charity case?" I asked Dr. P.

"No, just let's say, your case is very interesting," said Dr. P.

"My case. What do you mean my case? You writing me up as a special case for publication?" I asked.

"Yes, I am. Do you have the Diagnostic Service Manual handy? Turn to page 305 and I'll see you at 4:00 p.m. today," said Dr. P. and hung up.

    I decided not to open up the Diagnostic Service Manual. I wanted to, however, I didn't want to ruin the day. I had enough of right-wingers, evangelical Christians, John Birchers, nuts and therapy. Maybe I was just plain happy that Jordan was back safe in the United States. I started to laugh at my own expression "safe in the United States." My son just came back to the biggest nightmare that this world would see since the defeat of Adolph Hitler. Jordan poured himself a cup of coffee and joined me at the kitchen counter.

"Dad, did you read The New York Times today?" asked Jordan.

"No, not yet. I've been trying not to ruin my day. I'm sure Dr. P. will scramble my brains a little. I'm taking a brain day off," I told Jordan.

"Listen to this. In an article by Maureen Dowd entitled 'Casualties of Faith' she writes the following: 'What does it tell about a president that his grounds for war are so weak that the only way he can justify it is by believing God wants it?' She continues that 'evangelicals call the president a messenger of God' and Sam 'really believes he's the one.' Not only that, there's another article about Pat Robertson written by David Kirkpatrick that indicates that Pat Robertson felt as if Sam is on top of the world and said 'there wouldn't be any casualties in Iraq.' Anyway, it appears that Pat Robertson caught a lot of flack from other evangelicals. Dr. Richard Land, president of the Ethics and Religious Liberties Commission of the Southern Baptist Convention said about Robertson 'I think he speaks for an ever diminishing group of evangelicals on most issues.' It sounds like what you said last night. The Council has got three different wings battling it out," said Jordan. I started laughing to myself, first quietly and then out loud. Jordan implored me to tell him the joke but I couldn't stop laughing.

"I'm sorry Jordan. I had a funny thought. What we have here are dueling Messiah's," I said and then uttered the Dueling Banjos jingle from the movie Deliverance.

"Reverend Sun Myung Moon has been giving millions out to the conservative and evangelical community for thirty years. He paid his dues. For Christ's sake, he even bailed out Jerry Falwell for 2.5 million on his Liberty University deal. Now, along comes this little upstart and in a couple of years he thinks he's the one. Dueling, goddamn freaking Messiah's. But these white Supremacists wouldn't want a Korean Messiah when they can have a white boy. Think of the mess that this creates. Moon can blow the evangelical leaders out of the water with his extensive contacts with them. Sam owns the base so he thinks the leaders better play ball and the leaders are scared shit about Moon ratting on them," I said to Jordan and repeated the "Dueling Banjo's" jingle.

"What do you think is going to happen?" asked Jordan.

"Clearly, the Kingdom of God group that advocates worldwide expansion is going to win. The Constitution Party types will be there in support but not in control. They're going to follow the Fascist model. If I had money, I'd be investing in defense and security. Sam is not done. He's selling worldwide domination under the banner of liberty and freedom," I said.

"I guess you are in the zone on this stuff," said Jordan.

The balance of the day, Jordan and I spent reminiscing about our past experiences. Maki sat next to Jordan listening intently to every story. We shared memories that included Little League, Alaska, America's national parks, Thailand and wrestling. Maki enjoyed every story. Jordan and I laughed out loud throughout the day enjoying the details of our adventures together. I asked Maki what time it was. She told me that is was 2:45 p.m. I excused myself and retired to my office to look up page 305 in the Diagnostic Service Manual.

At the top of the page in bold letters was the following: "**297.3 Shared Psychotic Disorder (Folie a' Deux).**" Dr. P. definitely got my attention. I read on, it stated:

> "Diagnostic Features
>
> The essential feature of Shared Psychotic Disorder (Folie a' Deux) is a delusion that develops in an individual who is involved in a close relationship with another person (sometimes called the 'inducer' or 'primary case') who already has a Psychotic Disorder with prominent delusions (Criterion A). The individual comes to share the delusional beliefs of the primary case in whole or in part (Criterion B). The delusion is not better accounted for by another Psychotic Disorder (e.g. Schizophrenia) or a Mood Disorder with Psychotic Features and is not due to the direct physiological effects of a substance (e.g. amphetamine) or a general medical condition (e.g. brain tumor) (Criterion C). Schizophrenia is probably the most common diagnosis of the primary case, although other diagnoses may include Delusional Disorder or Mood Disorder with Psychotic Features. The Content of the shared delusional beliefs may be dependent on the diagnosis of the primary case and include relatively bizarre delusions (e.g., that radiation is being transmitted into an apartment from a hostile power, causing indigestion and diarrhea), mood congruent delusions (e.g., that the primary case will soon receive a film contract for $2 million, allowing the family to purchase a much larger home with a swimming pool), or the non-bizarre delusions that are characteristic of Delusional Disorder (e.g., the FBI is tapping the family telephone

and trailing family members when they go out). Usually the primary case in Shared Psychotic Disorder is dominant in the relationship and gradually imposes the delusional system on the more passive and initially healthy second person. Individuals who come to share delusional beliefs are often related by blood or marriage and have lived together for a long time, sometimes in relative social isolation. If the relationship with the primary case is interrupted, the delusional beliefs of the other individual usually diminish or disappear. Although most commonly seen in relationships on only two people, Shared Psychotic Disorder can occur among a larger number of individuals, especially in family situations in which the parent is the primary case and the children, sometimes to varying degrees, adopt the parent's delusional beliefs. Individuals with this disorder rarely seek treatment and usually are brought to clinical attention when the primary case receives treatment.

### Associated Features and Disorders

Aside from the delusional beliefs, behavior is usually not otherwise odd or unusual in Shared Psychotic Disorder. Impairment is often less severe in the individual with Shared Psychotic Disorder than in the primary case."

"Hello, Stan, how are you today?" asked Dr. P.

"I'm fine, Dr. P. I read the information on Shared Psychotic Disorder and I know why you're interested in not charging me. Number one, it's rare and number two, there are no reported cases of a psychologist and patient presenting themselves with Folie a' Deux. An article in some digest would be of some interest, that's for sure, but you will have a lot of naysayers out there claiming that it's merely a case of extreme counter transference," I said.

"It's not transference, Stan. You were delusional. You were nailed to the inside of Sam's skull and forced to keep silent. What makes it particularly interesting, is that you were, or thought you were, Sam's superego, his conscience, in a battle with Sam's id. Freud would love this," said Dr. P.

"The way I see it, Dr. P., you have two problems. One is that these cases usually involve two people in a close relationship, such as a husband and wife or mother and child. You can drag in both people for treatment. You can't drag in Sam in this case. The second is that in treating me you must, by necessity, ask me questions about Sam, my patient, and I can't disclose any information about him because it's privileged communications. I can't disclose the contents of our conversations. I don't suppose you want me to ask Sam to come to you?" I asked Dr. P.

"No. You can't ask Sam for permission. I thought about those issues, but we have to work around it. My research indicates that several drugs might work well. Accordingly, I'm going to prescribe Symbyax and put you on a strict news diet. No more political junkie. I don't want you to read newspapers, magazines, watch CNN, see or hear anything to do with Sam and politics. Read the old classics, go to museums, plays, do anything but receive information concerning Sam. I'm putting your brain on vacation. Jordan is back in town, hang with him," said Dr. P.

Dr. P. and I spent the rest of my hour discussing general issues and the research on Shared Psychotic Disorder. I could discuss money matters with Rueben. That was a relief. I arrived home at 5:30 p.m. Jordan and Maki were in the kitchen preparing dinner. Being an excellent cook, Jordan decided to prepare a Japanese style fish dish, head and all. It smelled delicious.

"Hey dad, how did it go?" asked Jordan.

"Not bad. You'll like the treatment to cure me. No more soapbox. I'm off the freaking soapbox. No Sam, no politics, no speeches, nothing. I bet you'll like that," I said.

"It's about time, however, can you make one exception. I've been out of the country for 2 ½ years and all I'm hearing is God and religion. What the hell is going on here in America? I can't believe it," said Jordan.

"I'll think about it, but if I decide to talk it's the last time. I really don't want to be delusional anymore. It's scary, Jordan, really scary," I said.

I poured myself a glass of white wine and stood next to Maki. She called me Stanley-San every time she spoke to me. Angelina walked in around 6:15 p.m., kissed me on the cheek, gave Jordan and Maki a hug and studied the wonderful meal that Jordan was preparing. Angie inquired about my meeting with Dr. P. and asked some non-threatening questions and let the issue drop. Angelina and I prepared the table on the deck. Jordan brought out a large platter with a beautiful whole red snapper prepared in chili sauce, garnished with scallions and wasabe mustard. Five bottles of white wine were on the table. I knew that we were going to get plastered. Jordan was into the slow food movement. If he prepared dinner, his guests had better be prepared to stay a long time. I told Angie that I was precluded from talking about religion, Sam, politics and current events. She wanted to know if I knew anything about anything else other than those subjects. "I don't know Angie, we'll find out," I told her and then added "how about making love." She smiled and kissed me on the lips. We continued eating, drinking and telling stories throughout the night. Finally, Jordan asked me a second time to answer his question about what was going on in America. Reluctantly, I agreed, but advised everyone that this was the last time. I told everyone to follow me into the office and typed in www.reformation.net and "Welcome to Coalition on Revival" appeared. I double clicked on "About COR" and permitted the group to read. It stated:

"The Coalition on Revival is a network of evangelical leaders from many major denominational and theological perspectives who share a vision for and commitment to revival, renewal, and reformation of the Church and society. COR's vision is to see Christians everywhere doing all they can in the power of the Holy Spirit to take every thought captive to the obedience of Christ in every aspect of life. COR's mission is "to help the Church rebuild civilization on the principles of the Bible so God's will may be done on earth as it is in heaven."

People of Anabaptist, Arminian, Lutheran, Calvinist, and Wesleyan denominational backgrounds are all represented among COR's leaders. Pre-, a-, and post-millennialists are cooperating with each other, sharing the exciting task of getting God's will to be done on earth as it is in heaven insofar as that is possible between now and whenever Christ comes back to Earth. Charismatics and non-charismatics, covenant and dispensationalist theologians, have joined arm in arm in prayer and hard work to see revival, renewal, and reformation in the Christian Church and the American culture.

COR's vision is to see Christians everywhere doing all they can in the power of the Holy Spirit to take every thought captive to the obedience of Christ (2 Cor. 10:5), in every aspect of life. Toward that end, we have developed a series of worldview documents that set forth what we believe are the fundamental and essential points of the total Christian world and life view. The COR worldview documents state what we believe are the biblical principles for all spheres of human life including theology, evangelism, discipleship, law, civil governments, economics, education, family, medicine, psychology and counseling, arts and media, business and professions, and science and technology. We believe that the

COR worldview documents state where the entire Church must stand and what action it must take to accomplish its task in the remaining years of the Twentieth Century and on into the next century.

COR has, in the past, brought together large groups of Christian leaders to produce a series of foundational documents to guide the Church in its return to historic orthodoxy. These documents include: <u>The Manifesto for the Christian Church</u>, the <u>42 Articles on Historic Christian Doctrine</u>, the <u>25 Articles of Affirmation and Denial on the Kingdom of God</u>, and a comprehensive series of <u>17 World View Documents</u> the outline the Christian world view in areas of life and thought. All of these documents are in turn based on the historic view of the Bible stated in The Chicago Statement on Biblical Inerrancy, created by the International Council on Biblical Inerrancy, which COR's director, <u>Dr. Jay Grimstead</u>, helped found and of which he was executive director in the early years. In addition, COR has organized a massive theological study and debate proposed to culminate in a global Church Council during the early years of the new millennium.

## Our Perspective

Wherever God's people, His willingly obedient subjects, are obeying Him in every aspect of their lives, there is where the King's Kingdom is being brought forth in this world in time and space.

It is inconceivable that it could be logical or that it could ever please the King to have His willing subjects bring their spiritual, theological, and ecclesiastical lives under His dominion without also bringing their families, finances, education, legal matters, professional life, voting choices, involvement in the arts and sciences, recreation, and physical health all under the King's dominion.

The Kingdom of God increases, advances, and becomes measurable in this space-time world in every sphere of life, as more and more individuals become truly regenerated, converted and discipled and let their Christianity and their commitment to the King's laws and values be expressed through the various facets and relationships of their lives.

Wherever and whenever and to whatever degree that Christians are making a united stand in their societal groupings for the concerns of their King, Jesus, and are operating according to His Kingdom's principles, exactly at that point is the

Kingdom of God in existence on this earth. When enough serious Christians thus influence, penetrate, and permeate enough various societal structures, and when those Christians are connected together in a common fellowship and commitment around their common Lord, that is when and where the Kingdom of God can be said to be advancing through society during this age."

"Everybody read that?" I asked. "Any questions?"

"Yes, I have a question?" said Maki. "What does all that stuff mean?"

"It means, let's stop bickering and have the Kingdom of God on earth right here and now, and that means the Kingdom of God in every aspect of life; families, finances, education, legal matters, professional life, voting choices, involvement in the arts and sciences, recreation, and physical health. Got it! A Fascist Christian state and anyone who doesn't go along with the program is a heretic and enemy of the state. COR has sponsored a new consensus effort to deal with serious heresies that challenge the new modern church. It's called the International Church Council and it's developing a new set of documents that set forth standards for all churches to follow. Now, listen to this, they have some interesting names on their National Steering Committee. For example, John Beckett, Robert Dugan, Michael Farris, Peter Gemma, Dr. Duane Gish, Dr. D. James Kennedy, Dr. Tim LaHaye, Ed McAteer, Dr. Gary North, Dr. J.I. Packer, Jerry Regier and Dr. R.J. Rushdoony. Do you know why I mention their names? Because they are all members of the Council on National Policy! At the center of this vast spider web is the Council and the web continues to expand outward interconnected by little threads forming ever—expanding circles around the inner circle. I'm telling you, it's a vast fascist right wing conspiracy. I'm not kidding. Take for example the Free Congress Foundation set up by Paul Weyrich, a big heavyweight on the Council. He also set up The Heritage Foundation, the most influential political think tank in Washington, D.C. The Free Congress Foundation evolved from the Committee for the Survival of a Free Congress and Free Congress Research and Education Foundation and was founded by Colorado beer magnate Joseph Coors. The Free Congress Foundation gets the bulk of its money from The Carthage Foundation, Sarah Scaife Foundation, The Lynde and Harry Bradley Foundation and The Castle Rock Foundation. Richard Mellon Scaife, a Council member, runs the Carthage and Scaife Foundations and The Castle Rock Foundation is a Coors foundation and the Coors are also Council members. The entire conspiracy always can be traced back to the Council on National Policy. It's huge, powerful, influential and moneyed. I mean, it's never ending. It just goes on and on and on. However, this is what makes me laugh the most. Sam's faith based initiatives. The Moonies are all over this and Sam is lining up more and more of his Council members and their abundant organizations to bring about the Kingdom of Christ. I mean we're paying to bring our own Fascist state to America. What a freaking joke. I'm paying for my own demise. It's brilliant. Just God inspired brilliancy and that's it. I'm done. No more Sam and politics and in the name of my favorite civil rights leader, Dr. Martin Luther King, let me say, 'free at last, free at last, thank God almighty, I'm free at last. O.K., boys and girls, now what do I do," I concluded. Everyone clapped. Jordan suggested a toast to freedom and Maki ran to get another bottle of wine. We all raised our glasses and toasted to "Freedom." "Religion is a cesspool of insanity. Let the delusions be over," I said. Everyone, said "amen," and laughed.

The next morning I called Rueben and told him I'm back in business and that I wanted him to come over for dinner and a resumption of the war room. "We're into money," I advised Rueben.

"You bet we are Doc. We're going to be floating in the stuff. Everything you told me is panning out, including the dollar. Yesterday, our April light crude contracts closed at $52.02. We bought in at $41.54. We're up $10.42 a barrel and we have 25,000 barrels. Doc, we're up $260,500.00. Gold is up, the market is down and our euro contracts are starting to make a big move," said Rueben.

"Rueben, what do you mean 'we're' in every sentence?" I asked.

"We're, as in you and I. We're partners. Don't you remember? When you were negotiating with Charles Westerfield about a signing bonus and you were going to use me to invest on your behalf you gave me $40,000.00. I put in my own $40,000.00 and we became buddies. You know, Semper Fi and all that,' said Rueben.

"Really, I gave you forty grand. I don't remember. I remember negotiating with Charles and then I walked out," I said.

"Doc, trust me. You gave me forty grand. Check your checking account," said Rueben.

"As soon as I get off the phone. By the way, how much do we have?" I asked.

"We're close to half a million. Your share is about $250,000.00," said Rueben and hung up the phone.

I immediately went into my office and went online to examine my bank account. Rueben was correct. I made out a check to him. I was delusional and up a quarter of a million dollars. Jordan and I spent the day at the Metropolitan Museum of Art. Maki stayed at home and contacted the United Nations seeking employment. On the way home, we passed the Mykonos Diner and waved to Angelina. She came outside and shouted "6:00 tonight" and I gave her the "o.k." sign with my fingers. At 4:00 p.m. I arrived promptly at Dr. P.'s office. We had an in-depth discussion about my delusions and discussed various theories of how we could get around the psychologist-patient privilege that existed between Sam and I. Half-jokingly Dr. P. told me to ask Sam if he would come to therapy. Half-jokingly, I told Dr. P. that Sam couldn't come because he was too busy being the Messiah. "After all, Messiah's are busy people," I told Dr. P. I told Dr. P. about my good fortune in having invested with Rueben. Dr. P. told me that early on Rueben mentioned my uncanny knack of picking trends and Dr. P. hinted at the possible disclosure to him of my picks. "Greed knows no boundaries," I said to Dr. P. He laughed. Dr. P. asked me if I had any noticeable reaction to the medication and I told him that I had not. "See ya tomorrow," he said as I walked out the door. "Yes, I'll let you in on some investment advice," I said to Dr. P. who smiled at being included in my new financial gang.

Rueben and Angelina showed up promptly at six o' clock. We had wine waiting for them. Maki took the day off from cooking and studied her English. Jordan and I manned the kitchen, as we had done a thousand times when he was growing up. It felt good to be together again. Declaring the dinner to be a celebration of my good fortune, Jordan and I decided to cook Chateaubriands and grilled asparagus. Over dinner, I explained to the group that we were all going into business, so to speak, because I wanted my newly constituted family to survive the upcoming financial catastrophe. A show of hands indicated that the group was content with money being the new soapbox topic and religion being off the table. Jordan and Maki promised to contribute $10,000.00 to the venture and Angelina was in for $25,000.00. Rueben advised everyone that he would set up books to keep accurate track of all contributions and distributions. We would each participate in profits to the percentage that our contribution made to the whole. I asked everyone if they felt secure permitting a delusional nut run the show and all nodded with approval. That was an easy answer because Rueben told the group how much he and I made in one month of investing. No one wanted Dr. P. included. "It's all about the Benjamins," shouted Jordan. "It's all about taking your wine and following me into the war room," I said. Everyone got up from the deck and marched triumphantly into the newly reconstituted war room. It's amazing how fast money makes friends. At the entrance to my office I stopped and said to the group, "is this real or this a delusion." Angelina pinched my arm that left a mark. "It's real," I said and continued to march into the room. Jordan, a map lover, picked up a world map and placed it on an easel. Rueben picked up a map of the Caspian Region and placed it on another easel.

"O.K. group. Before I proceed any further, I'm going to get Angelina, Jordan and Maki up to speed. Rueben and I are long gold; short the stock market, long euro and long oil. When I say 'long' I mean we're betting that it's going up and when I say 'short' we're betting that it's going down. Here is a brief scenario, an overview, if you will, of where we stand. America is broke. I don't know how many writers and books can explain this subject over and over, but we're broke. All obligations that America owes amount to approximately seventy four trillion dollars. We cannot repay that amount under any circumstances. There will be a deflationary depression within five years. America will repudiate its debt and the world will be in an economic disaster. Between now and then, we'll make millions, cash out and retire to the South of France. What will happen in America is as follows: the disaster will usher in the Kingdom of God, the lunatics will claim that is God's wrath that caused the disaster, they will blame the liberals for the disaster and the culmination of thirty years of work will be completed. If you want any help, you'll have to go to faith based Christian organizations, declare your allegiance to Jesus and beg for salvation. If you don't, you'll starve. Starvation is a great motivator. During this period of time we will make our money and get the hell out of here. I hate to tell you this but Sam will win in November. The world placed their bets during the beginning of October of this year, around October 5, 2004, and the dollar has been losing it's value ever since. They know Sam and expect more of the same. I expect the euro to go to $1.35 from its current position of $1.26. That's at least a nine-cent move. Accordingly, we'll take Jordan, Maki and Angelina's money and double up on our long euro position. Gold moves with interest rates until the world will start to see structural instability and get's freaked out. Then gold will move not with interest rates but out of fear. Everybody with me," I said. They all nodded in agreement. I could have been talking in Farsi; it would not have made a difference. Everyone was busy calculating his or her returns. Jordan, in the span of two minutes probably thought in terms of $30,000.00 on $10,000.00 and Angelina was probably up at $75,000.00.

"Now for the bad news. Don't cry one tear if the market goes against you for a day or a week. Have faith in the long term. Start to think like investors and ask serious questions. Don't think I'm a financial guru. You can get out anytime you want. Think, think, and then think again. Money is serious business. If financial people get on television and state day after day that they can't figure out how America is going to pay when the baby boomers start to retire, a light bulb should go off in your head. We're broke and the world's largest debtor nation. Our economy is financed by China and Japan. They buy all our securities with the money that comes from the trade imbalance. They own America. In August, they bought fewer securities than the month before. If a trend develops, we must move accordingly. That is a signal that China and Japan are demanding higher interest rates on their investments. Why? Because America is becoming an ever-increasing risk! Alan Greenspan is looking for any reason to raise interest rates and he can't. He knows that the auto and home markets will start to decline, which are the two biggest consumer purchases in the United States. Essentially, Sam is caught between a rock and hard place. However, as I told you before, Sam is a delusional psychopathic narcissist and he doesn't really care. He's one of Hegel's heroes. He's busy writing history and we're left to try to figure it out. But, but, but, this group is keyed into what's going on so we'll stay one step ahead. Let Sam write history. We're going to make money and I mean lots of money.

"Everyone raise a glass and toast to money," said Jordan.

"To money," said Angelina and smashed her glass against my office wall. Maki, Jordan and I turned around and imitated Angie, yelling to 'money' as we threw our glasses.

"This wine is too good to throw," said Rueben who took another gulp and then smashed his glass against the wall.

"Does everyone here kind of know what I'm talking about?" I asked.

"Dad, I think I do, but I'm not sure. It's going to be hard to get everyone into your mind set. I think the best thing to do is just begin. I'm sure we'll pick it up as you go along."

"Are you people sure this is not a delusion?" I asked. Angelina pinched my arm and left another mark that was clearly visible. "All right, let's start right here, right now. I think in terms of cartoons in my head. Many times I refer to China as the big Kung-Fu Master and Russia as the Great Bear. The Middle Eastern countries and the Caspian Sea Muslims I refer to as the, let me see, the Great Mullahs. All right, it's Friday, October 22, 2004 and the first article I see in the Business Day section of the New York Times is entitled 'Is is time to Stem Asia Deficits with a Weak Dollar?' The author states that America needs a weak dollar to stem the deficit in trade. Neither Sam nor his opponent is talking about our trade problem on the campaign trail. What this means is that the dollar must be pushed lower and thereby increase the cost of imports to American consumer. The bottom line is that out of necessity the dollar is going lower. To keep the dollar steady against Eastern countries, China, Japan, Hong Kong, South Korea, Taiwan and Singapore add to their treasury holdings at least half a billion dollars day. The Europeans don't do that and therefore, the euro heads higher. And that's why we're long euro. This one is for Rueben. It's about oil being weaponized to bring financial ruin to the United States. Did I tell you this stuff Rueben? Oh, never mind. High oil prices are a weapon. In the World Business Section there is an article entitled 'Safeguarding Columbia's Oil.' The article further states that 'Oil is Columbia's No. 1 export, providing nearly a third of the states revenues. Latin America's third largest exporter of oil, Columbia has long been among the top 10 suppliers of crude to the United States.' Here's the important part; 'But the Washington-backed offensive has another motive, oil and military authorities say, the one that Columbia and American officials only gingerly discuss: to make potentially oil rich regions safe for exploration by private companies and the government run oil company.' Blowing up pipelines has been legitimized as a target for terror. And why not? All the oil riches from oil never flow to poor people; they flow to the owners to enrich themselves. It doesn't hurt the rebels blowing up oil facilities. Now, all this commotion is going on because we have less oil and it is becoming scarcer. Wind power will never be a viable substitute to replace oil. However, nuclear energy will. We're going to look into uranium as a possible investment. Australia and Canada are the largest uranium producers. Therefore, tomorrow I will start researching Australian and Canadian mining companies as possible investments. Realizing that nuclear reactors are the quickest road to fulfilling energy needs, Sam wants to control uranium. Anyone who wants to build a reactor will be declared to have evil intentions. Take Iran for example. Iran states that it has no evil motive and Sam says that Iran is part of the axis of evil. Europe is trying to broker a deal and is telling Iran that it will supply Iran with its nuclear materials. Iran has told Sam and the Europeans, in easy to understand language to go shove it. Ain't no deal going to happen. Everybody has backed off, claiming that they will make progress after the elections. This is not going to happen. Iran is the largest oil supplier to the Grand Kung-Fu Master and Iran is protected. Iran has drawn a line in the sand. Iraq and no more advances. Sam better be prepared for war because Iran will not give in. Therefore, our gold position is strong because of the continued world turbulence. I had enough. I'm tired," I said and asked if anyone had any questions. It was late and my group decided to split up and call it a night. Angelina decided to sleep over which was a welcomed gift. I was tired but horny. Taz snuggled next to us on the couch. Angelina lied snuggled within my arms with her lips next to my ear. She kissed me gently and started to talk.

"How are you doing Doc? Is everything all right?" she asked.

"I don't know Angie. Having delusions is weird. It's like a big chunk of my life is missing and yet I had a certain reality that was just as real as you lying here in my arms. It's just that that reality didn't exist. I don't feel like I'm connecting to anyone. I feel like I'm barking at everybody, lecturing all the time and I'm all stirred up. I'm not feeling anybody. If I'm not ranting about Sam and his religious buddies, I'm delivering financial advice. I miss my quiet little practice and all my screwballs.

"Well, can we do anything about it?" asked Angelina.

"My shrink thinks that I have something called Shared Psychotic Disorder. I share a delusion with my former patient Sam, who, as you know, is head of this family. God speaks to Sam and I hear God as well because I'm mailed to the inside of Sam's skull," I said.

"You mean nailed, the same way Jesus was nailed to a cross?" asked Angelina.

"Exactly Angie, just like Jesus to a cross. In my case, I'm actually part of Sam's mind. I'm his superego and I'm battling his id. Freud would have a field day. I guess it's serious. I don't know. I do know that I haven't been myself lately. I used to be fun. I was a big flirt, believe it or not," I said.

"Come on Doc, you're talking to me. Don't you think I know that? We've been flirting for two years. We have to start having some fun. How about if we all go out dancing tomorrow night?" asked Angie.

"I'm up for that," I said to Angelina and kissed her gently on the forehead. Angelina started kissing me on the chest making her way south to my feet. I let out a big sigh.

## Chapter Twenty-Seven

Saturday morning, Jordan and Maki were up before Angie and I. They were sitting at the kitchen counter, thumbing through The New York Times.

"You only can have the financial section dad," said Jordan.

"Anything interesting this morning?" I asked.

"I'd say so. The market went down to new lows for 2004. It lost 107 points and I think our group is short the S & P, so we made lots of money there. Gold was up a little and oil busted through $55.00.

"Jordan, every time oil goes up a buck, we all make $25,000.00. How about the euro?" I asked.

"Euro is up. We're making money across the board," said Jordan.

"Jordan, give your dad some breathing room. He just got up. Why don't you and your dad go do something today? Take off and go play," said Angelina.

"Angie, great minds think alike. My fishing rod is already out. I have my baseball glove handy and I'm ready to rock and roll," said Jordan.

"Stan, what do you think?" said Angie.

"I don't have to think about that. We'll be out of here in twenty minutes. Do you know this is peak season for the fall leaves? Fishing, play catch, take a ride, I think I'm in heaven," I said to the group.

"And don't forget about dinner and dancing tonight" Angelina reminded me.

Thirty minutes later, Jordan and I were headed across the George Washington Bridge going up Route 17 to Camp-Moor to buy some fishing rods and worms. Our direction was north but our destination was unknown. I got off Route 17 near the New York border and took any small country road I could find. I was looking for those small narrow two lane highways that were enveloped with falls beautiful colors. The scenery was outstanding. Jordan rode shotgun and studied a map looking for a small lake within fifty miles. There was no reason to talk and generally all talk between Jordan and I was reserved for playing catch.

"Dad, about twenty miles up this road, it looks like that there's a small state park with a lake," said Jordan.

"Find me a river with no access so we can do a little bushwhacking," I said. Jordan went back to studying the map. I looked for a mellow Jazz station to compliment the colors of the season. Jordan and I stared out the window. Nothing was said between us. Jordan spotted a stream from the road. I drove until I found a spot where we could pull in and park. Walking down the embankment towards the stream, I slipped and Jordan started laughing. It was the beginning of one of our usual adventures.

"You're starting early," said Jordan. I knew what he meant. For the last ten years, whenever we went on one of our adventures, I usually wound up in trouble. One day in Thailand we took motorbikes down a dirt road for ten miles and stopped at an elephant village. For some reason, a baby elephant didn't like me and chased me around until he had me cornered and whipped his trunk across my thigh that left a welt for three days. The villagers and Jordan couldn't stop laughing. Thereafter, I stuck my hand in scalding water in a hot spring. I thought the steam emanating from the hot spring was morning mist. It was not. Jordan took control of our little ventures and always made sure that I had my afternoon medication, beer and a nap. Slipping down the embankment I envisioned that by the end of the day we would have to call Maki and Angie to make bail after being arrested for catching a blue gill without a license. I relished these little father-son adventures.

"Maki, how long do you know Jordan?" asked Angelina.

"Almost two years. We have been dating for year and half," Maki answered.

Angelina discovered through conversation that Maki was a regional javelin champion and in addition, an expert knife thrower. Maki was on a local salsa dance team in Northern Japan and met Jordan at an Aikido school. Angie was impressed with Maki's various life interests and her mannerisms, which exhibited a certain degree of kindness.

Jordan and I crossed a small stream and followed it up a valley to a larger feeder stream. Jordan rigged the rod for bottom fishing hoping to catch a Muskie. Neither of us ever caught a Muskellunge and I seriously doubted that a New York lake would have one. However, none of it mattered since the point was not to catch fish but to hang out with my son. Immediately after Jordan rigged the rod, he tackled me, and ten minutes of faux wrestling ensued. Neither of used full strength, just enough to make it seem like someone was trying to win. Rolling around in the leaves, "rastling," brought back many memories. When I stood up and told Jordan that I had had enough, he grabbed my hand, twisted it and bent it backwards. I asked Jordan if he missed Aikido and he told me that he continued his training in Japan and achieved black belt status, although he was reluctant to tell me that he had a black belt. It seemed every Aikido practitioner was always reluctant to talk about what color belt they had. It made no difference to them; Aikido people were always students, even the Masters. Picking up our baseball gloves, Jordan and I started throwing the ball back and forth. First, at a small distance and then adding several feet between us with each successive five throws. We were in a beautiful open area with all of fall's color thrust upon us. Brilliant yellows and reds, with occasional oranges surrounding our private "field of dreams." I stopped for a moment and looked at the rod to see if anything was tugging on the line.

"I told you we won't catch anything,' yelled Jordan.

"I haven't got skunked in twenty years," I yelled back. It only took twenty minutes of solid throwing before my shoulder started to ache. Jordan noticed that my pitches were getting softer and shorter and stopped throwing. We walked to the side of the stream sat down and checked our line. I reeled in the worm and felt a drag on the line. Jordan asked me if I had a fish but only a small Lilly pad was attached. Unbeknownst to me, beyond the Lilly pad was a six-inch yellow perch. Jordan was impressed. We hooked the fish with a "louie" which was Warlib speak meaning that the fish was hooked in the lip. Jordan gently removed the hook from the fish and urged the perch to swim away. We sat by the edge of the stream in silence until a chill descended upon the mountain and after twenty minutes decided to leave. Walking back towards the car in silence, Jordan said only one thing to me.

"Dad, if you really have this Shared Psychotic Disorder illness, you give Sam way to much power. If Sam thinks he powerful, then you by extension, think he's powerful. He's not that powerful and there isn't some vast fascist conspiracy to bring the Kingdom of God to America. You're sharing his delusion, that's all. Give it a break," said Jordan.

"You're wise beyond your years," I said and continued walking.

When Jordan and I arrived home, Angelina and Maki were on the back deck throwing knives. They were laughing at Angie's inability to hit the target, which was my chopping board.

"You women having a good time?" I asked.

"Yeah, we're having a blast," answered Angelina. "Catch any fish, boys?" asked Angie.

Jordan told Angelina that we caught a yellow perch and released it. I needed a nap. I went into my office and lied on the couch and within one minute, Angelina was lying next to me, snuggled up close.

"We're going dancing tonight, right?" she asked.

"Of course. I want to put Maki to the test. She claims that she's a great Salsa dancer." Jokingly, I asked Angelina if she lived with me. "Guess so," was all that she said. At six o' clock, Angie and I woke up. Jordan and Maki were sleeping in my bedroom. We snuck into the shower and started washing each other's hair. Angie grabbed my penis claiming that she was merely washing it, however, she was trying to get me hard. We were having such a good time that we woke Jordan and Maki up from their sleep. Jordan yelled, "stop fooling around in there," which made us only laugh more. At this point I realized that Dr. P. gave me sound advice. Removing myself from the incessant media barrage that I was living in only fed into my Shared Psychotic Disorder. In addition, I was sure that the medication was beginning to take hold. Life was better without being part of Sam's psychosis and I had a beautiful woman in my shower to prove it. I stood next to Angie as the water streamed down our faces and asked her if she was my girlfriend. She nodded her head and said "absolutely." She told me that she wanted to date me for two years but was precluded by the presence of Gabby. "Are you my boyfriend?" Angie asked. "Absolutely, positively, inexorably and yes," I said to Angie. Angie and I could feel Jordan and Maki waiting for us to stop having a great time in the shower. We got dressed and drank a glass of wine as we waited for Jordan and Maki. Dinner was wonderful. Our group agreed upon an Argentinean tappas bar where we drank and had appetizers. Later on, Maki proved every bit as good as she claimed. She was a *great* Salsa dancer. It was the most fun I had had in a long time. By two a.m., everyone was exhausted and we all agreed to go home. Angelina insisted on swinging by her apartment for several minutes to pick up some clothes. She came down with a briefcase and started laughing. "Oh well," she said as she entered into the cab.

Sunday, I went out to the store with Taz who seemed much happier the last several days. I believed that he was deeply affected by my delusional episodes as well. In any event, TazTwo was one happy puppy. Walking back home with my dog and The New York Times under my arm, I realized that I really wasn't meant to be rich like Mr. Westerfield. Big money is a corruptor and even though I was unemployed and in therapy I was having a great time. I picked up a dozen bagels, scallion cream cheese and lox at a neighborhood deli and walked home. I gave Taz the bag of bagels, which he dutifully carried proudly. Angie, Maki and Jordan were waiting at in the kitchen and asked aloud "what took me so long?"

Angie grabbed The New York Times as Jordan grabbed the bag of bagels out of Taz's mouth. Jordan asked, "who wants their bagel toasted?" to which everyone raised their hands. Maki helped Jordan set the kitchen counter. I made coffee. I was precluded from reading the paper, except that I was permitted to read the book review. There was an interesting article by Woody Allen about George S. Kaufman and not much else. Mitch Albom's Tuesday's with Morrie was still on the best-seller list having been on the list for 96 weeks. I read an article entitled "The People's Court," written by Laurence H. Tribe about a book entitled "The People Themselves" written by the new Dean of Stanford Law School, Larry D. Kramer. I was reading one paragraph: "The world according to Kramer is one in which 'we the people' not only shared in construing the Constitution but also rendered the final verdict on its meaning-until 'sometime in the past generation or so, when we were tricked into losing our constitutional voice and submitting meekly to judicial imperialism.' "They're here," I muttered to myself. Jordan heard the remark and leaned over my shoulder. As soon as he saw the article, he ripped the book review out of my hands and said "Doctors orders." He told me to stick to money, after all "you're unemployed," he said.

"Look dad, let me get serious for a minute," said Jordan. The room went silent. "I listen to people when they talk and I have been listening to your bullshit for several days. Did you know that Dr. James Dobson was promoting a Million Marriage March in Washington, D.C. for October 15, 2004? You know, the vast right wing conspiracy guys. Well, the organizers put the march at 1,000,000 people and the police put attendance at 100,000. Got it! Only one tenth of the expected crowd and that's exactly what their power is: one tenth of what you think they got. Besides, they're not the God damn problem, the stinking rich people are the problem," said Jordan. He was visibly upset and took his coffee and TazTwo out to the deck. Maki followed.

"What the hell got him so pissed off?" I asked Angelina.

"I don't know. Does he have a thing against rich people?" she asked.

"I never knew him to have," I said and added "Geez, I guess there's been a lot of growing up in the last 2 ½ years. Maybe I don't know my son as well as I thought I did." Through the kitchen window I watched as Maki put her hand on Jordan's shoulder and whispered into his ear. He smiled and returned to the kitchen. He stood behind me and whispered, "I'm sorry." Angelina and Maki went out to buy some finger food for the Jets-Pat game and the second game of the World Series.

I realized that if Angelina was going to hang out at my apartment, I needed to remove my desk from the office and buy a convertible couch for us to sleep in. My apartment was not user friendly for four people. The Patriots squeaked by the Jets and the Boston Red-Sox looked liked winners.

Monday morning the phone rang at 8:30 a.m. and I knew it was Rueben.

"Doc, we're looking good. There's some kind of strike threatened in Norway, which will effect off shore production. Norway is the world's third largest oil producer. Oil futures are up. Gold busted through $430.00 and the S & P futures index is down and the euro is almost at $1.28 to the dollar. We're up over $50,000.00 before the bell," said Rueben.

"How about saying hello first?" I said. I was half-kidding but Rueben apologized anyway. Clearly, he was excited and told me that he would be over in the evening. After I hung up, I told Jordan and Maki what Rueben had told me and I could see in their eyes that they were spending their profits. Angelina had gone to work at 6:00 a.m. and I thought that when I took TazTwo for a walk, I would pass the diner and let her know about the early morning financial gains. Jordan and Maki made plans to visit the Empire State Building and the Cloisters. By 10:00 a.m. I was alone and decided to resume my war room activities and in particular, studying my maps.

From my perspective, Sam's only reason to be in the Middle East was for oil. Having been kicked out of Saudi Arabia, Sam established a beachhead in Iraq for further excursions east towards Syria or west into the Caucasus region. It was important to note that Iraq had an estimated 112.5 billion barrels of crude oil in reserves. TazTwo stared at me as I laughed out loud at the thought of Sam not having an "exit strategy." After all, why should Sam have an exit strategy when he had no intention of exiting after toppling Saddam Hussein? Sam was there to stay. I realized that thinking of Sam in geo-political terms did not have the same effect on me as when I thought of him in terms of his domestic plans for the Kingdom of God. During the second debate, Sam's opponent stated that he thought that Sam was building ten to sixteen military bases that might be permanent in structure and I was convinced that that was the case. This particular subject was never discussed in the general media or on the cable stations. However, if sixteen permanent bases were indeed being built, it would be evidence of an intention to stay in Iraq and hence there would be no need for an exit strategy. Coupled with numerous statements from politicians to retired Generals, the collective opinion was that Sam would be in Iraq from five to twenty years. Sam's pronouncements of spreading liberty, democracy and free elections in Iraq were a sham in view of his backing of the current front-runner, interim leader Alwayi, a man with extensive C.I.A. ties. Their first choice was Chalabi, convicted in absentia by Jordan for being a bank embezzler. Sam's process of installing puppets loyal to him reminded me of Henry Ford who stated in the early years that a car buyer could have any color he wanted as long as it was black. In Afghanistan and Iraq, these alleged new democracies could have any democracy and leaders that they wanted as long as they were Sam's boys. Afghanistan's interim President Hamid Karzai, and now current President elected after the recent democratic vote had strong ties to Unocal, an American oil company. The maps that I was studying showed that the entire mess in Iraq revolved around the Middle East and the Caspian Sea region and in particular, the oil routes to get oil to Europe and America. In opposition, Russia, Iran and China were building strong coalitions for the same reasons and using northern oil routes controlled by Russia. Sam was betting on establishing Southern routes bypassing Iran and Russia and shipping oil via a Baku-Tblisi-Ceyhan route, the capitols of Azerbaijan, Georgia and Turkey, respectively to the west servicing Europe and America and a southern oil route east through Turkmenistan, Afghanistan and Pakistan, servicing India, Japan and hopefully China. Sam truly believed that his military strength would enable him to pull off this grandiose plan of controlling the last remaining viable region of oil. Exploration was out and invading sovereign countries was in. If Sam made another move, whatever remaining respect he had in the world would evaporate and alliances would form for his active destruction. I could envision the world dumping the dollar as the leading currency in favor of euros. The biggest dollar prop was China and Japan buying Sam's treasury securities and I was sure from their prospective, Sam looked like a drunk with a credit card running up his debt. Only one conclusion could be made: Sam had no intention of paying his debts and repudiating his debt entirely was not out of the question. Indeed, controlling oil and the course of the 21$^{st}$ century was enough incentive for any psychopathic narcissist. I needed a magnifying glass to view the very small dotted green lines on the map indicating oil and gas pipeline routes. The oil pipeline routes in Iraq proved most interesting. I decided to take a break and I took TazTwo out for walk past the Mykonos Diner. Angelina blew a kiss in my direction and mouthed six o' clock. I gave her the "o.k." sign and continued my stroll on Madison Avenue. I thought about how beautiful Angelina really was. She was a looker and no one could match her butt.

The main oil pipeline in Iraq started at the southern port of Al Faw on the Persian Gulf. It passed several miles west of Basrah, Fallujah, Karbarla and Ramadi. The pipeline ran generally northwest. At the town of Al Hadithah, a pipeline coming southwest from the northern oil fields of Kirkuk connected to the main pipeline. At Al Hadithah, the pipeline veered west towards and through Syria. Another pipeline, starting north of Baghdad, ran north parallel to the Tigris River and headed north to Turkey. In Turkey it veered west straight to the Mediterranean Sea and ended at the port of Iskenderun. In my opinion, Iran, China and Russia drew a line in the sand and presented a more dangerous threat to Sam than heading west to Syria. The pipeline split several miles from the coast and one leg ran into Lebanon and ended at the Mediterranean Port town of Tarabulus. The other leg ran into the Syrian port town of Baniyas. Having captured Iraq, the next move would be for Sam to reward his financial buddies with oil and oil related contracts to commence a rehabilitation of Iraq's oil fields and infrastructure. However, the most desired route for oil was not out of the port on the Persian Gulf and around Africa but through Syria to the Mediterranean Sea. This particular route would save an incredible amount of time and money. Syria was in Sam's crosshairs and was a walking target. Syria had to be shitting in its pants. Sam already exhibited his absolute willingness to invade a foreign country on dubious terms and Syria would be no exception. I envisioned the private meetings between Sam's Department of State and the Syrian government. It was not a negotiation but a threat: either you permit the United States to transport oil through Syria or my boss, Uncle Sam will invade your country. In Sam's language, you're either with me or against me. The question was: how does my group make money from this analysis? What was clear was that Osama bin Laden, Syria and Iran would never let up in their support for insurgents and sympathetic Iraqis against the occupation of Iraq by Sam. It just wasn't going to happen. Sam had better be prepared for a long extended deadly occupation with more of his young sons coming home in a box. Still, how was I going to make money? For sure, high oil was here to stay, instability would keep gold high and the market low and the euro made a major move towards new highs. If nothing else, we were positioned correctly. Maybe, I would suggest to the group that we keep steady and not venture into anything other than what our money was presently invested in. The necessity of a draft was clear if Sam continued on his expansionist policies. I thought about Jordan. He was twenty-five and would be drafted if Sam was reelected. The prospect of going to Canada or France became a viable possibility if Sam was reelected. I would not permit my son to participate in Sam's maniacal quest for world domination. It wouldn't happen on my watch.

My research discovered that on April 20, 2003, The New York Times ran an article citing unnamed sources that Sam was planning as many as four permanent military bases in Iraq. Sam's Secretary of Defense Donald Rumsfeld dismissed the story as inaccurate and unfortunate but never denied the contents. Maybe it was "inaccurate" in the sense that Sam's military planned ten bases? The names of the military bases were Al-Habbaniyah near the city of al-Fallujah, sixty-five kilometers west of Baghdad. The second airbase was named Ash-Sha'biyah Airbase in Basra, protecting the southern most exit port to the Persian Gulf. The third airbase was Ali ibn Abi Taleb Airbase on the outskirts of the city of an-Nasiriyah, mid-way between the southern port of Basra and Baghdad. The fourth airbase was al-Walid Airbase about 190 miles north-west of Baghdad, which had to be near the Syrian border where the pipeline runs into Syria and al-Ghazlani Camp in the city of Mosul, a major city north of Baghdad and near the border of Turkey. All bases were located near major highways and next to the pipeline. In addition, information existed to indicate that a permanent deployment of forces in the east of Iraq in what is known as the Hamrin mountain range that extends from Diyala Province, 36 miles west of Baghdad, and borders on Iran and extends to the oil-rich city of Kirkuk, protecting the oil fields in that region was taking place. Ahmad Chalabi, the C.I.A. backed Interim head of Iraq's governing council, told reporters on a September 30, 2003, visit to Washington D.C., that he would like Sam to establish permanent military bases in Iraq. My conclusion; Sam was there to stay and he needed an exit route for Iraq's oil. I was sure Sam was confident about the northern exit route through Turkey ending at the Mediterranean Turkish port city of Iskenderun. However, if Syria could not be secured, all oil would have to be piped through the Iraq-Turkey pipeline. Sam, by necessity, had to destabilize Syria under the banner of spreading freedom and democracy and protecting Israel from Lebanon groups.

After the election, Sam would make a move against Syria and if I had to guess, the January surprise that everyone talked about was not a surprise on a domestic issue but moving west against Syria. I was beginning to formulate an investment strategy, one that I would have never thought of. I was turning into a gold bug. The oil pits were shouting that $60.00 barrel oil was upon us. At that price, structural cracks would start to show up in world economies and the markets would conclude that recession dictated less demand and that oil would go down. Sam was going to write history and never listen to reason from anyone. He was going to invade Syria and screw anyone who got in his way. I could hear him shout "got enough balls, take me on." Instability would rule and instability causes gold to go up and I had the feeling that gold was going to go way up and then I realized that everything was going to go down, way down. We had to short everything in sight, including individual stocks. If my theory was correct, I was sure I could find evidence supporting Sam's intentions of turning west towards Syria. After all, if Sam fabricated Iraq's threat he would fabricate Syria's threat. Another desert kingdom was going under and if I knew it, so did they. Just today, after eighteen months of war, it was reported that 380 tons of weapons had disappeared from a weapons depot. Sam knew it and so did the International Atomic Energy Association. Why was it such big news now? One reason and one reason only! Sam was going to state that those nasty weapons were transported to Syria and they represented a direct threat to his troops in Iraq. "What a freaking mess," I thought to myself. Didn't anybody besides me see this shit? It was *all* so obvious. Were the Democrats in on this? Where was the media? To me it was a hot poker in the eye, how could one not know this crap. I was getting agitated and decided to walk away. If Dr. P. was correct in his analysis, another delusion might be only hours away. I turned on CNN and Sam was on one of his stump speeches telling a willing crowd that spreading freedom and democracy guaranteed their safety from terrorism. However, he added a new nuance: freedom and democracy wasn't his idea, it was everyone's rights granted by God. If that wasn't a call for a Christian crusade, then I wasn't a man. Indeed, gold was going up. "Come on Taz, we're going out," I said to TazTwo who eagerly awaited my fastening of the dog leash to his collar. As I was leaving, I heard a reporter on CNN state that the 380 tons of explosives could be used to set off nuclear bombs. There it was again, the nuclear mushroom cloud and I was sure that the next step was for all the right wing think tanks to advance their position that the weapons could be transferred to only one country-Syria. Fear, fear and more fear. Rationality never trumps a paranoid personality and walking down the steps of my stoop I was sure that in time, I would be known as the prophetic superego of Sam. I had to talk to Dr. P. I was starting to believe my own shit. The huge amounts of money to be reaped by the C.I.A., dummy corporations and insider corporations owned directly or indirectly by Sam and his buddies would be staggering. A lack of empathy is a hallmark trait of a narcissist and Sam didn't give a shit about his troops, their families or the dead civilian Iraqi's. A true Hegel hero writing history while the rest of the world studied his actions. I was back to my age-old question: at what point do you stand up to the bully on the block? Sam was betting that no one in the world would challenge him. I wasn't so sure. Walking down the block with Taz, I was firmly convinced that if Sam won reelection, the world would throw the first volley. Our financial markets would tumble; gold would get to $450.00 and ounce, oil prices would continue to advance and the euro would become a viable alternative to the dollar. My group was in a beautiful, bountiful position. I continued studying my map with a magnifying glass following the oil and gas pipelines.

"Boo," Jordan shouted as he grabbed me by the shoulders.

"What the hell are you doing? You could give me a heart attack," I said.

"Why do all you old people always say that?" asked Jordan.

"Cause it's true. How was your day?" I asked.

"Tiring and great. Maki really loves New York City and your apartment is perfectly located," said Jordan. My son studied all the hand written post-it notes that were on the maps.

"Not getting delusional are you?" he asked.

"No. Just trying to figure out our next financial move," I said. Jordan seemed content with my answer and told me that he and Maki were going to sleep and that I should wake him at 5:00 p.m. I continued studying the map and doing my research in an attempt to formulate a financial position going forward after the election. It was clear to me that Syria had a bull's eye on its back and that unless Syria gave Sam assurances of clear passage of using Iraq's pipeline to the Mediterranean ports, Sam would invade Syria after the Iraqi elections in January. I was confident that Sam had his Special Forces and C.I.A. already in Syria. For starters, Sam would threaten to stop the oil flow from Iraq. The simultaneous arrival of Rueben and the awakening of Jordan interrupted me. Maki continued her nap. Jordan ordered two pizza pies. I called Angelina and told her to pick up two six packs of beer.

The group assembled in my office at 6:00 p.m. and immediately started to eat. Rueben advised us that we lost money on our S & P position with very slight declines in oil, gold and the euro. He wasn't concerned and neither was anyone else. I advised the group that I didn't expect too much action the week prior to the election.

"Well, pops, the way I see it, somebody is going to make money if Sam wins and somebody will make money if his opponent wins. My question is; who is going to win the freaking election?" asked Jordan.

"I don't know. The polls indicate a close race," said Angie.

"It can go either way," said Rueben. "What's your take Doc?" asked Rueben.

"I know the polls are dead even and the only thing that no one knows is which way the newly registered voters will break. I've been racking my brain over this issue and I keep on coming back to my belief that under no circumstances will Sam lose this election. He just won't let it happen," I said.

"Come on dad. You mean Sam will rig a United States election. That's a little far-fetched, don't you think? Remember our conversation over the weekend? I told you that because of your Shared Psychotic Disorder you give Sam too much power. If he loses, he loses," said Jordan.

"All right, I'll tell you what I believe. Maybe I am crazy, but I believe that if Sam enters into this weekend with a clear positive trend that his opponent will win, he would think nothing about faking a domestic terror attack on Sunday. It will be all over the news from Sunday to Monday and Sam will give a national televised speech on Monday night claiming that he captured the terrorists and people will go into the polls on Tuesday and vote for him. That's how strongly I believe that Sam will do anything, and I mean anything, to win this election. He has too much riding on it. What's a little faked terror attack?" I asked.

"O.K., that's Stan's opinion. Anyone else have an opinion?" asked Angelina.

Maki raised her hand. "What's the difference who wins?" asked Maki.

"That's a good question Maki. Here's my take. If Sam wins on Tuesday, there will be a resounding vote of no confidence from the international community. Gold will go up. The euro will go up and oil will go up. The world will assume that it is in for another four years of militaristic aggressive policies initiated by Sam. Instability will be assumed by the major powers and they'll bid up gold, oil and the euro," I said.

"And our stock market?" asked Rueben.

"Well, American companies will bid up our market seeking another four years of corporate give a ways. After all, Sam just gave corporate America a one hundred and forty billion present," I said.

"Why don't we close out our position in the S & P on Monday, November 1 and hold our positions in oil, gas and the euro," said Jordan.

"That's not a bad idea," said Angelina.

"Yeah, and what happens if Sam's opponent wins? The race is dead even," added Rueben.

"Well, if he wins then I think the markets will go exactly the other way. Oil, gold and the euro will decline, as they will interpret the election of Sam's opponent as a step forward towards sanity. Our domestic market will drop if there's a change in the administration," said Jordan and added, "so, we're right back to where we started. Who will win this election?"

"I have an idea. Why don't we cash out this Friday and protect our money," said Angelina. "We don't have to take such a risk"

"That's true. I might consider that," said Rueben.

"Because, whoever has his chips on the table at the end of Tuesday night stands to make a lot of money Wednesday morning if he bet right," I said.

"I'm a gambler. I say let's figure this out, right here, right now and keep our chips on the table," said Jordan.

"Why don't we quantify it? What will happen to our money if either side wins?" asked Maki.

"That's a great question," said Rueben. Everyone looked at me as if I had an answer.

"Come on dad, you're the guru in this group. Your picks made you and Rueben a half-million dollars in about thirty days. So what do you think?" asked Jordan. I picked up another slice of pizza and gobbled it down.

"Here's what I think. I think you're all nuts listening to a man who has a Shared Psychotic Disorder. You know, anyone can be as nuts as they want to be as long as people can make money off them," I said.

"Grow up dad. You've been a screwball since I was five and I still love you. You can be delusional and a good trend picker, maybe even better because you're nuts. You're sitting on $500,000.00. The proof is in the pudding," said Jordan.

"All right, quantification if Sam wins. I think you're looking at $60.00 oil and $435.00 gold within one week after the election. The euro will hit $1.30 in that same period of time," I said and asked Rueben how much that would mean to us.

"Giving you a quick estimate, I would say about $200,000.00 in five days," said Rueben.

"And if Sam loses?" asked Maki.

"The euro goes to $1.23 and gold will decline to $415.00. The oil market will decline to $48.00 a barrel and the market slumps down a 100 points," I said.

"Rueben, what does that mean to us?" I asked.

"A rough estimate. I would say we lose about the same amount of money, mainly because the bulk of our money is in oil," said Rueben.

"That's great. Damned if we do and damned if we don't," said Angelina. Maki suggested cashing out Monday afternoon and liquidating all positions. She reminded everyone that the bulls make money and the bears make money, and the pigs get slaughtered. I stared at her.

"We have time to think about it and besides I want to kiss my man, right now," said Angelina who scrambled across the room and kissed me. "It's snuggling time for me," she said. Everyone agreed that we had time and that there was no immediacy to making a decision. We all decided to continue thinking about whether Sam would win or lose and agreed to meet Friday morning for breakfast and make our final decision. Jordan suggested that we all walk over to the steps of the Metropolitan Museum of Art and throw a Frisbee. We had fun.

Angelina had the day off and insisted upon making my office into living space. Maki and Jordan planned another sightseeing trip around New York City. After Jordan left, Angie helped me move my desk into another room. She decided that getting a convertible sofa and a club chair would work and we spent the next two hours shopping. I asked her if she was moving in and she shrugged her shoulders. "No, not really," she said. I didn't have any problems with Angie sleeping over at any time or all the time. I just didn't want it official as a matter of record, so to speak. The store promised same day delivery. Next, Angelina and I went to the West Village and she bought a bamboo curtain that she intended to place over the entryway of my office to give us a sense of privacy. We arrived back home at 2:00 p.m., made some lunch, made some love and hung the bamboo curtain. I remarked to Angelina that the apartment was taking on a hippy crash pad sixties feel and she laughed. Actually, my home reminded me of Seinfeld's apartment with all its various nutty and interesting characters. I was recreating all the nuts from my former psychology practice, except in a home setting. When Jordan and Maki arrived, Angie took Maki and a kitchen knife out to the back deck for knife throwing practice. I remained in my new bedroom studying my map of the Caspian region, examining all the pipeline routes that the former Soviet Union built during its empire days.

"Mind if I join you, dad?" asked Jordan.

"No, not at all. You're a traveler and I know you love maps. I'm following all the pipeline routes in Russia and the "Stan" countries. I need the magnifying glass to find them. I can't see small print anymore," I said. Jordan pulled up a chair and sat next to me. We were so close our cheeks almost touched. He needed the aid of the magnifying glass as well. He wore glasses.

"You know dad, parents have an incredible tool available to them," said Jordan.

"Yeah, what's that?" I asked.

"They get to create an image in their child's mind that they want to create and their son or daughter grows up believing whatever the image the parent wanted to create," said Jordan.

"What exactly are you talking about?" I asked.

"Take you, for example. When I was two, you were twenty-five. I have no idea of whom or what you were all about before I was born except what you presented to me later in life. Isn't that right?" asked Jordan.

"Absolutely. Every parent can create or mold his or her own image. A child would never know the truth unless of course the parent made the papers or something. Where are you going with all this?" I asked.

"You dad, you, for example. Who the hell were you before I was born?"

"Nobody too interesting. Just a regular guy trying to make a living," I said.

"Really, ever kill anyone?" asked Jordan. I turned and stared into my son's eyes.

"You've been talking to your mother too much. She tends to run dramatic. Growing up, you and I were very tight and she tried her best to fill your head with bullshit, including telling you I killed someone. It's a dramatic story and belongs in a fiction book and not in our conversation," I said.

"So, you're telling me my mom didn't overhear you talking to someone at 2:00 a.m. in the morning about a cocaine drug deal to raise money for guns and that guy was found dead two days later," said Jordan.

"What your mother heard was a frantic call from one of my law clients who I represented. He called me at two in the morning because he stole $25,000.00 from some drug guys and wanted to borrow the money to save his life," I said.

"That's not what I know," said Jordan.

"So, what the fuck do you think you know?" I angrily asked Jordan.

"Don't get mad at me. Don't kill the messenger," said Jordan.

"Are you threatening me?" I asked.

"The Statute of limitations never runs out on murder does it?" asked Jordan.

"I think this conversation is over," I said adamantly.

"Wait a minute dad. I'm not the enemy. I'm your son. Ever hear of S.E.A.? That was your group, The Students for an Enlightened Society. You set that up when the S.D.S. went down in the sixties. You remember, the Students for a Democratic Society. You never told me about S.E.A. did you?" asked Jordan. Angelina and Maki entered into the room and I yelled at them to take a walk. "Out of the fucking house," I demanded. Without question, both women marched out of the house. "And take Taz," I barked.

"I did some research on you guys, The Black Panthers, the S.D.S., Malcolm X, Symbianese Liberation Army and you. A whole mess of people dedicated to violence and overthrowing the government! Unfortunately, the only thing that anyone ever knew about the S.E.A. was nothing. I found only one line in a San Francisco paper on October 13, 1967, where the reporter found the initials S.E.A. carved into a park bench. You're not denying any of this, dad. Maybe you should start talking," said Jordan.

"I told you Jordan, your mother has an active imagination," I said.

"Not as active as your diary. Sixty-two murders in three years! Twenty-three armed robberies and eighteen bombings in the same period. My mom gave me the diary years ago. She never turned you in because she didn't want *my* father in jail and you threatened to kill her. The day you left the house, she burned a diary in front of you, but it wasn't your diary. It was a fake," said Jordan.

"And?" I asked.

"And the diary is in a bank vault in Switzerland. I made a side-trip on the way home from Japan. I want something from you," said Jordan.

"Money?" I asked.

"No, not money. You know dad, the apple never falls too far from the tree. I know you're still a warrior. A warrior's heart and soul never die. His body might fail, but his spirit never dies. You taught me that. The spirit is still inside you but like an old fighter, you're legs are gone. Let me be your body. I need you as the heart and soul of my movement," said Jordan.

"This conversation would be better outside. We'll take a hike in the woods someplace," I said and Jordan nodded in agreement. Jordan and I sat in silence for the next two hours, occasionally interrupted by either one of us pointing out a pipeline or making an innocuous geographical comment. Jordan brought me back to the darkest alley that I ever walked down. I could no longer remember the faces of the sixty-three people that I gunned down or any of the towns where I had set explosives. I never bothered to find out whether any one died in the explosions. During those two hours, I had flashes of faces in my mind but none of the flashes stayed long enough to remember the time, place or manner of death of my murder victims. Sometimes I shot them through the heart and sometimes in the head. Why I shot the particular people that I did, I couldn't recall. I was sure that I had a reason but I couldn't remember. Periodically, I stared at Jordan. I was his hero, someone he was proud of and wanted to emulate.

"Hi boys, finished arguing," said Angie as she separated the bamboo strings of the curtain.

"Yes. We finished discussing our mutual positions," I said.

"Dad's an intellectual," said Jordan. I decided that I needed to be alone and told Jordan to find something to do. He, Maki and Angie decided to make veal picatta, one of my favorite dishes. They left the house to go shopping. I needed to immerse myself in research and get out of my head. The memories were too appealing.

# Chapter Twenty-Eight

One thing that stuck in my head from Sam's recent statements was that our security rested upon spreading liberty and freedom throughout the world, as if having a democratic Iraq might make the Muslims love us. However, he went one step further and said that liberty and freedom are not American concepts but commands from God. The Fascist militaristic United States was selling the invasion of sovereign nations under the banner of God, after all, it is He that wants you to have those freedoms, and I, Sam, have been given this mission to bring you freedom and liberty. "The nuts are running the asylum," I said to myself, but I knew that the people behind Sam had all their wits about them.

In so far as Syria was concerned, the resurrected Team A/Team B approach was reborn in the Office of Special Plans that was actively preparing and drawing up plans to coerce Syria into submission or to invade Syria. It was reported that some of the same personnel who worked in the Pentagon's office of Special Plans, which reviewed and created the intelligence for evidence linking Saddam Hussein to al-Qaeda and weapons of mass destruction were reportedly working on a similar effort regarding Syria. I was confident that the 380 tons of weapons that was the cause of much tumult during the last week of Sam's campaign would be alleged to be in Syria and after all, these weapons can be used to detonate nuclear bombs. However, this was old news and I was more interested in Sam linking God's gift of freedom and liberty to the war on terrorism. Recently, Sam's State Department declared that China and Saudi Arabia violated the basic tenets of freedom and religion. Sam accused Saudi Arabia of particularly severe violations of religious freedom. The State Department releases an International Religious Freedom Report every year covering religious freedom in 191 countries. "Freedom of religion does not exist in China," a State Department spokesman said. China rejected the report with strong "displeasure" and "resolute objection." Chinese Foreign Ministry spokesman Kong Quan said the report "defied the facts, posed unreasonable criticism of China's religious policies, trampled the norms of international relations and interfered in China's affairs." Mr. Kong Quan further stated that, "It is groundless for the United States to make irresponsible remarks or criticize other countries internal affairs with the excuse of religion." I wondered what kind of report Sam would give himself when the Kingdom of God arrived in America and Christianity would be the de-facto state religion. Of course, America was always a Christian nation and other religions were permitted in America at the pleasure of the ruling Christians. I decided to research the law from which the State Department got its authority. I was doing anything to avoid thinking about my conversation with Jordan and in particular my last thought that those memories were appealing. Right then, I realized why I had such a visceral reaction to Sam. In my youth I was Sam. I was a delusional psychopathic narcissist who murdered sixty-three people in pursuit of my own messianic mission to overthrow the government of the United States. My mission was to "kill the pigs." Images of Huey Newton, Malcolm X and Martin Luther King flashed through my mind. I saw Newark, Detroit, Los Angeles and Brooklyn burning and lighting up the night sky. Heads were bashed and my brethren were murdered. We chanted as a nation, Chicago's famous line "that the whole world is watching" and sang Crosby, Stills, Nash & Young's lyric of "Tin soldiers and Nixon's coming." We were guardians of the truth and freedom. Malcolm X said that if you're not willing to die for freedom that you didn't deserve freedom. To repent for my sins, I decided to help people and that was the real reason I became a lawyer and psychologist. In 2004, I saw that same ugly Southern white man raising his fucking ugly Jim Crow head again, killing his nigger on Saturday and asking forgiveness in Church on Sunday. John Birch was back in my life with a vengeance and that was the basis for my delusions. I was Sam and that's how I knew exactly what he was doing and going to do.

The authority for the State Department's International Religious Freedom Report stemmed from Title 22, Chapter 73, Sec. 6401 of the United States Code. The relevant parts were as follows:

"Sec. 6401.-Findings; Policy

(a) Findings

Congress makes the following findings:

> (1) The right to freedom of religion undergirds the very origin and existence of the United States. Many of nation's founders fled religious persecution abroad, cherishing in their hearts and minds the ideal of religious freedom. They established in law, as a fundamental right and as a pillar of our Nation, the right to freedom of religion. From its birth to this day, the United States has prized this legacy of religious freedom and honored this heritage by standing for religious freedom and offering refuge to those suffering religious persecution.

(4) The right to freedom of religion is under renewed and, in some cases, increasing assault in many countries around the world...Among the many forms of such violations are state-sponsored slander campaigns, confiscations of property, surveillance by security police, including by special divisions of 'religious police', severe prohibitions against construction and repair of places of worship, denial of the right to assemble...or possessing religious materials."

I knew that I would do anything, including bullshit research, to avoid dwelling on the memories of the past. What frightened me the most were the visions of the smile on my face every time I blew up a building or committed armed robberies to get cash to buy guns. I felt alive. I was in a revolution for better reasons than the founding fathers of my country and should a revolution be born again, today's revolutionaries would have far better reasons than either George Washington or I. Sam wasn't an honest broker about his concern for religious freedom as I found out in the next two paragraphs.

"(7) Congress has recognized and denounced acts of religious persecution through the adoption of the following resolutions:

A. House Resolution 515 of the One Hundred Fourth Congress, expressing the sense of the House of Representatives with respect to the persecution of **Christians** worldwide.

B. Senate Concurrent Resolution 71 of the One Hundred Fourth Congress, expressing the sense of the Senate regarding persecution of **Christians** worldwide.

It shall be the policy of the United States, as follows:

1. To condemn violations of religious freedom, and to promote, and to assist other governments in the promotion of, the fundamental right to freedom of religion."

"What a cute piece of bullshit legislation," I thought to myself. It was nothing more than a bootstrap for Sam to mettle into the practices of other sovereign nations. Research was useless to take my mind off my fond memories. I sat back in my chair and put my feet up on the computer stand and drifted off into my mind. My friends, my allies and my Semper Fi buddies that got shot and brutalized walked across the stage that I created in my brain.

"Dad, the delivery men are here," shouted Jordan. I was embarrassed to look at Jordan but forced myself to exit from the room. Jordan knew his father was a killer and interestingly enough, he was impressed and I was depressed. "I'm proud of you dad. Let it go," he said as he opened the door to the delivery men in. "We need to take a walk in the woods real soon," I said, to which Jordan responded "no problem."

After the deliverymen arranged the furniture to my satisfaction, I grabbed a bottle of Jack Daniels and took two huge gulps. "Captain Jack will get me high tonight," I said to Jordan. "I think I'll join you," he said. Jordan took out two shot glasses and poured another round of Jack and proposed a toast. "To the revolution," he said. With great reluctance and hesitation I raised my glass and said, "to the revolution." Dinner was delicious and by the time it ended I was drunk. Conversation was subdued prior to dinner, during dinner and afterwards. It seemed that no one wanted to upset me. Maki's gift with a knife became clear. Jordan's completion of his Aikido studies became clear. In my drunken stupor I asked Angelina if she ever met Jordan to which she replied, "I have never met Jordan in my life." I passed out in my new bedroom as Angelina, Maki and Jordan made dessert. They saved me a slice of key lime pie.

The next morning I had a horrible hangover. Angelina had left for work. Jordan and Maki were in the kitchen making breakfast. The phone rang. It was Rueben.

"Doc, you know the market went up 138 points two days ago and yesterday it went up another 100 points. Gold slipped a little and crude oil tumbled. What do you think?" asked Rueben.

"Rueben, crude slipped because the Department of Energy claimed that there was an unexpected increase in the oil reserves. The consensus predicted a 1 million barrel increase and it was claimed that the increase was 3.9 million barrels, a 2.9 million barrel difference. We import ten million barrels a day so that increase is worth a stinking 8 hours worth of our energy needs. Every week we play the reserve number game. We have more, we have less, we have more and we have less. Rueben, there's an election in a couple of days and Sam's buddies want the Dow average over that psychologically important 10,000 level. Forget it; don't get worried, it's all election eve bullshit. For Christ's sake, even Matt Drudge reported a new tape claiming al-Qaeda would make the streets run with blood and the terrorist had an English accent. It's five days before election and I'm sure we'll have aliens from Mars telling everyone to vote for Sam. Goodbye, call me later," I said.

# Chapter Twenty-Nine

"Jesus Jordan, things are going to get weird this weekend," I said.

"How about a nice walk in the woods?" Jordan asked. Maki looked my way to check out my facial expressions.

"Not today, I got a whooper of a headache. Maybe this weekend we'll go for a hike. It might be a good idea to get out of the city," I said. Jordan told me that he and Maki were going to continue their tour of New York City. I asked him if he was visiting various sites for other reasons and he just smiled. I told Jordan that I was going back to sleep and then I was going to the Mykonos Diner for lunch. Jordan agreed to meet me there.

"Hi guys. How was your day? Stan, do you like our new bedroom?" asked Angie.

"Coffee and Mousaka, please," I said. Angelina planned on going back to her apartment to get more personal things, like her toothbrush, comb, hairbrush and razor. She suggested that I call Rueben and invite him, however, Rueben was coming for Friday's financial brunch and so I decided against inviting him for dinner.

"All the company is not wearing thin I hope?"

"No, Angie, I just have one big freaking headache," I told Angie.

After lunch I planned on going back to my apartment and check the recent polls concerning the Presidential race. Jordan wanted to join me and suggested that he and I continue our map research. I had no problem with that suggestion. The aspirin was starting to kick in and I began to feel better. He was particularly interested in the Caspian Sea region, as he had read a book entitled "The Great Game" which was about the centuries old struggle for dominance in the area. For a long time, many countries wanted to dominate the Caspian Sea region and it appeared that Sam was preparing to do the same. The polls indicated that Sam and his opponent were dead even and no one was venturing a guess as to who would win on Tuesday.

"Jordan, you have been out of the country and you missed the Republican Party's convention in New York City. Prominently on stage was a Senator named Sam Brownback who I never heard of before. I researched his website and he's one of those evangelical Christian types. Brownback is anti everything and right in line with winning the cultural war against the liberals. I figured he was just another screwball. I want to you look at what I found on the Internet. If you're interested in the Caspian Sea region, you'll be interested in this. I did a Goggle search and found what I was looking for and told Jordan to read it.

**BROWNBACK WELCOMES SILK ROAD HEADS OF STATE**
**Contact:** Erik Hotmire
Saturday, April 24, 1999

WASHINGTON—U.S. Sen. Sam Brownback made the following statement today welcoming heads of state from the South Caucasus, Central Asia and Eastern Europe in a Capitol Hill ceremony to show support for Brownbacks Silk Road Strategy Act of 1999.

Id like to welcome you here today to mark an historic occasion: the first time the leaders of the Silk Road countries have come together here in Washington as a region. Let me introduce you to the New Silk Road connecting, once again, Asia to Europe and the rest of the world.

The countries represented here today: The Republic of Armenia, the Republic of Azerbaijan, Georgia, the Republic Kazakhstan, the Kyrgyz Republic, the Republic of Tajikistan, the Republic of Turkmenistan and the Republic of Uzebekistan; along with our special guests from the Republic of Moldova, Romania and Turkey. Each are key nations in their own right, and as a cohesive region, they are also of significant strategic importance to the United States.

We have a unique window of opportunity to influence events there for the good. The U.S. must assume a broad-based and pro-active policy of engagement immediately. Time is of the essence. Other factors are at play in the region and they are attempting to destablize these nations. The Silk Road countries of the South Caucasus and Central Asia are at an historic crossroad: they are independent, they are at the juncture of many of todays major world forces, they are rich in natural resources and they are in the midst of nation building. The region is under increasing anti-western and anti-democratic pressures from outside forces, and they are looking to the United States as a partner in their growth and independence. It is clearly in our interest to support them. These countries are located in a strategic part of the globe, they are a major force in containing the spread of anti-western militant fundamentalism and terrorism from Iran, and other extremist nations. They are also at the forefront of stemming the flow of weapons of mass destruction. They are crucial in the fight against drug trafficking. And most importantly, after years of fighting communism in this region, the doors are open for the U.S. to promote institutions which will guarantee the rights of individuals and help create the conditions for the growth of pluralistic societies, including religious tolerance.

Our objective should be to insure that the nations of the Silk Road remain independent and become strong, economically viable and politically sovereign states. The single best way to achieve this goal is to promote regional cooperation and partnership. These countries and the U.S. need to work together to solve their most pressing problems: regional conflicts, defense and border protection, ethnic strife, water and energy distribution, compatible infrastructure development, ecological and environmental clean-up, trade agreements and more. Such cooperation and interdependence lie at the heart of maintaining long term regional stability and making the east-west links strong and successful. The long term independence of the region could well depend on it. The Silk Road countries have taken strong independent stances and shown their commitment to successful nation-building. We have the opportunity to help this rebuilding from the ground up. We have the ability to encourage the progress towards complete sovereignty. What we do in this area—promoting peaceful, open and sovereign governments, economic prosperity and mutually beneficial ties with the West—is in all our interests.

Participants today included former U.S. Secretary of State James Baker and former national security advisor Dr. Zbigniew Brzezinski, along with several U.S. Senators and members of Congress.

I went into the kitchen to make some coffee and give Jordan time to read the article. When I got back, Jordan was outlining the countries with a yellow marker.

"No wonder Vladimir Putin is a little concerned with Sam. It looks like Sam has a policy of containment in regard to Russia. Sam is blocking Russia's western border by forming alliances with Poland and Lithuania and surrounding Russia's southern flank," said Jordan.

"No shit! It is any wonder that Putin wants to snuggle up to China," I said.

"But dad, every time Putin opens his mouth, he's backing Sam. What the hell is that all about?" asked Jordan.

"I have a theory, but that's it. Only a theory," I said. "Now take a look at this piece of legislation that goes with that letter."

## Silk Road Strategy Act of 1999

106th CONGRESS

1st Session

S. 579

To amend the Foreign Assistance Act of 1961 to target assistance to support the economic and political independence of the countries of the South Caucasus and Central Asia.

IN THE SENATE OF THE UNITED STATES

March 10, 1999

Mr. BROWNBACK (for himself, Mr. SMITH of Oregon, Mr. BYRD, Mr. HAGEL, Mr. DODD, Mr. LUGAR, Mr. KYL, Mr. HATCH, Mr. GRAMS, Mr. CHAFEE, Mr. HELMS, Mr. THOMAS, and Mr. MCCAIN) introduced the following bill; which was read twice and referred to the Committee on Foreign Relations

A BILL

To amend the Foreign Assistance Act of 1961 to target assistance to support the economic and political independence of the countries of the South Caucasus and Central Asia.

Be it enacted by the Senate and House of Representatives of the United States of America in Congress assembled,

SECTION 1. SHORT TITLE.

This Act may be cited as the 'Silk Road Strategy Act of 1999'.

SEC. 2. FINDINGS.

Congress makes the following findings:

(1) The ancient Silk Road, once the economic lifeline of Central Asia and the South Caucasus, traversed much of the territory now within the countries of Armenia, Azerbaijan, Georgia, Kazakstan, Kyrgyzstan, Tajikistan, Turkmenistan, and Uzbekistan.

(2) Economic interdependence spurred mutual cooperation among the peoples along the Silk Road and restoration of the historic relationships and economic ties between those peoples is an important element of ensuring their sovereignty as well as the success of democratic and market reforms.

(3) The development of strong political, economic, and security ties among countries of the South Caucasus and Central Asia and the West will foster stability in this region, which is vulnerable to political and economic pressures from the south, north, and east.

(4) The development of open market economies and open democratic systems in the countries of the South Caucasus and Central Asia will provide positive incentives for international private investment, increased trade, and other forms of commercial interactions with the rest of the world.

(5) Many of the countries of the South Caucasus have secular Muslim governments that are seeking closer alliance with the United States and that have diplomatic and commercial relations with Israel.

(6) The region of the South Caucasus and Central Asia could produce oil and gas in sufficient quantities to reduce the dependence of the United States on energy from the volatile Persian Gulf region.

(7) United States foreign policy and international assistance should be narrowly targeted to support the economic and political independence as well as democracy building, free market policies, human rights, and regional economic integration of the countries of the South Caucasus and Central Asia.

SEC. 3. POLICY OF THE UNITED STATES.

It shall be the policy of the United States in the countries of the South Caucasus and Central Asia—

(1) to promote and strengthen independence, sovereignty, democratic government, and respect for human rights;

(2) to promote tolerance, pluralism, and understanding and counter racism and anti-Semitism;

(3) to assist actively in the resolution of regional conflicts and to facilitate the removal of impediments to cross-border commerce;

(4) to promote friendly relations and economic cooperation;

(5) to help promote market-oriented principles and practices;

(6) to assist in the development of the infrastructure necessary for communications, transportation, education, health, and energy and trade on an East-West axis in order to build strong international relations and commerce between those countries and the stable, democratic, and market-oriented countries of the Euro-Atlantic Community; and

(7) to support United States business interests and investments in the region.

SEC. 4. UNITED STATES EFFORTS TO RESOLVE CONFLICTS IN THE SOUTH CAUCASUS AND CENTRAL ASIA.

It is the sense of Congress that the President should use all diplomatic means practicable, including the engagement of senior United States Government officials, to press for an equitable, fair, and permanent resolution to the conflicts in the South Caucasus and Central Asia.

SEC. 5. AMENDMENT OF THE FOREIGN ASSISTANCE ACT OF 1961.

Part I of the Foreign Assistance Act of 1961 (22 U.S.C. 2151 et seq.) is amended by adding at the end the following new chapter:

'CHAPTER 12—SUPPORT FOR THE ECONOMIC AND POLITICAL INDEPENDENCE OF THE COUNTRIES OF THE SOUTH CAUCASUS AND CENTRAL ASIA

'SEC. 499. UNITED STATES ASSISTANCE TO PROMOTE RECONCILIATION AND RECOVERY FROM REGIONAL CONFLICTS.

'(a) PURPOSE OF ASSISTANCE—The purposes of assistance under this section include—

'(1) the creation of the basis for reconciliation between belligerents;

'(2) the promotion of economic development in areas of the countries of the South Caucasus and Central Asia impacted by civil conflict and war; and

'(3) the encouragement of broad regional cooperation among countries of the South Caucasus and Central Asia that have been destabilized by internal conflicts.

'(b) AUTHORIZATION FOR ASSISTANCE-

'(1) IN GENERAL—To carry out the purposes of subsection (a), the President is authorized to provide humanitarian assistance and economic reconstruction assistance for the countries of the South Caucasus and Central Asia to support the activities described in subsection (c).

`(2) DEFINITION OF HUMANITARIAN ASSISTANCE—In this subsection, the term 'humanitarian assistance' means assistance to meet humanitarian needs, including needs for food, medicine, medical supplies and equipment, education, and clothing.

`(c) ACTIVITIES SUPPORTED—Activities that may be supported by assistance under subsection (b) include—

`(1) providing for the humanitarian needs of victims of the conflicts;

`(2) facilitating the return of refugees and internally displaced persons to their homes; and

`(3) assisting in the reconstruction of residential and economic infrastructure destroyed by war.

`(d) POLICY—It is the sense of Congress that the United States should, where appropriate, support the establishment of neutral, multinational peacekeeping forces to implement peace agreements reached between belligerents in the countries of the South Caucasus and Central Asia.

`SEC. 499A. ECONOMIC ASSISTANCE.

`(a) PURPOSE OF ASSISTANCE—The purpose of assistance under this section is to foster economic growth and development, including the conditions necessary for regional economic cooperation, in the South Caucasus and Central Asia.

`(b) AUTHORIZATION FOR ASSISTANCE—To carry out the purpose of subsection (a), the President is authorized to provide assistance for the countries of the South Caucasus and Central Asia to support the activities described in subsection (c).

`(c) ACTIVITIES SUPPORTED—In addition to the activities described in section 498, activities supported by assistance under subsection (b) should support the development of the structures and means necessary for the growth of private sector economies based upon market principles.

`(d) POLICY—It is the sense of Congress that the United States should—

`(1) assist the countries of the South Caucasus and Central Asia to develop policies, laws, and regulations that would facilitate the ability of those countries to develop free market economies and to join the World Trade Organization to enjoy all the benefits of membership; and

'(2) consider the establishment of zero-to-zero tariffs between the United States and the countries of the South Caucasus and Central Asia.

'SEC. 499B. DEVELOPMENT OF INFRASTRUCTURE.

'(a) PURPOSE OF PROGRAMS—The purposes of programs under this section include—

'(1) to develop the physical infrastructure necessary for regional cooperation among the countries of the South Caucasus and Central Asia; and

'(2) to encourage closer economic relations and to facilitate the removal of impediments to cross-border commerce among those countries and the United States and other developed nations.

'(b) AUTHORIZATION FOR PROGRAMS—To carry out the purposes of subsection (a), the following types of programs for the countries of the South Caucasus and Central Asia may be used to support the activities described in subsection (c):

'(1) Activities by the Export-Import Bank to complete the review process for eligibility for financing under the Export-Import Bank Act of 1945.

'(2) The provision of insurance, reinsurance, financing, or other assistance by the Overseas Private Investment Corporation.

'(3) Assistance under section 661 of this Act (relating to the Trade and Development Agency).

'(c) ACTIVITIES SUPPORTED—Activities that may be supported by programs under subsection (b) include promoting actively the participation of United States companies and investors in the planning, financing, and construction of infrastructure for communications, transportation, including air transportation, and energy and trade including highways, railroads, port facilities, shipping, banking, insurance, telecommunications networks, and gas and oil pipelines.

'(d) POLICY—It is the sense of Congress that the United States representatives at the International Bank for Reconstruction and Development, the International Finance Corporation, and the European Bank for Reconstruction and Development should encourage lending to the countries of the

South Caucasus and Central Asia to assist the development of the physical infrastructure necessary for regional economic cooperation.

'SEC. 499C. BORDER CONTROL ASSISTANCE.

'(a) PURPOSE OF ASSISTANCE—The purpose of assistance under this section includes the assistance of the countries of the South Caucasus and Central Asia to secure their borders and implement effective controls necessary to prevent the trafficking of illegal narcotics and the proliferation of technology and materials related to weapons of mass destruction (as defined in section 2332a(c)(2) of title 18, United States Code), and to contain and inhibit transnational organized criminal activities.

'(b) AUTHORIZATION FOR ASSISTANCE—To carry out the purpose of subsection (a), the President is authorized to provide assistance to the countries of the South Caucasus and Central Asia to support the activities described in subsection (c).

'(c) ACTIVITIES SUPPORTED—Activities that may be supported by assistance under subsection (b) include assisting those countries of the South Caucasus and Central Asia in developing capabilities to maintain national border guards, coast guard, and customs controls.

'(d) POLICY—It is the sense of Congress that the United States should encourage and assist the development of regional military cooperation among the countries of the South Caucasus and Central Asia through programs such as the Central Asian Battalion and the Partnership for Peace of the North Atlantic Treaty Organization.

'SEC. 499D. STRENGTHENING DEMOCRACY, TOLERANCE, AND THE DEVELOPMENT OF CIVIL SOCIETY.

'(a) PURPOSE OF ASSISTANCE—The purpose of assistance under this section is to promote institutions of democratic government and to create the conditions for the growth of pluralistic societies, including religious tolerance and respect for internationally recognized human rights.

'(b) AUTHORIZATION FOR ASSISTANCE—To carry out the purpose of subsection (a), the President is authorized to provide the following types of assistance to the countries of the South Caucasus and Central Asia:

'(1) Assistance for democracy building, including programs to strengthen parliamentary institutions and practices.

`(2) Assistance for the development of nongovernmental organizations.

`(3) Assistance for development of independent media.

`(4) Assistance for the development of the rule of law, a strong independent judiciary, and transparency in political practice and commercial transactions.

`(5) International exchanges and advanced professional training programs in skill areas central to the development of civil society.

`(6) Assistance to promote increased adherence to civil and political rights under section 116(e) of this Act.

`(c) ACTIVITIES SUPPORTED—Activities that may be supported by assistance under subsection (b) include activities that are designed to advance progress toward the development of democracy.

`(d) POLICY—It is the sense of Congress that the Voice of America and RFE/RL, Incorporated, should maintain high quality broadcasting for the maximum duration possible in the native languages of the countries of the South Caucasus and Central Asia.

`SEC. 499E. INELIGIBILITY FOR ASSISTANCE.

`(a) IN GENERAL—Except as provided in subsection (b), assistance may not be provided under this chapter for the government of a country of the South Caucasus or Central Asia if the President determines and certifies to the appropriate congressional committees that the government of such country—

`(1) is engaged in a consistent pattern of gross violations of internationally recognized human rights;

`(2) has, on or after the date of enactment of this chapter, knowingly transferred to another country—

`(A) missiles or missile technology inconsistent with the guidelines and parameters of the Missile Technology Control Regime (as defined in section 11B(c) of the Export Administration Act of 1979 950 U.S.C. App. 2410b(c); or

`(B) any material, equipment, or technology that would contribute significantly to the ability of such country to manufacture any weapon of mass destruction (including nuclear, chemical, and biological weapons) if the

President determines that the material, equipment, or technology was to be used by such country in the manufacture of such weapons;

`(3) has repeatedly provided support for acts of international terrorism; or

`(4) is prohibited from receiving such assistance by chapter 10 of the Arms Export Control Act or section 306(a)(1) and 307 of the Chemical and Biological Weapons Control and Warfare Elimination Act of 1991 (22 U.S.C. 5604(a)(1), 5605).

`(b) EXCEPTIONS TO INELIGIBILITY-

`(1) EXCEPTIONS—Assistance prohibited by subsection (a) or any similar provision of law, other than assistance prohibited by the provisions referred to in paragraphs (2) and (4) of subsection (a), may be furnished under any of the following circumstances:

`(A) The President determines that furnishing such assistance is important to the national interest of the United States.

`(B) The President determines that furnishing such assistance will foster respect for internationally recognized human rights and the rule of law or the development of institutions of democratic governance.

`(C) The assistance is furnished for the alleviation of suffering resulting from a natural or man-made disaster.

`(D) The assistance is provided under the secondary school exchange program administered by the United States Information Agency.

`(2) REPORT TO CONGRESS—The President shall immediately report to Congress any determination under paragraph (1) (A) or (B) or any decision to provide assistance under paragraph (1)(C).

`SEC. 499F. ADMINISTRATIVE AUTHORITIES.

`(a) ASSISTANCE THROUGH GOVERNMENTS AND NONGOVERNMENTAL ORGANIZATIONS—Assistance under this chapter may be provided to governments or through nongovernmental organizations.

`(b) USE OF ECONOMIC SUPPORT FUNDS—Except as otherwise provided, any funds that have been allocated under chapter 4 of part II for assistance for the independent states of the former Soviet Union may be used in accordance with the provisions of this chapter.

`(c) TERMS AND CONDITIONS—Assistance under this chapter shall be provided on such terms and conditions as the President may determine.

`(d) AVAILABLE AUTHORITIES—The authority in this chapter to provide assistance for the countries of the South Caucasus and Central Asia is in addition to the authority to provide such assistance under the FREEDOM Support Act (22 U.S.C. 5801 et seq.) or any other Act, and the authorities applicable to the provision of assistance under chapter 11 may be used to provide assistance under this chapter.

`SEC. 499G. DEFINITIONS.

`In this chapter:

`(1) APPROPRIATE CONGRESSIONAL COMMITTEES—The term `appropriate congressional committees' means the Committee on Foreign Relations of the Senate and the Committee on International Relations of the House of Representatives.

`(2) COUNTRIES OF THE SOUTH CAUCASUS AND CENTRAL ASIA—The term `countries of the South Caucasus and Central Asia' means Armenia, Azerbaijan, Georgia, Kazakstan, Kyrgyzstan, Tajikistan, Turkmenistan, and Uzbekistan.'.

SEC. 6. RESTRICTION ON ASSISTANCE FOR GOVERNMENT OF AZERBAIJAN.

Section 907 of the Freedom Support Act (22 U.S.C. 5812 note) is amended—

(1) by inserting `(a) RESTRICTION—'; and

(2) by adding at the end the following:

`(b) WAIVER—The restriction on assistance in subsection (a) shall not apply if the President determines, and so certifies to Congress, that the application of the restriction would not be in the national interests of the United States.'.

SEC. 7. ANNUAL REPORT.

Section 104 of the FREEDOM Support Act (22 U.S.C. 5814) is amended—

(1) by striking `and' at the end of paragraph (3);

(2) by striking the period at the end of paragraph (4) and inserting `; and'; and

(3) by adding the following new paragraph:

`(5) with respect to the countries of the South Caucasus and Central Asia—

`(A) identifying the progress of United States foreign policy to accomplish the policy identified in section 3 of the Silk Road Strategy Act of 1999;

`(B) evaluating the degree to which the assistance authorized by chapter 12 of part I of the Foreign Assistance Act of 1961 has been able to accomplish the purposes identified in those sections; and

`(C) recommending any additional initiatives that should be undertaken by the United States to implement the policy and purposes contained in the Silk Road Strategy Act of 1999.'.

SEC. 8. CONFORMING AMENDMENTS.

Section 102(a) of the FREEDOM Support Act (Public Law 102-511) is amended in paragraphs (2) and (4) by striking each place it appears `this Act)' and inserting `this Act and the Silk Road Strategy Act of 1999)'.

SEC. 9. DEFINITIONS.

In this Act:

(1) APPROPRIATE CONGRESSIONAL COMMITTEES—The term `appropriate congressional committees' means the Committee on Foreign Relations of the Senate and the Committee on International Relations of the House of Representatives.

(2) COUNTRIES OF THE SOUTH CAUCASUS AND CENTRAL ASIA—The term `countries of the South Caucasus and Central Asia' means Armenia, Azerbaijan, Georgia, Kazakstan, Kyrgyzstan, Tajikistan, Turkmenistan, and Uzbekistan.

"What do you think?" I asked Jordan.

"It looks like the American taxpayer is going to pay for the infrastructure of those Caspian countries so Sam and his oil buddies don't have to," said Jordan.

"Pretty sweet deal, don't you think? I can't imagine Vladimir Putin is too happy about Sam surrounding his country and making deals permitting Sam entry into

Kazakhstan, for example. These countries don't have the financial wherewithal to finance the infrastructure that's needed for oil and gas exploration. Sam to the rescue at my expense, but what bothers me more than anything is the potential for regional conflict. Putin is in the same countries throwing his weight around. Something has to give. That's why Putin is snuggling up to China. Everybody is lining up everybody else," I said.

"So Putin wants Sam in office because he knows that Sam will continue to stay in Iraq and wear himself out," said Jordan.

"Exactly," I said and logged off the Internet. "By the way, you probably missed a very important man named in Brownback's letter. At the end of the letter it stated, 'Participants today included former U.S. Secretary of State James Baker…' Goggle James Baker, I'm sure you'll find him interesting," I said.

# Chapter Thirty

Angelina arrived at 6:00 o' clock and kissed everyone hello. It seemed as if she belonged there and indeed she did. I asked her how her day was and after telling me, she kissed me on the cheek and thanked me for asking. Maki wanted to go on the deck and throw knives but Angie waived her off. Dinner and the period afterwards could be described as quiet. I wasn't talking and Angie, Maki and Jordan avoided any subject that might be controversial. They were talking around me as if I didn't exist.

"What's wrong dad?" Jordan asked.

"Well, I just had memories suppressed for twenty-five years bust into my consciousness and result in a toast between my son and I to revolution. I think that's enough to make me quiet," I said. Everyone understood and nodded in agreement.

"What's really putting a chill on me though is that I'm trying to figure out if this another delusional episode or real, because if it's delusional I might commit horrible acts and hurt people and if it's real, we're all in trouble. Does anyone have any suggestions to prove to me that the last several days have not been part of a continuing delusion?" I asked.

"There's nothing you can do or I can do, or as a matter of fact, anyone sitting at this table can do to prove to you that this is real. You must have faith in your reality," said Jordan and added, "Dad, this is for real."

"I don't know. Maybe I do have to have faith. Am I functional?" I asked.

Everyone shook their heads "yes" and Jordan poured some red wine into our glasses.

"If I'm functional than the bottom line is this. If a delusional nut can run the country than I guess I can run my simple life," I said. Jordan raised his glass. Maki and Angelina followed and I was the last one to do so. "To the revolution," said Jordan and everyone chanted in unison "to the revolution."

The next morning Rueben arrived at 6:30 a.m. for brunch. Jordan and Maki prepared Mimosa's and eggs benedict. I immediately took control and told the group that I decided that we were going to stay put with our positions. After the elections, the federal deficit and trade deficit would still be there. The war in Iraq and possibly a war in Syria would still be there and in general, the world would still be a turbulent place. "My positions are based on financial and geo-political concerns that were good before this upcoming election and will be good after the election. We stay firm," I concluded. Everyone agreed.

Throughout the weekend, Jordan begged me to go hiking to finish our conversation. He wanted war stories from my past and I wasn't ready to reveal them nor did I want to. I avoided The New York Sunday Times and CNN over the next two days, following Dr. P.'s instructions to separate from Sam. I felt secure in my position that Sam and those behind him would not permit an election loss. I remembered telling Mr. Westerfield that I sincerely believed that Sam would go so far as creating a fake domestic terror attack if he thought it would help him and I still believed in my opinion. No way was Sam going to lose. Monday morning the phone rang.

"Jordan, get the phone, it's probably Rueben," I yelled from my office/bedroom.

"Hello, this is Jordan."

"Hello Jordan. This is Charles Westerfield. I've heard a lot about you. How was your trip? By the way, congratulations, you have two little half sisters. Gabby gave birth two days ago," said Mr. Westerfield.

"Really, two sisters. I always wanted a younger sister and now I have two," said Jordan. I overheard Jordan and immediately ran into the kitchen and grabbed the phone. Mr. Westerfield told me about the twins and invited Jordan, Maki and I over Monday night to see the babies. I didn't want to go because of the elections but I recalled Dr. P.'s advice of staying away from all matters concerning Sam. I questioned Charles Westerfield thoroughly because I was suspicious about the birth. Gabby didn't look that pregnant the last time I saw her. He explained to me that the babies were born prematurely and I asked him why they weren't in the hospital receiving medical attention. Mr. Westerfield reminded me of his wealth and stated that he had a team of doctors and nurses at the estate and turned the war room into an infant area. "Only the best" Mr. Westerfield stated. I agreed to Mr. Westerfield's invitation and told him that Jordan, Maki and I would arrive at 7:00 p.m. The rest of the day I felt uneasy. I didn't trust Westerfield, Gabby and in particular, Elicia. Jordan listened attentively and told me not to get delusional on him. He claimed that everything was under control.

The gates to the estate were open and we drove though.

"Holy shit dad. You lived here?" Who's that?" asked Jordan.

"Yes, I lived here and that's Harry the chauffeur," I said. The front door was open. I walked down the corridor and heard a voice.

"We're in daddy's study," yelled Gabriella. As we passed the war room we did not see any incubators for pre-mature arrivals nor any nurses or doctors.

"I don't like this dad," whispered Jordan. Entering Mr. Westerfield's study, Charles was standing behind his desk. Gabby and Elicia were five feet off to his right. They were holding hands.

"Where are my daughters Charles?" I asked.

"In due time Stan. Why don't you say hello first?" Charles asked. Jordan and Maki stood next to me in silence.

"Why don't we just get on with it," demanded Elicia. With that comment Jordan stood away from me. Maki separated from Jordan and we all stood, quietly facing Charles, Gabby and Elicia. The room was silent. Elicia leaned down towards a chair and removed two plastic bags and threw them at me. One bag landed on the floor in front of me and the other bag hit me in the chest. Both bags exploded open from the impact and two dead fetuses lie before us. I was soaked with blood stained mucous from my neck down to my belt.

"Fuck Stan, you're not even good as a sperm donor. You're useless. We had to abort these babies because they're defective. They were missing the little toe on their right foot. Let's get on with it," said Elicia.

"With what?" I asked.

"With your imminent demise," said Elicia who was the angriest of their group.

"Too bad you won't be around to see Sam win tomorrow," said Mr. Westerfield.

"Too bad you won't either," said Jordan. In the split second that Charles, Gabby and Elicia looked at each other, Jordan pulled a gun from behind his back and fired three shots that stuck Charles, Gabby and Elicia in the forehead. Maki stood next to me ready to throw her knife.

"Jordan, no bullshit, real or a delusion?" I asked.

"Real," answered Jordan. Harry came walking in and Maki threw her knife into Harry's heart. Within the span of a minute there were four dead bodies.

"Jordan, if this is real, I'm running towards the back door and I want you to shoot me in the back. If I'm not lying here, I'm a prime suspect," I said.

"The revolution will not be televised," shouted Jordan. I looked at him. He stopped his antics. I ran to the back door and Jordan shot me once in the back of the thigh and once up top shattering my collarbone. I told Jordan to leave and advised him that I would call the police. The story line was going to be outraged evangelicals in Westerfield's circle who were upset with his Lesbian daughter. The pain in my body was unbearable. I fainted and lied halfway out the back door.

"Maki, do have that note I gave you?" asked Jordan.

"Of course," Maki answered. Jordan placed a typewritten note in one hand of Charles. It read: *"and the multitude shall inherit the earth-Khan."*

978-0-595-35737-6
0-595-35737-7

Printed in the United States
43688LVS00003B/24